THE BEST SHORT STORIES
OF BRET HARTE

THE MODERN LIBRARY
OF THE WORLD'S BEST BOOKS

The publishers will be pleased to send, upon request, an illustrated folder setting forth the purpose and scope of THE MODERN LIBRARY, *and listing each volume in the series. Every reader of books will find titles he has been looking for, handsomely printed, in unabridged editions, and at an unusually low price.*

THE BEST SHORT STORIES

OF BRET HARTE

THE BEST
SHORT STORIES
OF
BRET HARTE

EDITED AND WITH AN

INTRODUCTION BY

ROBERT N. LINSCOTT

THE MODERN LIBRARY · NEW YORK

Random House IS THE PUBLISHER OF

THE MODERN LIBRARY

BENNETT A. CERF · DONALD S. KLOPFER · ROBERT K. HAAS

Manufactured in the United States of America

By H. Wolff

CONTENTS

Introduction	vii
The Luck of Roaring Camp	3
The Outcasts of Poker Flat	16
Tennessee's Partner	30
Brown of Calaveras	42
The Iliad of Sandy Bar	55
The Poet of Sierra Flat	69
How Santa Claus Came to Simpson's Bar	82
A Passage in the Life of Mr. John Oakhurst	100
An Heiress of Red Dog	127
An Ingenue of the Sierras	145
Chu Chu	166
The Devotion of Enriquez	192
A Yellow Dog	223
Salomy Jane's Kiss	235
Uncle Jim and Uncle Billy	259
Dick Spindler's Family Christmas	295
An Esmeralda of Rocky Cañon	316
The Boom in the "Calaveras Clarion"	332
The Youngest Miss Piper	353
Colonel Starbottle for the Plaintiff	373
Lanty Foster's Mistake	407
The Four Guardians of Lagrange	426
A Ward of Colonel Starbottle's	442
The Convalescence of Jack Hamlin	475
A Gentleman of La Porte	503

INTRODUCTION

FRANCIS BRETT HARTE (he was later to drop his first and the last letter of his middle name) was born in Albany, New York, in 1836, of English, Dutch and Hebrew descent. He was the son of an impecunious schoolteacher who died when the boy was nine, leaving four children and a widow dependent upon the charity of relatives. In 1853 the widow migrated to California, made an excellent marriage, and settled in Oakland, where she was joined a year later by her sixteen-year-old son.

The record of the next few years of Bret Harte's life is cloudy and his own reminiscences untrustworthy. For a time he worked for an Oakland apothecary. During a few months he taught in a village school. He may have served as an express messenger and tried a listless hand at mining. He certainly did odd jobs of tutoring and worked for a country paper. By 1860 he was a typesetter in San Francisco, the next year a federal employee, and soon after was married to Anna Griswold, formerly of New York.

During these years Bret Harte had not only absorbed the impressions upon which the work of his life was to be based, but had assiduously practiced the art of writing, and contributed dozens of stories, sketches and poems to California magazines. His earliest stories were snobbish, remote and unreal, but he had an eye for character and a gift for narrative. Gradually he became aware of the literary possibilities of the mining camp and learned to combine pathos and humor with a strong overlay of local color. By 1868 he was recognized as San Francisco's leading author, and, when a new magazine, *The Overland Monthly,* was established, he was made its editor.

In the second issue of the magazine, and over the objection of an outraged printer who (implausible as it may seem today) termed it "indecent, irreligious and improper," appeared "The Luck of Roaring Camp," and Harte's reputation was made. "The Outcasts of Poker Flat" and other California stories that followed were read and praised throughout the country, and in 1870 a poem entitled "Plain Language from Truthful James" swept like wildfire across the continent. A new star had risen; a new world had been revealed. Bret Harte was the literary man of the hour, and in 1871 he set out for New York like a king to his coronation.

His years in the East were disastrous. As a man, Harte was difficult, temperamental ("one of the pleasantest men I have ever known; also one of the unpleasantest," said Mark Twain), quick to incur obligations, slow to repay them. These are traits permissible, perhaps, to genius. What was fatal was a kind of shallowness and lack of creative conscience which led him to succumb to the get-rich-quick spirit of the age, and exploit his literary capital in the easiest way instead of taking pains to develop it. He played the literary lion, basked in his sudden fame, and vainly tried by lecturing, playwriting and the rapid production of potboilers to harmonize his income with his flamboyant tastes. His reputation suffered, his debts increased, his popularity declined. By 1877 he was glad to accept a consulate in a small German city, and crossed the Atlantic, never to return, leaving his wife and four children behind.

Three years later he was transferred to Glasgow, and, when

he was ousted in 1885 by a new administration, he settled in England where he could find a more profitable market for his stories than in his own country. Most of his income went to his family in America, and on the meager balance he lived quietly in London, an overworked hack, scraping the bottom of the California barrel to turn out his thousand words a day. Eventually his affairs were stabilized by an efficient literary agent, and his domestic life was tranquilized by a charming Frenchwoman in whose house he spent his last years. Under the care of his friend and the spurring of his agent he settled down to a sort of literary jog-trot, and turned out a long succession of competent and sometimes excellent stories before his death in 1902.

A re-examination of Bret Harte today leads to the conclusion that he is famous for the wrong stories; his best known are not his best. "The Luck of Roaring Camp," "The Outcasts of Poker Flat," "Tennessee's Partner," and "How Santa Claus Came to Simpson's Bar" had the impact of novelty; they achieved an immediate popularity and their reputation has endured. The stories written in later life dealt with the same scenes and characters and had no element of novelty. Published after the author's vogue had declined, they were neglected by his contemporaries and today are little known. Yet, reading in chronological order all twenty volumes of Bret Harte's collected works, it is evident that in such stories of his later years as "Colonel Starbottle for the Plaintiff," "A Gentleman of La Porte," and "An Ingenue of the Sierras" there is less sentimentality, a mellower humor, better writing and an easier competence than in their more celebrated predecessors.

Within his narrow range Bret Harte was an excellent storyteller; frugal in his ingredients but skillful in their use. He was the first of the local colorists and his colors today are still fresh and vivid. Above all he had the knack of painting characters with such reality and in such majestic dimensions that they became archetypes of the place and period. Jack Hamlin is *the* Western gambler and every stagecoach driver is Yuba Bill. In his youth Harte saw this fabulous America, and in the best of his stories he has made it immortal.

The first nine stories of this present volume were written during the decade from 1868 to 1878; the last sixteen, many years later during the author's residence in England. For permission to use these later stories I am indebted to Houghton Mifflin Company, Bret Harte's authorized publishers; for facts regarding his life, to the excellent biography of Harte by George R. Stewart.

ROBERT N. LINSCOTT

THE BEST SHORT STORIES
OF BRET HARTE

THE LUCK
OF ROARING CAMP

THERE was commotion in Roaring Camp. It could not have been a fight, for in 1850 that was not novel enough to have called together the entire settlement. The ditches and claims were not only deserted, but "Tuttle's grocery" had contributed its gamblers, who, it will be remembered, calmly continued their game the day that French Pete and Kanaka Joe shot each other to death over the bar in the front room. The whole camp was collected before a rude cabin on the outer edge of the clearing. Conversation was carried on in a low tone, but the name of a woman was frequently repeated. It was a name familiar enough in the camp,—"Cherokee Sal."

Perhaps the less said of her the better. She was a coarse and, it is to be feared, a very sinful woman. But at that time she was the only woman in Roaring Camp, and was just then lying in sore extremity, when she most needed the ministration of her own sex. Dissolute, abandoned, and irreclaimable, she was yet suffering a martyrdom hard enough to bear even when veiled by sympathizing womanhood, but now terrible in her loneliness. The primal curse had come to her in that original isolation which must have made the punishment of the first transgression so dreadful. It was, perhaps, part of the expiation of her sin that, at a moment when she most lacked her sex's intuitive tenderness and care, she met only the half-contemptuous faces of her masculine associates. Yet a few of the spectators were, I think, touched by her sufferings. Sandy Tipton thought it was "rough on Sal," and, in the contemplation of her condition, for a moment rose superior to the fact that he had an ace and two bowers in his sleeve.

It will be seen also that the situation was novel. Deaths were by no means uncommon in Roaring Camp, but a birth was a new thing. People had been dismissed from the camp effectively, finally, and with no possibility of return; but this was the first time that anybody had been introduced *ab initio*. Hence the excitement.

"You go in there, Stumpy," said a prominent citizen known as "Kentuck," addressing one of the loungers. "Go in there, and see what you kin do. You've had experience in them things."

Perhaps there was a fitness in the selection. Stumpy, in other climes, had been the putative head of two families; in fact, it was owing to some legal informality in these proceedings that Roaring Camp—a city of refuge—was indebted to his company. The crowd approved the choice, and Stumpy was wise enough to bow to the majority. The door closed on the extempore surgeon and midwife, and Roaring Camp sat down outside, smoked its pipe, and awaited the issue.

The assemblage numbered about a hundred men. One or two of these were actual fugitives from justice, some were criminal, and all were reckless. Physically they exhibited no indication of their past lives and character. The greatest scamp had a Raphael face, with a profusion of blonde hair; Oakhurst, a gambler, had the melancholy air and intellectual abstraction of a Hamlet; the coolest and most courageous man was scarcely over five feet in height, with a soft voice and an embarrassed, timid manner. The term "roughs" applied to them was a distinction rather than a definition. Perhaps in the minor details of fingers, toes, ears, etc., the camp may have been deficient, but these slight omissions did not detract from their aggregate force. The strongest man had but three fingers on his right hand; the best shot had but one eye.

Such was the physical aspect of the men that were dispersed around the cabin. The camp lay in a triangular valley between two hills and a river. The only outlet was a steep trail over the summit of a hill that faced the cabin, now illuminated by the rising moon. The suffering woman might have seen it from the rude bunk whereon she lay,—seen it winding like a silver thread until it was lost in the stars above.

A fire of withered pine boughs added sociability to the gathering. By degrees the natural levity of Roaring Camp returned. Bets were freely offered and taken regarding the result. Three to five that "Sal would get through with it"; even that the child would survive; side bets as to the sex and complexion of the coming stranger. In the midst of an excited discussion an exclamation came from those nearest the door, and the camp stopped to listen. Above the swaying and moaning of the pines, the swift rush of the river, and the crackling of the fire rose a sharp, querulous cry,—a cry unlike anything heard before in the camp. The pines stopped moaning, the river ceased to rush, and the fire to crackle. It seemed as if Nature had stopped to listen too.

The camp rose to its feet as one man! It was proposed to explode a barrel of gunpowder; but in consideration of the situation of the mother, better counsels prevailed, and only a few revolvers were discharged; for whether owing to the rude surgery of the camp, or some other reason, Cherokee Sal was sinking fast. Within an hour she had climbed, as it were, that rugged road that led to the stars, and so passed out of

Roaring Camp, its sin and shame, forever. I do not think that the announcement disturbed them much, except in speculation as to the fate of the child. "Can he live now?" was asked of Stumpy. The answer was doubtful. The only other being of Cherokee Sal's sex and maternal condition in the settlement was an ass. There was some conjecture as to fitness, but the experiment was tried. It was less problematical than the ancient treatment of Romulus and Remus, and apparently as successful.

When these details were completed, which exhausted another hour, the door was opened, and the anxious crowd of men, who had already formed themselves into a queue, entered in single file. Beside the low bunk or shelf, on which the figure of the mother was starkly outlined below the blankets, stood a pine table. On this a candle-box was placed, and within it, swathed in staring red flannel, lay the last arrival at Roaring Camp. Beside the candle-box was placed a hat. Its use was soon indicated. "Gentlemen," said Stumpy, with a singular mixture of authority and *ex officio* complacency,—"gentlemen will please pass in at the front door, round the table, and out at the back door. Them as wishes to contribute anything toward the orphan will find a hat handy." The first man entered with his hat on; he uncovered, however, as he looked about him, and so unconsciously set an example to the next. In such communities good and bad actions are catching. As the procession filed in comments were audible,—criticisms addressed perhaps rather to Stumpy in the character of showman: "Is that him?" "Mighty small specimen"; "Hasn't more'n got the color"; "Ain't bigger nor a derringer." The contributions were as characteristic: A silver tobacco box; a doubloon; a navy revolver, silver mounted; a gold specimen; a very beautifully embroidered lady's handkerchief (from Oakhurst the gambler); a diamond breastpin; a diamond ring (suggested by the pin, with the remark from the giver that he "saw that pin and went two diamonds better"); a slung-shot; a Bible (contributor not detected); a golden spur; a silver teaspoon (the initials, I regret to say, were not the giver's); a pair of surgeon's shears; a lancet; a Bank of England note for £5; and about $200 in loose gold and silver coin. During these proceedings Stumpy maintained a silence as impassive as the dead on his left, a gravity as inscrutable as that of the newly born on his right. Only one incident occurred to break the monotony of the curious procession. As Kentuck bent over the candle-box half curiously, the child turned, and, in a spasm of pain, caught at his groping finger, and held it fast for a moment. Kentuck looked foolish and embarrassed. Something like a blush tried to assert itself in his weather-beaten cheek. "The d—d little cuss!" he said, as he extricated his finger, with perhaps more tenderness and care than he might have been deemed capable of showing. He held that finger a little apart from its fellows as he went out, and examined it curiously. The examination provoked the same original remark in regard to the child. In fact, he seemed to enjoy repeating it. "He rastled with my finger," he remarked to Tipton, holding up the member, "the d—d little cuss!"

It was four o'clock before the camp sought repose. A light burnt in the cabin where the watchers sat, for Stumpy did not go to bed that night. Nor did Kentuck. He drank quite freely, and related with great gusto his experience, invariably ending with his characteristic condemnation of the newcomer. It seemed to relieve him of any unjust implication of sentiment, and Kentuck had the weaknesses of the nobler sex. When everybody else had gone to bed he walked down to the river and whistled reflectingly. Then he walked up the gulch past the cabin, still whistling with demonstrative unconcern. At a large redwood-tree he paused and retraced his steps, and again passed the cabin. Halfway down to the river's bank he again paused, and then returned and knocked at the door. It was opened by Stumpy. "How goes it?" said Kentuck, looking past Stumpy toward the candle-box. "All serene!" replied Stumpy. "Anything up?" "Nothing." There was a pause—an embarrassing one—Stumpy still holding the door. Then Kentuck had recourse to his finger, which he held up to Stumpy. "Rastled with it,—the d—d little cuss," he said, and retired.

The next day Cherokee Sal had such rude sepulture as Roaring Camp afforded. After her body had been committed to the hillside, there was a formal meeting of the camp to discuss what should be done with her infant. A resolution to adopt it was unanimous and enthusiastic. But an animated discussion in regard to the manner and feasibility of providing for its wants at once sprang up. It was remarkable that the argument partook of none of those fierce personalities with which discussions were usually conducted at Roaring Camp. Tipton proposed that they should send the child to Red Dog,—a distance of forty miles,—where female attention could be procured. But the unlucky suggestion met with fierce and unanimous opposition. It was evident that no plan which entailed parting from their new acquisition would for a moment be entertained. "Besides," said Tom Ryder, "them fellows at Red Dog would swap it, and ring in somebody else on us." A disbelief in the honesty of other camps prevailed at Roaring Camp, as in other places.

The introduction of a female nurse in the camp also met with objection. It was argued that no decent woman could be prevailed to accept Roaring Camp as her home, and the speaker urged that "they didn't want any more of the other kind." This unkind allusion to the defunct mother, harsh as it may seem, was the first spasm of propriety,—the first symptom of the camp's regeneration. Stumpy advanced nothing. Perhaps he felt a certain delicacy in interfering with the selection of a possible successor in office. But when questioned, he averred stoutly that he and "Jinny"—the mammal before alluded to—could manage to rear the child. There was something original, independent, and heroic about the plan that pleased the camp. Stumpy was retained. Certain articles were sent for to Sacramento. "Mind," said the treasurer, as he pressed a bag of gold-dust into the expressman's hand, "the best that can be got,—lace, you know, and filigree-work and frills,—d—n the cost!"

Strange to say, the child thrived. Perhaps the invigorating climate of the mountain camp was compensation for material deficiencies. Nature took the foundling to her broader breast. In that rare atmosphere of the Sierra foothills,—that air pungent with balsamic odor, that ethereal cordial at once bracing and exhilarating,—he may have found food and nourishment, or a subtle chemistry that transmuted ass's milk to lime and phosphorus. Stumpy inclined to the belief that it was the latter and good nursing. "Me and that ass," he would say, "has been father and mother to him! Don't you," he would add, apostrophizing the helpless bundle before him, "never go back on us."

By the time he was a month old the necessity of giving him a name became apparent. He had generally been known as "The Kid," "Stumpy's Boy," "The Coyote" (an allusion to his vocal powers), and even by Kentuck's endearing diminutive of "The d—d little cuss." But these were felt to be vague and unsatisfactory, and were at last dismissed under another influence. Gamblers and adventurers are generally superstitious, and Oakhurst one day declared that the baby had brought "the luck" to Roaring Camp. It was certain that of late they had been successful. "Luck" was the name agreed upon, with the prefix of Tommy for greater convenience. No allusion was made to the mother, and the father was unknown. "It's better," said the philosophical Oakhurst, "to take a fresh deal all round. Call him Luck, and start him fair." A day was accordingly set apart for the christening. What was meant by this ceremony the reader may imagine who has already gathered some idea of the reckless irreverence of Roaring Camp. The master of ceremonies was one "Boston," a noted wag, and the occasion seemed to promise the greatest facetiousness. This ingenious satirist had spent two days in preparing a burlesque of the Church service, with pointed local allusions. The choir was properly trained, and Sandy Tipton was to stand godfather. But after the procession had marched to the grove with music and banners, and the child had been deposited before a mock altar, Stumpy stepped before the expectant crowd. "It ain't my style to spoil fun, boys," said the little man, stoutly eying the faces around him, "but it strikes me that this thing ain't exactly on the squar. It's playing it pretty low down on this yer baby to ring in fun on him that he ain't goin' to understand. And ef there's goin' to be any godfathers round, I'd like to see who's got any better rights than me." A silence followed Stumpy's speech. To the credit of all humorists be it said that the first man to acknowledge its justice was the satirist thus stopped of his fun. "But," said Stumpy, quickly following up his advantage, "we're here for a christening, and we'll have it. I proclaim you Thomas Luck, according to the laws of the United States and the State of California, so help me God." It was the first time that the name of the Deity had been otherwise uttered than profanely in the camp. The form of christening was perhaps even more ludicrous than the satirist had conceived; but strangely enough, nobody saw it and nobody laughed. "Tommy" was christened as seriously as he would have been under a Christian roof, and cried and was comforted in as orthodox fashion.

And so the work of regeneration began in Roaring Camp. Almost imperceptibly a change came over the settlement. The cabin assigned to "Tommy Luck"—or "The Luck," as he was more frequently called—first showed signs of improvement. It was kept scrupulously clean and whitewashed. Then it was boarded, clothed, and papered. The rosewood cradle, packed eighty miles by mule, had, in Stumpy's way of putting it, "sorter killed the rest of the furniture." So the rehabilitation of the cabin became a necessity. The men who were in the habit of lounging in at Stumpy's to see "how 'The Luck' got on" seemed to appreciate the change, and in self-defense the rival establishment of "Tuttle's grocery" bestirred itself and imported a carpet and mirrors. The reflections of the latter on the appearance of Roaring Camp tended to produce stricter habits of personal cleanliness. Again Stumpy imposed a kind of quarantine upon those who aspired to the honor and privilege of holding The Luck. It was a cruel mortification to Kentuck—who, in the carelessness of a large nature and the habits of frontier life, had begun to regard all garments as a second cuticle, which, like a snake's, only sloughed off through decay—to be debarred this privilege from certain prudential reasons. Yet such was the subtle influence of innovation that he thereafter appeared regularly every afternoon in a clean shirt and face still shining from his ablutions. Nor were moral and social sanitary laws neglected. "Tommy," who was supposed to spend his whole existence in a persistent attempt to repose, must not be disturbed by noise. The shouting and yelling, which had gained the camp its infelicitous title, were not permitted within hearing distance of Stumpy's. The men conversed in whispers or smoked with Indian gravity. Profanity was tacitly given up in these sacred precincts, and throughout the camp a popular form of expletive, known as "D—n the luck!" and "Curse the luck!" was abandoned, as having a new personal bearing. Vocal music was not interdicted, being supposed to have a soothing, tranquilizing quality; and one song, sung by "Man-o'-War Jack," an English sailor from Her Majesty's Australian colonies, was quite popular as a lullaby. It was a lugubrious recital of the exploits of "The Arethusa, Seventy-four," in a muffled minor, ending with a prolonged dying fall at the burden of each verse, "On b-oo-o-ard of the Arethusa." It was a fine sight to see Jack holding The Luck, rocking from side to side as if with the motion of a ship, and crooning forth this naval ditty. Either through the peculiar rocking of Jack or the length of his song,—it contained ninety stanzas, and was continued with conscientious deliberation to the bitter end,— the lullaby generally had the desired effect. At such times the men would lie at full length under the trees in the soft summer twilight, smoking their pipes and drinking in the melodious utterances. An indistinct idea that this was pastoral happiness pervaded the camp. "This 'ere kind o' think," said the Cockney Simmons, meditatively reclining on his elbow, "is 'evingly." It reminded him of Greenwich.

On the long summer days The Luck was usually carried to the gulch from whence the golden store of Roaring Camp was taken. There, on a blanket spread over pine boughs, he would lie while the men were working in the ditches below. Latterly there was a rude attempt to decorate this bower with flowers and sweet-smelling shrubs, and generally some one would bring him a cluster of wild honeysuckles, azaleas, or the painted blossoms of Las Mariposas. The men had suddenly awakened to the fact that there were beauty and significance in these trifles, which they had so long trodden carelessly beneath their feet. A flake of glittering mica, a fragment of variegated quartz, a bright pebble from the bed of the creek, became beautiful to eyes thus cleared and strengthened, and were invariably put aside for The Luck. It was wonderful how many treasures the woods and hillsides yielded that "would do for Tommy." Surrounded by playthings such as never child out of fairyland had before, it is to be hoped that Tommy was content. He appeared to be serenely happy, albeit there was an infantine gravity about him, a contemplative light in his round gray eyes, that sometimes worried Stumpy. He was always tractable and quiet, and it is recorded that once, having crept beyond his "corral,"—a hedge of tessellated pine boughs, which surrounded his bed,—he dropped over the bank on his head in the soft earth, and remained with his mottled legs in the air in that position for at least five minutes with unflinching gravity. He was extricated without a murmur. I hesitate to record the many other instances of his sagacity, which rest, unfortunately, upon the statements of prejudiced friends. Some of them were not without a tinge of superstition. "I crep' up the bank just now," said Kentuck one day, in a breathless state of excitement, "and dern my skin if he wasn't a-talking to a jaybird as was a-sittin' on his lap. There they was, just as free and sociable as anything you please, a-jawin' at each other just like two cherrybums." Howbeit, whether creeping over the pine boughs or lying lazily on his back blinking at the leaves above him, to him the birds sang, the squirrels chattered, and the flowers bloomed. Nature was his nurse and playfellow. For him she would let slip between the leaves golden shafts of sunlight that fell just within his grasp; she would send wandering breezes to visit him with the balm of bay and resinous gum; to him the tall red-woods nodded familiarly and sleepily, the bumblebees buzzed, and the rooks cawed a slumbrous accompaniment.

Such was the golden summer of Roaring Camp. They were "flush times," and the luck was with them. The claims had yielded enormously. The camp was jealous of its privileges and looked suspiciously on strangers. No encouragement was given to immigration, and, to make their seclusion more perfect, the land on either side of the mountain wall that surrounded the camp they duly preëmpted. This, and a reputation for singular proficiency with the revolver, kept the reserve of Roaring Camp inviolate. The expressman—their only connecting link with the surrounding world—sometimes told wonderful stories of the camp. He would say, "They've a street up there in 'Roaring' that would lay over any street in Red Dog. They've got vines and flowers round their houses, and they wash themselves twice a day. But they're mighty rough on strangers, and they worship an Ingin baby."

With the prosperity of the camp came a desire for further improvement. It was proposed to build a hotel in the following spring, and to invite one or two decent families to reside there for the sake of The Luck, who might perhaps profit by female companionship. The sacrifice that this concession to the sex cost these men, who were fiercely skeptical in regard to its general virtue and usefulness, can only be accounted for by their affection for Tommy. A few still held out. But the resolve could not be carried into effect for three months, and the minority meekly yielded in the hope that something might turn up to prevent it. And it did.

The winter of 1851 will long be remembered in the foothills. The snow lay deep on the Sierras, and every mountain creek became a river, and every river a lake. Each gorge and gulch was transformed into a tumultuous watercourse that descended the hillsides, tearing down giant trees and scattering its drift and débris along the plain. Red Dog had been twice under water, and Roaring Camp had been forewarned. "Water put the gold into them gulches," said Stumpy. "It's been here once and will be here again!" And that night the North Fork suddenly leaped over its banks and swept up the triangular valley of Roaring Camp.

In the confusion of rushing water, crashing trees, and crackling timber, and the darkness which seemed to flow with the water and blot out the fair valley, but little could be done to collect the scattered camp. When the morning broke, the cabin of Stumpy, nearest the river-bank, was gone. Higher up the gulch they found the body of its unlucky owner; but the pride, the hope, the joy, The Luck, of Roaring Camp had disappeared. They were returning with sad hearts when a shout from the bank recalled them.

It was a relief-boat from down the river. They had picked up, they said, a man and an infant, nearly exhausted, about two miles below. Did anybody know them, and did they belong here?

It needed but a glance to show them Kentuck lying there, cruelly crushed and bruised, but still holding The Luck of Roaring Camp in his arms. As they bent over the strangely assorted pair, they saw that the child was cold and pulseless. "He is dead," said one. Kentuck opened his eyes. "Dead?" he repeated feebly. "Yes, my man, and you are dying too." A smile lit the eyes of the expiring Kentuck. "Dying!" he repeated; "he's a-taking me with him. Tell the boys I've got The Luck with me now"; and the strong man, clinging to the frail babe as a drowning man is said to cling to a straw, drifted away into the shadowy river that flows forever to the unknown sea.

THE OUTCASTS
OF POKER FLAT

As Mr. John Oakhurst, gambler, stepped into the main street of Poker Flat on the morning of the 23d of November, 1850, he was conscious of a change in its moral atmosphere since the preceding night. Two or three men, conversing earnestly together, ceased as he approached, and exchanged significant glances. There was a Sabbath lull in the air, which, in a settlement unused to Sabbath influences, looked ominous.

Mr. Oakhurst's calm, handsome face betrayed small concern in these indications. Whether he was conscious of any predisposing cause was another question. "I reckon they're after somebody," he reflected; "likely it's me." He returned to his pocket the handkerchief with which he had been whipping away the red dust of Poker Flat from his neat boots, and quietly discharged his mind of any further conjecture.

In point of fact, Poker Flat was "after somebody." It had lately suffered the loss of several thousand dollars, two valuable horses, and a prominent citizen. It was experiencing a spasm of virtuous reaction, quite as lawless and ungovernable as any of the acts that had provoked it. A secret committee had determined to rid the town of all improper persons. This was done permanently in regard to two men who were then hanging from the boughs of a sycamore in the gulch, and temporarily in the banishment of certain other objectionable characters. I regret to say that some of these were ladies. It is but due to the sex, however, to state that their impropriety was professional, and it was only in such easily established standards of evil that Poker Flat ventured to sit in judgment.

Mr. Oakhurst was right in supposing that he was included in this category. A few of the committee had urged hanging him as a possible example and a sure method of reimbursing themselves from his pockets of the sums he had won from them. "It's agin justice," said Jim Wheeler, "to let this yer young man from Roaring Camp—an entire stranger—carry away our money." But a crude sentiment of equity residing in the breasts of those who had been fortunate enough to win from Mr. Oakhurst overruled this narrower local prejudice.

Mr. Oakhurst received his sentence with philosophic calmness, none the less coolly that he was aware of the hesitation of his judges. He was too much of a gambler not to accept fate. With him life was at best an uncertain game, and he recognized the usual percentage in favor of the dealer.

A body of armed men accompanied the deported wickedness of Poker Flat to the outskirts of the settlement. Besides Mr. Oakhurst, who was known to be a coolly desperate man, and for whose intimidation the armed escort was intended, the expatriated party consisted of a young woman familiarly known as "the Duchess"; another who had won the title of "Mother Shipton"; and "Uncle Billy," a suspected sluice-robber and confirmed drunkard. The cavalcade provoked no comments from the spectators, nor was any word uttered by the escort. Only when the gulch which marked the uttermost limit of Poker Flat was reached, the leader spoke briefly and to the point. The exiles were forbidden to return at the peril of their lives.

As the escort disappeared, their pent-up feelings found

vent in a few hysterical tears from the Duchess, some bad language from Mother Shipton, and a Parthian volley of expletives from Uncle Billy. The philosophic Oakhurst alone remained silent. He listened calmly to Mother Shipton's desire to cut somebody's heart out, to the repeated statements of the Duchess that she would die in the road, and to the alarming oaths that seemed to be bumped out of Uncle Billy as he rode forward. With the easy good humor characteristic of his class, he insisted upon exchanging his own riding-horse, "Five-Spot," for the sorry mule which the Duchess rode. But even this act did not draw the party into any closer sympathy. The young woman readjusted her somewhat draggled plumes with a feeble, faded coquetry; Mother Shipton eyed the possessor of "Five-Spot" with malevolence, and Uncle Billy included the whole party in one sweeping anathema.

The road to Sandy Bar—a camp that, not having as yet experienced the regenerating influences of Poker Flat, consequently seemed to offer some invitation to the emigrants —lay over a steep mountain range. It was distant a day's severe travel. In that advanced season the party soon passed out of the moist, temperate regions of the foothills into the dry, cold, bracing air of the Sierras. The trail was narrow and difficult. At noon the Duchess, rolling out of her saddle upon the ground, declared her intention of going no farther, and the party halted.

The spot was singularly wild and impressive. A wooded amphitheatre, surrounded on three sides by precipitous cliffs of naked granite, sloped gently toward the crest of another precipice that overlooked the valley. It was, undoubtedly, the most suitable spot for a camp, had camping been advisable. But Mr. Oakhurst knew that scarcely half the journey to Sandy Bar was accomplished, and the party were not equipped or provisioned for delay. This fact he pointed out to his companions curtly, with a philosophic commentary on the folly of "throwing up their hand before the game was played out." But they were furnished with liquor, which in this emergency stood them in place of food, fuel, rest, and prescience. In spite of his remonstrances, it was not long before they were more or less under its influence. Uncle Billy passed rapidly from a bellicose state into one of stupor, the Duchess became maudlin, and Mother Shipton snored. Mr. Oakhurst alone remained erect, leaning against a rock, calmly surveying them.

Mr. Oakhurst did not drink. It interfered with a profession which required coolness, impassiveness, and presence of mind, and, in his own language, he "couldn't afford it." As he gazed at his recumbent fellow exiles, the loneliness begotten of his pariah trade, his habits of life, his very vices, for the first time seriously oppressed him. He bestirred himself in dusting his black clothes, washing his hands and face, and other acts characteristic of his studiously neat habits, and for a moment forgot his annoyance. The thought of deserting his weaker and more pitiable companions never perhaps occurred to him. Yet he could not help feeling the want of that excitement which, singularly enough, was most conducive to that calm equanimity for which he was notorious. He looked at the gloomy walls that rose a thousand feet sheer above the circling pines around him, at the sky ominously clouded, at the valley below, already deepening into shadow; and, doing so, suddenly he heard his own name called.

A horseman slowly ascended the trail. In the fresh, open face of the newcomer Mr. Oakhurst recognized Tom Simson, otherwise known as "The Innocent," of Sandy Bar. He had met him some months before over a "little game," and had, with perfect equanimity, won the entire fortune—amounting to some forty dollars—of that guileless youth. After the game was finished, Mr. Oakhurst drew the youthful speculator behind the door and thus addressed him: "Tommy, you're a good little man, but you can't gamble worth a cent. Don't try it over again." He then handed him his money back, pushed him gently from the room, and so made a devoted slave of Tom Simson.

There was a remembrance of this in his boyish and enthusiastic greeting of Mr. Oakhurst. He had started, he said, to go to Poker Flat to seek his fortune. "Alone?" No, not exactly alone; in fact (a giggle), he had run away with Piney Woods. Didn't Mr. Oakhurst remember Piney? She that used to wait on the table at the Temperance House? They had been engaged a long time, but old Jake Woods had objected, and so they had run away, and were going to Poker Flat to be married, and here they were. And they were tired out, and how lucky it was they had found a place to camp, and company. All this the Innocent delivered rapidly, while Piney, a stout, comely damsel of fifteen, emerged from behind the pine-tree, where she had been blushing unseen, and rode to the side of her lover.

Mr. Oakhurst seldom troubled himself with sentiment, still less with propriety; but he had a vague idea that the situation was not fortunate. He retained, however, his presence of mind sufficiently to kick Uncle Billy, who was about to say something, and Uncle Billy was sober enough to recognize in Mr. Oakhurst's kick a superior power that would not bear trifling. He then endeavored to dissuade Tom Simson from delaying further, but in vain. He even pointed out the fact that there was no provision, nor means of making a camp. But, unluckily, the Innocent met this objection by assuring the party that he was provided with an extra mule loaded with provisions, and by the discovery of a rude attempt at a log house near the trail. "Piney can stay with Mrs. Oakhurst," said the Innocent, pointing to the Duchess, "and I can shift for myself."

Nothing but Mr. Oakhurst's admonishing foot saved Uncle Billy from bursting into a roar of laughter. As it was, he felt compelled to retire up the cañon until he could recover his gravity. There he confided the joke to the tall pine-trees, with many slaps of his leg, contortions of his face, and the usual profanity. But when he returned to the party, he found them seated by a fire—for the air had grown strangely chill and the sky overcast—in apparently amicable conversation. Piney was actually talking in an impulsive girlish fashion to the Duchess, who was listening with an interest and animation she had not shown for many days. The Innocent was holding forth, apparently with equal effect, to Mr. Oakhurst and Mother Shipton, who was actually relaxing into amiability. "Is this yer a d—d picnic?" said Uncle Billy, with inward scorn, as he surveyed the sylvan group, the glancing firelight, and the tethered animals in the foreground. Suddenly an idea mingled with the alcoholic fumes that disturbed his brain. It was apparently of a jocular nature, for he felt impelled to slap his leg again and cram his fist into his mouth.

As the shadows crept slowly up the mountain, a slight breeze rocked the tops of the pine-trees and moaned through their long and gloomy aisles. The ruined cabin, patched and covered with pine boughs, was set apart for the ladies. As the lovers parted, they unaffectedly exchanged a kiss, so honest and sincere that it might have been heard above the swaying pines. The frail Duchess and the malevolent Mother Shipton were probably too stunned to remark upon this last evidence of simplicity, and so turned without a word to the hut. The fire was replenished, the men lay down before the door, and in a few minutes were asleep.

Mr. Oakhurst was a light sleeper. Toward morning he awoke benumbed and cold. As he stirred the dying fire, the wind, which was now blowing strongly, brought to his cheek that which caused the blood to leave it,—snow!

He started to his feet with the intention of awakening the sleepers, for there was no time to lose. But turning to where Uncle Billy had been lying, he found him gone. A suspicion leaped to his brain, and a curse to his lips. He ran to the spot where the mules had been tethered—they were no longer there. The tracks were already rapidly disappearing in the snow.

The momentary excitement brought Mr. Oakhurst back to the fire with his usual calm. He did not waken the sleepers. The Innocent slumbered peacefully, with a smile on his good-humored, freckled face; the virgin Piney slept beside her frailer sisters as sweetly as though attended by celestial guardians; and Mr. Oakhurst, drawing his blanket over his shoulders, stroked his mustaches and waited for the dawn. It came slowly in a whirling mist of snowflakes that dazzled and confused the eye. What could be seen of the landscape appeared magically changed. He looked over the valley, and summed up the present and future in two words, "Snowed in!"

A careful inventory of the provisions, which, fortunately for the party, had been stored within the hut, and so escaped the felonious fingers of Uncle Billy, disclosed the fact that with care and prudence they might last ten days longer. "That is," said Mr. Oakhurst *sotto voce* to the Innocent, "if you're willing to board us. If you ain't—and perhaps you'd better not—you can wait till Uncle Billy gets back with provisions." For some occult reason, Mr. Oakhurst could not

bring himself to disclose Uncle Billy's rascality, and so offered the hypothesis that he had wandered from the camp and had accidentally stampeded the animals. He dropped a warning to the Duchess and Mother Shipton, who of course knew the facts of their associate's defection. "They'll find out the truth about us *all* when they find out anything," he added significantly, "and there's no good frightening them now."

Tom Simson not only put all his worldly store at the disposal of Mr. Oakhurst, but seemed to enjoy the prospect of their enforced seclusion. "We'll have a good camp for a week, and then the snow'll melt, and we'll all go back together." The cheerful gayety of the young man and Mr. Oakhurst's calm infected the others. The Innocent, with the aid of pine boughs, extemporized a thatch for the roofless cabin, and the Duchess directed Piney in the rearrangement of the interior with a taste and tact that opened the blue eyes of that provincial maiden to their fullest extent. "I reckon now you're used to fine things at Poker Flat," said Piney. The Duchess turned away sharply to conceal something that reddened her cheeks through their professional tint, and Mother Shipton requested Piney not to "chatter." But when Mr. Oakhurst returned from a weary search for the trail, he heard the sound of happy laughter echoed from the rocks. He stopped in some alarm, and his thoughts first naturally reverted to the whiskey, which he had prudently cachéd. "And yet it don't somehow sound like whiskey," said the gambler. It was not until he caught sight of the blazing fire through the still blinding storm, and the group around it, that he settled to the conviction that it was "square fun."

Whether Mr. Oakhurst had cachéd his cards with the whiskey as something debarred the free access of the community, I cannot say. It was certain that, in Mother Shipton's words, he "didn't say 'cards' once" during that evening.

Haply the time was beguiled by an accordion, produced somewhat ostentatiously by Tom Simson from his pack. Notwithstanding some difficulties attending the manipulation of this instrument, Piney Woods managed to pluck several reluctant melodies from its keys, to an accompaniment by the Innocent on a pair of bone castanets. But the crowning festivity of the evening was reached in a rude camp-meeting hymn, which the lovers, joining hands, sang with great earnestness and vociferation. I fear that a certain defiant tone and Covenanter's swing to its chorus, rather than any devotional quality, caused it speedily to infect the others, who at last joined in the refrain:—

> *"I'm proud to live in the service of the Lord,*
> *And I'm bound to die in His army."*

The pines rocked, the storm eddied and whirled above the miserable group, and the flames of their altar leaped heavenward, as if in token of the vow.

At midnight the storm abated, the rolling clouds parted, and the stars glittered keenly above the sleeping camp. Mr. Oakhurst, whose professional habits had enabled him to live on the smallest possible amount of sleep, in dividing the watch with Tom Simson somehow managed to take upon himself the greater part of that duty. He excused himself to the Innocent by saying that he had "often been a week without sleep." "Doing what?" asked Tom. "Poker!" replied Oakhurst sententiously. "When a man gets a streak of luck, —nigger-luck,—he don't get tired. The luck gives in first. Luck," continued the gambler reflectively, "is a mighty queer thing. All you know about it for certain is that it's bound to change. And it's finding out when it's going to change that makes you. We've had a streak of bad luck since we left Poker Flat,—you come along, and slap you get into it, too. If

you can hold your cards right along you're all right. For," added the gambler, with cheerful irrelevance—

> " 'I'm proud to live in the service of the Lord,
> And I'm bound to die in His army.' "

The third day came, and the sun, looking through the white-curtained valley, saw the outcasts divide their slowly decreasing store of provisions for the morning meal. It was one of the peculiarities of that mountain climate that its rays diffused a kindly warmth over the wintry landscape, as if in regretful commiseration of the past. But it revealed drift on drift of snow piled high around the hut,—a hopeless, uncharted, trackless sea of white lying below the rocky shores to which the castaways still clung. Through the marvelously clear air the smoke of the pastoral village of Poker Flat rose miles away. Mother Shipton saw it, and from a remote pinnacle of her rocky fastness hurled in that direction a final malediction. It was her last vituperative attempt, and perhaps for that reason was invested with a certain degree of sublimity. It did her good, she privately informed the Duchess. "Just you go out there and cuss, and see." She then set herself to the task of amusing "the child," as she and the Duchess were pleased to call Piney. Piney was no chicken, but it was a soothing and original theory of the pair thus to account for the fact that she didn't swear and wasn't improper.

When night crept up again through the gorges, the reedy notes of the accordion rose and fell in fitful spasms and long-drawn gasps by the flickering campfire. But music failed to fill entirely the aching void left by insufficient food, and a new diversion was proposed by Piney,—story-telling. Neither Mr. Oakhurst nor his female companions caring to relate their personal experiences, this plan would have failed too, but for the Innocent. Some months before he had chanced upon a stray copy of Mr. Pope's ingenious translation of the *Iliad*. He now proposed to narrate the principal incidents of that poem—having thoroughly mastered the argument and fairly forgotten the words—in the current vernacular of Sandy Bar. And so for the rest of that night the Homeric demigods again walked the earth. Trojan bully and wily Greek wrestled in the winds, and the great pines in the cañon seemed to bow to the wrath of the son of Peleus. Mr. Oakhurst listened with quiet satisfaction. Most especially was he interested in the fate of "Ash-heels," as the Innocent persisted in denominating the "swift-footed Achilles."

So, with small food and much of Homer and the accordion, a week passed over the heads of the outcasts. The sun again forsook them, and again from leaden skies the snowflakes were sifted over the land. Day by day closer around them drew the snowy circle, until at last they looked from their prison over drifted walls of dazzling white, that towered twenty feet above their heads. It became more and more difficult to replenish their fires, even from the fallen trees beside them, now half hidden in the drifts. And yet no one complained. The lovers turned from the dreary prospect and looked into each other's eyes, and were happy. Mr. Oakhurst settled himself coolly to the losing game before him. The Duchess, more cheerful than she had been, assumed the care of Piney. Only Mother Shipton—once the strongest of the party—seemed to sicken and fade. At midnight on the tenth day she called Oakhurst to her side. "I'm going," she said, in a voice of querulous weakness, "but don't say anything about it. Don't waken the kids. Take the bundle from under my head, and open it." Mr. Oakhurst did so. It contained Mother Shipton's rations for the last week, untouched. "Give 'em to the child," she said, pointing to the sleeping Piney. "You've starved yourself," said the gambler. "That's what they call it," said the woman querulously, as she lay down again, and, turning her face to the wall, passed quietly away.

The accordion and the bones were put aside that day, and Homer was forgotten. When the body of Mother Shipton had been committed to the snow, Mr. Oakhurst took the Innocent aside, and showed him a pair of snowshoes, which he had fashioned from the old pack-saddle. "There's one chance in a hundred to save her yet," he said, pointing to Piney; "but it's there," he added, pointing toward Poker Flat. "If you can reach there in two days she's safe." "And you?" asked Tom Simson. "I'll stay here," was the curt reply.

The lovers parted with a long embrace. "You are not going, too?" said the Duchess, as she saw Mr. Oakhurst apparently waiting to accompany him. "As far as the cañon," he replied. He turned suddenly and kissed the Duchess, leaving her pallid face aflame, and her trembling limbs rigid with amazement.

Night came, but not Mr. Oakhurst. It brought the storm again and the whirling snow. Then the Duchess, feeding the fire, found that some one had quietly piled beside the hut enough fuel to last a few days longer. The tears rose to her eyes, but she hid them from Piney.

The women slept but little. In the morning, looking into each other's faces, they read their fate. Neither spoke, but Piney, accepting the position of the stronger, drew near and placed her arm around the Duchess's waist. They kept this attitude for the rest of the day. That night the storm reached its greatest fury, and, rending asunder the protecting vines, invaded the very hut.

Toward morning they found themselves unable to feed the fire, which gradually died away. As the embers slowly blackened, the Duchess crept closer to Piney, and broke the silence of many hours: "Piney, can you pray?" "No, dear," said Piney simply. The Duchess, without knowing exactly why, felt relieved, and, putting her head upon Piney's shoulder, spoke no more. And so reclining, the younger and purer pillowing the head of her soiled sister upon her virgin breast, they fell asleep.

The wind lulled as if it feared to waken them. Feathery drifts of snow, shaken from the long pine boughs, flew like white-winged birds, and settled about them as they slept. The moon through the rifted clouds looked down upon what had been the camp. But all human stain, all trace of earthly travail, was hidden beneath the spotless mantle mercifully flung from above.

They slept all that day and the next, nor did they waken when voices and footsteps broke the silence of the camp. And when pitying fingers brushed the snow from their wan faces, you could scarcely have told from the equal peace that dwelt upon them which was she that had sinned. Even the law of Poker Flat recognized this, and turned away, leaving them still locked in each other's arms.

But at the head of the gulch, on one of the largest pine-trees, they found the deuce of clubs pinned to the bark with a bowie-knife. It bore the following, written in pencil in a firm hand:—

†

BENEATH THIS TREE

LIES THE BODY

OF

JOHN OAKHURST,

WHO STRUCK A STREAK OF BAD LUCK

ON THE 23D OF NOVEMBER 1850,

AND

HANDED IN HIS CHECKS

ON THE 7TH DECEMBER, 1850.

†

And pulseless and cold, with a Derringer by his side and a bullet in his heart, though still calm as in life, beneath the snow lay he who was at once the strongest and yet the weakest of the outcasts of Poker Flat.

TENNESSEE'S PARTNER

I DO not think that we ever knew his real name. Our ignorance of it certainly never gave us any social inconvenience, for at Sandy Bar in 1854 most men were christened anew. Sometimes these appellatives were derived from some distinctiveness of dress, as in the case of "Dungaree Jack"; or from some peculiarity of habit, as shown in "Saleratus Bill," so called from an undue proportion of that chemical in his daily bread; or from some unlucky slip, as exhibited in "The Iron Pirate," a mild, inoffensive man, who earned that baleful title by his unfortunate mispronunciation of the term "iron pyrites." Perhaps this may have been the beginning of a rude heraldry; but I am constrained to think that it was because a man's real name in that day rested solely upon his own unsupported statement. "Call yourself Clifford, do you?" said Boston, addressing a timid newcomer with infinite scorn; "Hell is full of such Cliffords!" He then introduced the unfortunate man, whose name happened to be really Clifford, as "Jaybird Charley,"—an unhallowed inspiration of the moment that clung to him ever after.

But to return to Tennessee's Partner, whom we never knew by any other than this relative title. That he had ever existed as a separate and distinct individuality we only learned later. It seems that in 1853 he left Poker Flat to go to San Francisco, ostensibly to procure a wife. He never got any farther than Stockton. At that place he was attracted by a young person who waited upon the table at the hotel where he took his meals. One morning he said something to her which caused her to smile not unkindly, to somewhat coquettishly break a plate of toast over his upturned, serious, simple face, and to retreat to the kitchen. He followed her, and emerged a few moments later, covered with more toast and victory. That day week they were married by a justice of the peace, and returned to Poker Flat. I am aware that something more might be made of this episode, but I prefer to tell it as it was current at Sandy Bar,—in the gulches and bar-rooms,—where all sentiment was modified by a strong sense of humor.

Of their married felicity but little is known, perhaps for the reason that Tennessee, then living with his partner, one day took occasion to say something to the bride on his own account, at which, it is said, she smiled not unkindly and chastely retreated,—this time as far as Marysville, where Tennessee followed her, and where they went to housekeeping without the aid of a justice of the peace. Tennessee's Partner took the loss of his wife simply and seriously, as was his fashion. But to everybody's surprise, when Tennessee one day returned from Marysville, without his partner's wife,— she having smiled and retreated with somebody else,—Tennessee's Partner was the first man to shake his hand and greet him with affection. The boys who had gathered in the cañon to see the shooting were naturally indignant. Their indignation might have found vent in sarcasm but for a certain look in Tennessee's Partner's eye that indicated a lack of humorous appreciation. In fact, he was a grave man, with a steady application to practical detail which was unpleasant in a difficulty.

Meanwhile a popular feeling against Tennessee had grown up on the Bar. He was known to be a gambler; he was suspected to be a thief. In these suspicions Tennessee's Partner was equally compromised; his continued intimacy with Tennessee after the affair above quoted could only be accounted for on the hypothesis of a copartnership of crime. At last Tennessee's guilt became flagrant. One day he overtook a stranger on his way to Red Dog. The stranger afterward related that Tennessee beguiled the time with interesting anecdote and reminiscence, but illogically concluded the interview in the following words: "And now, young man, I'll trouble you for your knife, your pistols, and your money. You see your weppings might get you into trouble at Red Dog, and your money's a temptation to the evilly disposed. I think you said your address was San Francisco. I shall endeavor to call." It may be stated here that Tennessee had a fine flow of humor, which no business preoccupation could wholly subdue.

This exploit was his last. Red Dog and Sandy Bar made common cause against the highwayman. Tennessee was hunted in very much the same fashion as his prototype, the grizzly. As the toils closed around him, he made a desperate dash through the Bar, emptying his revolver at the crowd before the Arcade Saloon, and so on up Grizzly Cañon; but at its farther extremity he was stopped by a small man on a gray horse. The men looked at each other a moment in silence. Both were fearless, both self-possessed and independent, and both types of a civilization that in the seventeenth century would have been called heroic, but in the nineteenth simply "reckless."

"What have you got there?—I call," said Tennessee quietly.

"Two bowers and an ace," said the stranger as quietly, showing two revolvers and a bowie-knife.

"That takes me," returned Tennessee; and, with this gambler's epigram, he threw away his useless pistol and rode back with his captor.

It was a warm night. The cool breeze which usually sprang up with the going down of the sun behind the chaparral-crested mountain was that evening withheld from Sandy Bar. The little cañon was stifling with heated resinous odors, and the decaying driftwood on the Bar sent forth faint sickening exhalations. The feverishness of day and its fierce passions still filled the camp. Lights moved restlessly along the bank of the river, striking no answering reflection from its tawny current. Against the blackness of the pines the windows of the old loft above the express-office stood out staringly bright; and through their curtainless panes the loungers below could see the forms of those who were even then deciding the fate of Tennessee. And above all this, etched on the dark firmament, rose the Sierra, remote and passionless, crowned with remoter passionless stars.

The trial of Tennessee was conducted as fairly as was consistent with a judge and jury who felt themselves to some extent obliged to justify, in their verdict, the previous irregularities of arrest and indictment. The law of Sandy Bar was implacable, but not vengeful. The excitement and personal feeling of the chase were over; with Tennessee safe in their hands, they were ready to listen patiently to any defense, which they were already satisfied was insufficient. There being no doubt in their own minds, they were willing to give the prisoner the benefit of any that might exist. Secure in the hypothesis that he ought to be hanged on general principles, they indulged him with more latitude of defense than his reckless hardihood seemed to ask. The Judge appeared to be more anxious than the prisoner, who, otherwise unconcerned, evidently took a grim pleasure in the responsibility he had created. "I don't take any hand in this yer game," had been his invariable but good-humored reply to all questions. The Judge—who was also his captor—for a moment vaguely regretted that he had not shot him "on sight" that morning, but presently dismissed this human weakness as unworthy of the judicial mind. Nevertheless, when there was a tap at the door, and it was said that Tennessee's Partner was there on behalf of the prisoner, he was admitted at once without question. Perhaps the younger members of the jury, to whom the proceedings were becoming irksomely thoughtful, hailed him as a relief.

For he was not, certainly, an imposing figure. Short and stout, with a square face, sunburned into a preternatural redness, clad in a loose duck "jumper" and trousers streaked and splashed with red soil, his aspect under any circumstances would have been quaint, and was now even ridiculous. As he stooped to deposit at his feet a heavy carpetbag he was carrying, it became obvious, from partially developed legends and inscriptions, that the material with which his trousers had been patched had been originally intended for a less ambitious covering. Yet he advanced with great gravity, and after shaking the hand of each person in the room with labored cordiality, he wiped his serious perplexed face on a red bandana handkerchief, a shade lighter than his complexion, laid his powerful hand upon the table to steady himself, and thus addressed the Judge:—

"I was passin' by," he began, by way of apology, "and I thought I'd just step in and see how things was gittin' on with Tennessee thar,—my pardner. It's a hot night. I disremember any sich weather before on the Bar."

He paused a moment, but nobody volunteering any other meteorological recollection, he again had recourse to his pocket-handkerchief, and for some moments mopped his face diligently.

"Have you anything to say on behalf of the prisoner?" said the Judge finally.

"Thet's it," said Tennessee's Partner, in a tone of relief. "I come yar as Tennessee's pardner,—knowing him nigh on four year, off and on, wet and dry, in luck and out o' luck. His ways ain't aller my ways, but thar ain't any p'ints in that young man, thar ain't any liveliness as he's been up to, as I don't know. And you sez to me, sez you,—confidential-like, and between man and man,—sez you, 'Do you know anything in his behalf?' and I sez to you, sez I,—confidential-like, as between man and man,—'What should a man know of his pardner?'"

"Is this all you have to say?" asked the Judge impatiently, feeling, perhaps, that a dangerous sympathy of humor was beginning to humanize the court.

"Thet's so," continued Tennessee's Partner. "It ain't for me to say anything agin' him. And now, what's the case? Here's Tennessee wants money, wants it bad, and doesn't like to ask it of his old pardner. Well, what does Tennessee do? He lays for a stranger, and he fetches that stranger; and you lays for *him,* and you fetches *him;* and the honors is easy. And I put it to you, bein' a fa'r-minded man, and to you, gentlemen all, as fa'r-minded men, ef this isn't so."

"Prisoner," said the Judge, interrupting, "have you any questions to ask this man?"

"No! no!" continued Tennessee's Partner hastily. "I play this yer hand alone. To come down to the bed-rock, it's just this: Tennessee, thar, has played it pretty rough and ex-pensive-like on a stranger, and on this yer camp. And now, what's the fair thing? Some would say more, some would say less. Here's seventeen hundred dollars in coarse gold and a watch,—it's about all my pile,—and call it square!" And before a hand could be raised to prevent him, he had emptied the contents of the carpetbag upon the table.

For a moment his life was in jeopardy. One or two men

sprang to their feet, several hands groped for hidden weapons, and a suggestion to "throw him from the window" was only overridden by a gesture from the Judge. Tennessee laughed. And apparently oblivious of the excitement, Tennessee's Partner improved the opportunity to mop his face again with his handkerchief.

When order was restored, and the man was made to understand, by the use of forcible figures and rhetoric, that Tennessee's offense could not be condoned by money, his face took a more serious and sanguinary hue, and those who were nearest to him noticed that his rough hand trembled slightly on the table. He hesitated a moment as he slowly returned the gold to the carpetbag, as if he had not yet entirely caught the elevated sense of justice which swayed the tribunal, and was perplexed with the belief that he had not offered enough. Then he turned to the Judge, and saying, "This yer is a lone hand, played alone, and without my pardner," he bowed to the jury and was about to withdraw, when the Judge called him back:—

"If you have anything to say to Tennessee, you had better say it now."

For the first time that evening the eyes of the prisoner and his strange advocate met. Tennessee smiled, showed his white teeth, and saying, "Euchred, old man!" held out his hand. Tennessee's Partner took it in his own, and saying, "I just dropped in as I was passin' to see how things was gettin' on," let the hand passively fall, and adding that "it was a warm night," again mopped his face with his handkerchief, and without another word withdrew.

The two men never again met each other alive. For the unparalleled insult of a bribe offered to Judge Lynch—who, whether bigoted, weak, or narrow, was at least incorruptible —firmly fixed in the mind of that mythical personage any wavering determination of Tennessee's fate; and at the break of day he was marched, closely guarded, to meet it at the top of Marley's Hill.

How he met it, how cool he was, how he refused to say anything, how perfect were the arrangements of the committee, were all duly reported, with the addition of a warning moral and example to all future evil-doers, in the "Red Dog Clarion," by its editor, who was present, and to whose vigorous English I cheerfully refer the reader. But the beauty of that midsummer morning, the blessed amity of earth and air and sky, the awakened life of the free woods and hills, the joyous renewal and promise of Nature, and above all, the infinite serenity that thrilled through each, was not reported, as not being a part of the social lesson. And yet, when the weak and foolish deed was done, and a life, with its possibilities and responsibilities, had passed out of the misshapen thing that dangled between earth and sky, the birds sang, the flowers bloomed, the sun shone, as cheerily as before; and possibly the "Red Dog Clarion" was right.

Tennessee's Partner was not in the group that surrounded the ominous tree. But as they turned to disperse, attention was drawn to the singular appearance of a motionless donkey-cart halted at the side of the road. As they approached, they at once recognized the venerable "Jenny" and the two-wheeled cart as the property of Tennessee's Partner, used by him in carrying dirt from his claim; and a few paces distant the owner of the equipage himself, sitting under a buckeye-tree, wiping the perspiration from his glowing face. In answer to an inquiry, he said he had come for the body of the "diseased," "if it was all the same to the committee." He didn't wish to "hurry anything"; he could "wait." He was not working that day; and when the gentlemen were done with the "diseased," he would take him. "Ef thar is any present," he added, in his simple, serious way, "as would care to jine in the fun'l, they kin come." Perhaps it was from a sense of humor, which I have already intimated was a feature of Sandy Bar,—perhaps it was from something even better than that, but two thirds of the loungers accepted the invitation at once.

It was noon when the body of Tennessee was delivered into the hands of his partner. As the cart drew up to the fatal tree, we noticed that it contained a rough oblong box, —apparently made from a section of sluicing,—and half filled with bark and the tassels of pine. The cart was further decorated with slips of willow and made fragrant with buck-eye-blossoms. When the body was deposited in the box, Tennessee's Partner drew over it a piece of tarred canvas, and gravely mounting the narrow seat in front, with his feet upon the shafts, urged the little donkey forward. The equipage moved slowly on, at that decorous pace which was habitual with Jenny even under less solemn circumstances. The men—half curiously, half jestingly, but all good-humoredly—strolled along beside the cart, some in advance, some a little in the rear of the homely catafalque. But whether from the narrowing of the road or some present sense of decorum, as the cart passed on, the company fell to the rear in couples, keeping step, and otherwise assuming the external show of a formal procession. Jack Folinsbee, who had at the outset played a funeral march in dumb show upon an imaginary trombone, desisted from a lack of sympathy and appreciation,—not having, perhaps, your true humorist's capacity to be content with the enjoyment of his own fun.

The way led through Grizzly Cañon, by this time clothed in funereal drapery and shadows. The redwoods, burying their moccasined feet in the red soil, stood in Indian file along the track, trailing an uncouth benediction from their bending boughs upon the passing bier. A hare, surprised into helpless inactivity, sat upright and pulsating in the ferns by the roadside as the cortége went by. Squirrels hastened to gain a secure outlook from higher boughs; and the blue-jays, spreading their wings, fluttered before them like outriders, until the outskirts of Sandy Bar were reached, and the solitary cabin of Tennessee's Partner.

Viewed under more favorable circumstances, it would not have been a cheerful place. The unpicturesque site, the rude and unlovely outlines, the unsavory details, which distinguish the nest-building of the California miner, were all here with the dreariness of decay superadded. A few paces from the cabin there was a rough inclosure, which, in the brief days of Tennessee's Partner's matrimonial felicity, had been used as a garden, but was now overgrown with fern. As we approached it, we were surprised to find that what we had taken for a recent attempt at cultivation was the broken soil about an open grave.

The cart was halted before the inclosure, and rejecting the offers of assistance with the same air of simple self-reliance he had displayed throughout, Tennessee's Partner lifted the rough coffin on his back, and deposited it unaided within the shallow grave. He then nailed down the board which served as a lid, and mounting the little mound of earth beside it, took off his hat and slowly mopped his face with his handkerchief. This the crowd felt was a preliminary to speech, and they disposed themselves variously on stumps and boulders, and sat expectant.

"When a man," began Tennessee's Partner slowly, "has been running free all day, what's the natural thing for him to do? Why, to come home. And if he ain't in a condition to go home, what can his best friend do? Why, bring him home. And here's Tennessee has been running free, and we brings him home from his wandering." He paused and picked up a fragment of quartz, rubbed it thoughtfully on his sleeve, and went on: "It ain't the first time that I've packed him on my back, as you see'd me now. It ain't the first time that I brought him to this yer cabin when he couldn't help himself; it ain't the first time that I and Jinny have waited for him on yon hill, and picked him up and so fetched him home, when he couldn't speak and didn't know me. And now that it's the last time, why"—he paused and rubbed the quartz gently on his sleeve—"you see it's sort of rough on his pardner. And now, gentlemen," he added abruptly, picking up his long-handled shovel, "the fun'l's over; and my thanks, and Tennessee's thanks, to you for your trouble."

Resisting any proffers of assistance, he began to fill in the grave, turning his back upon the crowd, that after a few moments' hesitation gradually withdrew. As they crossed the little ridge that hid Sandy Bar from view, some, looking back, thought they could see Tennessee's Partner, his work done, sitting upon the grave, his shovel between his knees, and his face buried in his red bandana handkerchief. But it was argued by others that you couldn't tell his face from his handkerchief at that distance, and this point remained undecided.

In the reaction that followed the feverish excitement of that day, Tennessee's Partner was not forgotten. A secret investigation had cleared him of any complicity in Tennessee's guilt, and left only a suspicion of his general sanity. Sandy Bar made a point of calling on him, and proffering various uncouth but well-meant kindnesses. But from that day his rude health and great strength seemed visibly to decline; and when the rainy season fairly set in, and the tiny grass-blades were beginning to peep from the rocky mound above Tennessee's grave, he took to his bed.

One night, when the pines beside the cabin were swaying in the storm and trailing their slender fingers over the roof, and the roar and rush of the swollen river were heard below, Tennessee's Partner lifted his head from the pillow, saying, "It is time to go for Tennessee; I must put Jinny in the cart"; and would have risen from his bed but for the restraint of his attendant. Struggling, he still pursued his singular fancy: "There, now, steady, Jinny,—steady, old girl. How dark it is! Look out for the ruts,—and look out for him, too, old gal. Sometimes, you know, when he's blind drunk, he drops down right in the trail. Keep on straight up to the pine on the top of the hill. Thar! I told you so!— thar he is,—coming this way, too,—all by himself, sober, and his face a-shining. Tennessee! Pardner!"

And so they met.

BROWN OF
CALAVERAS

A SUBDUED tone of conversation, and the absence of cigar-smoke and boot-heels at the windows of the Wingdam stagecoach, made it evident that one of the inside passengers was a woman. A disposition on the part of loungers at the stations to congregate before the window, and some concern in regard to the appearance of coats, hats, and collars, further indicated that she was lovely. All of which Mr. Jack Hamlin, on the box-seat, noted with the smile of cynical philosophy. Not that he depreciated the sex, but that he recognized therein a deceitful element, the pursuit of which sometimes drew mankind away from the equally uncertain blandishments of poker,—of which it may be remarked that Mr. Hamlin was a professional exponent.

So that, when he placed his narrow boot on the wheel and leaped down, he did not even glance at the window from which a green veil was fluttering, but lounged up and down with that listless and grave indifference of his class, which was, perhaps, the next thing to good-breeding. With his closely buttoned figure and self-contained air he was a marked contrast to the other passengers, with their feverish restlessness and boisterous emotion; and even Bill Masters, a graduate of Harvard, with his slovenly dress, his overflowing vitality, his intense appreciation of lawlessness and barbarism, and his mouth filled with crackers and cheese, I fear cut but an unromantic figure beside this lonely calculator of chances, with his pale Greek face and Homeric gravity.

The driver called "All aboard!" and Mr. Hamlin returned to the coach. His foot was upon the wheel, and his face raised to the level of the open window, when, at the same moment, what appeared to him to be the finest eyes in the world suddenly met his. He quietly dropped down again, addressed a few words to one of the inside passengers, effected an exchange of seats, and as quietly took his place inside. Mr. Hamlin never allowed his philosophy to interfere with decisive and prompt action.

I fear that this irruption of Jack cast some restraint upon the other passengers, particularly those who were making themselves most agreeable to the lady. One of them leaned forward, and apparently conveyed to her information regarding Mr. Hamlin's profession in a single epithet. Whether Mr. Hamlin heard it, or whether he recognized in the informant a distinguished jurist, from whom, but a few evenings before, he had won several thousand dollars, I cannot say. His colorless face betrayed no sign; his black eyes, quietly observant, glanced indifferently past the legal gentleman, and rested on the much more pleasing features of his neighbor. An Indian stoicism—said to be an inheritance from his maternal ancestor—stood him in good service, until the rolling wheels rattled upon the river gravel at Scott's Ferry, and the stage drew up at the International Hotel for dinner. The legal gentleman and a member of Congress leaped out, and stood ready to assist the descending goddess, while Colonel Starbottle of Siskiyou took charge of her parasol and shawl. In this multiplicity of attention there was a momentary confusion and delay. Jack Hamlin quietly opened the *opposite* door of the coach, took the lady's hand, with that decision and positiveness which a hesitating and undecided sex knows how to admire, and in an instant had dexterously and gracefully swung her to the ground and again lifted her to the platform. An audible chuckle on the box, I fear, came from that other cynic, Yuba Bill, the driver. "Look keerfully arter that baggage, Kernel," said the expressman, with affected concern, as he looked after Colonel Starbottle, gloomily bringing up the rear of the triumphant procession to the waiting-room.

Mr. Hamlin did not stay for dinner. His horse was already saddled and awaiting him. He dashed over the ford, up the gravelly hill, and out into the dusty perspective of the Wingdam road, like one leaving an unpleasant fancy behind him. The inmates of dusty cabins by the roadside shaded their eyes with their hands and looked after him, recognizing the man by his horse, and speculating what "was up with Comanche Jack." Yet much of this interest centred in the horse, in a community where the time made by "French Pete's" mare, in his run from the Sheriff of Calaveras, eclipsed all concern in the ultimate fate of that worthy.

The sweating flanks of his gray at length recalled him to himself. He checked his speed, and turning into a byroad, sometimes used as a cut-off, trotted leisurely along, the reins hanging listlessly from his fingers. As he rode on, the character of the landscape changed and became more pastoral. Openings in groves of pine and sycamore disclosed some rude attempts at cultivation,—a flowering vine trailed over the porch of one cabin, and a woman rocked her cradled babe under the roses of another. A little farther on, Mr. Hamlin came upon some bare-legged children wading in the willowy creek, and so wrought upon them with a badinage peculiar to himself, that they were emboldened to climb up his horse's legs and over his saddle, until he was fain to develop an exaggerated ferocity of demeanor, and to escape, leaving behind some kisses and coin. And then, advancing deeper into the woods, where all signs of habitation failed, he began to sing, uplifting a tenor so singularly sweet, and shaded by a pathos so subdued and tender, that I wot the robins and linnets stopped to listen. Mr. Hamlin's voice was not cultivated; the subject of his song was some sentimental lunacy, borrowed from the Negro minstrels; but there thrilled through all some occult quality of tone and expression that was unspeakably touching. Indeed, it was a wonderful sight to see this sentimental blackleg, with a pack of cards in his pocket and a revolver at his back, sending his voice before him through the dim woods with a plaint about his "Nelly's grave," in a way that overflowed the eyes of the listener. A sparrow-hawk, fresh from his sixth victim, possibly recognizing in Mr. Hamlin a kindred spirit, stared at him in surprise, and was fain to confess the superiority of man. With a superior predatory capacity *he* couldn't sing.

But Mr. Hamlin presently found himself again on the highroad and at his former pace. Ditches and banks of gravel, denuded hillsides, stumps, and decayed trunks of trees, took the place of woodland and ravine, and indicated his approach to civilization. Then a church-steeple came in sight, and he knew that he had reached home. In a few moments he was clattering down the single narrow street that lost itself in a chaotic ruin of races, ditches, and tailings at the foot of the hill, and dismounted before the gilded windows of the Magnolia saloon. Passing through the long bar-room, he pushed open a green-baize door, entered a dark passage, opened another door with a passkey, and found himself in a dimly lighted room, whose furniture, though elegant and costly for the locality, showed signs of abuse. The inlaid centre-table was overlaid with stained disks that were not contemplated in the original design, the embroidered armchairs were discolored, and the green velvet lounge, on which Mr. Hamlin threw himself, was soiled at the foot with the red soil of Wingdam.

Mr. Hamlin did not sing in his cage. He lay still, looking at a highly colored painting above him, representing a young creature of opulent charms. It occurred to him then, for the first time, that he had never seen exactly that kind of a woman, and that, if he should, he would not, probably, fall in love with her. Perhaps he was thinking of another style of beauty. But just then some one knocked at the door. Without rising, he pulled a cord that apparently shot back a bolt, for the door swung open, and a man entered.

The new-comer was broad-shouldered and robust,—a vigor not borne out in the face, which, though handsome, was singularly weak and disfigured by dissipation. He appeared to be, also, under the influence of liquor, for he started on seeing Mr. Hamlin, and said, "I thought Kate was here"; stammered, and seemed confused and embarrassed.

Mr. Hamlin smiled the smile which he had before worn on the Wingdam coach, and sat up, quite refreshed and ready for business.

"You didn't come up on the stage," continued the new-comer, "did you?"

"No," replied Hamlin. "I left it at Scott's Ferry. It isn't due for half an hour yet. But how's luck, Brown?"

"D—d bad," said Brown, his face suddenly assuming an expression of weak despair. "I'm cleaned out again, Jack," he continued, in a whining tone, that formed a pitiable contrast to his bulky figure; "can't you help me with a hundred till to-morrow's clean-up? You see I've got to send money home to the old woman, and—you've won twenty times that amount from me."

The conclusion was, perhaps, not entirely logical, but Jack overlooked it, and handed the sum to his visitor. "The old-woman business is about played out, Brown," he added, by way of commentary; "why don't you say you want to buck ag'in' faro? You know you ain't married!"

"Fact, sir," said Brown, with a sudden gravity, as if the mere contact of the gold with the palm of the hand had imparted some dignity to his frame. "I've got a wife—a d—d good one, too, if I do say it—in the States. It's three years since I've seen her, and a year since I've writ to her. When things is about straight, and we get down to the lead, I'm going to send for her."

"And Kate?" queried Mr. Hamlin, with his previous smile.

Mr. Brown of Calaveras essayed an archness of glance to cover his confusion, which his weak face and whiskey-muddled intellect but poorly carried out, and said,—

"D—n it, Jack, a man must have a little liberty, you know. But come, what do you say to a little game? Give us a show to double this hundred."

Jack Hamlin looked curiously at his fatuous friend. Perhaps he knew that the man was predestined to lose the money, and preferred that it should flow back into his own coffers rather than any other. He nodded his head, and drew his chair toward the table. At the same moment there came a rap upon the door.

"It's Kate," said Mr. Brown.

Mr. Hamlin shot back the bolt and the door opened. But, for the first time in his life, he staggered to his feet utterly unnerved and abashed, and for the first time in his life the hot blood crimsoned his colorless cheeks to his forehead. For before him stood the lady he had lifted from the Wingdam coach, whom Brown, dropping his cards with a hysterical laugh, greeted as,—

"My old woman, by thunder!"

They say that Mrs. Brown burst into tears and reproaches

of her husband. I saw her in 1857 at Marysville, and disbelieve the story. And the "Wingdam Chronicle" of the next week, under the head of "Touching Reunion," said: "One of those beautiful and touching incidents, peculiar to California life, occurred last week in our city. The wife of one of Wingdam's eminent pioneers, tired of the effete civilization of the East and its inhospitable climate, resolved to join her noble husband upon these golden shores. Without informing him of her intention, she undertook the long journey, and arrived last week. The joy of the husband may be easier imagined than described. The meeting is said to have been indescribably affecting. We trust her example may be followed."

Whether owing to Mrs. Brown's influence, or to some more successful speculations, Mr. Brown's financial fortune from that day steadily improved. He bought out his partners in the "Nip and Tuck" lead, with money which was said to have been won at poker a week or two after his wife's arrival, but which rumor, adopting Mrs. Brown's theory that Brown had forsworn the gaming-table, declared to have been furnished by Mr. Jack Hamlin. He built and furnished the Wingdam House, which pretty Mrs. Brown's great popularity kept overflowing with guests. He was elected to the Assembly, and gave largess to churches. A street in Wingdam was named in his honor.

Yet it was noted that in proportion as he waxed wealthy and fortunate, he grew pale, thin, and anxious. As his wife's popularity increased, he became fretful and impatient. The most uxorious of husbands, he was absurdly jealous. If he did not interfere with his wife's social liberty, it was because it was maliciously whispered that his first and only attempt was met by an outburst from Mrs. Brown that terrified him into silence. Much of this kind of gossip came from those of her own sex whom she had supplanted in the chivalrous attentions of Wingdam, which, like most popular chivalry, was devoted to an admiration of power, whether of masculine force or feminine beauty. It should be remembered, too, in her extenuation, that, since her arrival, she had been the unconscious priestess of a mythological worship, perhaps not more ennobling to her womanhood than that which distinguished an older Greek democracy. I think that Brown was dimly conscious of this. But his only confidant was Jack Hamlin, whose infelix reputation naturally precluded any open intimacy with the family, and whose visits were infrequent.

It was midsummer and a moonlit night, and Mrs. Brown, very rosy, large-eyed, and pretty, sat upon the piazza, enjoying the fresh incense of the mountain breeze, and, it is to be feared, another incense which was not so fresh nor quite as innocent. Beside her sat Colonel Starbottle and Judge Boompointer, and a later addition to her court in the shape of a foreign tourist. She was in good spirits.

"What do you see down the road?" inquired the gallant Colonel, who had been conscious, for the last few minutes, that Mrs. Brown's attention was diverted.

"Dust." said Mrs. Brown, with a sigh. "Only Sister Anne's 'flock of sheep.'"

The Colonel, whose literary recollections did not extend farther back than last week's paper, took a more practical view. "It ain't sheep," he continued; "it's a horseman. Judge, ain't that Jack Hamlin's gray?"

But the Judge didn't know; and, as Mrs. Brown suggested the air was growing too cold for further investigations, they retired to the parlor.

Mr. Brown was in the stable, where he generally retired after dinner. Perhaps it was to show his contempt for his wife's companions; perhaps, like other weak natures, he found pleasure in the exercise of absolute power over inferior animals. He had a certain gratification in the training of a chestnut mare, whom he could beat or caress as pleased him, which he couldn't do with Mrs. Brown. It was here that he recognized a certain gray horse which had just come in, and, looking a little farther on, found his rider. Brown's greeting was cordial and hearty; Mr. Hamlin's somewhat restrained. But, at Brown's urgent request, he followed him up the back stairs to a narrow corridor, and thence to a small room looking out upon the stable-yard. It was plainly furnished with a bed, a table, a few chairs, and a rack for guns and whips.

"This yer's my home, Jack," said Brown with a sigh, as he threw himself upon the bed and motioned his companion to a chair. "Her room's t' other end of the hall. It's more'n six months since we've lived together, or met, except at meals. It's mighty rough papers on the head of the house, ain't it?" he said with a forced laugh. "But I'm glad to see you, Jack, d—d glad," and he reached from the bed, and again shook the unresponsive hand of Jack Hamlin.

"I brought ye up here, for I didn't want to talk in the stable; though, for the matter of that, it's all round town. Don't strike a light. We can talk here in the moonshine. Put up your feet on that winder and sit here beside me. Thar's whiskey in that jug."

Mr. Hamlin did not avail himself of the information. Brown of Calaveras turned his face to the wall, and continued,—

"If I didn't love the woman, Jack, I wouldn't mind. But it's loving her, and seeing her day arter day goin' on at this rate, and no one to put down the brake; that's what gits me! But I'm glad to see ye, Jack, d—d glad."

In the darkness he groped about until he had found and wrung his companion's hand again. He would have detained it, but Jack slipped it into the buttoned breast of his coat, and asked listlessly, "How long has this been going on?"

"Ever since she came here; ever since the day she walked into the Magnolia. I was a fool then; Jack, I'm a fool now; but I didn't know how much I loved her till then. And she hasn't been the same woman since.

"But that ain't all, Jack; and it's what I wanted to see you about, and I'm glad you've come. It ain't that she doesn't love me any more; it ain't that she fools with every chap that comes along; for perhaps I staked her love and lost it, as I did everything else at the Magnolia; and perhaps foolin' is nateral to some women, and thar ain't no great harm done, 'cept to the fools. But, Jack, I think,—I think she loves somebody else. Don't move, Jack! don't move; if your pistol hurts ye, take it off.

"It's been more'n six months now that she's seemed unhappy and lonesome, and kinder nervous and scared-like. And sometimes I've ketched her lookin' at me sort of timid and pitying. And she writes to somebody. And for the last week she's been gathering her own things,—trinkets, and furbelows, and jew'lry,—and, Jack, I think she's goin' off. I could stand all but that. To have her steal away like a thief!" He put his face downward to the pillow, and for a few moments there was no sound but the ticking of a clock on the mantel. Mr. Hamlin lit a cigar, and moved to the open window. The moon no longer shone into the room, and the bed and its occupant were in shadow. "What shall I do, Jack?" said the voice from the darkness.

The answer came promptly and clearly from the window side, "Spot the man, and kill him on sight."

"But, Jack"—

"He's took the risk!"

"But will that bring *her* back?"

Jack did not reply, but moved from the window towards the door.

"Don't go yet, Jack; light the candle and sit by the table. It's a comfort to see ye, if nothin' else."

Jack hesitated and then complied. He drew a pack of cards from his pocket and shuffled them, glancing at the bed. But Brown's face was turned to the wall. When Mr. Hamlin had shuffled the cards, he cut them, and dealt one card on the opposite side of the table towards the bed, and another on his side of the table for himself. The first was a deuce; his own card a king. He then shuffled and cut again. This time "dummy" had a queen and himself a four-spot. Jack brightened up for the third deal. It brought his adversary a deuce and himself a king again. "Two out of three," said Jack audibly.

"What's that, Jack?" said Brown.

"Nothing."

Then Jack tried his hand with dice; but he always threw sixes and his imaginary opponent aces. The force of habit is sometimes confusing.

Meanwhile some magnetic influence in Mr. Hamlin's presence, or the anodyne of liquor, or both, brought surcease of sorrow, and Brown slept. Mr. Hamlin moved his chair to the window and looked out on the town of Wingdam, now sleeping peacefully, its harsh outlines softened and subdued, its glaring colors mellowed and sobered in the moonlight that flowed over all. In the hush he could hear the gurgling of water in the ditches and the sighing of the pines beyond the hill. Then he looked up at the firmament, and as he did so a star shot across the twinkling field. Presently another, and then another. The phenomenon suggested to Mr. Hamlin a fresh augury. If in another fifteen minutes another star should fall— He sat there, watch in hand, for twice that time, but the phenomenon was not repeated.

The clock struck two, and Brown still slept. Mr. Hamlin approached the table and took from his pocket a letter, which he read by the flickering candlelight. It contained only a single line, written in pencil, in a woman's hand,—

"Be at the corral with the buggy at three."

The sleeper moved uneasily and then awoke. "Are you there, Jack?"

"Yes."

"Don't go yet. I dreamed just now, Jack,—dreamed of old times. I thought that Sue and me was being married agin, and that the parson, Jack, was—who do you think?— you!"

The gambler laughed, and seated himself on the bed, the paper still in his hand.

"It's a good sign, ain't it?" queried Brown.

"I reckon! Say, old man, hadn't you better get up?"

The "old man," thus affectionately appealed to, rose, with the assistance of Hamlin's outstretched hand.

"Smoke?"

Brown mechanically took the proffered cigar.

"Light?"

Jack had twisted the letter into a spiral, lit it, and held it for his companion. He continued to hold it until it was consumed, and dropped the fragment—a fiery star—from the open window. He watched it as it fell, and then returned to his friend.

"Old man," he said, placing his hands upon Brown's shoulders, "in ten minutes I'll be on the road, and gone like that spark. We won't see each other agin; but, before I go, take a fool's advice: sell out all you've got, take your wife with you, and quit the country. It ain't no place for you nor her. Tell her she must go; make her go if she won't. Don't whine because you can't be a saint and she ain't an angel. Be a man, and treat her like a woman. Don't be a d—d fool. Good-by."

He tore himself from Brown's grasp and leaped down the stairs like a deer. At the stable-door he collared the half-sleeping hostler, and backed him against the wall. "Saddle my horse in two minutes, or I'll"— The ellipsis was frightfully suggestive.

"The missis said you was to have the buggy," stammered the man.

"D—n the buggy!"

The horse was saddled as fast as the nervous hands of the astounded hostler could manipulate buckle and strap.

"Is anything up, Mr. Hamlin?" said the man, who, like all his class, admired the élan of his fiery patron, and was really concerned in his welfare.

"Stand aside!"

The man fell back. With an oath, a bound, and clatter, Jack was into the road. In another moment, to the man's half-awakened eyes, he was but a moving cloud of dust in the distance, towards which a star just loosed from its brethren was trailing a stream of fire.

But early that morning the dwellers by the Wingdam turnpike, miles away, heard a voice, pure as a sky-lark's, singing afield. They who were asleep turned over on their rude couches to dream of youth, and love, and olden days. Hard-faced men and anxious gold-seekers, already at work, ceased their labors and leaned upon their picks to listen to a romantic vagabond ambling away against the rosy sunrise.

BEFORE nine o'clock it was pretty well known all along the river that the two parties of the "Amity Claim" had quarreled and separated at daybreak. At that time the attention of their nearest neighbor had been attracted by the sounds of altercations and two consecutive pistol-shots. Running out, he had seen dimly in the gray mist that rose from the river the tall form of Scott, one of the partners, descending the hill toward the cañon; a moment later, York, the other partner, had appeared from the cabin, and walked in an opposite direction toward the river, passing within a few feet of the curious watcher. Later it was discovered that a serious Chinaman, cutting wood before the cabin, had witnessed part of the quarrel. But John was stolid, indifferent, and reticent. "Me choppee wood, me no fightee," was his serene response to all anxious queries. "But what did they *say*, John?" John did not *sabe*. Colonel Starbottle deftly ran over the various popular epithets which a generous public sentiment might accept as reasonable provocation for an assault. But John did not recognize them. "And this yer's the cattle," said the Colonel, with some severity, "that some thinks oughter be allowed to testify agin a White Man! Git—you heathen!"

Still the quarrel remained inexplicable. That two men, whose amiability and grave tact had earned for them the title of "The Peacemakers," in a community not greatly given to the passive virtues,—that these men, singularly devoted to each other, should suddenly and violently quarrel, might well excite the curiosity of the camp. A few of the more inquisitive visited the late scene of conflict, now deserted by its former occupants. There was no trace of disorder or confusion in the neat cabin. The rude table was arranged as if for breakfast; the pan of yellow biscuit still sat upon that hearth whose dead embers might have typified the evil passions that had raged there but an hour before. But Colonel Starbottle's eye, albeit somewhat bloodshot and rheumy, was more intent on practical details. On examination, a bullet-hole was found in the doorpost, and another nearly opposite in the casing of the window. The Colonel called attention to the fact that the one "agreed with" the bore of Scott's revolver, and the other with that of York's derringer. "They must hev stood about yer," said the Colonel, taking position; "not more'n three feet apart, and—missed!" There was a fine touch of pathos in the falling inflection of the Colonel's voice, which was not without effect. A delicate perception of wasted opportunity thrilled his auditors.

But the Bar was destined to experience a greater disappointment. The two antagonists had not met since the quarrel, and it was vaguely rumored that, on the occasion of a second meeting, each had determined to kill the other "on sight." There was, consequently, some excitement—and, it is to be feared, no little gratification—when, at ten o'clock, York stepped from the Magnolia Saloon into the one long straggling street of the camp, at the same moment that Scott left the blacksmith's shop at the forks of the road. It was evident, at a glance, that a meeting could only be avoided by the actual retreat of one or the other.

In an instant the doors and windows of the adjacent saloons were filled with faces. Heads unaccountably appeared above the river banks and from behind boulders. An empty wagon at the cross-road was suddenly crowded with people, who seemed to have sprung from the earth. There was much running and confusion on the hillside. On the mountain-road, Mr. Jack Hamlin had reined up his horse and was standing upright on the seat of his buggy. And the two objects of this absorbing attention approached each other.

"York's got the sun," "Scott'll line him on that tree," "He's waiting to draw his fire," came from the cart; and then it was silent. But above this human breathlessness the river rushed and sang, and the wind rustled the tree-tops with an indifference that seemed obtrusive. Colonel Starbottle felt it, and in a moment of sublime preoccupation, without looking around, waved his cane behind him warningly to all Nature, and said, "Shu!"

The men were now within a few feet of each other. A hen ran across the road before one of them. A feathery seed vessel, wafted from a wayside tree, fell at the feet of the other. And, unheeding this irony of Nature, the two opponents came nearer, erect and rigid, looked in each other's eyes, and —passed!

Colonel Starbottle had to be lifted from the cart. "This yer camp is played out," he said gloomily, as he affected to be supported into the Magnolia. With what further expression he might have indicated his feelings it was impossible to say, for at that moment Scott joined the group. "Did you speak to me?" he asked of the Colonel, dropping his hand, as if with accidental familiarity, on that gentleman's shoulder. The Colonel, recognizing some occult quality in the touch, and some unknown quantity in the glance of his questioner, contented himself by replying, "No, sir," with dignity. A few rods away, York's conduct was as characteristic and peculiar. "You had a mighty fine chance; why didn't you plump him?" said Jack Hamlin, as York drew near the buggy. "Because I hate him," was the reply, heard only by Jack. Contrary to popular belief, this reply was not hissed between the lips of the speaker, but was said in an ordinary tone. But Jack Hamlin, who was an observer of mankind, noticed that the speaker's hands were cold and his lips dry, as he helped him into the buggy, and accepted the seeming paradox with a smile.

When Sandy Bar became convinced that the quarrel between York and Scott could not be settled after the usual local methods, it gave no further concern thereto. But presently it was rumored that the "Amity Claim" was in litigation, and that its possession would be expensively disputed by each of the partners. As it was well known that the claim in question was "worked out" and worthless, and that the partners whom it had already enriched had talked of abandoning it but a day or two before the quarrel, this proceeding could only be accounted for as gratuitous spite. Later, two San Francisco lawyers made their appearance in this guileless Arcadia, and were eventually taken into the saloons, and—what was pretty much the same thing—the confidences of the inhabitants. The results of this unhallowed intimacy were many subpœnas; and, indeed, when the "Amity Claim" came to trial, all of Sandy Bar that was not in compulsory attendance at the county seat came there from curiosity. The gulches and ditches for miles around were deserted. I do not propose to describe that already famous trial. Enough that, in the language of the plaintiff's counsel, "it was one of no ordinary significance, involving the inherent rights of that untiring industry which had developed the Pactolian resources of this golden land"; and, in the homelier phrase of Colonel Starbottle, "a fuss that gentlemen might hev settled in ten minutes over a social glass, ef they meant business; or in ten seconds with a revolver, ef they meant fun." Scott got a verdict, from which York instantly appealed. It was said that he had sworn to spend his last dollar in the struggle.

In this way Sandy Bar began to accept the enmity of the former partners as a lifelong feud, and the fact that they had ever been friends was forgotten. The few who expected to learn from the trial the origin of the quarrel were disappointed. Among the various conjectures, that which ascribed some occult feminine influence as the cause was naturally popular in a camp given to dubious compliment of the sex. "My word for it, gentlemen," said Colonel Starbottle, who had been known in Sacramento as a Gentleman of the Old School, "there's some lovely creature at the bottom of this." The gallant Colonel then proceeded to illustrate his theory by divers sprightly stories, such as Gentlemen of the Old School are in the habit of repeating, but which, from deference to the prejudices of gentlemen of a more recent school, I refrain from transcribing here. But it would appear that even the Colonel's theory was fallacious. The only woman who personally might have exercised any influence over the partners was the pretty daughter of "old man Folinsbee," of Poverty Flat, at whose hospitable house—which exhibited some comforts and refinements rare in that crude civilization —both York and Scott were frequent visitors. Yet into this charming retreat York strode one evening a month after the quarrel, and, beholding Scott sitting there, turned to the fair hostess with the abrupt query, "Do you love this man?" The young woman thus addressed returned that answer—at once spirited and evasive—which would occur to most of my fair readers in such an emergency. Without another word, York left the house. "Miss Jo" heaved the least possible sigh as the door closed on York's curls and square shoulders, and then, like a good girl, turned to her insulted guest. "But would you believe it, dear?" she afterwards related to an intimate friend, "the other creature, after glowering at me for a moment, got up on its hind legs, took its hat, and left too; and that's the last I've seen of either."

The same hard disregard of all other interests or feelings in the gratification of their blind rancor characterized all their actions. When York purchased the land below Scott's new claim, and obliged the latter, at a great expense, to make a long détour to carry a "tail-race" around it, Scott retaliated by building a dam that overflowed York's claim on the river. It was Scott who, in conjunction with Colonel Starbottle, first organized that active opposition to the Chinamen which resulted in the driving off of York's Mongolian laborers; it was York who built the wagon-road and established the express which rendered Scott's mules and pack-trains obsolete; it was Scott who called into life the Vigilance Committee which expatriated York's friend, Jack Hamlin; it was York who created the "Sandy Bar Herald," which characterized the act as "a lawless outrage" and Scott as a "Border Ruffian"; it was Scott, at the head of twenty masked men, who, one moonlight night, threw the offending "forms" into the yellow river, and scattered the types in the dusty road. These proceedings were received in the distant and more civilized outlying towns as vague indications of progress and vitality. I have before me a copy of the "Poverty Flat Pioneer" for the week ending August 12, 1856, in which the editor, under the head of "County Improvements," says: "The new Presbyterian Church on C Street, at Sandy Bar, is completed. It stands upon the lot formerly occupied by the Magnolia Saloon, which was so mysteriously burnt last month. The temple, which now rises like a Phœnix from the ashes of the Magnolia, is virtually the free gift of H. J. York, Esq., of Sandy Bar, who purchased the lot and donated the lumber. Other buildings are going up in the vicinity, but the most noticeable is the 'Sunny South Saloon,' erected by Captain Mat. Scott, nearly opposite the church. Captain Scott has spared no expense in the furnishing of this saloon, which promises to be one of the most agreeable places of resort in old Tuolumne. He has recently imported two new first-class billiard-tables with cork cushions. Our old friend, 'Mountain Jimmy,' will dispense liquors at the bar. We refer our readers to the advertisement in another column. Visitors to Sandy Bar cannot do better than give 'Jimmy' a call." Among the local items occurred the following: "H. J. York, Esq., of Sandy Bar, has offered a reward of $100 for the detection of the parties who hauled away the steps of the new Presbyterian Church, C Street, Sandy Bar, during divine service on Sabbath evening last. Captain Scott adds another hundred for the capture of the miscreants who broke the magnificent plate-glass windows of the new saloon on the following evening. There is some talk of reorganizing the old Vigilance Committee at Sandy Bar."

When, for many months of cloudless weather, the hard, unwinking sun of Sandy Bar had regularly gone down on the unpacified wrath of these men, there was some talk of mediation. In particular, the pastor of the church to which I have just referred—a sincere, fearless, but perhaps not fully enlightened man—seized gladly upon the occasion of York's liberality to attempt to reunite the former partners. He preached an earnest sermon on the abstract sinfulness of discord and rancor. But the excellent sermons of the Rev. Mr. Daws were directed to an ideal congregation that did not exist at Sandy Bar,—a congregation of beings of unmixed vices and virtues, of single impulses, and perfectly logical motives, of preternatural simplicity, of childlike faith, and grown-up responsibilities. As unfortunately the people who actually attended Mr. Daws's church were mainly very human, somewhat artful, more self-excusing than self-accusing, rather good-natured, and decidedly weak, they quietly shed that portion of the sermon which referred to themselves, and accepting York and Scott—who were both in defiant attendance—as curious examples of those ideal beings above referred to, felt a certain satisfaction—which, I fear, was not altogether Christian-like—in their "raking-down." If Mr. Daws expected York and Scott to shake hands after the sermon, he was disappointed. But he did not relax his purpose. With that quiet fearlessness and determination which had won for him the respect of men who were too apt to regard piety as synonymous with effeminacy, he attacked Scott in his own house. What he said has not been recorded, but it is to be feared that it was part of his sermon. When he had concluded, Scott looked at him, not unkindly, over the glasses of his bar, and said, less irreverently than the words might convey, "Young man, I rather like your style; but when you know York and me as well as you do God Almighty, it'll be time to talk."

And so the feud progressed; and so, as in more illustrious examples, the private and personal enmity of two representative men led gradually to the evolution of some crude, half-expressed principle or belief. It was not long before it was made evident that those beliefs were identical with certain broad principles laid down by the founders of the American Constitution, as expounded by the statesmanlike A., or were the fatal quicksands on which the ship of state might be wrecked, warningly pointed out by the eloquent B. The practical result of all which was the nomination of York and Scott to represent the opposite factions of Sandy Bar in legislative councils.

For some weeks past the voters of Sandy Bar and the ad-

jacent camps had been called upon, in large type, to "RALLY!"
In vain the great pines at the cross-roads—whose trunks were
compelled to bear this and other legends—moaned and protested from their windy watch-towers. But one day, with fife
and drum and flaming transparency, a procession filed into
the triangular grove at the head of the gulch. The meeting was
called to order by Colonel Starbottle, who, having once enjoyed legislative functions, and being vaguely known as
"war-horse," was considered to be a valuable partisan of
York. He concluded an appeal for his friend with an
enunciation of principles, interspersed with one or two anec-
dotes so gratuitously coarse that the very pines might have
been moved to pelt him with their cast-off cones as he stood
there. But he created a laugh, on which his candidate rode
into popular notice; and when York rose to speak, he was
greeted with cheers. But, to the general astonishment, the
new speaker at once launched into bitter denunciation of his
rival. He not only dwelt upon Scott's deeds and example as
known to Sandy Bar, but spoke of facts connected with his
previous career hitherto unknown to his auditors. To great
precision of epithet and directness of statement, the speaker
added the fascination of revelation and exposure. The crowd
cheered, yelled, and were delighted; but when this astounding philippic was concluded, there was a unanimous call for
"Scott!" Colonel Starbottle would have resisted this mani-
fest impropriety, but in vain. Partly from a crude sense of
justice, partly from a meaner craving for excitement, the assemblage was inflexible; and Scott was dragged, pushed, and
pulled upon the platform. As his frowsy head and unkempt
beard appeared above the railing, it was evident that he was
drunk. But it was also evident, before he opened his lips, that
the orator of Sandy Bar—the one man who could touch their
vagabond sympathies (perhaps because he was not above

appealing to them)—stood before them. A consciousness of this power lent a certain dignity to his figure, and I am not sure but that his very physical condition impressed them as a kind of regal unbending and large condescension. Howbeit, when this unexpected Hector arose from this ditch, York's myrmidons trembled. "There's naught, gentlemen," said Scott, leaning forward on the railing,—"there's naught as that man hez said as isn't true. I *was* run outer Cairo; I *did* belong to the Regulators; I *did* desert from the army; I *did* leave a wife in Kansas. But thar's one thing he didn't charge me with, and maybe he's forgotten. For three years, gentlemen, I was that man's pardner!" Whether he intended to say more, I cannot tell; a burst of applause artistically rounded and enforced the climax, and virtually elected the speaker. That fall he went to Sacramento, York went abroad, and for the first time in many years distance and a new atmosphere isolated the old antagonists.

With little of change in the green wood, gray rock, and yellow river, but with much shifting of human landmarks and new faces in its habitations, three years passed over Sandy Bar. The two men, once so identified with its character, seemed to have been quite forgotten. "You will never return to Sandy Bar," said Miss Folinsbee, the "Lily of Poverty Flat," on meeting York in Paris, "for Sandy Bar is no more. They call it Riverside now; and the new town is built higher up on the river bank. By the bye, 'Jo' says that Scott has won his suit about the 'Amity Claim,' and that he lives in the old cabin, and is drunk half his time. Oh, I beg your pardon," added the lively lady, as a flush crossed York's sallow cheek; "but, bless me, I really thought that old grudge was made up. I'm sure it ought to be."

It was three months after this conversation, and a pleasant summer evening, that the Poverty Flat coach drew up before the veranda of the Union Hotel at Sandy Bar. Among its passengers was one, apparently a stranger, in the local distinction of well-fitting clothes and closely shaven face, who demanded a private room and retired early to rest. But before sunrise next morning he arose, and, drawing some clothes from his carpet-bag, proceeded to array himself in a pair of white duck trousers, a white duck overshirt, and straw hat. When his toilet was completed, he tied a red bandana handkerchief in a loop and threw it loosely over his shoulders. The transformation was complete. As he crept softly down the stairs and stepped into the road, no one would have detected in him the elegant stranger of the previous night, and but few have recognized the face and figure of Henry York, of Sandy Bar.

In the uncertain light of that early hour, and in the change that had come over the settlement, he had to pause for a moment to recall where he stood. The Sandy Bar of his recollection lay below him, nearer the river; the buildings around him were of later date and newer fashion. As he strode toward the river, he noticed here a schoolhouse and there a church. A little farther on, the "Sunny South" came in view, transformed into a restaurant, its gilding faded and its paint rubbed off. He now knew where he was; and running briskly down a declivity, crossed a ditch, and stood upon the lower boundary of the "Amity Claim."

The gray mist was rising slowly from the river, clinging to the tree-tops and drifting up the mountain-side until it was caught among these rocky altars, and held a sacrifice to the ascending sun. At his feet the earth, cruelly gashed and scarred by his forgotten engines, had, since the old days, put on a show of greenness here and there, and now smiled forgivingly up at him, as if things were not so bad after all. A few birds were bathing in the ditch with a pleasant suggestion of its being a new and special provision of Nature, and a hare ran into an inverted sluice-box as he approached, as if it were put there for that purpose.

He had not yet dared to look in a certain direction. But the sun was now high enough to paint the little eminence on which the cabin stood. In spite of his self-control, his heart beat faster as he raised his eyes toward it. Its window and door were closed, no smoke came from its adobe chimney, but it was else unchanged. When within a few yards of it, he picked up a broken shovel, and shouldering it with a smile, he strode toward the door and knocked. There was no sound from within. The smile died upon his lips as he nervously pushed the door open.

A figure started up angrily and came toward him,—a figure whose bloodshot eyes suddenly fixed into a vacant stare, whose arms were at first outstretched and then thrown up in warning gesticulation,—a figure that suddenly gasped, choked, and then fell forward in a fit.

But before he touched the ground, York had him out into the open air and sunshine. In the struggle, both fell and rolled over on the ground. But the next moment York was sitting up, holding the convulsed frame of his former partner on his knee, and wiping the foam from his inarticulate lips. Gradually the tremor became less frequent and then ceased, and the strong man lay unconscious in his arms.

For some moments York held him quietly thus, looking in his face. Afar, the stroke of a woodman's axe—a mere phantom of sound—was all that broke the stillness. High up the mountain, a wheeling hawk hung breathlessly above them. And then came voices, and two men joined them.

"A fight?" No, a fit; and would they help him bring the sick man to the hotel?

And there for a week the stricken partner lay, unconscious

of aught but the visions wrought by disease and fear. On the eighth day at sunrise he rallied, and opening his eyes, looked upon York and pressed his hand; and then he spoke:—

"And it's you. I thought it was only whiskey."

York replied by only taking both of his hands, boyishly working them backward and forward, as his elbow rested on the bed, with a pleasant smile.

"And you've been abroad. How did you like Paris?"

"So, so! How did *you* like Sacramento?"

"Bully!"

And that was all they could think to say. Presently Scott opened his eyes again.

"I'm mighty weak."

"You'll get better soon."

"Not much."

A long silence followed, in which they could hear the sounds of wood-chopping, and that Sandy Bar was already astir for the coming day. Then Scott slowly and with difficulty turned his face to York and said,—

"I might hev killed you once."

"I wish you had."

They pressed each other's hands again, but Scott's grasp was evidently failing. He seemed to summon his energies for a special effort.

"Old man!"

"Old chap."

"Closer!"

York bent his head toward the slowly fading face.

"Do ye mind that morning?"

"Yes."

A gleam of fun slid into the corner of Scott's blue eyes as he whispered,—

"Old man, thar *was* too much saleratus in that bread!"

It is said that these were his last words. For when the sun, which had so often gone down upon the idle wrath of these foolish men, looked again upon them reunited, it saw the hand of Scott fall cold and irresponsive from the yearning clasp of his former partner, and it knew that the feud of Sandy Bar was at an end.

THE POET
OF SIERRA FLAT

As the enterprising editor of the "Sierra Flat Record" stood at his case setting type for his next week's paper, he could not help hearing the woodpeckers who were busy on the roof above his head. It occurred to him that possibly the birds had not yet learned to recognize in the rude structure any improvement on Nature, and this idea pleased him so much that he incorporated it in the editorial article which he was then doubly composing. For the editor was also printer of the "Record"; and although that remarkable journal was reputed to exert a power felt through all Calaveras and a great part of Tuolumne County, strict economy was one of the conditions of its beneficent existence.

Thus preoccupied, he was startled by the sudden irruption of a small roll of manuscript, which was thrown through the open door and fell at his feet. He walked quickly to the threshold and looked down the tangled trail which led to the highroad. But there was nothing to suggest the presence of his mysterious contributor. A hare limped slowly away, a green-and-gold lizard paused upon a pine stump, the woodpeckers ceased their work. So complete had been his sylvan seclusion, that he found it difficult to connect any human agency with the act; rather the hare seemed to have an inexpressibly guilty look, the woodpeckers to maintain a significant silence, and the lizard to be conscience-stricken into stone.

An examination of the manuscript, however, corrected this injustice to defenseless Nature. It was evidently of human origin,—being verse, and of exceeding bad quality. The editor laid it aside. As he did so he thought he saw a face at the window. Sallying out in some indignation, he penetrated the surrounding thicket in every direction, but his search was as fruitless as before. The poet, if it were he, was gone.

A few days after this the editorial seclusion was invaded by voices of alternate expostulation and entreaty. Stepping to the door, the editor was amazed at beholding Mr. Morgan McCorkle, a well-known citizen of Angel's and a subscriber to the "Record," in the act of urging, partly by force and partly by argument, an awkward young man toward the building. When he had finally effected his object, and, as it were, safely landed his prize in a chair, Mr. McCorkle took off his hat, carefully wiped the narrow isthmus of forehead which divided his black brows from his stubby hair, and, with an explanatory wave of his hand toward his reluctant companion, said, "A borned poet, and the cussedest fool you ever seed!"

Accepting the editor's smile as a recognition of the introduction, Mr. McCorkle panted and went on: "Didn't want to come! 'Mister Editor don't want to see me, Morg,' sez he. 'Milt,' sez I, 'he do; a borned poet like you and a gifted genius like he oughter come together sociable!' And I fetched him. Ah, will yer?" The born poet had, after exhibiting signs of great distress, started to run. But Mr. McCorkle was down upon him instantly, seizing him by his long linen coat, and settled him back in his chair. " 'T ain't no use stampeding. Yer ye are and yer ye stays. For yer a borned poet,—ef ye are as shy as a jackass rabbit. Look it 'im now!"

He certainly was not an attractive picture. There was

hardly a notable feature in his weak face, except his eyes, which were moist and shy, and not unlike the animal to which Mr. McCorkle had compared him. It was the face that the editor had seen at the window.

"Knowed him for fower year,—since he war a boy," continued Mr. McCorkle in a loud whisper. "Allers the same, bless you! Can jerk a rhyme as easy as turnin' jack. Never had any eddication; lived out in Missooray all his life. But he's chock full o' poetry. On'y this mornin' sez I to him,—he camps along o' me,—'Milt!' sez I, 'are breakfast ready?' and he up and answers back quite peart and chipper, 'The breakfast it is ready, and the birds is singing free, and it's risin' in the dawnin' light is happiness to me!' When a man," said Mr. McCorkle, dropping his voice with deep solemnity, "gets off things like them, without any call to do it, and handlin' flapjacks over a cookstove at the same time,—that man's a borned poet."

There was an awkward pause. Mr. McCorkle beamed patronizingly on his protégé. The born poet looked as if he were meditating another flight,—not a metaphorical one. The editor asked if he could do anything for them.

"In course you can," responded Mr. McCorkle, "that's jest it. Milt, where's that poetry?"

The editor's countenance fell as the poet produced from his pocket a roll of manuscript. He, however, took it mechanically and glanced over it. It was evidently a duplicate of the former mysterious contribution.

The editor then spoke briefly but earnestly. I regret that I cannot recall his exact words, but it appeared that never before, in the history of the "Record," had the pressure been so great upon its columns. Matters of paramount importance, deeply affecting the material progress of Sierra, questions touching the absolute integrity of Calaveras and Tuolumne as social communities, were even now waiting expression. Weeks, nay, months, must elapse before that pressure would be removed, and the "Record" could grapple with any but the sternest of topics. Again, the editor had noticed with pain the absolute decline of poetry in the foothills of the Sierras. Even the works of Byron and Moore attracted no attention in Dutch Flat, and a prejudice seemed to exist against Tennyson in Grass Valley. But the editor was not without hope for the future. In the course of four or five years, when the country was settled—

"What would be the cost to print this yer?" interrupted Mr. McCorkle quietly.

"About fifty dollars, as an advertisement," responded the editor with cheerful alacrity.

Mr. McCorkle placed the sum in the editor's hand. "Yer see thet's what I sez to Milt. 'Milt,' sez I, 'pay as you go, for you are a borned poet. Hevin' no call to write, but doin' it free and spontaneous like, in course you pays. Thet's why Mr. Editor never printed your poetry.'"

"What name shall I put to it?" asked the editor.

"Milton."

It was the first word that the born poet had spoken during the interview, and his voice was so very sweet and musical that the editor looked at him curiously, and wondered if he had a sister.

"Milton! Is that all?"

"Thet's his furst name," exclaimed Mr. McCorkle.

The editor here suggested that as there had been another poet of that name—

"Milt might be took for him! Thet's bad," reflected Mr. McCorkle with simple gravity. "Well, put down his full name,—Milton Chubbuck."

The editor made a note of the fact. "I'll set it up now," he said. This was also a hint that the interview was ended. The poet and patron, arm in arm, drew towards the door. "In next week's paper," said the editor smilingly, in answer to the childlike look of inquiry in the eyes of the poet, and in another moment they were gone.

The editor was as good as his word. He straightway betook himself to his case, and, unrolling the manuscript, began his task. The woodpeckers on the roof recommenced theirs, and in a few moments the former sylvan seclusion was restored. There was no sound in the barren, barn-like room but the birds above, and below the click of the composing-rule as the editor marshaled the types into lines in his stick, and arrayed them in solid columns on the galley. Whatever might have been his opinion of the copy before him, there was no indication of it in his face, which wore the stolid indifference of his craft. Perhaps this was unfortunate, for as the day wore on and the level rays of the sun began to pierce the adjacent thicket, they sought out and discovered an anxious ambush figure drawn up beside the editor's window,—a figure that had sat there motionless for hours. Within, the editor worked on as steadily and impassively as Fate. And without, the born poet of Sierra Flat sat and watched him as waiting its decree.

The effect of the poem on Sierra Flat was remarkable and unprecedented. The absolute vileness of its doggerel, the gratuitous imbecility of its thought, and above all the crowning audacity of the fact that it was the work of a citizen and published in the county paper, brought it instantly into popularity. For many months Calaveras had languished for a sensation; since the last Vigilance Committee nothing had transpired to dispel the listless ennui begotten of stagnant business and growing civilization. In more prosperous moments the office of the "Record" would have been simply gutted and the editor deported; at present the paper was in such demand that the edition was speedily exhausted. In brief, the poem of Mr. Milton Chubbuck came like a special providence to Sierra Flat. It was read by camp-fires, in lonely cabins, in flaring bar-rooms and noisy saloons, and declaimed from the boxes of stage-coaches. It was sung in Poker Flat with the addition of a local chorus, and danced as an unhallowed rhythmic dance by the Pyrrhic phalanx of One Horse Gulch, known as "The Festive Stags of Calaveras." Some unhappy ambiguities of expression gave rise to many new readings, notes, and commentaries, which, I regret to state, were more often marked by ingenuity than delicacy of thought or expression.

Never before did poet acquire such sudden local reputation. From the seclusion of McCorkle's cabin and the obscurity of culinary labors he was haled forth into the glowing sunshine of Fame. The name of Chubbuck was written in letters of chalk on unpainted walls and carved with a pick on the sides of tunnels. A drink known variously as "The Chubbuck Tranquilizer" or "The Chubbuck Exalter" was dispensed at the bars. For some weeks a rude design for a Chubbuck statue, made up of illustrations from circus and melodeon posters, representing the genius of Calaveras in brief skirts on a flying steed in the act of crowning the poet Chubbuck, was visible at Keeler's Ferry. The poet himself was overborne with invitations to drink and extravagant congratulations. The meeting between Colonel Starbottle of Siskiyou and Chubbuck, as previously arranged by our "Boston," late of Roaring Camp, is said to have been indescribably affecting. The Colonel embraced him unsteadily. "I could not return to my constituents at Siskiyou, sir, if this hand, which has grasped that of the gifted Prentice and the lamented Poe, should not have been honored by the touch of the godlike

Chubbuck. Gentlemen, American literature is looking up. Thank you! I will take sugar in mine." It was "Boston" who indited letters of congratulations from H. W. Longfellow, Tennyson, and Browning to Mr. Chubbuck, deposited them in the Sierra Flat post-office, and obligingly consented to dictate the replies.

The simple faith and unaffected delight with which these manifestations were received by the poet and his patron might have touched the hearts of these grim masters of irony, but for the sudden and equal development in both of the variety of weak natures. Mr. McCorkle basked in the popularity of his protégé, and became alternately supercilious or patronizing toward the dwellers of Sierra Flat; while the poet, with hair carefully oiled and curled, and bedecked with cheap jewelry and flaunting neck-handkerchief, paraded himself before the single hotel. As may be imagined, this new disclosure of weakness afforded intense satisfaction to Sierra Flat, gave another lease of popularity to the poet, and suggested another idea to the facetious "Boston."

At that time a young lady popularly and professionally known as the "California Pet" was performing to enthusiastic audiences in the interior. Her specialty lay in the personation of youthful masculine character; as a *gamin* of the street she was irresistible, as a Negro-dancer she carried the honest miner's heart by storm. A saucy, pretty brunette, she had preserved a wonderful moral reputation even under the Jove-like advances of showers of gold that greeted her appearance on the stage at Sierra Flat. A prominent and delighted member of that audience was Milton Chubbuck. He attended every night. Every day he lingered at the door of the Union Hotel for a glimpse of the "California Pet." It was not long before he received a note from her,—in "Boston's" most popular and approved female hand,—acknowledging his admiration. It was not long before "Boston" was called upon to indite a suitable reply. At last, in furtherance of his facetious design, it became necessary for "Boston" to call upon the young actress herself and secure her personal participation. To her he unfolded a plan, the successful carrying out of which he felt would secure his fame to posterity as a practical humorist. The "California Pet's" black eyes sparkled approvingly and mischievously. She only stipulated that she should see the man first,—a concession to her feminine weakness which years of dancing Juba and wearing trousers and boots had not wholly eradicated from her willful breast. By all means, it should be done. And the interview was arranged for the next week.

It must not be supposed that during this interval of popularity Mr. Chubbuck had been unmindful of his poetic qualities. A certain portion of each day he was absent from town,— "a-communin' with natur'," as Mr. McCorkle expressed it, —and actually wandering in the mountain trails, or lying on his back under the trees, or gathering fragrant herbs and the bright-colored berries of the Manzanita. These and his company he generally brought to the editor's office late in the afternoon, often to that enterprising journalist's infinite weariness. Quiet and uncommunicative, he would sit there patiently watching him at his work until the hour for closing the office arrived, when he would as quietly depart. There was something so humble and unobtrusive in these visits, that the editor could not find it in his heart to deny them, and accepting them, like the woodpeckers, as a part of his sylvan surroundings, often forgot even his presence. Once or twice, moved by some beauty of expression in the moist, shy eyes, he felt like seriously admonishing his visitor of his idle folly; but his glance falling upon the oiled hair and the gorgeous necktie he invariably thought better of it. The case was evidently hopeless.

The interview between Mr. Chubbuck and the "California Pet" took place in a private room of the Union Hotel; propriety being respected by the presence of that arch-humorist, "Boston." To this gentleman we are indebted for the only true account of the meeting. However reticent Mr. Chubbuck might have been in the presence of his own sex, toward the fairer portion of humanity he was, like most poets, exceedingly voluble. Accustomed as the "California Pet" had been to excessive compliment, she was fairly embarrassed by the extravagant praises of her visitor. Her personation of boy characters, her dancing of the "champion jig," were particularly dwelt upon with fervid but unmistakable admiration. At last, recovering her audacity and emboldened by the presence of "Boston," the "California Pet" electrified her hearers by demanding, half jestingly, half viciously, if it were as a boy or a girl that she was the subject of his flattering admiration.

"That knocked him out o' time," said the delighted "Boston," in his subsequent account of the interview. "But do you believe the d—d fool actually asked her to take him with her; wanted to engage in the company."

The plan, as briefly unfolded by "Boston," was to prevail upon Mr. Chubbuck to make his appearance in costume (already designed and prepared by the inventor) before a Sierra Flat audience, and recite an original poem at the Hall immediately on the conclusion of the "California Pet's" performance. At a given signal the audience were to rise and deliver a volley of unsavory articles (previously provided by the originator of the scheme); then a select few were to rush on the stage, seize the poet, and, after marching him in triumphal procession through the town, were to deposit him beyond its uttermost limits, with strict injunctions never to enter it again. To the first part of the plan the poet was committed; for the latter portion it was easy enough to find participants.

The eventful night came, and with it an audience that packed the long narrow room with one dense mass of human beings. The "California Pet" never had been so joyous, so reckless, so fascinating and audacious before. But the applause was tame and weak compared to the ironical outburst that greeted the second rising of the curtain and the entrance of the born poet of Sierra Flat. Then there was a hush of expectancy, and the poet stepped to the footlights and stood with his manuscript in his hand.

His face was deadly pale. Either there was some suggestion of his fate in the faces of his audience, or some mysterious instinct told him of his danger. He attempted to speak, but faltered, tottered, and staggered to the wings.

Fearful of losing his prey, "Boston" gave the signal and leaped upon the stage. But at the same moment a light figure darted from behind the scenes, and delivering a kick that sent the discomfited humorist back among the musicians, cut a pigeon-wing, executed a double-shuffle, and then advancing to the footlights with that inimitable look, that audacious swagger and utter abandon which had so thrilled and fascinated them a moment before, uttered the characteristic speech, "Wot are you goin' to hit a man fur when he's down, s-a-a-y?"

The look, the drawl, the action, the readiness, and above all the downright courage of the little woman, had an effect. A roar of sympathetic applause followed the act. "Cut and run while you can," she whispered hurriedly over her one shoulder, without altering the other's attitude of pert and saucy defiance toward the audience. But even as she spoke, the poet tottered and sank fainting upon the stage. Then she threw a despairing whisper behind the scenes, "Ring down the curtain."

There was a slight movement of opposition in the audience, but among them rose the burly shoulders of Yuba Bill, the tall, erect figure of Henry York, of Sandy Bar, and the color- less, determined face of John Oakhurst. The curtain came down.

Behind it knelt the "California Pet" beside the prostrate poet. "Bring me some water. Run for a doctor. Stop!! CLEAR OUT, ALL OF YOU!"

She had unloosed the gaudy cravat and opened the shirt- collar of the insensible figure before her. Then she burst into an hysterical laugh.

"Manuela!"

Her tiring-woman, a Mexican half-breed, came toward her.

"Help me with him to my dressing-room, quick; then stand outside and wait. If any one questions you, tell them he's gone. Do you hear? HE's gone."

The old woman did as she was bade. In a few moments the audience had departed. Before morning so also had the "California Pet," Manuela, and the poet of Sierra Flat.

But, alas! with them also had departed the fair fame of the "California Pet." Only a few, and these, it is to be feared, of not the best moral character themselves, still had faith in the stainless honor of their favorite actress. "It was a mighty foolish thing to do, but it'll all come out right yet." On the other hand, a majority gave her full credit and approbation for her undoubted pluck and gallantry, but deplored that she should have thrown it away upon a worth- less object. To elect for a lover the despised and ridiculed vagrant of Sierra Flat, who had not even the manliness to stand up in his own defense, was not only evidence of inherent moral depravity, but was an insult to the community. Colonel Starbottle saw in it only another instance of extreme frailty of the sex; he had known similar cases; and remembered distinctly, sir, how a well known Philadelphia heiress, one of the finest women that ever rode in her kerridge, that, gad, sir! had thrown over a Southern member of Congress to consort with a d—d nigger. The Colonel had also noticed a singular look in the dog's eye which he did not entirely fancy. He would not say anything against the lady, sir, but he had noticed— And here, haply, the Colonel became so mysterious and darkly confidential as to be unintelligible and inaudible to the bystanders.

A few days after the disappearance of Mr. Chubbuck a singular report reached Sierra Flat, and it was noticed that "Boston," who since the failure of his elaborate joke had been even more depressed in spirits than is habitual with great humorists, suddenly found that his presence was required in San Francisco. But as yet nothing but the vaguest surmises were afloat, and nothing definite was known.

It was a pleasant afternoon when the editor of the "Sierra Flat Record" looked up from his case and beheld the figure of Mr. Morgan McCorkle standing in the doorway. There was a distressed look on the face of that worthy gentleman that at once enlisted the editor's sympathizing attention. He held an open letter in his hand as he advanced toward the middle of the room.

"As a man as has allers borne a fair reputation," began Mr. McCorkle slowly, "I should like, if so be as I could, Mister Editor, to make a correction in the columns of your valooable paper."

Mr. Editor begged him to proceed.

"Ye may not disremember that about a month ago I fetched

here what so be as we'll call a young man whose name might be as it were Milton—Milton Chubbuck."

Mr. Editor remembered perfectly.

"Thet same party I'd knowed better nor fower year, two on 'em campin' out together. Not that I'd known him all the time, fur he war shy and strange at spells, and had odd ways that I took war nat'ral to a borned poet. Ye may remember that I said he was a borned poet?"

The editor distinctly did.

"I picked this same party up in St. Jo., taking a fancy to his face, and kinder calklating he'd runned away from home; for I'm a married man, Mr. Editor, and hev children of my own,—and thinkin' belike he was a borned poet."

"Well," said the editor.

"And as I said before, I should like now to make a correction in the columns of your valooable paper."

"What correction?" asked the editor.

"I said, ef you remember my words, as how he was a borned poet."

"Yes."

"From statements in this yer letter it seems as how I war wrong."

"Well?"

"She war a woman."

It had been raining in the valley of the Sacramento. The North Fork had overflowed its banks, and Rattlesnake Creek was impassable. The few boulders that had marked the summer ford at Simpson's Crossing were obliterated by a vast sheet of water stretching to the foothills. The up-stage was stopped at Granger's; the last mail had been abandoned in the *tules,* the rider swimming for his life. "An area," remarked the "Sierra Avalanche," with pensive local pride, "as large as the State of Massachusetts is now under water."

Nor was the weather any better in the foothills. The mud lay deep on the mountain road; wagons that neither physical force nor moral objurgation could move from the evil ways into which they had fallen encumbered the track, and the way to Simpson's Bar was indicated by broken-down teams and hard swearing. And further on, cut off and inaccessible, rained upon and bedraggled, smitten by high winds and threatened by high water, Simpson's Bar, on the eve of Christmas Day, 1862, clung like a swallow's nest to the rocky entablature and splintered capitals of Table Mountain, and shook in the blast.

As night shut down on the settlement, a few lights gleamed through the mist from the windows of cabins on either side of the highway, now crossed and gullied by lawless streams and swept by marauding winds. Happily most of the population were gathered at Thompson's store, clustered around a red-hot stove, at which they silently spat in some accepted sense of social communion that perhaps rendered conversation unnecessary. Indeed, most methods of diversion had long since been exhausted on Simpson's Bar; high water had suspended the regular occupations on gulch and on river, and a consequent lack of money and whiskey had taken the zest from most illegitimate recreation. Even Mr. Hamlin was fain to leave the Bar with fifty dollars in his pocket—the only amount actually realized of the large sums won by him in the successful exercise of his arduous profession. "Ef I was asked," he remarked somewhat later,—"ef I was asked to pint out a purty little village where a retired sport as didn't care for money could exercise hisself, frequent and lively, I'd say Simpson's Bar; but for a young man with a large family depending on his exertions, it don't pay." As Mr. Hamlin's family consisted mainly of female adults, this remark is quoted rather to show the breadth of his humor than the exact extent of his responsibilities.

Howbeit, the unconscious objects of this satire sat that evening in the listless apathy begotten of idleness and lack of excitement. Even the sudden splashing of hoofs before the door did not arouse them. Dick Bullen alone paused in the act of scraping out his pipe, and lifted his head, but no other one of the group indicated any interest in, or recognition of, the man who entered.

It was a figure familiar enough to the company, and known in Simpson's Bar as "The Old Man." A man of perhaps fifty years; grizzled and scant of hair, but still fresh and youthful of complexion. A face full of ready but not very powerful sympathy, with a chameleon-like aptitude for taking on the shade and color of contiguous moods and feelings.

He had evidently just left some hilarious companions, and did not at first notice the gravity of the group, but clapped the shoulder of the nearest man jocularly, and threw himself into a vacant chair.

"Jest heard the best thing out, boys! Ye know Smiley, over yar—Jim Smiley—funniest man in the Bar? Well, Jim was jest telling the richest yarn about"—

"Smiley's a —— fool," interrupted a gloomy voice.

"A particular —— skunk," added another in sepulchral accents.

A silence followed these positive statements. The Old Man glanced quickly around the group. Then his face slowly changed. "That's so," he said reflectively, after a pause, "certainly a sort of a skunk and suthin' of a fool. In course." He was silent for a moment, as in painful contemplation of the unsavoriness and folly of the unpopular Smiley. "Dismal weather, ain't it?" he added, now fully embarked on the current of prevailing sentiment. "Mighty rough papers on the boys, and no show for money this season. And to-morrow's Christmas."

There was a movement among the men at this announcement, but whether of satisfaction or disgust was not plain. "Yes," continued the Old Man in the lugubrious tone he had, within the last few moments, unconsciously adopted, —"yes, Christmas, and to-night's Christmas Eve. Ye see, boys, I kinder thought—that is, I sorter had an idee, jest passin' like, you know—that maybe ye'd all like to come over to my house to-night and have a sort of tear round. But I suppose, now, you wouldn't? Don't feel like it, maybe?" he added with anxious sympathy, peering into the faces of his companions.

"Well, I don't know," responded Tom Flynn with some cheerfulness. "P'r'aps we may. But how about your wife, Old Man? What does *she* say to it?"

The Old Man hesitated. His conjugal experience had not been a happy one, and the fact was known to Simpson's Bar. His first wife, a delicate, pretty little woman, had suffered keenly and secretly from the jealous suspicions of her husband, until one day he invited the whole Bar to his house to expose her infidelity. On arriving, the party found the shy, petite creature quietly engaged in her household duties, and retired abashed and discomfited. But the sensitive woman did not easily recover from the shock of this extraordinary outrage. It was with difficulty she regained her equanimity sufficiently to release her lover from the closet in which he was concealed, and escape with him. She left a boy of three years to comfort her bereaved husband. The Old Man's present wife had been his cook. She was large, loyal, and aggressive.

Before he could reply, Joe Dimmick suggested with great directness that it was the "Old Man's house," and that, invoking the Divine Power, if the case were his own, he would invite whom he pleased, even if in so doing he imperiled his salvation. The Powers of Evil, he further remarked, should contend against him vainly. All this delivered with a terseness and vigor lost in this necessary translation.

"In course. Certainly. Thet's it," said the Old Man with a sympathetic frown. "Thar's no trouble about thet. It's my own house, built every stick on it myself. Don't you be afeard o' her, boys. She *may* cut up a trifle rough—ez wimmin do —but she'll come round." Secretly the Old Man trusted to the exaltation of liquor and the power of courageous example to sustain him in such an emergency.

As yet, Dick Bullen, the oracle and leader of Simpson's Bar, had not spoken. He now took his pipe from his lips, "Old Man, how's that yer Johnny gettin' on? Seems to me he didn't look so peart last time I seed him on the bluff

heavin' rocks at Chinamen. Didn't seem to take much interest in it. Thar was a gang of 'em by yar yesterday—
drownded out up the river—and I kinder thought o' Johnny,
and how he'd miss 'em! Maybe now, we'd be in the way ef
he wus sick?"

The father, evidently touched not only by this pathetic
picture of Johnny's deprivation, but by the considerate delicacy of the speaker, hastened to assure him that Johnny was
better, and that a "little fun might 'liven him up." Whereupon
Dick arose, shook himself, and saying, "I'm ready. Lead the
way, Old Man: here goes," himself led the way with a leap,
a characteristic howl, and darted out into the night. As he
passed through the outer room he caught up a blazing brand
from the hearth. The action was repeated by the rest of the
party, closely following and elbowing each other, and before
the astonished proprietor of Thompson's grocery was aware
of the intention of his guests, the room was deserted.

The night was pitchy dark. In the first gust of wind
their temporary torches were extinguished, and only the red
brands dancing and flitting in the gloom like drunken will-
o'-the-wisps indicated their whereabouts. Their way led up
Pine-Tree Cañon, at the head of which a broad, low, bark-
thatched cabin burrowed in the mountain-side. It was the
home of the Old Man, and the entrance to the tunnel in
which he worked when he worked at all. Here the crowd
paused for a moment, out of delicate deference to their host,
who came up panting in the rear.

"P'r'aps ye'd better hold on a second out yer, whilst I go
in and see that things is all right," said the Old Man, with
an indifference he was far from feeling. The suggestion was
graciously accepted, the door opened and closed on the host,
and the crowd, leaning their backs against the wall and
cowering under the eaves, waited and listened.

For a few moments there was no sound but the dripping of water from the eaves, and the stir and rustle of wrestling boughs above them. Then the men became uneasy, and whispered suggestion and suspicion passed from the one to the other. "Reckon she's caved in his head the first lick!" "Decoyed him inter the tunnel and barred him up, likely." "Got him down and sittin' on him." "Prob'ly biling suthin' to heave on us: stand clear the door, boys!" For just then the latch clicked, the door slowly opened, and a voice said, "Come in out o' the wet."

The voice was neither that of the Old Man nor of his wife. It was the voice of a small boy, its weak treble broken by that preternatural hoarseness which only vagabondage and the habit of premature self-assertion can give. It was the face of a small boy that looked up at theirs,—a face that might have been pretty, and even refined, but that it was darkened by evil knowledge from within, and dirt and hard experience from without. He had a blanket around his shoulders, and had evidently just risen from his bed. "Come in," he repeated, "and don't make no noise. The Old Man's in there talking to mar," he continued, pointing to an adjacent room which seemed to be a kitchen, from which the Old Man's voice came in deprecating accents. "Let me be," he added querulously, to Dick Bullen, who had caught him up, blanket and all, and was affecting to toss him into the fire, "let go o' me, you d—d old fool, d' ye hear?"

Thus adjured, Dick Bullen lowered Johnny to the ground with a smothered laugh, while the men, entering quietly, ranged themselves around a long table of rough boards which occupied the centre of the room. Johnny then gravely proceeded to a cupboard and brought out several articles, which he deposited on the table. "Thar's whiskey. And crackers. And red herons. And cheese." He took a bite of the latter on his way to the table. "And sugar." He scooped up a mouthful *en route* with a small and very dirty hand. "And terbacker. Thar's dried appils too on the shelf, but I don't admire 'em. Appils is swellin'. Thar," he concluded, "now wade in, and don't be afeard. *I* don't mind the old woman. She don't b'long to *me*. S'long."

He had stepped to the threshold of a small room, scarcely larger than a closet, partitioned off from the main apart-ment, and holding in its dim recess a small bed. He stood there a moment looking at the company, his bare feet peep-ing from the blanket, and nodded.

"Hello, Johnny! You ain't goin' to turn in agin, are ye?" said Dick.

"Yes, I are," responded Johnny decidedly.

"Why, wot's up, old fellow?"

"I'm sick."

"How sick?"

"I've got a fevier. And childblains. And roomatiz," re-turned Johnny, and vanished within. After a moment's pause, he added in the dark, apparently from under the bedclothes, —"And biles!"

There was an embarrassing silence. The men looked at each other and at the fire. Even with the appetizing banquet before them, it seemed as if they might again fall into the despondency of Thompson's grocery, when the voice of the Old Man, incautiously lifted, came deprecatingly from the kitchen.

"Certainly! Thet's so. In course they is. A gang o' lazy, drunken loafers, and that ar Dick Bullen's the orneriest of all. Didn't hev no more *sabe* than to come round yar with sickness in the house and no provision. Thet's what I said: 'Bullen,' sez I, 'it's crazy drunk you are, or a fool,' sez I, 'to think o' such a thing.' 'Staples,' I sez, 'be you a man, Staples,

and 'spect to raise h—ll under my roof and invalids lyin'
round?' But they would come,—they would. Thet's wot you
must 'spect o' such trash as lays round the Bar."

A burst of laughter from the men followed this unfortunate
exposure. Whether it was overheard in the kitchen, or
whether the Old Man's irate companion had just then exhausted all other modes of expressing her contemptuous indignation, I cannot say, but a back door was suddenly
slammed with great violence. A moment later and the Old
Man reappeared, haply unconscious of the cause of the late
hilarious outburst, and smiled blandly.

"The old woman thought she'd jest run over to Mrs. Mac-
Fadden's for a sociable call," he explained with jaunty indifference, as he took a seat at the board.

Oddly enough it needed this untoward incident to relieve
the embarrassment that was beginning to be felt by the
party, and their natural audacity returned with their host. I
do not propose to record the convivialities of that evening.
The inquisitive reader will accept the statement that the conversation was characterized by the same intellectual exaltation, the same cautious reverence, the same fastidious delicacy, the same rhetorical precision, and the same logical and
coherent discourse somewhat later in the evening, which
distinguish similar gatherings of the masculine sex in more
civilized localities and under more favorable auspices. No
glasses were broken in the absence of any; no liquor was
uselessly spilt on the floor or table in the scarcity of that
article.

It was nearly midnight when the festivities were interrupted. "Hush," said Dick Bullen, holding up his hand.
It was the querulous voice of Johnny from his adjacent
closet: "O dad!"

The Old Man arose hurriedly and disappeared in the

closet. Presently he reappeared. "His rheumatiz is coming on agin bad," he explained, "and he wants rubbin'." He lifted the demijohn of whiskey from the table and shook it. It was empty. Dick Bullen put down his tin cup with an embarrassed laugh. So did the others. The Old Man examined their contents and said hopefully, "I reckon that's enough; he don't need much. You hold on all o' you for a spell, and I'll be back"; and vanished in the closet with an old flannel shirt and the whiskey. The door closed but imperfectly, and the following dialogue was distinctly audible:

"Now, sonny, whar does she ache worst?"

"Sometimes over yar and sometimes under yer; but it's most powerful from yer to yer. Rub yer, dad."

A silence seemed to indicate a brisk rubbing. Then Johnny:

"Hevin' a good time out yer, dad?"

"Yes, sonny."

"To-morrer's Chrismiss,—ain't it?"

"Yes, sonny. How does she feel now?"

"Better. Rub a little furder down. Wot's Chrismiss, anyway? Wot's it all about?"

"Oh, it's a day."

This exhaustive definition was apparently satisfactory, for there was a silent interval of rubbing. Presently Johnny again:

"Mar sez that everywhere else but yer everybody gives things to everybody Chrismiss, and then she jist waded inter you. She sez thar's a man they call Sandy Claws, not a white man, you know, but a kind o' Chinemin, comes down the chimbley night afore Chrismiss and gives things to chillern,—boys like me. Puts 'em in their butes! Thet's what she tried to play upon me. Easy now, pop, whar are you rubbin' to,—thet's a mile from the place. She jest made that up,

lidn't she, jest to aggrewate me and you? Don't rub thar. . . .
Why, dad!"

In the great quiet that seemed to have fallen upon the
house the sigh of the near pines and the drip of leaves without was very distinct. Johnny's voice, too, was lowered as he
went on, "Don't you take on now, for I'm gettin' all right
fast. Wot's the boys doin' out thar?"

The Old Man partly opened the door and peered through.
His guests were sitting there sociably enough, and there
were a few silver coins and a lean buckskin purse on the
table. "Bettin' on suthin'—some little game or 'nother.
They're all right," he replied to Johnny, and recommenced
his rubbing.

"I'd like to take a hand and win some money," said
Johnny reflectively after a pause.

The Old Man glibly repeated what was evidently a familiar
formula, that if Johnny would wait until he struck it rich
in the tunnel he'd have lots of money, etc., etc.

"Yes," said Johnny, "but you don't. And whether you
strike it or I win it, it's about the same. It's all luck. But
it's mighty cur'o's about Chrismiss—ain't it? Why do they
call it Chrismiss?"

Perhaps from some instinctive deference to the overhear-
ing of his guests, or from some vague sense of incongruity,
the Old Man's reply was so low as to be inaudible beyond the
room.

"Yes," said Johnny, with some slight abatement of interest,
"I've heerd o' *him* before. Thar, that'll do, dad. I don't ache
near so bad as I did. Now wrap me tight in this yer blanket.
So. Now," he added in a muffled whisper, "sit down yer by
me till I go asleep." To assure himself of obedience, he disengaged one hand from the blanket, and, grasping his father's
sleeve, again composed himself to rest.

For some moments the Old Man waited patiently. Then the unwonted stillness of the house excited his curiosity, and without moving from the bed he cautiously opened the door with his disengaged hand, and looked into the main room. To his infinite surprise it was dark and deserted. But even then a smouldering log on the hearth broke, and by the upspringing blaze he saw the figure of Dick Bullen sitting by the dying embers.

"Hello!"

Dick started, rose, and came somewhat unsteadily toward him.

"Whar's the boys?" said the Old Man.

"Gone up the cañon on a little *pasear*. They're coming back for me in a minit. I'm waitin' round for 'em. What are you starin' at, Old Man?" he added, with a forced laugh; "do you think I'm drunk?"

The Old Man might have been pardoned the supposition, for Dick's eyes were humid and his face flushed. He loitered and lounged back to the chimney, yawned, shook himself, buttoned up his coat and laughed. "Liquor ain't so plenty as that, Old Man. Now don't you git up," he continued, as the Old Man made a movement to release his sleeve from Johnny's hand. "Don't you mind manners. Sit jest whar you be; I'm goin' in a jiffy. Thar, that's them now."

There was a low tap at the door. Dick Bullen opened it quickly, nodded "Good-night" to his host, and disappeared. The Old Man would have followed him but for the hand that still unconsciously grasped his sleeve. He could have easily disengaged it: it was small, weak, and emaciated. But perhaps because it *was* small, weak, and emaciated he changed his mind, and, drawing his chair closer to the bed, rested his head upon it. In this defenseless attitde the potency of his earlier potations surprised him. The room flickered and faded before his eyes, reappeared, faded again, went out, and left him—asleep.

Meantime Dick Bullen, closing the door, confronted his companions. "Are you ready?" said Staples. "Ready," said Dick; "what's the time?" "Past twelve," was the reply; "can you make it?—it's nigh on fifty miles, the round trip hither and yon." "I reckon," returned Dick shortly. "Whar's the mare?" "Bill and Jack's holdin' her at the crossin'." "Let 'em hold on a minit longer," said Dick.

He turned and reëntered the house softly. By the light of the guttering candle and dying fire he saw that the door of the little room was open. He stepped toward it on tip-toe and looked in. The Old Man had fallen back in his chair, snoring, his helpless feet thrust out in a line with his collapsed shoulders, and his hat pulled over his eyes. Beside him, on a narrow wooden bedstead, lay Johnny, muffled tightly in a blanket that hid all save a strip of forehead and a few curls damp with perspiration. Dick Bullen made a step forward, hesitated, and glanced over his shoulder into the deserted room. Everything was quiet. With a sudden resolution he parted his huge mustaches with both hands and stooped over the sleeping boy. But even as he did so a mischievous blast, lying in wait, swooped down the chimney, rekindled the hearth, and lit up the room with a shameless glow from which Dick fled in bashful terror.

His companions were already waiting for him at the crossing. Two of them were struggling in the darkness with some strange misshapen bulk, which as Dick came nearer took the semblance of a great yellow horse.

It was the mare. She was not a pretty picture. From her Roman nose to her rising haunches, from her arched spine hidden by the stiff *machillas* of a Mexican saddle, to her thick, straight bony legs, there was not a line of equine grace. In

her half-blind but wholly vicious white eyes, in her protruding under-lip, in her monstrous color, there was nothing
but ugliness and vice.

"Now then," said Staples, "stand cl'ar of her heels, boys,
and up with you. Don't miss your first holt of her mane,
and mind ye get your off stirrup *quick*. Ready!"

There was a leap, a scrambling struggle, a bound, a wild
retreat of the crowd, a circle of flying hoofs, two springless
leaps that jarred the earth, a rapid play and jingle of spurs,
a plunge, and then the voice of Dick somewhere in the
darkness. "All right!"

"Don't take the lower road back onless you're hard pushed
for time! Don't hold her in down hill. We'll be at the ford
at five. G'lang! Hoopa! Mula! GO!"

A splash, a spark struck from the ledge in the road, a
clatter in the rocky cut beyond, and Dick was gone.

Sing, O Muse, the ride of Richard Bullen! Sing, O Muse,
of chivalrous men! the sacred quest, the doughty deeds, the
battery of low churls, the fearsome ride and gruesome perils
of the Flower of Simpson's Bar! Alack! she is dainty, this
Muse! She will have none of this bucking brute and swagger-
ing, ragged rider, and I must fain follow him in prose, afoot!

It was one o'clock, and yet he had only gained Rattlesnake Hill. For in that time Jovita had rehearsed to him
all her imperfections and practiced all her vices. Thrice
had she stumbled. Twice had she thrown up her Roman
nose in a straight line with the reins, and, resisting bit and
spur, struck out madly across country. Twice had she reared,
and, rearing, fallen backward; and twice had the agile Dick,
unharmed, regained his seat before she found her vicious legs
again. And a mile beyond them, at the foot of a long hill,
was Rattlesnake Creek. Dick knew that here was the crucial

test of his ability to perform his enterprise, set his teeth grimly, put his knees well into her flanks, and changed his defensive tactics to brisk aggression. Bullied and maddened, Jovita began the descent of the hill. Here the artful Richard pretended to hold her in with ostentatious objurgation and well-feigned cries of alarm. It is unnecessary to add that Jovita instantly ran away. Nor need I state the time made in the descent; it is written in the chronicles of Simpson's Bar. Enough that in another moment, as it seemed to Dick, she was splashing on the overflowed banks of Rattlesnake Creek. As Dick expected, the momentum she had acquired carried her beyond the point of balking, and, holding her well together for a mighty leap, they dashed into the middle of the swiftly flowing current. A few moments of kicking, wading, and swimming, and Dick drew a long breath on the opposite bank.

The road from Rattlesnake Creek to Red Mountain was tolerably level. Either the plunge in Rattlesnake Creek had dampened her baleful fire, or the art which led to it had shown her the superior wickedness of her rider, for Jovita no longer wasted her surplus energy in wanton conceits. Once she bucked, but it was from force of habit; once she shied, but it was from a new, freshly painted meeting-house at the crossing of the county road. Hollows, ditches, gravelly deposits, patches of freshly springing grasses, flew from beneath her rattling hoofs. She began to smell unpleasantly, once or twice she coughed slightly, but there was no abatement of her strength or speed. By two o'clock he had passed Red Mountain and begun the descent to the plain. Ten minutes later the driver of the fast Pioneer coach was overtaken and passed by a "man on a Pinto hoss,"—an event sufficiently notable for remark. At half past two Dick rose in his stirrups with a great shout. Stars were glittering through the rifted clouds, and beyond him, out of the plain, rose two spires, a flagstaff, and a straggling line of black objects. Dick jingled his spurs and swung his *riata,* Jovita bounded forward, and in another moment they swept into Tuttleville, and·drew up before the wooden piazza of "The Hotel of All Nations."

What transpired that night at Tuttleville is not strictly a part of this record. Briefly I may state, however, that after Jovita had been handed over to a sleepy ostler, whom she at once kicked into unpleasant consciousness, Dick sallied out with the barkeeper for a tour of the sleeping town. Lights still gleamed from a few saloons and gambling-houses; but, avoiding these, they stopped before several closed shops, and by persistent tapping and judicious outcry roused the proprietors from their beds, and made them unbar the doors of their magazines and expose their wares. Sometimes they were met by curses, but oftener by interest and some concern in their needs, and the interview was invariably concluded by a drink. It was three o'clock before this pleasantry was given over, and with a small waterproof bag of India-rubber strapped on his shoulders, Dick returned to the hotel. But here he was waylaid by Beauty,—Beauty opulent in charms, affluent in dress, persuasive in speech, and Spanish in accent! In vain she repeated the invitation in "Excelsior," happily scorned by all Alpine-climbing youth, and rejected by this child of the Sierras,—a rejection softened in this instance by a laugh and his last gold coin. And then he sprang to the saddle and dashed down the lonely street and out into the lonelier plain, where presently the lights, the black line of houses, the spires, and the flagstaff sank into the earth behind him again and were lost in the distance.

The storm had cleared away, the air was brisk and cold, the outlines of adjacent landmarks were distinct, but it was half-past four before Dick reached the meeting-house and the crossing of the county road. To avoid the rising grade he had taken a longer and more circuitous road, in whose viscid mud Jovita sank fetlock deep at every bound. It was a poor preparation for a steady ascent of five miles more; but Jovita, gathering her legs under her, took it with her usual blind, unreasoning fury, and a half-hour later reached the long level that led to Rattlesnake Creek. Another half-hour would bring him to the creek. He threw the reins lightly upon the neck of the mare, chirruped to her, and began to sing.

Suddenly Jovita shied with a bound that would have unseated a less practiced rider. Hanging to her rein was a figure that had leaped from the bank, and at the same time from the road before her arose a shadowy horse and rider.

"Throw up your hands," commanded the second apparition, with an oath.

Dick felt the mare tremble, quiver, and apparently sink under him. He knew what it meant and was prepared.

"Stand aside, Jack Simpson. I know you, you d—d thief! Let me pass, or"—

He did not finish the sentence. Jovita rose straight in the air with a terrific bound, throwing the figure from her bit with a single shake of her vicious head, and charged with deadly malevolence down on the impediment before her. An oath, a pistol-shot, horse and highwayman rolled over in the road, and the next moment Jovita was a hundred yards away. But the good right arm of her rider, shattered by a bullet, dropped helplessly at his side.

Without slacking his speed he shifted the reins to his left hand. But a few moments later he was obliged to halt and tighten the saddle-girths that had slipped in the onset. This in his crippled condition took some time. He had no fear of pursuit, but looking up he saw that the eastern stars were already paling, and that the distant peaks had lost their ghostly whiteness, and now stood out blackly against a lighter sky. Day was upon him. Then completely absorbed in a single idea, he forgot the pain of his wound, and mounting again dashed on toward Rattlesnake Creek. But now Jovita's breath came broken by gasps, Dick reeled in his saddle, and brighter and brighter grew the sky.

Ride, Richard; run, Jovita; linger, O day!

For the last few rods there was a roaring in his ears. Was it exhaustion from loss of blood, or what? He was dazed and giddy as he swept down the hill, and did not recognize his surroundings. Had he taken the wrong road, or was this Rattlesnake Creek?

It was. But the brawling creek he had swam a few hours before had risen, more than doubled its volume, and now rolled a swift and resistless river between him and Rattlesnake Hill. For the first time that night Richard's heart sank within him. The river, the mountain, the quickening east, swam before his eyes. He shut them to recover his self-control. In that brief interval, by some fantastic mental process, the little room at Simpson's Bar and the figures of the sleeping father and son rose upon him. He opened his eyes wildly, cast off his coat, pistol, boots, and saddle, bound his precious pack tightly to his shoulders, grasped the bare flanks of Jovita with his bared knees, and with a shout dashed into the yellow water. A cry rose from the opposite bank as the head of a man and horse struggled for a few moments against the battling current, and then were swept away amidst uprooted trees and whirling driftwood.

The Old Man started and woke. The fire on the hearth was dead, the candle in the outer room flickering in its socket, and somebody was rapping at the door. He opened it, but

fell back with a cry before the dripping, half-naked figure
that reeled against the doorpost.

"Dick?"

"Hush! Is he awake yet?"

"No; but, Dick"—

"Dry up, you old fool! Get me some whiskey, *quick*!"
The Old Man flew and returned with—an empty bottle!
Dick would have sworn, but his strength was not equal to
the occasion. He staggered, caught at the handle of the
door, and motioned to the Old Man.

"Thar's suthin' in my pack yer for Johnny. Take it off.
I can't."

The Old Man unstrapped the pack, and laid it before
the exhausted man.

"Open it, quick."

He did so with trembling fingers. It contained only a
few poor toys,—cheap and barbaric enough, goodness knows,
but bright with paint and tinsel. One of them was broken;
another, I fear, was irretrievably ruined by water, and on
the third—ah me! there was a cruel spot.

"It don't look like much, that's a fact," said Dick rue-
fully. . . . "But it's the best we could do. . . . Take 'em,
Old Man, and put 'em in his stocking, and tell him—tell him,
you know—hold me, Old Man"— The Old Man caught at
his sinking figure. "Tell him," said Dick, with a weak little
laugh,—"tell him Sandy Claus has come."

And even so, bedraggled, ragged, unshaven and unshorn,
with one arm hanging helplessly at his side, Santa Claus
came to Simpson's Bar and fell fainting on the first threshold.
The Christmas dawn came slowly after, touching the remoter peaks with the rosy warmth of ineffable love. And
it looked so tenderly on Simpson's Bar that the whole mountain, as if caught in a generous action, blushed to the skies.

```
⌠⌠⌠⌠⌠⌠⌠⌠                                    ⌡⌡⌡⌡⌡⌡⌡⌡
```

A PASSAGE IN
THE LIFE OF
MR. JOHN OAKHURST

He always thought it must have been Fate. Certainly nothing could have been more inconsistent with his habits than to have been in the Plaza at seven o'clock of that midsummer morning. The sight of his colorless face in Sacramento was rare at that season, and indeed at any season, anywhere, publicly, before two o'clock in the afternoon. Looking back upon it in after years, in the light of a chanceful life, he determined, with the characteristic philosophy of his profession, that it must have been Fate.

Yet it is my duty, as a strict chronicler of facts, to state that Mr. Oakhurst's presence there that morning was due to a very simple cause. At exactly half past six, the bank being then a winner to the amount of twenty thousand dollars, he had risen from the faro-table, relinquished his seat to an accomplished assistant, and withdrawn quietly, without attracting a glance from the silent, anxious faces bowed over the table. But when he entered his luxurious sleeping-room, across the passageway, he was a little shocked at finding the sun streaming through an inadvertently opened window. Something in the rare beauty of the morning, perhaps something in the novelty of the idea, struck him as he was about to close the blinds, and he hesitated. Then, taking his hat from the table, he stepped down a private staircase into the street.

The people who were abroad at that early hour were of a class quite unknown to Mr. Oakhurst. There were milkmen and hucksters delivering their wares, small tradespeople opening their shops, housemaids sweeping doorsteps, and occasionally a child. These Mr. Oakhurst regarded with a certain cold curiosity, perhaps quite free from the cynical disfavor with which he generally looked upon the more pretentious of his race whom he was in the habit of meeting. Indeed, I think he was not altogether displeased with the admiring glances which these humble women threw after his handsome face and figure, conspicuous even in a country of fine-looking men. While it is very probable that this wicked vagabond, in the pride of his social isolation, would have been coldly indifferent to the advances of a fine lady, a little girl who ran admiringly by his side in a ragged dress had the power to call a faint flush into his colorless cheek. He dismissed her at last, but not until she had found out—what sooner or later her large-hearted and discriminating sex inevitably did—that he was exceedingly free and open-handed with his money, and also—what perhaps none other of her sex ever did—that the bold black eyes of this fine gentleman were in reality of a brownish and even tender gray.

There was a small garden before a white cottage in a side-street that attracted Mr. Oakhurst's attention. It was filled with roses, heliotrope, and verbena,—flowers familiar enough to him in the expensive and more portable form of bouquets, but, as it seemed to him then, never before so notably lovely. Perhaps it was because the dew was yet fresh upon them, perhaps it was because they were unplucked, but Mr. Oakhurst admired them, not as a possible future tribute to the fascinating and accomplished Miss Ethelinda, then performing at the Varieties, for Mr. Oakhurst's especial benefit, as she had often assured him; nor yet as a *douceur* to the enthralling

Miss Montmorrissy, with whom Mr. Oakhurst expected to sup that evening, but simply for himself, and mayhap for the flowers' sake. Howbeit, he passed on, and so out into the open plaza, where, finding a bench under a cottonwood tree, he first dusted the seat with his handkerchief, and then sat down.

It was a fine morning. The air was so still and calm that a sigh from the sycamores seemed like the deep-drawn breath of the just awakening tree, and the faint rustle of its boughs as the outstretching of cramped and reviving limbs. Far away the Sierras stood out against a sky so remote as to be of no positive color,—so remote that even the sun despaired of ever reaching it, and so expended its strength recklessly on the whole landscape, until it fairly glittered in a white and vivid contrast. With a very rare impulse, Mr. Oakhurst took off his hat, and half reclined on the bench, with his face to the sky. Certain birds who had taken a critical attitude on a spray above him apparently began an animated discussion regarding his possible malevolent intentions. One or two, emboldened by the silence, hopped on the ground at his feet, until the sound of wheels on the gravel walk frightened them away.

Looking up, he saw a man coming slowly towards him, wheeling a nondescript vehicle in which a woman was partly sitting, partly reclining. Without knowing why, Mr. Oakhurst instantly conceived that the carriage was the invention and workmanship of the man, partly from its oddity, partly from the strong, mechanical hand that grasped it, and partly from a certain pride and visible consciousness in the manner in which the man handled it. Then Mr. Oakhurst saw something more,—the man's face was familiar. With that regal faculty of not forgetting a face that had ever given him professional audience, he instantly classified it under the following mental formula: "At 'Frisco, Polka Saloon. Lost his week's wages. I reckon seventy dollars—on red. Never came again." There was, however, no trace of this in the calm eyes and unmoved face that he turned upon the stranger, who, on the contrary, blushed, looked embarrassed, hesitated, and then stopped with an involuntary motion that brought the carriage and its fair occupant face to face with Mr. Oakhurst.

I should hardly do justice to the position she will occupy in this veracious chronicle by describing the lady now—if, indeed, I am able to do it at all. Certainly, the popular estimate was conflicting. The late Colonel Starbottle—to whose large experience of a charming sex I have before been indebted for many valuable suggestions—had, I regret to say, depreciated her fascinations. "A yellow-faced cripple, by dash—a sick woman, with mahogany eyes. One of your blanked spiritual creatures, with no flesh on her bones." On the other hand, however, she enjoyed later much complimentary disparagement from her own sex. Miss Celestina Howard, second leader in the ballet at the Varieties, had, with great alliterative directness, in after years, denominated her as an "aquiline asp." Mlle. Brimborion remembered that she had always warned "Mr. Jack" that this woman would "empoison" him. But Mr. Oakhurst, whose impressions are perhaps the most important, only saw a pale, thin, deep-eyed woman, raised above the level of her companion by the refinement of long suffering and isolation, and a certain shy virginity of manner. There was a suggestion of physical purity in the folds of her fresh-looking robe, and a certain picturesque tastefulness in the details, that, without knowing why, made him think that the robe was her invention and handiwork, even as the carriage she occupied was evidently the work of her companion. Her own hand, a trifle too thin, but well-shaped, subtle-fingered, and gentlewomanly, rested on the side of the carriage, the counterpart of the strong mechanical grasp of her companion's.

There was some obstruction to the progress of the vehicle, and Mr. Oakhurst stepped forward to assist. While the wheel was being lifted over the curbstone, it was necessary that she should hold his arm, and for a moment her thin hand rested there, light and cold as a snowflake, and then—as it seemed to him—like a snowflake melted away. Then there was a pause, and then conversation—the lady joining occasionally and shyly.

It appeared that they were man and wife. That for the past two years she had been a great invalid, and had lost the use of her lower limbs from rheumatism. That until lately she had been confined to her bed, until her husband—who was a master carpenter—had bethought himself to make her this carriage. He took her out regularly for an airing before going to work, because it was his only time, and—they attracted less attention. They had tried many doctors, but without avail. They had been advised to go to the Sulphur Springs, but it was expensive. Mr. Decker, the husband, had once saved eighty dollars for that purpose, but while in San Francisco had his pocket picked—Mr. Decker was so senseless. (The intelligent reader need not be told that it is the lady who is speaking.) They had never been able to make up the sum again, and they had given up the idea. It was a dreadful thing to have one's pocket picked. Did he not think so?

Her husband's face was crimson, but Mr. Oakhurst's countenance was quite calm and unmoved, as he gravely agreed with her, and walked by her side until they passed the little garden that he had admired. Here Mr. Oakhurst commanded a halt, and, going to the door, astounded the proprietor by a preposterously extravagant offer for a choice of the flowers. Presently he returned to the carriage with his arms full of roses, heliotrope, and verbena, and cast them in the lap of the invalid. While she was bending over them with childish delight, Mr. Oakhurst took the opportunity of drawing her husband aside.

"Perhaps," he said in a low voice, and a manner quite free from any personal annoyance,—"perhaps it's just as well that you lied to her as you did. You can say now that the pickpocket was arrested the other day, and you got your money back." Mr. Oakhurst quietly slipped four twenty-dollar gold-pieces into the broad hand of the bewildered Mr. Decker. "Say that—or anything you like—but the truth. Promise me you won't say that!"

The man promised. Mr. Oakhurst quietly returned to the front of the little carriage. The sick woman was still eagerly occupied with the flowers, and as she raised her eyes to his, her faded cheek seemed to have caught some color from the roses, and her eyes some of their dewy freshness. But at that instant Mr. Oakhurst lifted his hat, and before she could thank him was gone.

I grieve to say that Mr. Decker shamelessly broke his promise. That night, in the very goodness of his heart and uxorious self-abnegation, he, like all devoted husbands, not only offered himself, but his friend and benefactor, as a sacrifice on the family altar. It is only fair, however, to add that he spoke with great fervor of the generosity of Mr. Oakhurst, and dealt with an enthusiasm quite common with his class on the mysterious fame and prodigal vices of the gambler.

"And now, Elsie, dear, say that you'll forgive me," said Mr. Decker, dropping on one knee beside his wife's couch. "I did it for the best. It was for you, dearey, that I put that money on them cards that night in 'Frisco. I thought to win a heap,—enough to take you away, and enough left to get you a new dress."

Mrs. Decker smiled and pressed her husband's hand. "I do forgive you, Joe, dear," she said, still smiling, with eyes abstractedly fixed on the ceiling; "and you ought to be whipped for deceiving me so, you bad boy, and making me make such a speech. There, say no more about it. If you'll be very good hereafter, and will just now hand me that cluster of roses, I'll forgive you." She took the branch in her fingers, lifted the roses to her face, and presently said, behind their leaves,—

"Joe!"

"What is it, lovey?"

"Do you think that this Mr. — what do you call him?—Jack Oakhurst would have given that money back to you if I hadn't made that speech?"

"Yes."

"If he hadn't seen me at all?"

Mr. Decker looked up. His wife had managed in some way to cover up her whole face with the roses, except her eyes, which were dangerously bright.

"No; it was you, Elsie—it was all along of seeing you that made him do it."

"A poor sick woman like me?"

"A sweet, little, lovely, pooty Elsie—Joe's own little wifey! How could he help it?"

Mrs. Decker fondly cast one arm around her husband's neck, still keeping the roses to her face with the other. From behind them she began to murmur gently and idiotically, "Dear, ole square Joey. Elsie's oney booful big bear." But, really, I do not see that my duty as a chronicler of facts compels me to continue this little lady's speech any further, and out of respect to the unmarried reader I stop.

Nevertheless, the next morning Mrs. Decker betrayed some slight and apparently uncalled-for irritability on reaching the Plaza, and presently desired her husband to wheel her back home. Moreover, she was very much astonished at meeting Mr. Oakhurst just as they were returning, and even doubted if it were he, and questioned her husband as to his identity with the stranger of yesterday as he approached. Her manner to Mr. Oakhurst, also, was quite in contrast with her husband's frank welcome. Mr. Oakhurst instantly detected it. "Her husband has told her all, and she dislikes me," he said to himself, with that fatal appreciation of the half-truths of a woman's motives that causes the wisest masculine critic to stumble. He lingered only long enough to take the business address of the husband, and then, lifting his hat gravely, without looking at the lady, went his way. It struck the honest master carpenter as one of the charming anomalies of his wife's character that, although the meeting was evidently very much constrained and unpleasant, instantly afterward his wife's spirits began to rise. "You was hard on him—a leetle hard, wasn't you, Elsie?" said Mr. Decker deprecatingly. "I'm afraid he may think I've broke my promise." "Ah, indeed," said the lady indifferently. Mr. Decker instantly stepped round to the front of the vehicle. "You look like an A 1 first-class lady riding down Broadway in her own carriage, Elsie," said he; "I never seed you lookin' so peart and sassy before."

A few days later the proprietor of the San Isabel Warm Sulphur Springs received the following note in Mr. Oakhurst's well-known dainty hand:—

DEAR STEVE,—I've been thinking over your proposition to buy Nichols's quarter interest and have concluded to go in. But I don't see how the thing will pay until you have more accommodation down there, and for the best class—I mean *my* customers. What we want is an extension to the main building, and two or three cottages put up. I send down a builder to take hold of the job at once. He takes his sick wife with him, and you are to look after them as you would for one of us.

I may run down there myself, after the races, just to look after things; but I sha'n't set upon any game this season.

Yours always,

JOHN OAKHURST.

It was only the last sentence of this letter that provoked criticism. "I can understand," said Mr. Hamlin, a professional brother, to whom Mr. Oakhurst's letter was shown,—"I can understand why Jack goes in heavy and builds, for it's a sure spec, and is bound to be a mighty soft thing in time, if he comes here regularly. But why in blank he don't set up a bank this season and take the chance of getting some of the money back that he puts into circulation in building, is what gets me. I wonder now," he mused deeply, "what *is* his little game."

The season had been a prosperous one to Mr. Oakhurst, and proportionally disastrous to several members of the Legislature, judges, colonels, and others who had enjoyed but briefly the pleasure of Mr. Oakhurst's midnight society. And yet Sacramento had become very dull to him. He had lately formed a habit of early morning walks,—so unusual and startling to his friends, both male and female, as to occasion the intensest curiosity. Two or three of the latter set spies upon his track, but the inquisition resulted only in the discovery that Mr. Oakhurst walked to the Plaza, sat down upon one particular bench for a few moments, and then returned without seeing anybody, and the theory that there was a woman in the case was abandoned. A few superstitious gentlemen of his own profession believed that he did it for "luck." Some others, more practical, declared that he went out to "study points."

After the races at Marysville, Mr. Oakhurst went to San Francisco; from that place he returned to Marysville, but a few days after was seen at San José, Santa Cruz, and Oakland. Those who met him declared that his manner was restless and feverish, and quite unlike his ordinary calmness and phlegm. Colonel Starbottle pointed out the fact that at San Francisco, at the Club, Jack had declined to deal. "Hand shaky, sir—depend upon it; don't stimulate enough—blank him!"

From San José he started to go to Oregon by land with a rather expensive outfit of horses and camp equipage, but on reaching Stockton he suddenly diverged, and four hours later found him, with a single horse, entering the cañon of the San Isabel Warm Sulphur Springs.

It was a pretty triangular valley lying at the foot of three sloping mountains, dark with pines and fantastic with madroño and manzanita. Nestling against the mountain-side, the straggling buildings and long piazza of the hotel glittered through the leaves; and here and there shone a white toy-like cottage. Mr. Oakhurst was not an admirer of nature, but he felt something of the same novel satisfaction in the view that he experienced in his first morning walk in Sacramento. And now carriages began to pass him on the road filled with gayly dressed women, and the cold California outlines of the landscape began to take upon themselves somewhat of a human warmth and color. And then the long hotel piazza came in view, efflorescent with the full-toileted fair. Mr. Oakhurst, a good rider after the California fashion, did not check his speed as he approached his destination, but charged the hotel at a gallop, threw his horse on his haunches within a foot of the piazza, and then quietly emerged from the cloud of dust that veiled his dismounting.

Whatever feverish excitement might have raged within, all his habitual calm returned as he stepped upon the piazza. With the instinct of long habit he turned and faced the battery of eyes with the same cold indifference with which he had for years encountered the half-hidden sneers of men and the half-frightened admiration of women. Only one person stepped forward to welcome him. Oddly enough, it was Dick Hamilton, perhaps the only one present who, by birth, education, and position, might have satisfied the most fastidious social critic. Happily for Mr. Oakhurst's reputation, he was also a very rich banker and social leader. "Do you know who that is you spoke to?" asked young Parker, with an alarmed expression. "Yes," replied Hamilton, with characteristic effrontery; "the man you lost a thousand dollars to last week. *I* only know him *socially*." "But isn't he a gambler?" queried the youngest Miss Smith. "He is," replied Hamilton; "but I wish, my dear young lady, that we all played as open and honest a game as our friend yonder, and were as willing as he is to abide by its fortunes."

But Mr. Oakhurst was happily out of hearing of this colloquy, and was even then lounging listlessly, yet watchfully, along the upper hall. Suddenly he heard a light footstep behind him, and then his name called in a familiar voice that drew the blood quickly to his heart. He turned, and she stood before him.

But how transformed! If I have hesitated to describe the hollow-eyed cripple,—the quaintly dressed artisan's wife, a few pages ago,—what shall I do with this graceful, shapely, elegantly attired gentlewoman into whom she has been merged within these two months? In good faith she was very pretty. You and I, my dear madam, would have been quick to see that those charming dimples were misplaced for true beauty, and too fixed in their quality for honest mirthfulness; that the delicate lines around those aquiline nostrils were cruel and selfish; that the sweet, virginal surprise of those lovely eyes was as apt to be opened on her plate as upon the gallant speeches of her dinner partner; that her sympathetic color came and went more with her own spirits than yours. But you and I are not in love with her, dear madam, and Mr. Oakhurst is. And even in the folds of her Parisian gown, I am afraid this poor fellow saw the same subtle strokes of purity that he had seen in her homespun robe. And then there was the delightful revelation that she could walk, and that she had dear little feet of her own in the tiniest slippers of her French shoemaker, with such preposterous blue bows, and Chappell's own stamp, Rue de something or other, Paris, on the narrow sole.

He ran towards her with a heightened color and outstretched hands. But she whipped her own behind her, glanced rapidly up and down the long hall, and stood looking at him with a half-audacious, half-mischievous admiration in utter contrast to her old reserve.

"I've a great mind not to shake hands with you at all. You passed me just now on the piazza without speaking, and I ran after you, as I suppose many another poor woman has done."

Mr. Oakhurst stammered that she was so changed.

"The more reason why you should know me. Who changed me? You. You have re-created me. You found a helpless, crippled, sick, poverty-stricken woman, with one dress to her back, and that her own make, and you gave her life, health, strength, and fortune. You did, and you know it, sir. How do you like your work?" She caught the side seams of her gown in either hand and dropped him a playful courtesy. Then, with a sudden, relenting gesture, she gave him both her hands.

Outrageous as this speech was, and unfeminine, as I trust every fair reader will deem it, I fear it pleased Mr. Oakhurst. Not but that he was accustomed to a certain frank female admiration; but then it was of the *coulisses* and not of the cloister, with which he always persisted in associating Mrs. Decker. To be addressed in this way by an invalid Puritan, a sick saint, with the austerity of suffering still clothing her, —a woman who had a Bible on the dressing-table, who went to church three times a day, and was devoted to her husband, completely bowled him over. He still held her hands as she went on,—

"Why didn't you come before? What were you doing in Marysville, in San José, in Oakland? You see I have followed you. I saw you as you came down the cañon, and knew you at once. I saw your letter to Joseph, and knew you were coming. Why didn't you write to me? You will some time! Good-evening, Mr. Hamilton."

She had withdrawn her hands, but not until Hamilton, ascending the staircase, was nearly abreast of them. He raised his hat to her with well-bred composure, nodded familiarly to Oakhurst, and passed on. When he had gone Mrs. Decker lifted her eyes to Mr. Oakhurst. "Some day I shall ask a great favor of you!"

Mr. Oakhurst begged that it should be now. "No, not until you know me better. Then, some day, I shall want you to— kill that man!"

She laughed, such a pleasant little ringing laugh, such a display of dimples,—albeit a little fixed in the corners of her mouth,—such an innocent light in her brown eyes, and such a lovely color in her cheeks, that Mr. Oakhurst—who seldom laughed—was fain to laugh too. It was as if a lamb had pro-posed to a fox a foray into a neighboring sheepfold.

A few evenings after this, Mrs. Decker arose from a charmed circle of her admirers on the hotel piazza, excused herself for a few moments, laughingly declined an escort, and ran over to her little cottage—one of her husband's creation —across the road. Perhaps from the sudden and unwonted exercise in her still convalescent state, she breathed hurriedly and feverishly as she entered her boudoir, and once or twice placed her hand upon her breast. She was startled on turning up the light to find her husband lying on the sofa.

"You look hot and excited, Elsie, love." said Mr. Decker; "You ain't took worse, are you?"

Mrs. Decker's face had paled, but now flushed again. "No," she said, "only a little pain here," as she again placed her hand upon her corsage.

"Can I do anything for you?" said Mr. Decker, rising with affectionate concern.

"Run over to the hotel and get me some brandy, quick!"

Mr. Decker ran. Mrs. Decker closed and bolted the door, and then putting her hand to her bosom, drew out the pain. It was folded foursquare, and was, I grieve to say, in Mr. Oakhurst's handwriting.

She devoured it with burning eyes and cheeks until there came a step upon the porch. Then she hurriedly replaced it in her bosom and unbolted the door. Her husband entered; she raised the spirits to her lips and declared herself better.

"Are you going over there again to-night?" asked Mr. Decker submissively.

"No," said Mrs. Decker, with her eyes fixed dreamily on the floor.

"I wouldn't if I was you," said Mr. Decker with a sigh of relief. After a pause he took a seat on the sofa, and drawing his wife to his side, said, "Do you know what I was thinking of when you came in, Elsie?" Mrs. Decker ran her fingers through his stiff black hair, and couldn't imagine.

"I was thinking of old times, Elsie; I was thinking of the days when I built that kerridge for you, Elsie—when I used to take you out to ride, and was both hoss and driver! We was poor then, and you was sick, Elsie, but we was happy. We've got money now, and a house, and you're quite another woman. I may say, dear, that you're a *new* woman. And that's where the trouble comes in. I could build you a kerridge, Elsie; I could build you a house, Elsie—but there I stopped. I couldn't build up *you*. You're strong and pretty, Elsie, and fresh and new. But somehow, Elsie, you ain't no work of mine!"

He paused. With one hand laid gently on his forehead and the other pressed upon her bosom as if to feel certain of the presence of her pain, she said sweetly and soothingly:—

"But it was your work, dear."

Mr. Decker shook his head sorrowfully. "No, Elsie, not mine. I had the chance to do it once and I let it go. It's done now; but not by me."

Mrs. Decker raised her surprised, innocent eyes to his. He kissed her tenderly, and then went on in a more cheerful voice.

"That ain't all I was thinking of, Elsie. I was thinking that maybe you give too much of your company to that Mr. Hamilton. Not that there's any wrong in it, to you or him. But it might make people talk. You're the only one here, Elsie," said the master carpenter, looking fondly at his wife, "who isn't talked about; whose work ain't inspected or condemned."

Mrs. Decker was glad he had spoken about it. She had thought so, too, but she could not well be uncivil to Mr

Hamilton, who was a fine gentleman, without making a powerful enemy. "And he's always treated me as if I was a born lady in his own circle," added the little woman, with a certain pride that made her husband fondly smile. "But I have thought of a plan. He will not stay here if I should go away. If, for instance, I went to San Francisco to visit ma for a few days, he would be gone before I should return."

Mr. Decker was delighted. "By all means," he said; "go to-morrow. Jack Oakhurst is going down, and I'll put you in his charge."

Mrs. Decker did not think it was prudent. "Mr. Oakhurst is our friend, Joseph, but you know his reputation." In fact, she did not know that she ought to go now, knowing that he was going the same day; but with a kiss Mr. Decker overcame her scruples. She yielded gracefully. Few women, in fact, knew how to give up a point as charmingly as she.

She stayed a week in San Francisco. When she returned she was a trifle thinner and paler than she had been. This she explained as the result of perhaps too active exercise and excitement. "I was out of doors nearly all the time, as ma will tell you," she said to her husband, "and always alone. I am getting quite independent now," she added gayly. "I don't want any escort—I believe, Joey dear, I could get along even without you—I'm so brave!"

But her visit, apparently, had not been productive of her impelling design. Mr. Hamilton had not gone, but had remained, and called upon them that very evening. "I've thought of a plan, Joey, dear," said Mrs. Decker when he had departed. "Poor Mr. Oakhurst has a miserable room at the hotel—suppose you ask him when he returns from San Francisco to stop with us. He can have our spare room. I don't think," she added archly, "that Mr. Hamilton will call often." Her husband laughed, intimated that she was a little coquette, pinched her cheek, and complied. "The queer thing about a woman," he said afterwards confidentially to Mr. Oakhurst, "is, that without having any plan of her own, she'll take anybody's and build a house on it entirely differ-ent to suit herself. And dern my skin, if you'll be able to say whether or not you didn't give the scale and measurements yourself. That's what gets me."

The next week Mr. Oakhurst was installed in the Deckers' cottage. The business relations of her husband and himself were known to all, and her own reputation was above sus-picion. Indeed, few women were more popular. She was domestic, she was prudent, she was pious. In a country of great feminine freedom and latitude, she never rode or walked with anybody but her husband; in an epoch of slang and ambiguous expression, she was always precise and formal in her speech; in the midst of a fashion of ostentatious decora-tion she never wore a diamond, nor a single valuable jewel. She never permitted an indecorum in public; she never coun-tenanced the familiarities of California society. She declaimed against the prevailing tone of infidelity and skepticism in religion. Few people who were present will ever forget the dignified yet stately manner with which she rebuked Mr. Hamilton in the public parlor for entering upon the discus-sion of a work on materialism, lately published; and some among them, also, will not forget the expression of amused surprise on Mr. Hamilton's face, that gradually changed to sardonic gravity as he courteously waived his point. Cer-tainly, not Mr. Oakhurst, who from that moment began to be uneasily impatient of his friend, and even—if such a term could be applied to any moral quality in Mr. Oakhurst—to fear him.

For, during this time, Mr. Oakhurst had begun to show symptoms of a change in his usual habits. He was seldom, if ever, seen in his old haunts, in a bar-room, or with his old associates. Pink and white notes, in distracted handwriting, accumulated on the dressing-table in his rooms at Sacramento. It was given out in San Francisco that he had some organic disease of the heart, for which his physician had prescribed perfect rest. He read more, he took long walks, he sold his fast horses, he went to church.

I have a very vivid recollection of his first appearance there. He did not accompany the Deckers, nor did he go into their pew, but came in as the service commenced, and took a seat quietly in one of the back pews. By some mysterious instinct his presence became presently known to the congregation, some of whom so far forgot themselves, in their curiosity, as to face around and apparently address their responses to him. Before the service was over it was pretty well understood that "miserable sinners" meant Mr. Oakhurst. Nor did this mysterious influence fail to affect the officiating clergyman, who introduced an allusion to Mr. Oakhurst's calling and habits in a sermon on the architecture of Solomon's Temple, and in a manner so pointed and yet labored as to cause the youngest of us to flame with indignation. Happily, however, it was lost upon Jack; I do not think he even heard it. His handsome, colorless face—albeit a trifle worn and thoughtful—was inscrutable. Only once, during the singing of a hymn, at a certain note in the contralto's voice, there crept into his dark eyes a look of wistful tenderness, so yearning and yet so hopeless that those who were watching him felt their own glisten. Yet I retain a very vivid remembrance of his standing up to receive the benediction, with the suggestion, in his manner and tightly buttoned coat, of taking the fire of his adversary at ten paces. After church he disappeared as quietly as he had entered, and fortunately escaped hearing the comments on his rash act. His appearance was generally considered as an impertinence—attributable only to some wanton fancy—or possibly a bet. One or two thought that the sexton was exceedingly remiss in not turning him out after discovering who he was; and a prominent pewholder remarked that if he couldn't take his wife and daughters to that church without exposing them to such an influence, he would try to find some church where he could. Another traced Mr. Oakhurst's presence to certain Broad Church radical tendencies, which he regretted to say he had lately noted in their pastor. Deacon Sawyer, whose delicately organized, sickly wife had already borne him eleven children, and died in an ambitious attempt to complete the dozen, avowed that the presence of a person of Mr. Oakhurst's various and indiscriminate gallantries was an insult to the memory of the deceased that, as a man, he could not brook.

It was about this time that Mr. Oakhurst, contrasting himself with a conventional world in which he had hitherto rarely mingled, became aware that there was something in his face, figure, and carriage quite unlike other men,—something that if it did not betray his former career, at least showed an individuality and originality that was suspicious. In this belief he shaved off his long, silken mustache, and religiously brushed out his clustering curls every morning. He even went so far as to affect a negligence of dress, and hid his small, slim, arched feet in the largest and heaviest walking-shoes. There is a story told that he went to his tailor in Sacramento, and asked him to make him a suit of clothes like everybody else. The tailor, familiar with Mr. Oakhurst's fastidiousness, did not know what he meant. "I mean," said Mr. Oakhurst savagely, "something *respectable*,—something that doesn't exactly fit me, you know." But however Mr. Oakhurst might hide his shapely limbs in homespun and home-made garments, there was something in his carriage, something in the pose of his beautiful head, something in the strong and fine manliness of his presence, something in the perfect and utter discipline and control of his muscles, something in the high repose of his nature—a repose not so much a matter of intellectual ruling as of his very nature—that go where he would, and with whom, he was always a notable man in ten thousand. Perhaps this was never so clearly intimated to Mr. Oakhurst as when, emboldened by Mr. Hamilton's advice and assistance and his predilections, he became a San Francisco broker. Even before objection was made to his presence in the Board—the objection, I remember, was urged very eloquently by Watt Sanders, who was supposed to be the inventor of the "freezing-out" system of disposing of poor stockholders, and who also enjoyed the reputation of having been the impelling cause of Briggs of Tuolumne's ruin and suicide—even before this formal protest of respectability against lawlessness, the aquiline suggestions of Mr. Oakhurst's mien and countenance not only prematurely fluttered the pigeons, but absolutely occasioned much uneasiness among the fish-hawks, who circled below him with their booty. "Dash me! but he's as likely to go after us as anybody," said Joe Fielding.

It wanted but a few days before the close of the brief summer season at San Isabel Warm Sulphur Springs. Already there had been some migration of the more fashionable, and there was an uncomfortable suggestion of dregs and lees in the social life that remained. Mr. Oakhurst was moody; it was hinted that even the secure reputation of Mrs. Decker could no longer protect her from the gossip which his presence excited. It is but fair to her to say that during the last few weeks of this trying ordeal she looked like a sweet, pale martyr, and conducted herself toward her traducers with the gentle, forgiving manner of one who relied not upon the idle homage of the crowd, but upon the security of a principle that was dearer than popular favor. "They talk about myself and Mr. Oakhurst, my dear," she said to a friend, "but Heaven and my husband can best answer their calumny. It never shall be said that my husband ever turned his back upon a friend in the moment of his adversity because the position was changed, because his friend was poor and he was rich." This was the first intimation to the public that Jack had lost money, although it was known generally that the Deckers had lately bought some valuable property in San Francisco.

A few evenings after this an incident occurred which seemed to unpleasantly discord with the general social harmony that had always existed at San Isabel. It was at dinner, and Mr. Oakhurst and Mr. Hamilton, who sat together at a separate table, were observed to rise in some agitation. When they reached the hall, by a common instinct they stepped into a little breakfast-room which was vacant, and closed the door. Then Mr. Hamilton turned, with a half-amused, half-serious smile, toward his friend, and said,—

"If we are to quarrel, Jack Oakhurst,—you and I,—in the name of all that is ridiculous, don't let it be about a"—

I do not know what was the epithet intended. It was either unspoken or lost. For at that very instant Mr. Oakhurst raised a wine-glass and dashed its contents into Hamilton's face.

As they faced each other the men seemed to have changed natures. Mr. Oakhurst was trembling with excitement, and the wine-glass that he returned to the table shivered between his fingers. Mr. Hamilton stood there, grayish white, erect, and dripping. After a pause he said coldly,—

"So be it. But remember! our quarrel commences here. If I fall by your hand, you shall not use it to clear her character; if you fall by mine, you shall not be called a martyr. I am sorry it has come to this, but amen!—the sooner now the better."

He turned proudly, dropped his lids over his cold steel-blue eyes, as if sheathing a rapier, bowed, and passed coldly out.

They met twelve hours later in a little hollow two miles from the hotel, on the Stockton road. As Mr. Oakhurst received his pistol from Colonel Starbottle's hands he said to him in a low voice, "Whatever turns up or down I shall not return to the hotel. You will find some directions in my room. Go there"—but his voice suddenly faltered, and he turned his glistening eyes away, to his second's intense astonishment. "I've been out a dozen times with Jack Oakhurst," said Colonel Starbottle afterwards, "and I never saw him anyways cut before. Blank me if I didn't think he was losing his sand, till he walked to position."

The two reports were almost simultaneous. Mr. Oakhurst's right arm dropped suddenly to his side, and his pistol would have fallen from his paralyzed fingers, but the discipline of trained nerve and muscle prevailed, and he kept his grasp until he had shifted it to the other hand, without changing his position. Then there was a silence that seemed interminable, a gathering of two or three dark figures where a smoke curl still lazily floated, and then the hurried, husky, panting voice of Colonel Starbottle in his ear, "He's hit hard—through the lungs—you must run for it!"

Jack turned his dark, questioning eyes upon his second, but did not seem to listen; rather seemed to hear some other voice, remoter in the distance. He hesitated, and then made a step forward in the direction of the distant group. Then he paused again as the figures separated, and the surgeon came hastily toward him.

"He would like to speak with you a moment," said the

man. "You have little time to lose, I know; but," he added in a lower voice, "it is my duty to tell you he has still less."

A look of despair so hopeless in its intensity swept over Mr. Oakhurst's usually impassive face that the surgeon started. "You are hit," he said, glancing at Jack's helpless arm.

"Nothing—a mere scratch," said Jack hastily. Then he added, with a bitter laugh, "I'm not in luck to-day. But come! We'll see what he wants."

His long feverish stride outstripped the surgeon's, and in another moment he stood where the dying man lay—like most dying men—the one calm, composed, central figure of an anxious group. Mr. Oakhurst's face was less calm as he dropped on one knee beside him and took his hand. "I want to speak with this gentleman alone," said Hamilton, with something of his old imperious manner, as he turned to those about him. When they drew back, he looked up in Oakhurst's face.

"I've something to tell you, Jack."

His own face was white, but not so white as that which Mr. Oakhurst bent over him—a face so ghastly, with haunting doubts and a hopeless presentiment of coming evil, a face so piteous in its infinite weariness and envy of death, that the dying man was touched, even in the languor of dissolution, with a pang of compassion, and the cynical smile faded from his lips.

"Forgive me, Jack," he whispered more feebly, "for what I have to say. I don't say it in anger, but only because it must be said. I could not do my duty to you—I could not die contented until you knew it all. It's a miserable business at best, all around. But it can't be helped now. Only I ought to have fallen by Decker's pistol and not yours."

A flush like fire came into Jack's cheek, and he would have risen, but Hamilton held him fast.

"Listen! in my pocket you will find two letters. Take them—there! You will know the handwriting. But promise you will not read them until you are in a place of safety. Promise me!"

Jack did not speak, but held the letters between his fingers as if they had been burning coals.

"Promise me," said Hamilton faintly.

"Why?" asked Oakhurst, dropping his friend's hand coldly.

"Because," said the dying man with a bitter smile,—"because—when you have read them—you—will—go back—to capture—and death!"

They were his last words. He pressed Jack's hand faintly. Then his grasp relaxed, and he fell back a corpse.

It was nearly ten o'clock at night, and Mrs. Decker reclined languidly upon the sofa with a novel in her hand, while her husband discussed the politics of the country in the bar-room of the hotel. It was a warm night, and the French window looking out upon a little balcony was partly open. Suddenly she heard a foot upon the balcony, and she raised her eyes from the book with a slight start. The next moment the window was hurriedly thrust wide and a man entered.

Mrs. Decker rose to her feet with a little cry of alarm.

"For Heaven's sake, Jack, are you mad? He has only gone for a little while—he may return at any moment. Come an hour later—to-morrow—any time when I can get rid of him—but go, now, dear, at once."

Mr. Oakhurst walked toward the door, bolted it, and then faced her without a word. His face was haggard, his coat-sleeve hung loosely over an arm that was bandaged and bloody.

Nevertheless, her voice did not falter as she turned again

toward him. "What has happened, Jack? Why are you here?"

He opened his coat, and threw two letters in her lap.

"To return your lover's letters—to kill you—and then myself," he said in a voice so low as to be almost inaudible.

Among the many virtues of this admirable woman was invincible courage. She did not faint, she did not cry out. She sat quietly down again, folded her hands in her lap, and said calmly,—

"And why should you not?"

Had she recoiled, had she shown any fear or contrition, had she essayed an explanation or apology, Mr. Oakhurst would have looked upon it as an evidence of guilt. But there is no quality that courage recognizes so quickly as courage, there is no condition that desperation bows before but desperation; and Mr. Oakhurst's power of analysis was not so keen as to prevent him from confounding her courage with a moral quality. Even in his fury he could not help admiring this dauntless invalid.

"Why should you not?" she repeated with a smile. "You gave me life, health, and happiness, Jack. You gave me your love. Why should you not take what you have given? Go on. I am ready."

She held out her hands with that same infinite grace of yielding with which she had taken his own on the first day of their meeting at the hotel. Jack raised his head, looked at her for one wild moment, dropped upon his knees beside her, and raised the folds of her dress to his feverish lips. But she was too clever not to instantly see her victory; she was too much of a woman, with all her cleverness, to refrain from pressing that victory home. At the same moment, as with the impulse of an outraged and wounded woman, she rose, and with an imperious gesture pointed to the window. Mr. Oakhurst rose in his turn, cast one glance upon her, and without another word passed out of her presence forever.

When he had gone, she closed the window and bolted it, and going to the chimneypiece placed the letters, one by one, in the flame of the candle until they were consumed. I would not have the reader think that during this painful operation she was unmoved. Her hand trembled and—not being a brute—for some minutes (perhaps longer) she felt very badly, and the corners of her sensitive mouth were depressed. When her husband arrived it was with a genuine joy that she ran to him, and nestled against his broad breast with a feeling of security that thrilled the honest fellow to the core.

"But I've heard dreadful news to-night, Elsie," said Mr. Decker, after a few endearments were exchanged.

"Don't tell me anything dreadful, dear; I'm not well to-night," she pleaded sweetly.

"But it's about Mr. Oakhurst and Hamilton."

"Please!" Mr. Decker could not resist the petitionary grace of those white hands and that sensitive mouth, and took her to his arms. Suddenly he said, "What's that?"

He was pointing to the bosom of her white dress. Where Mr. Oakhurst had touched her there was a spot of blood.

It was nothing, she had slightly cut her hand in closing the window; it shut so hard! If Mr. Decker had remembered to close and bolt the shutter before he went out, he might have saved her this. There was such a genuine irritability and force in this remark that Mr. Decker was quite overcome by remorse. But Mrs. Decker forgave him with that graciousness which I have before pointed out in these pages, and with the halo of that forgiveness and marital confidence still lingering above the pair, with the reader's permission we will leave them and return to Mr. Oakhurst.

But not for two weeks. At the end of that time he walked into his rooms in Sacramento, and in his old manner took his seat at the faro-table.

"How's your arm, Jack?" asked an incautious player.

There was a smile followed the question, which, however, ceased as Jack looked up quietly at the speaker.

"It bothers my dealing a little, but I can shoot as well with my left."

The game was continued in that decorous silence which usually distinguished the table at which Mr. John Oakhurst presided.

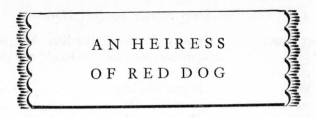

AN HEIRESS
OF RED DOG

THE first intimation given of the eccentricity of the testator was, I think, in the spring of 1854. He was at that time in possession of a considerable property, heavily mortgaged to one friend, and a wife of some attraction, on whose affections another friend held an encumbering lien. One day it was found that he had secretly dug, or caused to be dug, a deep trap before the front door of his dwelling, into which a few friends, in the course of the evening, casually and familiarly dropped. This circumstance, slight in itself, seemed to point to the existence of a certain humor in the man, which might eventually get into literature, although his wife's lover—a man of quick discernment, whose leg was broken by the fall —took other views. It was some weeks later that, while dining with certain other friends of his wife, he excused himself from the table to quietly reappear at the front window with a three-quarter-inch hydraulic pipe, and a stream of water projected at the assembled company. An attempt was made to take public cognizance of this, but a majority of the citizens of Red Dog who were not at the dinner, decided that a man had a right to choose his own methods of diverting his company. Nevertheless, there were some hints of his insanity; his wife recalled other acts clearly attributable to *dementia;* the crippled lover argued from his own experience that the integrity of her limbs could only be secured by leaving her husband's house; and the mortgagee, fearing a further damage to his property, foreclosed. But here the cause of all this anxiety took matters into his own hands, and disappeared.

When we next heard from him, he had, in some mysterious way, been relieved alike of his wife and property, and was living alone at Rockville, fifty miles away, and editing a newspaper. But that originality he had displayed when dealing with the problems of his own private life, when applied to politics in the columns of the "Rockville Vanguard" was singularly unsuccessful. An amusing exaggeration, purporting to be an exact account of the manner in which the opposing candidate had murdered his Chinese laundryman, was, I regret to say, answered only by assault and battery. A gratuitous and purely imaginative description of a great religious revival in Calaveras, in which the sheriff of the county—a notoriously profane skeptic—was alleged to have been the chief exhorter, resulted only in the withdrawal of the county advertising from the paper. In the midst of this practical confusion he suddenly died. It was then discovered, as a crowning proof of his absurdity, that he had left a will, bequeathing his entire effects to a freckle-faced maidservant at the Rockville Hotel. But that absurdity became serious when it was also discovered that among these effects were a thousand shares in the Rising Sun Mining Co., which, a day or two after his demise, and while people were still laughing at his grotesque benefaction, suddenly sprang into opulence and celebrity. Three millions of dollars was roughly estimated as the value of the estate thus wantonly sacrificed! For it is only fair to state, as a just tribute to the enterprise and energy of that young and thriving settlement, that there was not probably a single citizen who did not feel himself better able to control the deceased humorist's property. Some had expressed a doubt of their ability to support a family; others had felt perhaps too keenly the deep responsibility resting upon them when chosen from the panel as jurors, and had evaded their public duties; a few had declined office and a low salary; but no one shrank from the possibility of having been called upon to assume the functions of Peggy Moffat—the heiress.

The will was contested. First by the widow, who, it now appeared, had never been legally divorced from the deceased; next by four of his cousins, who awoke, only too late, to a consciousness of his moral and pecuniary worth. But the humble legatee—a singularly plain, unpretending, uneducated Western girl—exhibited a dogged pertinacity in claiming her rights. She rejected all compromises. A rough sense of justice in the community, while doubting her ability to take care of the whole fortune, suggested that she ought to be content with three hundred thousand dollars. "She's bound to throw even *that* away on some derned skunk of a man, natoorally; but three millions is too much to give a chap for makin' her onhappy. It's offering a temptation to cussedness." The only opposing voice to this counsel came from the sardonic lips of Mr. Jack Hamlin. "Suppose," suggested that gentleman, turning abruptly on the speaker,—"suppose, when you won twenty thousand dollars of me last Friday night—suppose that instead of handing you over the money as I did—suppose I'd got up on my hind legs and said, 'Look yer, Bill Wethersbee, you're a damned fool. If I give ye that twenty thousand you'll throw it away in the first skin game in 'Frisco, and hand it over to the first short card-sharp you'll meet. There's a thousand—enough for you to fling away—take it and get!' Suppose what I'd said to you was the frozen truth, and you'd know'd it—would that have been the square thing to play on you?" But here Wethersbee quickly pointed out the inefficiency of the comparison by stating that *he* had won the money fairly with a *stake*. "And how do you know," demanded Hamlin savagely, bending his black eyes on the astounded casuist,—"how do you know that the gal hezn't put down a stake?" The man stammered an unintelligible reply. The gambler laid his white hand on Wethersbee's shoulder. "Look yer, old man," he said, "every gal stakes her *whole* pile—you can bet your life on that—whatever's her little game. If she took to keerds instead of her feelings—if she'd put up 'chips' instead o' body and soul, she'd bust every bank 'twixt this and 'Frisco! You hear me?"

Somewhat of this idea was conveyed, I fear not quite as sentimentally, to Peggy Moffat herself. The best legal wisdom of San Francisco retained by the widow and relatives took occasion, in a private interview with Peggy, to point out that she stood in the quasi-criminal attitude of having unlawfully practiced upon the affections of an insane elderly gentleman, with a view of getting possession of his property, and suggested to her that no vestige of her moral character would remain after the trial—if she persisted in forcing her claims to that issue. It is said that Peggy, on hearing this, stopped washing the plate she had in her hands, and, twisting the towel around her fingers, fixed her small pale blue eyes at the lawyer.

"And ez that the kind o' chirpin' the critters keep up?"

"I regret to say, my dear young lady," responded the lawyer, "that the world is censorious. I must add," he continued, with engaging frankness, "that we professional lawyers are apt to study the opinion of the world—and that such will be the theory of—our side."

"Then," said Peggy stoutly, "ez I allow I've got to go into court to defend my character, I might as well pack in them three millions too."

There is hearsay evidence that Peg added to this speech a

wish and desire to "bust the crust" of her traducers, and, re-marking that "that was the kind of hairpin" she was, closed the conversation with an unfortunate accident to the plate, that left a severe contusion on the legal brow of her companion. But this story, popular in the bar-rooms and gulches, lacked confirmation in higher circles. Better authenticated was the legend related of an interview with her own lawyer. That gentleman had pointed out to her the advantage of being able to show some reasonable cause for the singular generosity of the testator.

"Although," he continued, "the law does not go back of the will for reason or cause for its provisions, it would be a strong point with the judge and jury—particularly if the theory of insanity were set up—for us to show that the act was logical and natural. Of course you have—I speak confidentially, Miss Moffat—certain ideas of your own why the late Mr. Byways was so singularly generous to you."

"No, I haven't," said Peg decidedly.

"Think again. Had he not expressed to you—you understand that this is confidential between us, although I protest, my dear young lady, that I see no reason why it should not be made public—had he not given utterance to sentiments of a nature consistent with some future matrimonial relations?" But here Miss Peg's large mouth, which had been slowly relaxing over her irregular teeth, stopped him.

"If you mean he wanted to marry me—no!"

"I see. But were there any conditions—of course you know the law takes no cognizance of any not expressed in the will; but still, for the sake of mere corroboration of the bequest—do you know of any conditions on which he gave you the property?"

"You mean, did he want anything in return?"

"Exactly, my dear young lady."

Peg's face on one side turned a deep magenta color, on the other a lighter cherry, while her nose was purple, and her forehead an Indian red. To add to the effect of this awkward and discomposing dramatic exhibition of embarrassment, she began to wipe her hands on her dress, and sat silent.

"I understand," said the lawyer hastily. "No matter—the conditions *were* fulfilled."

"No," said Peg amazedly; "how could they be until he was dead?"

It was the lawyer's turn to color and grow embarrassed.

"He *did* say something, and make some conditions," continued Peg, with a certain firmness through her awkwardness; "but that's nobody's business but mine and his'n. And it's no call o' yours or theirs."

"But, my dear Miss Moffat, if these very conditions were proofs of his right mind, you surely would not object to make them known, if only to enable you to put yourself in a condition to carry them out."

"But," said Peg cunningly, "'spose you and the Court didn't think 'em satisfactory? 'Spose you thought 'em *queer*? Eh?"

With this helpless limitation on the part of the defense, the case came to trial. Everybody remembers it: how for six weeks it was the daily food of Calaveras County; how for six weeks the intellectual and moral and spiritual competency of Mr. James Byways to dispose of his property was discussed with learned and formal obscurity in the Court, and with unlettered and independent prejudice by camp-fires and in bar-rooms. At the end of that time, when it was logically established that at least nine tenths of the population of Calaveras were harmless lunatics, and everybody else's reason seemed to totter on its throne, an exhausted jury succumbed one day to the presence of Peg in the court-room. It was not a prepossessing presence at any time; but the excitement, and an injudicious attempt to ornament herself, brought her defects into a glaring relief that was almost unreal. Every freckle on her face stood out and asserted itself singly; her pale blue eyes, that gave no indication of her force of character, were weak and wandering, or stared blankly at the judge; her over-sized head, broad at the base, terminating in the scantiest possible light-colored braid in the middle of her narrow shoulders, was as hard and uninteresting as the wooden spheres that topped the railing against which she sat. The jury, who for six weeks had had her described to them by the plaintiffs as an arch, wily enchantress, who had sapped the failing reason of Jim Byways, revolted to a man. There was something so appallingly gratuitous in her plainness, that it was felt that three millions was scarcely a compensation for it. "Ef that money was give to her, she earned it *sure,* boys; it wasn't no softness of the old man," said the foreman. When the jury retired, it was felt that she had cleared her character. When they reëntered the room with their verdict, it was known that she had been awarded three millions damages for its defamation.

She got the money. But those who had confidently expected to see her squander it were disappointed. On the contrary, it was presently whispered that she was exceedingly penurious. That admirable woman, Mrs. Stiver of Red Dog, who accompanied her to San Francisco to assist her in making purchases, was loud in her indignation. "She cares more for two bits than I do for five dollars. She wouldn't buy anything at the 'City of Paris' because it was 'too expensive,' and at last rigged herself out, a perfect guy, at some cheap slop-shops in Market Street. And after all the care Jane and me took of her, giving up our time and experience to her, she never so much as made Jane a single present." Popular opin-

ion, which regarded Mrs. Stiver's attention as purely specu-
lative, was not shocked at this unprofitable dénouement;
but when Peg refused to give anything to clear the mortgage
off the Presbyterian Church, and even declined to take shares
in the Union Ditch, considered by many as an equally sacred
and safe investment, she began to lose favor. Nevertheless,
she seemed to be as regardless of public opinion as she had
been before the trial; took a small house, in which she lived
with an old woman, who had once been a fellow servant, on,
apparently, terms of perfect equality, and looked after her
money. I wish I could say that she did this discreetly, but the
fact is, she blundered. The same dogged persistency she had
displayed in claiming her rights was visible in her unsuccessful ventures. She sunk two hundred thousand dollars in
a worn-out shaft originally projected by the deceased testator.
She prolonged the miserable existence of the "Rockville Vanguard" long after it had ceased to interest even its enemies;
she kept the doors of the Rockville Hotel open when its custom had departed; she lost the coöperation and favor of a
fellow capitalist through a trifling misunderstanding in
which she was derelict and impenitent; she had three law-
suits on her hands that could have been settled for a trifle. I
note these defects to show that she was by no means a heroine. I
quote her affair with Jack Folinsbee to show that she was
scarcely the average woman.

That handsome, graceless vagabond had struck the outskirts of Red Dog in a cyclone of dissipation, which left him
a stranded but still rather interesting wreck in a ruinous
cabin not far from Peg Moffat's virgin bower. Pale, crippled
from excesses, with a voice quite tremulous from sympathetic
emotion more or less developed by stimulants, he lingered
languidly, with much time on his hands, and only a few
neighbors. In this fascinating kind of general deshabille of

morals, dress, and the emotions, he appeared before Peg Moffat. More than that, he occasionally limped with her through the settlement. The critical eye of Red Dog took in the singular pair,—Jack, voluble, suffering, apparently overcome by remorse, conscience, vituperation, and disease; and Peg, open-mouthed, high-colored, awkward, yet delighted; and the critical eye of Red Dog, seeing this, winked meaningly at Rockville. No one knew what passed between them. But all observed that one summer day Jack drove down the main street of Red Dog in an open buggy, with the heiress of that town beside him. Jack, albeit a trifle shaky, held the reins with something of his old dash; and Mistress Peggy, in an enormous bonnet with pearl-colored ribbons, a shade darker than her hair, holding in her short pink-gloved fingers a bouquet of yellow roses, absolutely glowed crimson in distressful gratification over the dashboard. So these two fared on—out of the busy settlement, into the woods, against the rosy sunset. Possibly it was not a pretty picture; nevertheless, as the dim aisles of the solemn pines opened to receive them, miners leaned upon their spades, and mechanics stopped in their toil to look after them. The critical eye of Red Dog, perhaps from the sun, perhaps from the fact that it had itself once been young and dissipated, took on a kindly moisture as it gazed.

The moon was high when they returned. Those who had waited to congratulate Jack on this near prospect of a favorable change in his fortunes were chagrined to find that, having seen the lady safe home, he had himself departed from Red Dog. Nothing was to be gained from Peg, who, on the next day and ensuing days, kept the even tenor of her way, sunk a thousand or two more in unsuccessful speculation, and made no change in her habits of personal economy. Weeks passed without any apparent sequel to this romantic idyl. Nothing was known definitely until Jack, a month later, turned up in Sacramento, with a billiard-cue in his hand, and a heart overcharged with indignant emotion. "I don't mind saying to you gentlemen, in confidence," said Jack, to a circle of sympathizing players,—"I don't mind telling you regarding this thing, that I was as soft on that freckled-faced, red-eyed, tallow-haired gal as if she'd been— a—a—an actress. And I don't mind saying, gentlemen, that, as far as I understand women, she was just as soft on me! You kin laugh, but it's so. One day I took her out buggy-riding,—in style, too,—and out on the road I offered to do the square thing—just as if she'd been a lady—offered to marry her then and there! And what did she do?" said Jack with an hysterical laugh. "Why, blank it all! *offered me twenty-five dollars a week allowance—pay to be stopped when I wasn't at home!*" The roar of laughter that greeted this frank confession was broken by a quiet voice asking, "And what did *you* say?" "Say?" screamed Jack. "I just told her to—with her money." "They say," continued the quiet voice, "that you asked her for the loan of two hundred and fifty dollars to get you to Sacramento—and that you got it." "Who says so?" roared Jack. "Show me the blank liar." There was a dead silence. Then the possessor of the quiet voice, Mr. Jack Hamlin, languidly reached under the table, took the chalk, and rubbing the end of his billiard-cue, began with gentle gravity: "It was an old friend of mine in Sacramento,—a man with a wooden leg, a game eye, three fingers on his right hand, and a consumptive cough. Being unable naturally to back himself, he leaves things to me. So for the sake of argument," continued Hamlin, suddenly laying down his cue, and fixing his wicked black eyes on the speaker, "say it's *me!*"

I am afraid that this story, whether truthful or not, did

not tend to increase Peg's popularity in a community where recklessness or generosity condoned for the absence of all the other virtues; and it is possible also that Red Dog was no more free from prejudice than other more civilized but equally disappointed match-makers. Likewise, during the following years, she made several more foolish ventures, and lost heavily. In fact, a feverish desire to increase her store at almost any risk seemed to possess her. At last it was announced that she intended to reopen the infelix Rockville Hotel, and keep it herself. Wild as this scheme appeared in theory, when put into practical operation there seemed to be some chance of success. Much, doubtless, was owing to her practical knowledge of hotel-keeping, but more to her rigid economy and untiring industry. The mistress of millions, she cooked, washed, waited on table, made the beds, and labored like a common menial. Visitors were attracted by this novel spectacle. The income of the house increased as their respect for the hostess lessened. No anecdote of her avarice was too extravagant for current belief. It was even alleged that she had been known to carry the luggage of guests to their rooms, that she might anticipate the usual porter's gratuity. She denied herself the ordinary necessaries of life. She was poorly clad, she was ill fed—but the hotel was making money.

A few hinted at insanity; others shook their heads, and said a curse was entailed on the property. It was believed also, from her appearance, that she could not long survive this tax on her energies, and already there was discussion as to the probable final disposition of her property. It was the particular fortune of Mr. Jack Hamlin to be able to set the world right on this and other questions regarding her.

A stormy December evening had set in when he chanced to be a guest of the Rockville Hotel. He had during the past week been engaged in the prosecution of his noble profession at Red Dog, and had, in the graphic language of a coadjutor, "cleared out the town, except his fare in the pockets of the stage-driver." The Red Dog "Standard" had bewailed his departure in playful obituary verse, beginning, "Dear Johnny, thou hast left us," wherein the rhymes "bereft us," and "deplore" carried a vague allusion to "a thousand dollars more." A quiet contentment naturally suffused his personality, and he was more than usually lazy and deliberate in his speech. At midnight, when he was about to retire, he was a little surprised, however, by a tap on his door, followed by the presence of Mistress Peg Moffat, heiress, and landlady of Rockville Hotel.

Mr. Hamlin, despite his previous defense of Peg, had no liking for her. His fastidious taste rejected her uncomeliness; his habits of thought and life were all antagonistic to what he had heard of her niggardliness and greed. As she stood there, in a dirty calico wrapper, still redolent with the day's cuisine, crimson with embarrassment and the recent heat of the kitchen range, she certainly was not an alluring apparition. Happily for the lateness of the hour, her loneliness, and the infelix reputation of the man before her, she was at least a safe one. And I fear the very consciousness of this scarcely relieved her embarrassment.

"I wanted to say a few words to ye alone, Mr. Hamlin," she began, taking an unoffered seat on the end of his portmanteau, "or I shouldn't hev intruded. But it's the only time I can ketch you, or you me, for I'm down in the kitchen from sun-up till now."

She stopped awkwardly, as if to listen to the wind which was rattling against the windows, and spreading a film of rain against the opaque darkness without. Then, smoothing her wrapper over her knees, she remarked, as if opening a desultory conversation, "Thar's a power of rain outside."

Mr. Hamlin's only response to this meteorological observation was a yawn, and a preliminary tug at his coat as he began to remove it.

"I thought ye couldn't mind doin' me a favor," continued Peg, with a hard, awkward laugh; "partik'ly seein' ez folks allowed you'd sorter been a friend o' mine, and hed stood up for me at times when you hedn't any partikler call to do it. I hevn't," she continued, looking down on her lap, and following with her finger and thumb a seam of her gown,— "I hevn't so many friends ez slings a kind word for me these times that I disremember them." Her under lip quivered a little here, and after vainly hunting for a forgotten handkerchief, she finally lifted the hem of her gown, wiped her snub nose upon it, but left the tears still in her eyes as she raised them to the man.

Mr. Hamlin, who had by this time divested himself of his coat, stopped unbuttoning his waistcoat, and looked at her.

"Like ez not thar'll be high water on the North Fork, ef this rain keeps on," said Peg, as if apologetically, looking toward the window.

The other rain having ceased, Mr. Hamlin began to unbutton his waistcoat again.

"I wanted to ask ye a favor about Mr.—about—Jack Folinsbee," began Peg again, hurriedly. "He's ailin' agin', and is mighty low. And he's losin' a heap o' money here and thar, and mostly to *you*. You cleaned him out of two thousand dollars last night—all he had."

"Well," said the gambler coldly.

"Well, I thought ez you woz a friend o' mine, I'd ask ye to let up a little on him," said Peg, with an affected laugh. "You kin do it. Don't let him play with ye."

"Mistress Margaret Moffat," said Jack with lazy deliberation, taking off his watch and beginning to wind it up; "ef you're that much stuck after Jack Folinsbee *you* kin keep him off of me much easier than I kin. You're a rich woman! Give him enough money to break my bank, or break himself for good and all; but don't keep him foolin' round me, in hopes to make a raise. It don't pay, Mistress Moffat,—it don't pay!"

A finer nature than Peg's would have misunderstood or resented the gambler's slang, and the miserable truths that underlay it. But she comprehended him instantly, and sat hopelessly silent.

"Ef you'll take my advice," continued Jack, placing his watch and chain under his pillow, and quietly unloosing his cravat, "you'll quit this yer foolin', marry that chap, and hand over to him the money and the money-makin' that's killin' you. He'll get rid of it soon enough. I don't say this because *I* expect to git it, for when he's got that much of a raise, he'll make a break for 'Frisco, and lose it to some first-class sport *there*. I don't say neither that you mayn't be in luck enough to reform him. I don't say neither—and it's a derned sight more likely—that you mayn't be luckier yet—and he'll up and die afore he gits rid of your money. But I do say you'll make him happy *now;* and ez I reckon you're about ez badly stuck after that chap ez I ever saw any woman, you won't be hurtin' your own feelin's either!"

The blood left Peg's face as she looked up. "But that's *why* I can't give him the money—and he won't marry me without it."

Mr. Hamlin's hand dropped from the last button of his waistcoat. "Can't—give—him—the—money?" he repeated slowly.

"No."

"Why?"

"Because—because I *love* him."

Mr. Hamlin rebuttoned his waistcoat, and sat down patiently on the bed. Peg rose, and awkwardly drew the portmanteau a little bit nearer to him.

"When Jim Byways left me this yer property," she began, looking cautiously around, "he left it to me on *conditions*. Not conditions ez was in his *written* will—but conditions ez was *spoken*. A promise I made him in this very room, Mr. Hamlin,—this very room, and on that very bed you're sittin' on, in which he died."

Like most gamblers, Mr. Hamlin was superstitious. He rose hastily from the bed, and took a chair beside the window. The wind shook it as if the discontented spirit of Mr. Byways were without, reinforcing his last injunction.

"I don't know if you remember him," said Peg feverishly. "He was a man ez hed suffered. All that he loved—wife, fammerly, friends—had gone back on him! He tried to make light of it afore folk; but with me, being a poor gal, he let himself out. I never told anybody this—I don't know why he told *me*—I don't know," continued Peg with a sniffle, "why he wanted to make me unhappy too. But he made me promise that if he left me his fortune I'd *never—never*, so help me, God—never share it with any man or woman that I *loved*! I didn't think it would be hard to keep that promise then, Mr. Hamlin, for I was very poor, and hedn't a friend nor a living bein' that was kind to me but *him*."

"But you've as good as broken your promise already," said Hamlin; "you've given Jack money—as I know."

"Only what I made myself! Listen to me, Mr. Hamlin. When Jack proposed to me, I offered him about what I kalkilated I could earn myself. When he went away, and was sick and in trouble, I came here and took this hotel. I knew that by hard work I could make it pay. Don't laugh at me, please. I *did* work hard, and *did* make it pay—without takin' one cent of the fortin'. And all I made, workin' by night and day, I gave to him. I did, Mr. Hamlin. I ain't so hard to him as you think; though I might be kinder, I know."

Mr. Hamlin rose, deliberately resumed his coat, watch, hat, and overcoat. When he was completely dressed again, he turned to Peg.

"Do you mean to say that you've been givin' all the money you make here to this A 1 first-class cherubim?"

"Yes, but he didn't know where I got it. O Mr. Hamlin, he didn't know that!"

"Do I understand you that he's bin bucking agin faro with the money that you raised on hash? And *you* makin' the hash?"

"But he didn't know that—he wouldn't hev took it if I'd told him."

"No; he'd hev died fust!" said Mr. Hamlin gravely. "Why, he's that sensitive—is Jack Folinsbee—that it nearly kills him to take money even of *me*. But where does this angel reside when he isn't fightin' the tiger, and is, so to speak, visible to the naked eye?"

"He—he—stops here," said Peg, with an awkward blush.

"I see. Might I ask the number of his room, or should I be a—disturbing him in his meditations?" continued Jack Hamlin with grave politeness.

"Oh, then you'll promise? And you'll talk to him, and make *him* promise?"

"Of course," said Hamlin quietly.

"And you'll remember he's sick—very sick? His room's No. 44, at the end of the hall. Perhaps I had better go with you?"

"I'll find it."

"And you won't be too hard on him?"

"I'll be a father to him," said Hamlin demurely, as he opened the door and stepped into the hall. But he hesitated a moment, and then turned and gravely held out his hand. Peg took it timidly; he did not seem quite in earnest—and his black eyes, vainly questioned, indicated nothing. But he shook her hand warmly, and the next moment was gone.

He found the room with no difficulty. A faint cough from within, and a querulous protest, answered his knock. Mr. Hamlin entered without further ceremony. A sickening smell of drugs, a palpable flavor of stale dissipation, and the wasted figure of Jack Folinsbee, half dressed, extended upon the bed, greeted him. Mr. Hamlin was, for an instant, startled. There were hollow circles round the sick man's eyes, there was palsy in his trembling limbs, there was dissolution in his feverish breath.

"What's up?" he asked huskily and nervously.

"I am; and I want *you* to get up too."

"I can't, Jack. I'm regularly done up." He reached his shaking hand towards a glass half filled with suspicious, pungent-smelling liquid, but Mr. Hamlin stayed it.

"Do you want to get back that two thousand dollars you lost?"

"Yes."

"Well, get up and marry that woman downstairs."

Folinsbee laughed half hysterically, half sardonically.

"She won't give it to me."

"No, but *I* will."

"*You?*"

"Yes."

Folinsbee, with an attempt at a reckless laugh, rose, trembling and with difficulty, to his swollen feet. Hamlin eyed him narrowly, and then bade him lie down again. "To-morrow will do," he said, "and then"—

"If I don't"—

"If you don't," responded Hamlin, "why, I'll just wade in and *cut you out!*"

But on the morrow Mr. Hamlin was spared that possible act of disloyalty. For in the night the already hesitating spirit of Mr. Jack Folinsbee took flight on the wings of the south-east storm. When or how it happened, nobody knew. Whether this last excitement and the near prospect of matri-mony, or whether an over-dose of anodyne had hastened his end was never known. I only know that when they came to awaken him the next morning, the best that was left of him —a face still beautiful and boylike—looked up tearful at the eyes of Peg Moffat. "It serves me right—it's a judgment," she said in a low whisper to Jack Hamlin; "for God knew that I'd broken my word and willed all my property to him."

She did not long survive him. Whether Mr. Hamlin ever clothed with action the suggestion indicated in his speech to the lamented Jack that night is not on record. He was always her friend, and on her demise became her executor. But the bulk of her property was left to a distant relation of handsome Jack Folinsbee, and so passed out of the control of Red Dog forever.

AN INGENUE
OF THE SIERRAS

I

WE all held our breath as the coach rushed through the
semi-darkness of Galloper's Ridge. The vehicle itself was
only a huge lumbering shadow; its side-lights were carefully
extinguished, and Yuba Bill had just politely removed from
the lips of an outside passenger even the cigar with which
he had been ostentatiously exhibiting his coolness. For it had
been rumored that the Ramon Martinez gang of "road
agents" were "laying" for us on the second grade, and would
time the passage of our lights across Galloper's in order to
intercept us in the "brush" beyond. If we could cross the
ridge without being seen, and so get through the brush
before they reached it, we were safe. If they followed, it
would only be a stern chase with the odds in our favor.

The huge vehicle swayed from side to side, rolled, dipped,
and plunged, but Bill kept the track, as if, in the whispered
words of the Expressman, he could "feel and smell" the
road he could no longer see. We knew that at times we hung
perilously over the edge of slopes that eventually dropped
a thousand feet sheer to the tops of the sugar-pines below,
but we knew that Bill knew it also. The half visible heads of
the horses, drawn wedge-wise together by the tightened
reins, appeared to cleave the darkness like a ploughshare,
held between his rigid hands. Even the hoof-beats of the six
horses had fallen into a vague, monotonous, distant roll.
Then the ridge was crossed, and we plunged into the still
blacker obscurity of the brush. Rather we no longer seemed

to move—it was only the phantom night that rushed by us. The horses might have been submerged in some swift Lethean stream; nothing but the top of the coach and the rigid bulk of Yuba Bill arose above them. Yet even in that awful moment our speed was unslackened; it was as if Bill cared no longer to *guide* but only to drive, or as if the direction of his huge machine was determined by other hands than his. An incautious whisperer hazarded the paralyzing suggestion of our "meeting another team." To our great astonishment Bill overheard it; to our greater astonishment he replied. "It 'ud be only a neck and neck race which would get to h—ll first," he said quietly. But we were relieved —for he had *spoken*! Almost simultaneously the wider turnpike began to glimmer faintly as a visible track before us; the wayside trees fell out of line, opened up, and dropped off one after another; we were on the broader tableland, out of danger, and apparently unperceived and unpursued.

Nevertheless in the conversation that broke out again with the relighting of the lamps, and the comments, congratulations, and reminiscences that were freely exchanged, Yuba Bill preserved a dissatisfied and even resentful silence. The most generous praise of his skill and courage awoke no response. "I reckon the old man waz just spilin' for a fight, and is feelin' disappointed," said a passenger. But those who knew that Bill had the true fighter's scorn for any purely purposeless conflict were more or less concerned and watchful of him. He would drive steadily for four or five minutes with thoughtfully knitted brows, but eyes still keenly observant under his slouched hat, and then, relaxing his strained attitude, would give way to a movement of impatience. "You ain't uneasy about anything, Bill, are you?" asked the Expressman confidentially. Bill lifted his eyes with a slightly contemptuous surprise. "Not about anything ter *come*. It's what *hez* happened that I don't exactly *sabe*. I don't see no signs of Ramon's gang ever havin' been out at all, and ef they were out I don't see why they didn't go for us."

"The simple fact is that our ruse was successful," said an outside passenger. "They waited to see our lights on the ridge, and, not seeing them, missed us until we had passed. That's my opinion."

"You ain't puttin' any price on that opinion, air ye?" inquired Bill politely.

"No."

" 'Cos thar's a comic paper in 'Frisco pays for them things, and I've seen worse things in it."

"Come off, Bill," retorted the passenger, slightly nettled by the tittering of his companions. "Then what did you put out the lights for?"

"Well," returned Bill grimly, "it mout have been because I didn't keer to hev you chaps blazin' away at the first bush you *thought* you saw move in your skeer, and bringin' down their fire on us."

The explanation, though unsatisfactory, was by no means an improbable one, and we thought it better to accept it with a laugh. Bill, however, resumed his abstracted manner.

"Who got in at the Summit?" he at last asked abruptly of the Expressman.

"Derrick and Simpson of Cold Spring, and one of the 'Excelsior' boys," responded the Expressman.

"And that Pike County girl from Dow's Flat, with her bun·dles. Don't forget her," added the outside passenger ironically.

"Does anybody here know her?" continued Bill, ignoring the irony.

"You'd better ask Judge Thompson; he was mighty attentive to her; gettin' her a seat by the off window, and lookin' after her bundles and things."

"Gettin' her a seat by the *window?*" repeated Bill.

"Yes, she wanted to see everything, and wasn't afraid of the shooting."

"Yes," broke in a third passenger, "and he was so d—d civil that when she dropped her ring in the straw, he struck a match agin all your rules, you know, and held it for her to find it. And it was just as we were crossin' through the brush, too. I saw the hull thing through the window, for I was hanging over the wheels with my gun ready for action. And it wasn't no fault of Judge Thompson's if his d—d foolishness hadn't shown us up, and got us a shot from the gang."

Bill gave a short grunt, but drove steadily on without further comment or even turning his eyes to the speaker.

We were now not more than a mile from the station at the crossroads where we were to change horses. The lights already glimmered in the distance, and there was a faint suggestion of the coming dawn on the summits of the ridge to the west. We had plunged into a belt of timber, when suddenly a horseman emerged at a sharp canter from a trail that seemed to be parallel with our own. We were all slightly startled; Yuba Bill alone preserving his moody calm.

"Hullo!" he said.

The stranger wheeled to our side as Bill slackened his speed. He seemed to be a "packer" or freight muleteer.

"Ye didn't get 'held up' on the Divide?" continued Bill cheerfully.

"No," returned the packer, with a laugh. "*I* don't carry treasure. But I see you're all right, too. I saw you crossin' over Galloper's."

"*Saw* us?" said Bill sharply. "We had our lights out."

"Yes, but there was suthin' white—a handkerchief or woman's veil, I reckon—hangin' from the window. It was only a movin' spot agin the hillside, but ez I was lookin' out for ye I knew it was you by that. Good-night!"

He cantered away. We tried to look at each other's faces, and at Bill's expression in the darkness, but he neither spoke nor stirred until he threw down the reins when we stopped before the station. The passengers quickly descended from the roof; the Expressman was about to follow, but Bill plucked his sleeve.

"I'm goin' to take a look over this yer stage and these yer passengers with ye, afore we start."

"Why, what's up?"

"Well," said Bill, slowly disengaging himself from one of his enormous gloves, "when we waltzed down into the brush up there I saw a man, ez plain ez I see you, rise up from it. I thought our time had come and the band was goin' to play, when he sorter drew back, made a sign, and we just scooted past him."

"Well?"

"Well," said Bill, "it means that this yer coach was *passed through free* to-night."

"You don't object to *that*—surely? I think we were deucedly lucky."

Bill slowly drew off his other glove. "I've been riskin' my everlastin' life on this d—d line three times a week," he said with mock humility, "and I'm allus thankful for small mercies. *But*," he added grimly, "when it comes down to being passed free by some pal of a hoss thief, and thet called a speshal Providence, *I ain't in it*! No, sir, I ain't in it!"

II

IT was with mixed emotions that the passengers heard that a delay of fifteen minutes to tighten certain screw-bolts had been ordered by the autocratic Bill. Some were anxious to get their breakfast at Sugar Pine, but others were not averse to linger for the daylight that promised greater safety on the road. The Expressman, knowing the real cause of Bill's delay, was nevertheless at a loss to understand the object of it. The passengers were all well known; any idea of complicity with the road agents was wild and impossible, and, even if there was a confederate of the gang among them, he would have been more likely to precipitate a robbery than to check it. Again, the discovery of such a confederate— to whom they clearly owned their safety—and his arrest would have been quite against the Californian sense of justice, if not actually illegal. It seemed evident that Bill's quixotic sense of honor was leading him astray.

The station consisted of a stable, a wagon shed, and a building containing three rooms. The first was fitted up with "bunks" or sleeping berths for the employees; the second was the kitchen; and the third and larger apartment was dining-room or sitting-room, and was used as general waiting-room for the passengers. It was not a refreshment station, and there was no "bar." But a mysterious command from the omnipotent Bill produced a demijohn of whiskey, with which he hospitably treated the company. The seductive influence of the liquor loosened the tongue of the gallant Judge Thompson. He admitted to having struck a match to enable the fair Pike Countian to find her ring, which, however, proved to have fallen in her lap. She was "a fine, healthy young woman—a type of the Far West, sir; in fact, quite a prairie blossom! yet simple and guileless as a child." She was on her way to Marysville, he believed, "although she expected to meet friends—a friend, in fact—later on." It was her first visit to a large town—in fact, any civilized centre—since she crossed the plains three years ago. Her girlish curiosity was quite touching, and her innocence irresistible. In fact, in a country whose tendency was to produce "frivolity and forwardness in young girls, he found her a most interesting young person." She was even then out in the stable-yard watching the horses being harnessed, "preferring to indulge a pardonable healthy young curiosity than to listen to the empty compliments of the younger passengers."

The figure which Bill saw thus engaged, without being otherwise distinguished, certainly seemed to justify the Judge's opinion. She appeared to be a well-matured country girl, whose frank gray eyes and large laughing mouth expressed a wholesome and abiding gratification in her life and surroundings. She was watching the replacing of luggage in the boot. A little feminine start, as one of her own parcels was thrown somewhat roughly on the roof, gave Bill his opportunity. "Now there," he growled to the helper, "ye ain't carting stone! Look out, will yer! Some of your things, miss?" he added, with gruff courtesy, turning to her. "These yer trunks, for instance?"

She smiled a pleasant assent, and Bill, pushing aside the helper, seized a large square trunk in his arms. But from excess of zeal, or some other mischance, his foot slipped, and he came down heavily, striking the corner of the trunk on the ground and loosening its hinges and fastenings. It was a cheap, common-looking affair, but the accident discovered in its yawning lid a quantity of white, lace-edged feminine apparel of an apparently superior quality. The young lady uttered another cry and came quickly forward, but Bill was profuse in his apologies, himself girded the broken box with a strap, and declared his intention of having the company "make it good" to her with a new one. Then he casually accompanied her to the door of the waiting-room, entered, made a place for her before the fire by simply lifting the nearest and most youthful passenger by the coat collar from the stool that he was occupying, and, having installed the lady in it, displaced another man who was standing before the chimney, and, drawing himself up to his full six feet of height in front of her, glanced down upon his fair passenger as he took his waybill from his pocket.

"Your name is down here as Miss Mullins?" he said.

She looked up, became suddenly aware that she and her questioner were the centre of interest to the whole circle of passengers, and, with a slight rise of color, returned, "Yes."

"Well, Miss Mullins, I've got a question or two to ask ye. I ask it straight out afore this crowd. It's in my rights to take ye aside and ask it—but that ain't my style; I'm no detective. I needn't ask it at all, but act as ef I knowed the answer, or I might leave it to be asked by others. Ye needn't answer it ef ye don't like; ye've got a friend over there—Judge Thompson —who is a friend to ye, right or wrong, jest as any other man here is—as though ye'd packed your own jury. Well, the simple question I've got to ask ye is *this:* Did you signal to anybody from the coach when we passed Galloper's an hour ago?"

We all thought that Bill's courage and audacity had reached its climax here. To openly and publicly accuse a "lady" before a group of chivalrous Californians, and that lady possessing the further attractions of youth, good looks, and innocence, was little short of desperation. There was an evident movement of adhesion towards the fair stranger, a slight muttering broke out on the right, but the very boldness of the act held them in stupefied surprise. Judge Thompson, with a bland propitiatory smile began: "Really, Bill, I must protest on behalf of this young lady"—when the fair accused, raising her eyes to her accuser, to the consternation of everybody answered with the slight but convincing hesitation of conscientious truthfulness:—

"*I did.*"

"Ahem!" interposed the Judge hastily, "er—that is—er—you allowed your handkerchief to flutter from the window,—I noticed it myself,—casually—one might say even playfully—but without any particular significance."

The girl, regarding her apologist with a singular mingling of pride and impatience, returned briefly:—

"I signaled."

"Who did you signal to?" asked Bill gravely.

"The young gentleman I'm going to marry."

A start, followed by a slight titter from the younger passengers, was instantly suppressed by a savage glance from Bill.

"What did you signal to him for?" he continued.

"To tell him I was here, and that it was all right," returned the young girl, with a steadily rising pride and color.

"Wot was all right?" demanded Bill.

"That I wasn't followed, and that he could meet me on the road beyond Cass's Ridge Station." She hesitated a moment, and then, with a still greater pride, in which a youthful defiance was still mingled, said: "I've run away from home to marry him. And I mean to! No one can stop me. Dad didn't like him just because he was poor, and dad's got money. Dad wanted me to marry a man I hate, and got a lot of dresses and things to bribe me."

"And you're taking them in your trunk to the other feller?" said Bill grimly.

"Yes, he's poor," returned the girl defiantly.

"Then your father's name is Mullins?" asked Bill.

"It's not Mullins. I—I—took that name," she hesitated, with her first exhibition of self-consciousness.

"Wot *is* his name?"

"Eli Hemmings."

A smile of relief and significance went round the circle. The fame of Eli or "Skinner" Hemmings, as a notorious miser and usurer, had passed even beyond Galloper's Ridge.

"The step that you're taking, Miss Mullins, I need not tell you, is one of great gravity," said Judge Thompson, with a certain paternal seriousness of manner, in which, however, we were glad to detect a glaring affectation; "and I trust that you and your affianced have fully weighed it. Far be it from me to interfere with or question the natural affections of two young people, but may I ask you what you know of the—er—young gentleman for whom you are sacrificing so much, and, perhaps, imperiling your whole future? For instance, have you known him long?"

The slightly troubled air of trying to understand,—not unlike the vague wonderment of childhood,—with which Miss Mullins had received the beginning of this exordium, changed to a relieved smile of comprehension as she said quickly, "Oh yes, nearly a whole year."

"And," said the Judge, smiling, "has he a vocation—is he in business?"

"Oh yes," she returned; "he's a collector."

"A collector?"

"Yes; he collects bills, you know,—money," she went on, with childish eagerness, "not for himself,—*he* never has any money, poor Charley,—but for his firm. It's dreadful hard work, too; keeps him out for days and nights, over bad roads and baddest weather. Sometimes, when he's stole over to the ranch just to see me, he's been so bad he could scarcely keep his seat in the saddle, much less stand. And he's got to take mighty big risks, too. Times the folks are cross with him and won't pay; once they shot him in the arm, and he came to me, and I helped do it up for him. But he don't mind. He's real brave,—jest as brave as he's good." There was such a wholesome ring of truth in this pretty praise that we were touched in sympathy with the speaker.

"What firm does he collect for?" asked the Judge gently.

"I don't know exactly—he won't tell me; but I think it's a Spanish firm. You see"—she took us all into her confidence with a sweeping smile of innocent yet half-mischievous artfulness—"I only know because I peeped over a letter he once got from his firm, telling him he must hustle up and be ready for the road the next day; but I think the name was Martinez—yes, Ramon Martinez."

In the dead silence that ensued—a silence so profound that we could hear the horses in the distant stable-yard rattling their harness—one of the younger "Excelsior" boys burst into a hysteric laugh, but the fierce eye of Yuba Bill was down upon him, and seemed to instantly stiffen him into a silent, grinning mask. The young girl, however, took no note of it. Following out, with lover-like diffusiveness, the reminiscences thus awakened, she went on:—

"Yes, it's mighty hard work, but he says it's all for me, and as soon as we're married he'll quit it. He might have quit it before, but he won't take no money of me, nor what I told him I could get out of dad! That ain't his style. He's mighty proud—if he is poor—is Charley. Why, thar's all ma's money which she left me in the Savin's Bank that I wanted to draw out—for I had the right—and give it to him, but he wouldn't hear of it! Why, he wouldn't take one of the things I've got with me, if he knew it. And so he goes on ridin' and ridin', here and there and everywhere, and gettin' more and more played out and sad, and thin and pale as a spirit, and always so uneasy about his business, and startin' up at times when we're meetin' out in the South Woods or in the far clearin'.

and sayin': 'I must be goin' now, Polly,' and yet always tryin' to be chiffle and chipper afore me. Why, he must have rid miles and miles to have watched for me thar in the brush at the foot of Galloper's to-night, jest to see if all was safe; and Lordy! I'd have given him the signal and showed a light if I'd died for it the next minit. There! That's what I know of Charley—that's what I'm running away from home for—that's what I'm running to him for, and I don't care who knows it! And I only wish I'd done it afore—and I would—if —if—if—he'd only *asked me*! There now!" She stopped, panted, and choked. Then one of the sudden transitions of youthful emotion overtook the eager, laughing face; it clouded up with the swift change of childhood, a. lightning quiver of expression broke over it, and—then came the rain!

I think this simple act completed our utter demoralization! We smiled feebly at each other with that assumption of masculine superiority which is miserably conscious of its own helplessness at such moments. We looked out of the window, blew our noses, said: "Eh—what?" and "I say," vaguely to each other, and were greatly relieved, and yet apparently astonished, when Yuba Bill, who had turned his back upon the fair speaker, and was kicking the logs in the fireplace, suddenly swept down upon us and bundled us all into the road, leaving Miss Mullins alone. Then he walked aside with Judge Thompson for a few moments; returned to us, autocratically demanded of the party a complete reticence towards Miss Mullins on the subject-matter under discussion, reëntered the station, reappeared with the young lady, suppressed a faint idiotic cheer which broke from us at the spectacle of her innocent face once more cleared and rosy, climbed the box, and in another moment we were under way.

"Then she don't know what her lover is yet?" asked the Expressman eagerly.

"No."

"Are *you* certain it's one of the gang?"

"Can't say *for sure*. It mout be a young chap from Yolo who bucked agin the tiger [1] at Sacramento, got regularly cleaned out and busted, and joined the gang for a flier. They say thar was a new hand in that job over at Keeley's,—and a mighty game one, too; and ez there was some buckshot onloaded that trip, he might hev got his share, and that would tally with what the girl said about his arm. See! Ef that's the man, I've heered he was the son of some big preacher in the States, and a college sharp to boot, who ran wild in 'Frisco, and played himself for all he was worth. They're the wust kind to kick when they once get a foot over the traces. For stiddy, comf'ble kempany," added Bill reflectively, "give *me* the son of a man that was *hanged*!"

"But what are you going to do about this?"

"That depends upon the feller who comes to meet her."

"But you ain't going to try to take him? That would be playing it pretty low down on them both."

"Keep your hair on, Jimmy! The Judge and me are only going to rastle with the sperrit of that gay young galoot, when he drops down for his girl—and exhort him pow'ful! Ef he allows he's convicted of sin and will find the Lord, we'll marry him and the gal offhand at the next station, and the Judge will officiate himself for nothin'. We're goin' to have this yer elopement done on the square—and our waybill clean —you bet!"

"But you don't suppose he'll trust himself in your hands?"

"Polly will signal to him that it's all square."

"Ah!" said the Expressman. Nevertheless in tnose few moments the men seemed to have exchanged dispositions. The Expressman looked doubtfully, critically, and even

[1] Gambled at faro.

cynically before him. Bill's face had relaxed, and something like a bland smile beamed across it, as he drove confidently and unhesitatingly forward.

Day, meantime, although full blown and radiant on the mountain summits around us, was yet nebulous and uncertain in the valleys into which we were plunging. Lights still glimmered in the cabins and few ranch buildings which began to indicate the thicker settlements. And the shadows were heaviest in a little copse, where a note from Judge Thompson in the coach was handed up to Yuba Bill, who at once slowly began to draw up his horses. The coach stopped finally near the junction of a small crossroad. At the same moment Miss Mullins slipped down from the vehicle, and, with a parting wave of her hand to the Judge, who had assisted her from the steps, tripped down the crossroad, and disappeared in its semi-obscurity. To our surprise the stage waited, Bill holding the reins listlessly in his hands. Five minutes passed—an eternity of expectation, and, as there was that in Yuba Bill's face which forbade idle questioning, an aching void of silence also! This was at last broken by a strange voice from the road:—

"Go on—we'll follow."

The coach started forward. Presently we heard the sound of other wheels behind us. We all craned our necks backward to get a view of the unknown, but by the growing light we could only see that we were followed at a distance by a buggy with two figures in it. Evidently Polly Mullins and her lover! We hoped that they would pass us. But the vehicle, although drawn by a fast horse, preserved its distance always, and it was plain that its driver had no desire to satisfy our curiosity. The Expressman had recourse to Bill.

"Is it the man you thought of?" he asked eagerly.

"I reckon," said Bill briefly.

"But," continued the Expressman, returning to his former skepticism, "what's to keep them both from levanting together now?"

Bill jerked his hand towards the boot with a grim smile. "Their baggage."

"Oh!" said the Expressman.

"Yes," continued Bill. "We'll hang on to that gal's little frills and fixin's until this yer job's settled, and the ceremony's over, jest as ef we waz her own father. And, what's more, young man," he added, suddenly turning to the Expressman, "*you'll* express them trunks of hers *through to Sacramento* with your kempany's lables, and hand her the receipts and checks for them, so she *can get 'em there.* That'll keep *him* outer temptation and the reach o' the gang, until they get away among white men and civilization again. When your hoary-headed ole grandfather, or, to speak plainer, that partikler old whiskey-soaker known as Yuba Bill, wot sits on this box," he continued, with a diabolical wink at the Expressman, "waltzes in to pervide for a young couple jest startin' in life, thar's nothin' mean about his style, you bet. He fills the bill every time! Speshul Providences take a back seat when he's around."

When the station hotel and straggling settlement of Sugar Pine, now distinct and clear in the growing light, at last rose within rifleshot on the plateau, the buggy suddenly darted swiftly by us, so swiftly that the faces of the two occupants were barely distinguishable as they passed, and keeping the lead by a dozen lengths, reached the door of the hotel. The young girl and her companion leaped down and vanished within as we drew up. They had evidently determined to elude our curiosity, and were successful.

But the material appetites of the passengers, sharpened by the keen mountain air, were more potent than their curiosity, and, as the breakfast-bell rang out at the moment the stage stopped, a majority of them rushed into the dining-room and scrambled for places without giving much heed to the vanished couple or to the Judge and Yuba Bill, who had disappeared also. The through coach to Marysville and Sacramento was likewise waiting, for Sugar Pine was the limit of Bill's ministration, and the coach which we had just left went no farther. In the course of twenty minutes, however, there was a slight and somewhat ceremonious bustling in the hall and on the veranda, and Yuba Bill and the Judge reappeared. The latter was leading, with some elaboration of manner and detail, the shapely figure of Miss Mullins, and Yuba Bill was accompanying her companion to the buggy. We all rushed to the windows to get a good view of the mysterious stranger and probable ex-brigand whose life was now linked with our fair fellow-passenger. I am afraid, however, that we all participated in a certain impression of disappointment and doubt. Handsome and even cultivated-looking, he assuredly was—young and vigorous in appearance. But there was a certain half-shamed, half-defiant suggestion in his expression, yet coupled with a watchful lurking uneasiness which was not pleasant and hardly becoming in a bridegroom—and the possessor of such a bride. But the frank, joyous, innocent face of Polly Mullins, resplendent with a simple, happy confidence, melted our hearts again, and condoned the fellow's shortcomings. We waved our hands; I think we would have given three rousing cheers as they drove away if the omnipotent eye of Yuba Bill had not been upon us. It was well, for the next moment we were summoned to the presence of that soft-hearted autocrat.

We found him alone with the Judge in a private sitting-room, standing before a table on which there were a decanter and glasses. As we filed expectantly into the room and the door closed behind us, he cast a glance of hesitating tolerance over the group.

"Gentlemen," he said slowly, "you was all present at the beginnin' of a little game this mornin', and the Judge thar thinks that you oughter be let in at the finish. *I* don't see that it's any of *your* d—d business—so to speak; but ez the Judge here allows you're all in the secret, I've called you in to take a partin' drink to the health of Mr. and Mrs. Charley Byng— ez is now comf'ably off on their bridal tower. What *you* know or what *you* suspects of the young galoot that's married the gal ain't worth shucks to anybody, and I wouldn't give it to a yaller pup to play with, but the Judge thinks you ought all to promise right here that you'll keep it dark. That's his opinion. Ez far as my opinion goes, gen'l'men," continued Bill, with greater blandness and apparent cordiality, "I wanter simply remark, in a keerless, offhand gin'ral way, that ef I ketch any God-forsaken, lop-eared, chuckleheaded blath-erin' idjet airin' *his* opinion"—

"One moment, Bill," interposed Judge Thompson with a grave smile; "let me explain. You understand, gentlemen," he said, turning to us, "the singular, and I may say affecting, situation which our good-hearted friend here has done so much to bring to what we hope will be a happy termination. I want to give here, as my professional opinion, that there is nothing in his request which, in your capacity as good citizens and law-abiding men, you may not grant. I want to tell you, also, that you are condoning no offense against the statutes; that there is not a particle of legal evidence before us of the criminal antecedents of Mr. Charles Byng, except that which has been told you by the innocent lips of his betrothed, which the law of the land has now sealed forever in the mouth of his wife, and that our own actual experience of his acts has been in the main exculpatory of any previous irregularity—if not incompatible with it. Briefly, no judge would charge, no jury convict, on such evidence. When I add that the young girl is of legal age, that there is no evidence of any previous undue influence, but rather of the reverse, on the part of the bridegroom, and that I was content, as a magistrate, to perform the ceremony, I think you will be satisfied to give your promise, for the sake of the bride, and drink a happy life to them both."

I need not say that we did this cheerfully, and even extorted from Bill a grunt of satisfaction. The majority of the company, however, who were going with the through coach to Sacramento, then took their leave, and, as we accompanied them to the veranda, we could see that Miss Polly Mullins's trunks were already transferred to the other vehicle under the protecting seals and labels of the all-potent Express Company. Then the whip cracked, the coach rolled away, and the last traces of the adventurous young couple disappeared in the hanging red dust of its wheels.

But Yuba Bill's grim satisfaction at the happy issue of the episode seemed to suffer no abatement. He even exceeded his usual deliberately regulated potations, and, standing comfortably with his back to the centre of the now deserted barroom, was more than usually loquacious with the Expressman. "You see," he said, in bland reminiscence, "when your old Uncle Bill takes hold of a job like this, he puts it straight through without changin' hosses. Yet thar was a moment, young feller, when I thought I was stompt! It was when we'd made up our mind to make that chap tell the gal fust all what he was! Ef she'd rared or kicked in the traces, or hung back only ez much ez that, we'd hev given him jest five minits' law to get up and get and leave her, and we'd hev toted that gal and her fixin's back to her dad again! But she jest gave a little scream and start, and then went off inter hysterics, right on his buzzum, laughin' and cryin' and sayin' that nothin' should part 'em. Gosh! if I didn't think *he* woz more cut up than she about it; a minit it looked as ef *he* didn't allow to marry her arter all, but that passed, and they was married hard and fast—you bet! I reckon he's had enough of stayin' out o' nights to last him, and ef the valley settlements hevn't got hold of a very shinin' member, at least the foot-hills hev got shut of one more of the Ramon Martinez gang."

"What's that about the Ramon Martinez gang?" said a quiet potential voice.

Bill turned quickly. It was the voice of the Divisional Superintendent of the Express Company,—a man of eccentric determination of character, and one of the few whom the autocratic Bill recognized as an equal,—who had just entered the bar-room. His dusty pongee cloak and soft hat indicated that he had that morning arrived on a round of inspection.

"Don't care if I do, Bill," he continued, in response to Bill's invitatory gesture, walking to the bar. "It's a little raw out on the road. Well, what were you saying about Ramon Martinez gang? You haven't come across one of 'em, have you?"

"No," said Bill, with a slight blinking of his eye, as he ostentatiously lifted his glass to the light.

"And you *won't*," added the Superintendent, leisurely sipping his liquor. "For the fact is, the gang is about played out. Not from want of a job now and then, but from the difficulty of disposing of the results of their work. Since the new instructions to the agents to identify and trace all dust and bullion offered to them went into force, you see, they can't get rid of their swag. All the gang are spotted at the offices, and it costs too much for them to pay a fence or a middleman of any standing. Why, all that flaky river gold they took from the Excelsior Company can be identified as easy as if it was stamped with the company's mark. They can't melt it down themselves; they can't get others to do it for them; they can't ship it to the Mint or Assay Offices in Marysville and 'Frisco, for they won't take it without our certificate and seals; and *we* don't take any undeclared freight *within* the lines that we've drawn around their beat, except from people and agents known. Why, *you* know that well enough, Jim," he said, suddenly appealing to the Expressman, "don't you?"

Possibly the suddenness of the appeal caused the Expressman to swallow his liquor the wrong way, for he was overtaken with a fit of coughing, and stammered hastily as he laid down his glass, "Yes—of course—certainly."

"No, sir," resumed the Superintendent cheerfully, "they're pretty well played out. And the best proof of it is that they've lately been robbing ordinary passengers' trunks. There was a freight wagon 'held up' near Dow's Flat the other day, and a lot of baggage gone through. I had to go down there to look into it. Darned if they hadn't lifted a lot o' woman's wedding things from that rich couple who got married the other day out at Marysville. Looks as if they were playing it rather low down, don't it? Coming down to hardpan and the bed rock —eh?"

The Expressman's face was turned anxiously towards Bill, who, after a hurried gulp of his remaining liquor, still stood staring at the window. Then he slowly drew on one of his large gloves. "Ye didn't," he said, with a slow, drawling, but perfectly distinct, articulation, "happen to know old 'Skinner' Hemmings when you were over there?"

"Yes."

"And his daughter?"

"He hasn't got any."

"A sort o' mild, innocent, guileless child of nature?" persisted Bill, with a yellow face, a deadly calm, and Satanic deliberation.

"No. I tell you he *hasn't* any daughter. Old man Hemmings is a confirmed old bachelor. He's too mean to support more than one."

"And you didn't happen to know any o' that gang, did ye?" continued Bill, with infinite protraction.

"Yes. Knew 'em all. There was French Pete, Cherokee Bob, Kanaka Joe, One-eyed Stillson, Softy Brown, Spanish Jack, and two or three Greasers."

"And ye didn't know a man by the name of Charley Byng?"

"No," returned the Superintendent, with a slight suggestion of weariness and a distraught glance towards the door.

"A dark, stylish chap, with shifty black eyes and a curled-up merstache?" continued Bill, with dry, colorless persistence.

"No. Look here, Bill, I'm in a little bit of a hurry—but I suppose you must have your little joke before we part. Now, what *is* your little game?"

"Wot you mean?" demanded Bill, with sudden brusqueness.

"Mean? Well, old man, you know as well as I do. You're giving me the very description of Ramon Martinez himself, ha! ha! No—Bill! you didn't play me this time. You're mighty spry and clever, but you didn't catch on just then."

He nodded and moved away with a light laugh. Bill turned a stony face to the Expressman. Suddenly a gleam of mirth came into his gloomy eyes. He bent over the young man, and said in a hoarse, chuckling whisper:—

"But I got even after all!"

"How?"

"He's tied up to that lying little she-devil, hard and fast!"

CHU CHU

I DO not believe that the most enthusiastic lover of that "useful and noble animal," the horse, will claim for him the charm of geniality, humor, or expansive confidence. Any creature who will not look you squarely in the eye— whose only oblique glances are inspired by fear, distrust, or a view to attack; who has no way of returning caresses, and whose favorite expression is one of head-lifting disdain, may be "noble" or "useful," but can be hardly said to add to the gayety of nations. Indeed it may be broadly stated that, with the single exception of gold-fish, of all animals kept for the recreation of mankind the horse is alone capable of exciting a passion that shall be absolutely hopeless. I deem these general remarks necessary to prove that my unreciprocated affection for Chu Chu was not purely individual or singular. And I may add that to these general characteristics she brought the waywardness of her capricious sex.

She came to me out of the rolling dust of an emigrant wagon, behind whose tail-board she was gravely trotting. She was a half-broken colt—in which character she had at different times unseated everybody in the train—and, although covered with dust, she had a beautiful coat, and the most lambent gazelle-like eyes I had ever seen. I think she kept these latter organs purely for ornament—apparently looking at things with her nose, her sensitive ears, and, sometimes, even a slight lifting of her slim near foreleg. On our first interview I thought she favored me with a coy glance, but as it was accompanied by an irrelevant "Look out!" from her owner, the teamster, I was not certain. I only know that after some conversation, a good deal of mental reservation, and the disbursement of considerable coin, I found myself standing in the dust of the departing emigrant wagon with one end of a forty-foot riata in my hand, and Chu Chu at the other.

I pulled invitingly at my own end, and even advanced a step or two toward her. She then broke into a long disdainful pace, and began to circle round me at the extreme limit of her tether. I stood admiring her free action for some moments—not always turning with her, which was tiring—until I found that she was gradually winding herself up *on me*! Her frantic astonishment when she suddenly found herself thus brought up against me was one of the most remarkable things I ever saw, and nearly took me off my legs. Then, when she had pulled against the riata until her narrow head and prettily arched neck were on a perfectly straight line with it. she as suddenly slackened the tension and condescended to follow me, at an angle of her own choosing. Sometimes it was on one side of me, sometimes on the other. Even then the sense of my dreadful contiguity apparently would come upon her like a fresh discovery, and she would become hysterical. But I do not think that she really *saw* me. She looked at the riata and sniffed it disparagingly; she pawed some pebbles that were near me tentatively with her small hoof; she started back with a Robinson Crusoe-like horror of my footprints in the wet gully, but my actual personal presence she ignored. She would sometimes pause, with her head thoughtfully between her forelegs, and apparently say: "There is some extraordinary presence here: animal, vegetable, or mineral—I can't make out which— but it's not good to eat, and I loathe and detest it."

When I reached my house in the suburbs, before entering the "fifty vara" lot inclosure, I deemed it prudent to leave her outside while I informed the household of my purchase; and with this object I tethered her by the long riata to a solitary sycamore which stood in the centre of the road, the crossing of two frequented thoroughfares. It was not long, however, before I was interrupted by shouts and screams from that vicinity, and on returning thither I found that Chu Chu, with the assistance of her riata, had securely wound up two of my neighbors to the tree, where they presented the appearance of early Christian martyrs. When I released them it appeared that they had been attracted by Chu Chu's graces, and had offered her overtures of affection, to which she had characteristically rotated with this miserable result. I led her, with some difficulty, warily keeping clear of the riata, to the inclosure, from whose fence I had previously removed several bars. Although the space was wide enough to have admitted a troop of cavalry she affected not to notice it, and managed to kick away part of another section on entering. She resisted the stable for some time, but after carefully examining it with her hoofs, and an affectedly meek outstretching of her nose, she consented to recognize some oats in the feed-box—without looking at them—and was formally installed. All this while she had resolutely ignored my presence. As I stood watching her she suddenly stopped eating; the same reflective look came over her. "Surely I am not mistaken, but that same obnoxious creature is somewhere about here!" she seemed to say, and shivered at the possibility.

It was probably this which made me confide my unreciprocated affection to one of my neighbors—a man supposed to be an authority on horses, and particularly of that wild species to which Chu Chu belonged. It was he who, leaning over the edge of the stall where she was compla- cently and, as usual, obliviously munching, absolutely dared to toy with a pet lock of hair which she wore over the pretty star on her forehead.

"Ye see, captain," he said, with jaunty easiness, "hosses is like wimmen; ye don't want ter use any standoffishness or shyness with *them;* a stiddy but keerless sort o' famil- iarity, a kind o' free but firm handlin', jess like this, to let her see who's master"—

We never clearly knew *how* it happened; but when I picked up my neighbor from the doorway, amid the broken splinters of the stall rail, and a quantity of oats that mys- teriously filled his hair and pockets, Chu Chu was found to have faced around the other way, and was contemplating her forelegs, with her hind ones in the other stall. My neighbor spoke of damages while he was in the stall, and of physical coercion when he was out of it again. But here Chu Chu, in some marvelous way, righted herself, and my neighbor departed hurriedly with a brimless hat and an unfinished sentence.

My next intermediary was Enriquez Saltello—a youth of my own age, and the brother of Consuelo Saltello, whom I adored. As a Spanish Californian he was presumed, on account of Chu Chu's half-Spanish origin, to have superior knowledge of her character, and I even vaguely believed that his language and accent would fall familiarly on her ear. There was the drawback, however, that he always pre- ferred to talk in a marvelous English, combining Castilian precision with what he fondly believed to be Californian slang.

"To confer then as to thees horse, which is not—observe

me—a Mexican plug! Ah, no! you can your boots bet on that. She is of Castilian stock—believe me and strike me dead! I will myself at different times overlook and affront her in the stable, examine her as to the assault, and why she should do thees thing. When she is of the exercise I will also accost and restrain her. Remain tranquil, my friend! When a few days shall pass much shall be changed, and she will be as another. Trust your oncle to do thees thing! Comprehend me? Everything shall be lovely, and the goose hang high!"

Conformably with this he "overlooked" her the next day, with a cigarette between his yellow-stained fingertips, which made her sneeze in a silent pantomimic way, and certain Spanish blandishments of speech which she received with more complacency. But I don't think she ever even looked at him. In vain he protested that she was the "dearest" and "littlest" of his "little loves"—in vain he asserted that she was his patron saint, and that it was his soul's delight to pray to her; she accepted the compliment with her eyes fixed upon the manger. When he had exhausted his whole stock of endearing diminutives, adding a few playful and more audacious sallies, she remained with her head down, as if inclined to meditate upon them. This he declared was at least an improvement on her former performances. It may have been my own jealousy, but I fancied she was only saying to herself, "Gracious! can there be *two* of them?"

"Courage and patience, my friend," he said, as we were slowly quitting the stable. "Thees horse is yonge, and has not yet the habitude of the person. To-morrow, at another season, I shall give to her a foundling" ("fondling," I have reason to believe, was the word intended by Enriquez)—"and we shall see. It shall be as easy as to fall away from a log. A leetle more of this chin music which your friend Enriquez possesses, and some tapping of the head and neck, and you are there. You are ever the right side up. Houp la! But let us not precipitate this thing. The more haste, we do not so much accelerate ourselves."

He appeared to be suiting the action to the word as he lingered in the doorway of the stable. "Come on," I said.

"Pardon," he returned, with a bow that was both elaborate and evasive, "but you shall yourself precede me—the stable is *yours*."

"Oh, come along!" I continued impatiently. To my surprise he seemed to dodge back into the stable again. After an instant he reappeared.

"Pardon! but I am re-strain! Of a truth, in this instant I am grasp by the mouth of thees horse in the coattail of my dress! She will that I should remain. It would seem"—he disappeared again—"that"—he was out once more—"the experiment is a sooccess! She reciprocate! She is, of a truth, gone on me. It is lofe!"—a stronger pull from Chu Chu here sent him in again—"but"—he was out now triumphantly with half his garment torn away—"I shall coquet."

Nothing daunted, however, the gallant fellow was back next day with a Mexican saddle, and attired in the complete outfit of a vaquero. Overcome though *he* was by heavy deerskin trousers, open at the side from the knees down, and fringed with bullion buttons, an enormous flat sombrero, and a stiff, short embroidered velvet jacket, I was more concerned at the ponderous saddle and equipments intended for the slim Chu Chu. That these would hide and conceal her beautiful curves and contour, as well as overweight her, seemed certain; that she would resist them all to the last seemed equally clear. Nevertheless, to my surprise, when she was led out, and the saddle thrown deftly across her back, she was passive. Was it possible that some drop of her old Spanish blood responded to its clinging embrace? She did not either look at it or smell it. But when Enriquez began to tighten the cinch or girth a more singular thing occurred. Chu Chu visibly distended her slender barrel to twice its dimensions; the more he pulled the more she swelled, until I was actually ashamed of her. Not so Enriquez. He smiled at us, and complacently stroked his thin mustache.

"Eet is ever so! She is the child of her grandmother! Even when you shall make saddle thees old Castilian stock, it will make large—it will become a balloon! Eet is a trick —eet is a leetle game—believe me. For why?"

I had not listened, as I was at that moment astonished to see the saddle slowly slide under Chu Chu's belly, and her figure resume, as if by magic, its former slim proportions. Enriquez followed my eyes, lifted his shoulders, shrugged them, and said smilingly, "Ah, you see!"

When the girths were drawn in again with an extra pull or two from the indefatigable Enriquez, I fancied that Chu Chu nevertheless secretly enjoyed it, as her sex is said to appreciate tight lacing. She drew a deep sigh, possibly of satisfaction, turned her neck, and apparently tried to glance at her own figure—Enriquez promptly withdrawing to enable her to do so easily. Then the dread moment arrived. Enriquez, with his hand on her mane, suddenly paused and, with exaggerated courtesy, lifted his hat and made an inviting gesture.

"You will honor me to precede."

I shook my head laughingly.

"I see," responded Enriquez gravely. "You have to attend the obsequies of your aunt who is dead, at two of the clock. You have to meet your broker who has bought you feefty share of the Comstock lode—at thees moment—or you are loss! You are excuse! Attend! Gentlemen, make your bets! The band has arrived to play! 'Ere we are!"

With a quick movement the alert young fellow had vaulted into the saddle. But, to the astonishment of both of us, the mare remained perfectly still. There was Enriquez bolt upright in the stirrups, completely overshadowing by his saddle-flaps, leggings, and gigantic spurs the fine proportions of Chu Chu, until she might have been a placid Rosinante, bestridden by some youthful Quixote. She closed her eyes, she was going to sleep! We were dreadfully disappointed. This clearly would not do. Enriquez lifted the reins cautiously! Chu Chu moved forward slowly—then stopped, apparently lost in reflection.

"Affront her on thees side."

I approached her gently. She shot suddenly into the air, coming down again on perfectly stiff legs with a springless jolt. This she instantly followed by a succession of other rocket-like propulsions, utterly unlike a leap, all over the inclosure. The movements of the unfortunate Enriquez were equally unlike any equitation I ever saw. He appeared occasionally over Chu Chu's head, astride of her neck and tail, or in the free air, but never *in* the saddle. His rigid legs, however, never lost the stirrups, but came down regularly, accentuating her springless hops. More than that, the disproportionate excess of rider, saddle, and accoutrements was so great that he had, at times, the appearance of lifting Chu Chu forcibly from the ground by superior strength, and of actually contributing to her exercise! As they came toward me, a wild tossing and flying mass of hoofs and spurs, it was not only difficult to distinguish them apart, but to ascertain how much of the jumping was done by Enriquez separately. At last Chu Chu brought matters to a close by making for the low-stretching branches of an oak-tree which stood at the corner of the lot. In a few moments she emerged from it—but without Enriquez.

I found the gallant fellow disengaging himself from the fork of a branch in which he had been firmly wedged, but still smiling and confident, and his cigarette between his teeth. Then for the first time he removed it, and seating himself easily on the branch with his legs dangling down, he blandly waved aside my anxious queries with a gentle reassuring gesture.

"Remain tranquil, my friend. Thees does not count! I have conquer—you observe—for why? I have *never* for once *arrive at the ground*! Consequent she is disappoint! She will ever that I *should*! But I have got her when the hair is not long! Your oncle Henry"—with an angelic wink—"is fly! He is ever a bully boy, with the eye of glass! Believe me. Behold! I am here! Big Injun! Whoop!"

He leaped lightly to the ground. Chu Chu, standing watchfully at a little distance, was evidently astonished at his appearance. She threw out her hind hoofs violently, shot up into the air until the stirrups crossed each other high above the saddle, and made for the stable in a succession of rabbit-like bounds—taking the precaution to remove the saddle, on entering, by striking it against the lintel of the door.

"You observe," said Enriquez blandly, "she would make that thing of *me*. Not having the good occasion, she ees dissatisfied. Where are you now?"

Two or three days afterwards he rode her again with the same result—accepted by him with the same heroic complacency. As we did not, for certain reasons, care to use the open road for this exercise, and as it was impossible to remove the tree, we were obliged to submit to the inevitable. On the following day I mounted her—undergoing the same experience as Enriquez, with the individual sensation of falling from a third-story window on top of a counting-house stool, and the variation of being projected over the fence. When I found that Chu Chu had not accompanied me, I saw Enriquez at my side.

"More than ever it is become necessary that we should do thees things again," he said gravely, as he assisted me to my feet. "Courage, my noble General! God and Liberty! Once more on to the breach! Charge, Chestare, charge! Come on, Don Stanley! 'Ere we are!"

He helped me none too quickly to catch my seat again, for it apparently had the effect of the turned peg on the enchanted horse in the Arabian Nights, and Chu Chu instantly rose into the air. But she came down this time before the open window of the kitchen, and I alighted easily on the dresser. The indefatigable Enriquez followed me.

"Won't this do?" I asked meekly.

"It ees *better*—for you arrive *not* on the ground," he said cheerfully; "but you should not once but a thousand times make trial! Ha! Go and win! Nevare die and say so! 'Eave ahead! 'Eave! There you are!"

Luckily, this time I managed to lock the rowels of my long spurs under her girth, and she could not unseat me. She seemed to recognize the fact after one or two plunges, when, to my great surprise, she suddenly sank to the ground and quietly rolled over me. The action disengaged my spurs, but, righting herself without getting up, she turned her beautiful head and absolutely *looked* at me!—still in the saddle. I felt myself blushing! But the voice of Enriquez was at my side.

"Errise, my friend; you have conquer! It is *she* who has arrive at the ground! *You* are all right. It is done; believe me, it is feenish! No more shall she make thees thing. From thees instant you shall ride her as the cow—as the rail of thees fence—and remain tranquil. For she is a-broke! Ta-ta! Regain your hats, gentlemen! Pass in your checks! It is ovar! How are you now?" He lit a fresh cigarette, put his hands in his pockets, and smiled at me blandly.

For all that, I ventured to point out that the habit of alighting in the fork of a tree, or the disengaging of one's self from the saddle on the ground, was attended with inconvenience, and even ostentatious display. But Enriquez swept the objections away with a single gesture. "It is the *preencipal*—the bottom fact—at which you arrive. The next come of himself! Many horse have achieve to mount the rider by the knees, and relinquish after thees same fashion. My grandfather had a barb of thees kind—but she has gone dead, and so have my grandfather. Which is sad and strange! Otherwise I shall make of them both an instant example!"

I ought to have said that although these performances were never actually witnessed by Enriquez's sister—for reasons which he and I thought sufficient—the dear girl displayed the greatest interest in them, and, perhaps aided by our mutually complimentary accounts of each other, looked upon us both as invincible heroes. It is possible also that she overestimated our success, for she suddenly demanded that I should *ride* Chu Chu to her house, that she might see her. It was not far; by going through a back lane I could avoid the trees which exercised such a fatal fascination for Chu Chu. There was a pleading, childlike entreaty in Consuelo's voice that I could not resist, with a slight flash from her lustrous dark eyes that I did not care to encourage. So I resolved to try it at all hazards.

My equipment for the performance was modeled after Enriquez's previous costume, with the addition of a few fripperies of silver and stamped leather out of compliment to Consuelo, and even with a faint hope that it might appease Chu Chu. *She* certainly looked beautiful in her glittering accoutrements, set off by her jet-black shining coat. With an air of demure abstraction she permitted me to mount her, and even for a hundred yards or so indulged in a mincing maidenly amble that was not without a touch of coquetry. Encouraged by this, I addressed a few terms of endearment to her, and in the exuberance of my youthful enthusiasm I even confided to her my love for Consuelo, and begged her to be "good" and not disgrace herself and me before my Dulcinea. In my foolish trustfulness I was rash enough to add a caress, and to pat her soft neck. She stopped instantly with an hysteric shudder. I knew what was passing through her mind: she had suddenly become aware of my baleful existence.

The saddle and bridle Chu Chu was becoming accustomed to, but who was this living, breathing object that had actually touched her? Presently her oblique vision was attracted by the fluttering movement of a fallen oak-leaf in the road before her. She had probably seen many oak-leaves many times before; her ancestors had no doubt been familiar with them on the trackless hills and in field and paddock, but this did not alter her profound conviction that I and the leaf were identical, that our baleful touch was something indissolubly connected. She reared before that innocent leaf, she revolved round it, and then fled from it at the top of her speed.

The lane passed before the rear wall of Saltellos' garden. Unfortunately, at the angle of the fence stood a beautiful madroño-tree, brilliant with its scarlet berries, and endeared to me as Consuelo's favorite haunt, under whose protecting shade I had more than once avowed my youthful passion. By the irony of fate Chu Chu caught sight of it, and with a succession of spirited bounds instantly made for it. In another moment I was beneath it, and Chu Chu shot like a rocket into the air. I had barely time to withdraw my feet from the stirrups, to throw up one arm to protect my glazed sombrero and grasp an overhanging branch with the other, before Chu Chu darted off. But to my consternation, as I gained a secure perch on the tree, and looked about me, I saw her—instead of running away—quietly trot through the open gate into Saltellos' garden.

Need I say that it was to the beneficent Enriquez that I again owed my salvation? Scarcely a moment elapsed before his bland voice rose in a concentrated whisper from the corner of the garden below me. He had divined the dreadful truth!

"For the love of God, collect to yourself many kinds of thees berry! All you can! Your full arms round! Rest tranquil. Leave to your ole oncle to make for you a delicate exposure. At the instant!"

He was gone again. I gathered, wonderingly, a few of the larger clusters of parti-colored fruit, and patiently waited. Presently he reappeared, and with him the lovely Consuelo —her dear eyes filled with an adorable anxiety.

"Yes," continued Enriquez to his sister, with a confidential lowering of tone but great distinctness of utterance, "it is ever so with the American! He will ever make *first* the salutation of the flower or the fruit, picked to himself by his own hand, to the lady where he call. It is the custom of the American hidalgo! My God—what will you? *I* make it not—it is so! Without doubt he is in this instant doing thees thing. That is why he have let go his horse to precede him here; it is always the etiquette to offer these things on the feet. Ah! behold! it is he!—Don Francisco! Even now he will descend from thees tree! Ah! You make the blush, little sister (archly)! I will retire! I am discreet; two is not company for the one! I make tracks! I am gone!"

How far Consuelo entirely believed and trusted her ingenious brother I do not know, nor even then cared to inquire. For there was a pretty mantling of her olive cheek, as I came forward with my offering, and a certain significant shyness in her manner that were enough to throw me into a state of hopeless imbecility. And I was always miserably conscious that Consuelo possessed an exalted sentimentality, and a predilection for the highest mediæval romance, in which I knew I was lamentably deficient. Even in our most confidential moments I was always aware that I weakly lagged behind this daughter of a gloomily distinguished ancestry, in her frequent incursions into a vague but poetic past. There was something of the dignity of the Spanish châtelaine in the sweetly grave little figure that advanced to accept my specious offering. I think I should have fallen on my knees to present it, but for the presence of the all-seeing Enriquez. But why did I even at that moment remember that he had early bestowed upon her the nickname of "Pomposa?" This, as Enriquez himself might have observed, was "sad and strange."

I managed to stammer out something about the madroño berries being at her "disposicion" (the tree was in her own garden!), and she took the branches in her little brown hand with a soft response to my unutterable glances.

But here Chu Chu, momentarily forgotten, executed a happy diversion. To our astonishment she gravely walked up to Consuelo and, stretching out her long slim neck, not only sniffed curiously at the berries, but even protruded a black under lip towards the young girl herself. In another instant Consuelo's dignity melted. Throwing her arms around Chu Chu's neck she embraced and kissed her. Young as I was, I understood the divine significance of a girl's vicarious effusiveness at such a moment, and felt delighted. But I was the more astonished that the usually sensitive horse not only submitted to these caresses, but actually responded to the extent of affecting to nip my mistress's little right ear.

This was enough for the impulsive Consuelo. She ran hastily into the house, and in a few moments reappeared in a bewitching riding-skirt gathered round her jimp waist. In vain Enriquez and myself joined in earnest entreaty: the horse was hardly broken for even a man's riding yet; the saints alone could tell what the nervous creature might do with a woman's skirt flapping at her side! We begged for delay, for reflection, for at least time to change the saddle —but with no avail! Consuelo was determined, indignant, distressingly reproachful! Ah, well! if Don Pancho (an ingenious diminutive of my Christian name) valued his horse so highly—if he were jealous of the evident devotion of the animal to herself, he would— But here I succumbed! And then I had the felicity of holding that little foot for one brief moment in the hollow of my hand, of readjusting the skirt as she threw her knee over the saddle-horn, of clasping her tightly—only half in fear—as I surrendered the reins to her grasp. And to tell the truth, as Enriquez and I fell back, although I had insisted upon still keeping hold of the end of the riata, it was a picture to admire. The petite figure of the young girl, and the graceful folds of her skirt, admirably harmonized with Chu Chu's lithe contour, and as the mare arched her slim neck and raised her slender head under the pressure of the reins, it was so like the lifted velvet-capped toreador crest of Consuelo herself, that they seemed of one race.

"I would not that you should hold the riata," said Consuelo petulantly.

I hesitated—Chu Chu looked certainly very amiable— I let go. She began to amble towards the gate, not mincingly as before, but with a freer and fuller stride. In spite of the incongruous saddle the young girl's seat was admirable. As they neared the gate she cast a single mischievous glance at me, jerked at the rein, and Chu Chu sprang into the road at a rapid canter. I watched them fearfully and breathlessly, until at the end of the lane I saw Consuelo rein in slightly, wheel easily, and come flying back. There was no doubt about it; the horse was under perfect control. Her second subjugation was complete and final!

Overjoyed and bewildered, I overwhelmed them with congratulations; Enriquez alone retaining the usual brotherly attitude of criticism, and a superior toleration of a lover's enthusiasm. I ventured to hint to Consuelo (in what I believed was a safe whisper) that Chu Chu only showed my own feelings towards her.

"Without doubt," responded Enriquez gravely. "She have of herself assist you to climb to the tree to pull to yourself the berry for my sister."

But I felt Consuelo's little hand return my pressure, and I forgave and even pitied him.

From that day forward, Chu Chu and Consuelo were not only firm friends but daily companions. In my devotion I would have presented the horse to the young girl, but with flattering delicacy she preferred to call it mine.

"I shall erride it for you, Pancho," she said. "I shall feel," she continued, with exalted although somewhat vague poetry, "that it is of *you*! You lofe the beast—it is therefore of a necessity *you*, my Pancho! It is *your* soul I shall erride like the wings of the wind—your lofe in this beast shall be my only cavalier forever."

I would have preferred something whose vicarious qualities were less uncertain than I still felt Chu Chu's to be, but I kissed the girl's hand submissively. It was only when I attempted to accompany her in the flesh, on another horse, that I felt the full truth of my instinctive fears. Chu Chu would not permit any one to approach her mistress's side. My mounted presence revived in her all her old blind astonishment and disbelief in my existence; she would start suddenly, face about, and back away from me in utter amazement as if I had been only recently created, or with an affected modesty as if I had been just guilty of some grave indecorum towards her sex which she really could not stand. The frequency of these exhibitions in the public highway were not only distressing to me as a simple escort, but as it had the effect on the casual spectators of making Consuelo seem to participate in Chu Chu's objections, I felt that, as a lover, it could not be borne. Any attempt to coerce Chu Chu ended in her running away. And my frantic pursuit of her was open to equal misconstruction.

"Go it, miss, the little dude is gainin' on you!" shouted by a drunken teamster to the frightened Consuelo, once checked me in mid-career.

Even the dear girl herself saw the uselessness of my real presence, and after a while was content to ride with "my soul."

Notwithstanding this, I am not ashamed to say that it was my custom, whenever she rode out, to keep a slinking and distant surveillance of Chu Chu on another horse, until she had fairly settled down to her pace. A little nod of Consuelo's round black-and-red toreador hat, or a kiss tossed from her riding-whip, was reward enough!

I remember a pleasant afternoon when I was thus awaiting her in the outskirts of the village. The eternal smile of the Californian summer had begun to waver and grow less fixed; dust lay thick on leaf and blade; the dry hills were clothed in russet leather; the trade-winds were shifting to the south with an ominous warm humidity; a few days longer and the rains would be here. It so chanced that this afternoon my seclusion on the roadside was accidentally invaded by a village belle—a Western young lady somewhat older than myself, and of flirtatious reputation. As she persistently and—as I now have reason to believe—mischievously lingered, I had only a passing glimpse of Consuelo riding past at an unaccustomed speed which surprised me at the moment. But as I reasoned later that she was only trying to avoid a merely formal meeting, I thought no more about it. It was not until I called at the house to fetch Chu Chu at the usual hour, and found that Consuelo had not yet returned, that a recollection of Chu Chu's furious pace again troubled me. An hour passed—it was getting towards sunset, but there were no signs of Chu Chu or her mistress. I became seriously alarmed. I did not care to reveal my fears to the family, for I felt myself responsible for Chu Chu. At last I desperately saddled my horse, and galloped off in the direction she had taken. It was the road to Rosario and the hacienda of one of her relations, where she sometimes halted.

The road was a very unfrequented one, twisting like a mountain river; indeed, it was the bed of an old watercourse, between brown hills of wild oats, and debouching at last into a broad blue lake-like expanse of alfalfa meadows. In vain I strained my eyes over the monotonous level; nothing appeared to rise above or move across it. In the faint hope that she might have lingered at the hacienda, I was spurring on again when I heard a slight splashing on my left. I looked around. A broad patch of fresher-colored herbage and a cluster of dwarfed alders indicated a hidden spring. I cautiously approached its quaggy edges, when I was shocked by what appeared to be a sudden vision! Mid-leg deep in the centre of a greenish pool stood Chu Chu! But without a strap or buckle of harness upon her—as naked as when she was foaled!

For a moment I could only stare at her in bewildered terror. Far from recognizing me, she seemed to be absorbed in a nymph-like contemplation of her own graces in the pool. Then I called, "Consuelo!" and galloped frantically around the spring. But there was no response, nor was there anything to be seen but the all-unconscious Chu Chu. The pool, thank Heaven! was not deep enough to have drowned any one; there were no signs of a struggle on its quaggy edges. The horse might have come from a distance! I galloped on, still calling. A few hundred yards further I detected the vivid glow of Chu Chu's scarlet saddle-blanket, in the brush near the trail. My heart leaped—I was on the track. I called again; this time a faint reply, in accents I knew too well, came from the field beside me!

Consuelo was there! reclining beside a manzanita bush which screened her from the road, in what struck me, even at that supreme moment, as a judicious and picturesquely selected couch of scented Indian grass and dry tussocks. The velvet hat with its balls of scarlet plush was laid carefully aside; her lovely blue-black hair retained its tight coils undisheveled, her eyes were luminous and tender. Shocked as I was at her apparent helplessness, I remember being impressed with the fact that it gave so little indication of violent usage or disaster.

I threw myself frantically on the ground beside her.

"You are hurt, Consita! For Heaven's sake, what has happened?"

She pushed my hat back with her little hand, and tumbled my hair gently.

"Nothing. *You* are here, Pancho—eet is enofe! What shall come after thees—when I am perhaps gone among the grave—make nothing! *You* are here—I am happy. For a little, perhaps—not mooch."

"But," I went on desperately, "was it an accident? Were you thrown? Was it Chu Chu?"—for somehow, in spite of her languid posture and voice, I could not, even in my fears, believe her seriously hurt.

"Beat not the poor beast, Pancho. It is not from *her* comes thees thing. She have make nothing—believe me! I have come upon your assignation with Miss Essmith! I make but to pass you—to fly—to never come back! I have say to Chu Chu, 'Fly!' We fly many miles. Sometimes together, sometimes not so mooch! Sometimes in the saddle, sometimes on the neck! Many things remain in the road; at the end, I myself remain! I have say, 'Courage, Pancho will come!' Then I say, 'No, he is talk with Miss Essmith!' I remember not more. I have creep here on the hands. Eet is feenish!"

I looked at her distractedly. She smiled tenderly, and slightly smoothed down and rearranged a fold of her dress to cover her delicate little boot.

"But," I protested, "you are not much hurt, dearest. You have broken no bones. Perhaps," I added, looking at the boot, "only a slight sprain. Let me carry you to my horse; I will walk beside you, home. Do, dearest Consita!"

She turned her lovely eyes towards me sadly.

"You comprehend not, my poor Pancho! It is not of the foot, the ankle, the arm, or the head that I can say, 'She is broke!' I would it were even so. But"—she lifted her sweet lashes slowly—"I have derrange my inside. It is an affair of my family. My grandfather have once toomble over the bull at a rodeo. He speak no more; he is dead. For why? He has derrange his inside. Believe me, it is of the family. You comprehend? The Saltellos are not as the other peoples for this. When I am gone, you will bring to me the berry to grow upon my tomb, Pancho; the berry you have picked for me. The little flower will come too, the little star will arrive, but

Consuelo, who lofe you, she will come not more! When you are happy and talk in the road to the Essmith, you will not think of me. You will not see my eyes, Pancho; thees little grass"—she ran her plump little fingers through a tussock—"will hide them; and the small animals in the black coats that lif here will have much sorrow—but you will not. It ees better so! My father will not that I, a Catholique, should marry into a camp-meeting, and lif in a tent, and make howl like the coyote." (It was one of Consuelo's bewildering beliefs that there was only one form of dissent,—Methodism!) "He will not that I should marry a man who possess not the many horses, ox, and cow, like him. But *I* care not. *You* are my only religion, Pancho! I have enofe of the horse, and ox, and cow when *you* are with me! Kiss me, Pancho. Perhaps it is for the last time—the feenish! Who knows?"

There were tears in her lovely eyes; I felt that my own were growing dim; the sun was sinking over the dreary plain to the slow rising of the wind; an infinite loneliness had fallen upon us, and yet I was miserably conscious of some dreadful unreality in it all. A desire to laugh, which I felt must be hysterical, was creeping over me; I dared not speak. But her dear head was on my shoulder, and the situation was not unpleasant.

Nevertheless, something must be done! This was the more difficult as it was by no means clear what had already been done. Even while I supported her drooping figure I was straining my eyes across her shoulder for succor of some kind. Suddenly the figure of a rapid rider appeared upon the road. It seemed familiar. I looked again—it was the blessed Enriquez! A sense of deep relief came over me. I loved Consuelo; but never before had lover ever hailed the irruption of one of his beloved's family with such complacency. "You are safe, dearest; it is Enriquez!"

I thought she received the information coldly. Suddenly she turned upon me her eyes, now bright and glittering.

"Swear to me at the instant, Pancho, that you will not again look upon Miss Essmith, even for once."

I was simple and literal. Miss Smith was my nearest neighbor, and, unless I was stricken with blindness, compliance was impossible. I hesitated—but swore.

"Enofe—you have hesitate—I will no more."

She rose to her feet with grave deliberation. For an instant, with the recollection of the delicate internal organization of the Saltellos on my mind, I was in agony lest she should totter and fall, even then, yielding up her gentle spirit on the spot. But when I looked again she had a hairpin between her white teeth, and was carefully adjusting her toreador hat. And beside us was Enriquez—cheerful, alert, voluble, and undaunted.

"Eureka! I have found! We are all here! Eet is a leetle public—eh? a leetle to much of a front seat for a tête-à-tête, my yonge friends," he said, glancing at the remains of Consuelo's bower, "but for the accounting of taste there is none. What will you? The meat of the one man shall envenom the meat of the other. But" (in a whisper to me) "as to thees horse—thees Chu Chu, which I have just pass—why is she undress? Surely you would not make an exposition of her to the traveler to suspect! And if not, why so?"

I tried to explain, looking at Consuelo, that Chu Chu had run away, that Consuelo had met with a terrible accident, had been thrown, and I feared had suffered serious internal injury. But to my embarrassment Consuelo maintained a half-scornful silence, and an inconsistent freshness of healthful indifference, as Enriquez approached her with an engaging smile.

"Ah, yes, she have the headache, and the molligrubs. She

will sit on the damp stone when the gentle dew is falling. I comprehend. Meet me in the lane when the clock strike nine! But," in a lower voice, "of thees undress horse I comprehend nothing! Look you—it is sad and strange."

He went off to fetch Chu Chu, leaving me and Consuelo alone. I do not think I ever felt so utterly abject and bewildered before in my life. Without knowing why, I was miserably conscious of having in some way offended the girl for whom I believed I would have given my life, and I had made her and myself ridiculous in the eyes of her brother. I had again failed in my slower Western nature to understand her high romantic Spanish soul! Meantime she was smoothing out her riding-habit, and looking as fresh and pretty as when she first left her house.

"Consita," I said hesitatingly, "you are not angry with me?"

"Angry?" she repeated haughtily, without looking at me. "Oh, no! Of a possibility eet is Mees Essmith who is angry that I have interroopt her tête-à-tête with you, and have send here my brother to make the same with me."

"But," I said eagerly, "Miss Smith does not even know Enriquez!"

Consuelo turned on me a glance of unutterable significance.

"Ah!" she said darkly, "you *tink*!"

Indeed I *knew*. But here I believed I understood Consuelo, and was relieved. I even ventured to say gently, "And you are better?"

She drew herself up to her full height, which was not much.

"Of my health, what is it? A nothing. Yes! Of my soul let us not speak."

Nevertheless, when Enriquez appeared with Chu Chu she

ran towards her with outstretched arms. Chu Chu protruded about six inches of upper lip in response—apparently under the impression, which I could quite understand, that her mistress was edible. And, I may have been mistaken, but their beautiful eyes met in an absolute and distinct glance of intelligence!

During the home journey Consuelo recovered her spirits, and parted from me with a magnanimous and forgiving pressure of the hand. I do not know what explanation of Chu Chu's original escapade was given to Enriquez and the rest of the family; the inscrutable forgiveness extended to me by Consuelo precluded any further inquiry on my part. I was willing to leave it a secret between her and Chu Chu. But, strange to say, it seemed to complete our own understanding, and precipitated, not only our love-making, but the final catastrophe which culminated that romance. For we had resolved to elope. I do not know that this heroic remedy was absolutely necessary from the attitude of either Consuelo's family or my own; I am inclined to think we preferred it, because it involved no previous explanation or advice. Need I say that our confidant and firm ally was Consuelo's brother —the alert, the linguistic, the ever happy, ever ready Enriquez! It was understood that his presence would not only give a certain mature respectability to our performance—but I do not think we would have contemplated this step without it. During one of our riding excursions we were to secure the services of a Methodist minister in the adjoining county, and later, that of the mission padre—when the secret was out.

"I will gif her away," said Enriquez confidently; "it will on the instant propitiate the old shadbelly who shall perform the affair, and withhold his jaw. A little chin music from your oncle 'Arry shall finish it! Remain tranquil and forget not a ring! One does not always, in the agony and dissatisfaction of the moment, a ring remember. I shall bring two in the pocket of my dress."

If I did not entirely participate in this roseate view it may have been because Enriquez, although a few years my senior, was much younger-looking, and with his demure deviltry of eye, and his upper lip close shaven for this occasion, he suggested a depraved acolyte rather than a responsible member of a family. Consuelo had also confided to me that her father—possibly owing to some rumors of our previous escapade—had forbidden any further excursions with me alone. The innocent man did not know that Chu Chu had forbidden it also, and that even on this momentous occasion both Enriquez and myself were obliged to ride in opposite fields like out-flankers. But we nevertheless felt the full guilt of disobedience added to our desperate enterprise. Meanwhile, although pressed for time, and subject to discovery at any moment, I managed at certain points of the road to dismount and walk beside Chu Chu (who did not seem to recognize me on foot), holding Consuelo's hand in my own, with the discreet Enriquez leading my horse in the distant field. I retain a very vivid picture of that walk—the ascent of a gentle slope towards a prospect as yet unknown, but full of glorious possibilities; the tender dropping light of an autumn sky, slightly filmed with the promise of the future rains, like foreshadowed tears, and the half-frightened, half-serious talk into which Consuelo and I had insensibly fallen. And then, I don't know how it happened, but as we reached the summit Chu Chu suddenly reared, wheeled, and the next moment was flying back along the road we had just traveled, at the top of her speed! It might have been that, after her abstracted fashion, she only at that moment detected my presence; but so sudden and complete was her evolution that before I could regain my horse from the astonished Enriquez she was already a quarter of a mile on the homeward stretch, with the frantic Consuelo pulling hopelessly at the bridle. We started in pursuit. But a horrible despair seized us. To attempt to overtake her, to even follow at the same rate of speed, would only excite Chu Chu and endanger Consuelo's life. There was absolutely no help for it, nothing could be done; the mare had taken her determined long, continuous stride; the road was a straight, steady descent all the way back to the village; Chu Chu had the bit between her teeth, and there was no prospect of swerving her. We could only follow hopelessly, idiotically, furiously, until Chu Chu dashed triumphantly into the Saltellos' courtyard, carrying the half-fainting Consuelo back to the arms of her assembled and astonished family.

It was our last ride together. It was the last I ever saw of Consuelo before her transfer to the safe seclusion of a convent in Southern California. It was the last I ever saw of Chu Chu, who in the confusion of that rencontre was overlooked in her half-loosed harness, and allowed to escape through the back gate to the fields. Months afterwards it was said that she had been identified among a band of wild horses in the Coast Range, as a strange and beautiful creature who had escaped the brand of the rodeo and had become a myth. There was another legend that she had been seen, sleek, fat, and gorgeously caparisoned, issuing from the gateway of the Rosario patio, before a lumbering Spanish cabriolé in which a short, stout matron was seated—but I will have none of it. For there are days when she still lives, and I can see her plainly still climbing the gentle slope towards the summit, with Consuelo on her back, and myself at her side, pressing eagerly forward towards the illimitable prospect that opens in the distance.

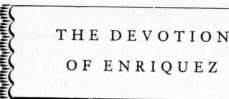

THE DEVOTION
OF ENRIQUEZ

In another chronicle which dealt with the exploits of Chu Chu, a Californian mustang, I gave some space to the accomplishments of Enriquez Saltello, who assisted me in training her, and who was also brother to Consuelo Saltello, the young lady to whom I had freely given both the mustang and my youthful affections. I consider it a proof of the superiority of masculine friendship that neither the subsequent desertion of the mustang nor the young lady ever made the slightest difference to Enriquez or me in our exalted amity. To a wondering doubt as to what I ever could possibly have seen in his sister to admire he joined a tolerant skepticism of the whole sex. This he was wont to express in that marvelous combination of Spanish precision and California slang for which he was justly famous.

"As to thees women and their little game," he would say, "believe me, my friend, your old oncle 'Enry is not in it. No; he will ever take a back seat when lofe is around. For why? Regard me here! If she is a horse you shall say, 'She will buck-jump,' 'She will ess-shy,' 'She will not arrive,' or 'She will arrive too quick.' But if it is thees women, where are you? For when you shall say, 'She will ess-shy,' look you, she will walk straight; or she will remain tranquil when you think she buck-jump; or else she will arrive and, look you, you will not. You shall get left. It is ever so. My father and the brother of my father have both make court to my

mother when she was but a señorita. My father think she
have lofe his brother more. So he say to her: 'It is enofe;
tranquilize yourself. I will go. I will efface myself. Adios!
Shake hands! Ta-ta! So long! See you again in the fall.' And
what make my mother? Regard me! She marry my father—
on the instant! Of thees women, believe me, Pancho, you
shall know nothing. Not even if they shall make you the son
of your father or his nephew."

I have recalled this characteristic speech to show the general tendency of Enriquez's convictions at the opening of
this little story. It is only fair to say, however, that his usual
attitude toward the sex he so cheerfully maligned exhibited
little apprehension or caution in dealing with them. Among
the frivolous and light-minded intermixture of his race he
moved with great freedom and popularity. He danced well;
when we went to fandangos together his agility and the
audacity of his figures always procured him the prettiest
partners, his professed sentiments, I presume, shielding him
from subsequent jealousies, heart-burnings, or envy. I have
a vivid recollection of him in the mysteries of the semicuacua,
a somewhat corybantic dance which left much to the invention of the performers, and very little to the imagination of
the spectator. In one of the figures a gaudy handkerchief,
waved more or less gracefully by dancer and danseuse before
the dazzled eyes of each other, acted as love's signal, and was
used to express alternate admiration and indifference, shyness and audacity, fear and transport, coyness and coquetry,
as the dance proceeded. I need not say that Enriquez's pantomimic illustration of these emotions was peculiarly extravagant; but it was always performed and accepted with
a gravity that was an essential feature of the dance. At such
times sighs would escape him which were supposed to por-
tray the incipient stages of passion; snorts of jealousy burst

from him at the suggestion of a rival; he was overtaken by a sort of St. Vitus's dance that expressed his timidity in making the first advances of affection; the scorn of his lady-love struck him with something like a dumb ague; and a single gesture of invitation from her produced marked delirium. All this was very like Enriquez; but on the particular occasion to which I refer, I think no one was prepared to see him begin the figure with the waving of *four* handkerchiefs! Yet this he did, pirouetting, capering, brandishing his silken signals like a ballerina's scarf in the languishment or fire of passion, until, in a final figure, where the conquered and submitting fair one usually sinks into the arms of her partner, need it be said that the ingenious Enriquez was found in the centre of the floor supporting four of the dancers! Yet he was by no means unduly excited either by the plaudits of the crowd or by his evident success with the fair.

"Ah, believe me, it is nothing," he said quietly, rolling a fresh cigarette as he leaned against the doorway. "Possibly, I shall have to offer the chocolate or the wine to thees girls, or make to them a promenade in the moonlight on the veranda. It is ever so. Unless, my friend," he said, suddenly turning toward me in an excess of chivalrous self-abnegation, "unless you shall yourself take my place. Behold, I gif them to you! I vamos! I vanish! I make track! I skedaddle!"

I think he would have carried his extravagance to the point of summoning his four gypsy witches of partners, and committing them to my care, if the crowd had not at that moment parted before the remaining dancers, and left one of the onlookers, a tall, slender girl, calmly surveying them through gold-rimmed eye-glasses in complete critical absorption. I stared in amazement and consternation; for I recognized in the fair stranger Miss Urania Mannersley, the Congregational minister's niece!

Everybody knew Rainie Mannersley throughout the length and breadth of the Encinal. She was at once the envy and the goad of the daughters of those Southwestern and Eastern immigrants who had settled in the valley. She was correct, she was critical, she was faultless and observant. She was proper, yet independent; she was highly educated; she was suspected of knowing Latin and Greek; she even spelled correctly! She could wither the plainest field nosegay in the hands of other girls by giving the flowers their botanical names. She never said, "Ain't you?" but "Aren't you?" She looked upon "Did I which?" as an incomplete and imperfect form of "What did I do?" She quoted from Browning and Tennyson, and was believed to have read them. She was from Boston. What could she possibly be doing at a free-and-easy fandango?

Even if these facts were not already familiar to every one there, her outward appearance would have attracted attention. Contrasted with the gorgeous red, black, and yellow skirts of the dancers, her plain, tightly fitting gown and hat, all of one delicate gray, were sufficiently notable in themselves, even had they not seemed, like the girl herself, a kind of quiet protest to the glaring flounces before her. Her small, straight waist and flat back brought into greater relief the corsetless, waistless, swaying figures of the Mexican girls, and her long, slim, well-booted feet, peeping from the stiff, white edges of her short skirt, made their broad, low-quartered slippers, held on by the big toe, appear more preposterous than ever. Suddenly she seemed to realize that she was standing there alone, but without fear or embarrassment. She drew back a little, glancing carelessly behind her as if missing some previous companion, and then her eyes fell upon mine. She smiled an easy recognition; then, a moment later, her glance rested more curiously upon Enriquez, who was still by my side. I disengaged myself and instantly joined her, particularly as I noticed that a few of the other bystanders were beginning to stare at her with little reserve.

"Isn't it the most extraordinary thing you ever saw?" she said quietly. Then, presently noticing the look of embarrassment on my face, she went on, more by way of conversation than of explanation: "I just left uncle making a call on a parishioner next door, and was going home with Jocasta" (a peon servant of her uncle's), "when I heard the music, and dropped in. I don't know what has become of her," she added, glancing round the room again; "she seemed perfectly wild when she saw that creature over there bounding about with his handkerchiefs. You were speaking to him just now. Do tell me—is he real?"

"I should think there was little doubt of that," I said with a vague laugh.

"You know what I mean," she said simply. "Is he quite sane? Does he do that because he likes it, or is he paid for it?"

This was too much. I pointed out somewhat hurriedly that he was a scion of one of the oldest Castilian families, that the performance was a national gypsy dance which he had joined in as a patriot and a patron, and that he was my dearest friend. At the same time I was conscious that I wished she hadn't seen his last performance.

"You don't mean to say that all that he did was in the dance?" she said. "I don't believe it. It was only like him." As I hesitated over this palpable truth, she went on: "I do wish he'd do it again. Don't you think you could make him?"

"Perhaps he might if *you* asked him," I said a little maliciously.

"Of course I shouldn't do that," she returned quietly. "All the same, I do believe he is really going to do it—or something else. Do look!"

I looked, and to my horror saw that Enriquez, possibly incited by the delicate gold eye-glasses of Miss Mannersley, had divested himself of his coat, and was winding the four handkerchiefs, tied together, picturesquely around his waist, preparatory to some new performance. I tried furtively to give him a warning look, but in vain.

"Isn't he really too absurd for anything!" said Miss Mannersley, yet with a certain comfortable anticipation in her voice. "You know, I never saw anything like this before. I wouldn't have believed such a creature could have existed."

Even had I succeeded in warning him, I doubt if it would have been of any avail. For, seizing a guitar from one of the musicians, he struck a few chords, and suddenly began to zigzag into the centre of the floor, swaying his body languishingly from side to side in time with the music and the pitch of a thin Spanish tenor. It was a gypsy love-song. Possibly Miss Mannersley's lingual accomplishments did not include a knowledge of Castilian, but she could not fail to see that the gestures and illustrative pantomime were addressed to her. Passionately assuring her that she was the most favored daughter of the Virgin, that her eyes were like votive tapers, and yet in the same breath accusing her of being a "brigand" and "assassin" in her attitude toward "his heart," he balanced with quivering timidity toward her, threw an imaginary cloak in front of her neat boots as a carpet for her to tread on, and with a final astonishing pirouette and a languishing twang of his guitar, sank on one knee, and blew, with a rose, a kiss at her feet.

If I had been seriously angry with him before for his grotesque extravagance, I could have pitied him now for the young girl's absolute unconsciousness of anything but his utter ludicrousness. The applause of dancers and bystanders was instantaneous and hearty; her only contribution to it was a slight parting of her thin red lips in a half-incredulous smile. In the silence that followed the applause, as Enriquez walked pantingly away, I heard her saying, half to herself, "Certainly a most extraordinary creature!" In my indignation I could not help turning suddenly upon her and looking straight into her eyes. They were brown, with that peculiar velvet opacity common to the pupils of near-sighted persons, and seemed to defy internal scrutiny. She only repeated carelessly, "Isn't he?" and added: "Please see if you can find Jocasta. I suppose we ought to be going now; and I dare say he won't be doing it again. Ah! there she is. Good gracious, child! what have you got there?"

It was Enriquez's rose which Jocasta had picked up, and was timidly holding out toward her mistress.

"Heavens! I don't want it. Keep it yourself."

I walked with them to the door, as I did not fancy a certain glitter in the black eyes of the Señoritas Manuela and Pepita, who were watching her curiously. But I think she was as oblivious of this as she was of Enriquez's particular attentions. As we reached the street I felt that I ought to say something more.

"You know," I began casually, "that although those poor people meet here in this public way, their gathering is really quite a homely pastoral and a national custom; and these girls are all honest, hard-working peons or servants, enjoying themselves in quite the old idyllic fashion."

"Certainly," said the young girl, half abstractedly. "Of course it's a Moorish dance, originally brought over, I suppose, by those old Andalusian immigrants two hundred years ago. It's quite Arabic in its suggestions. I have got something like it in an old cancionero I picked up at a bookstall in Boston. But," she added, with a gasp of reminiscent satisfaction, "that's not like *him*! Oh, no! *he* is decidedly original. Heavens! yes."

I turned away in some discomfiture to join Enriquez, who was calmly awaiting me, with a cigarette in his mouth, outside the sala. Yet he looked so unconscious of any previous absurdity that I hesitated in what I thought was a necessary warning. He, however, quickly precipitated it. Glancing after the retreating figures of the two women, he said, "Thees mees from Boston is return to her house. You do not accompany her? I shall. Behold me—I am there."

But I linked my arm firmly in his. Then I pointed out, first, that she was already accompanied by a servant; secondly, that if I, who knew her, had hesitated to offer myself as an escort, it was hardly proper for him, a perfect stranger, to take that liberty; that Miss Mannersley was very punctilious of etiquette, which he, as a Castilian gentleman, ought to appreciate.

"But will she not regard lofe—the admiration excessif?" he said, twirling his thin little mustache meditatively.

"No; she will not," I returned sharply; "and you ought to understand that she is on a different level from your Manuelas and Carmens."

"Pardon, my friend," he said gravely; "thees women are ever the same. There is a proverb in my language. Listen: 'Whether the sharp blade of the Toledo pierce the satin or the goatskin, it shall find behind it ever the same heart to wound.' I am that Toledo blade—possibly it is you, my friend. Wherefore, let us together pursue this girl of Boston on the instant."

But I kept my grasp on Enriquez's arm, and succeeded in restraining his mercurial impulses for the moment. He halted, and puffed vigorously at his cigarette; but the next instant he started forward again.

"Let us, however, follow with discretion in the rear; we shall pass her house; we shall gaze at it; it shall touch her heart."

Ridiculous as was this following of the young girl we had only just parted from, I nevertheless knew that Enriquez was quite capable of attempting it alone, and I thought it better to humor him by consenting to walk with him in that direction; but I felt it necessary to say:—

"I ought to warn you that Miss Mannersley already looks upon your performances at the sala as something outré and peculiar, and if I were you I shouldn't do anything to deepen that impression."

"You are saying she ees shock?" said Enriquez gravely.

I felt I could not conscientiously say that she was shocked, and he saw my hesitation.

"Then she have jealousy of the señoritas," he observed, with insufferable complacency. "You observe! I have already said. It is ever so."

I could stand it no longer.

"Look here, Harry," I said, "if you must know it, she looks upon you as an acrobat—a paid performer."

"Ah!"—his black eyes sparkled—"the torero, the man who fights the bull, he is also an acrobat."

"Yes; but she thinks you a clown!—a gracioso de teatro,—there!"

"Then I have make her laugh?" he said coolly.

I don't think he had; but I shrugged my shoulders.

"Bueno!" he said cheerfully. "Lofe, he begin with a laugh, he make feenish with a sigh."

I turned to look at him in the moonlight. His face presented its habitual Spanish gravity—a gravity that was almost ironical. His small black eyes had their characteristic irresponsible audacity—the irresponsibility of the vivacious young animal. It could not be possible that he was really touched with the placid frigidities of Miss Mannersley. I remembered his equally elastic gallantries with Miss Pinky Smith, a blond Western belle, from which both had harmlessly rebounded. As we walked on slowly I continued more persuasively:—

"Of course this is only your nonsense; but don't you see, Miss Mannersley thinks it all in earnest and really your nature?" I hesitated, for it suddenly struck me that it *was* really his nature. "And—hang it all!—you don't want her to believe you a common buffoon, or some intoxicated muchacho."

"Intoxicated?" repeated Enriquez, with exasperating languishment. "Yes; that is the word that shall express itself. My friend, you have made a shot in the centre—you have ring the bell every time! It is intoxication—but not of aguardiente. Look! I have long time an ancestor of whom is a pretty story. One day in church he have seen a young girl—a mere peasant girl—pass to the confessional. He look her in her eye, he stagger,"—here Enriquez wobbled pantomimically into the road,—"he fall!"—he would have suited the action to the word if I had not firmly held him up. "They have take him home, where he have remain without his clothes, and have dance and sing. But it was the drunkenness of lofe. And, look you, thees village girl was a nothing, not even pretty. The name of my ancestor was"—

"Don Quixote de la Mancha," I suggested maliciously. "I suspected as much. Come along. That will do."

"My ancestor's name," continued Enriquez gravely, "was Antonio Hermenegildo de Salvatierra, which is not the same. Thees Don Quixote of whom you speak exist not at all."

"Never mind. Only, for Heaven's sake, as we are nearing the house, don't make a fool of yourself again."

It was a wonderful moonlight night. The deep redwood porch of the Mannersley parsonage, under the shadow of a great oak,—the largest in the Encinal,—was diapered in black and silver. As the women stepped upon the porch their shadows were silhouetted against the door. Miss Mannersley paused for an instant, and turned to give a last look at the beauty of the night as Jocasta entered. Her glance fell upon us as we passed. She nodded carelessly and unaffectedly to me, but as she recognized Enriquez she looked a little longer at him with her previous cold and invincible curiosity. To my horror Enriquez began instantly to affect a slight tremulousness of gait and a difficulty of breathing; but I gripped his arm savagely, and managed to get him past the house as the door closed finally on the young lady.

"You do not comprehend, friend Pancho," he said gravely, "but those eyes in their glass are as the espejo ustorio, the burning mirror. They burn, they consume me here like paper. Let us affix to ourselves thees tree. She will, without doubt, appear at her window. We shall salute her for good-night."

"We will do nothing of the kind," I said sharply.

Finding that I was determined, he permitted me to lead him away. I was delighted to notice, however, that he had indicated the window which I knew was the minister's study, and that as the bedrooms were in the rear of the house, this later incident was probably not overseen by the young lady or the servant. But I did not part from Enriquez until I saw him safely back to the sala, where I left him sipping chocolate, his arm alternating around the waists of his two previous partners in a delightful Arcadian and childlike simplicity, and an apparent utter forgetfulness of Miss Mannersley.

The fandangos were usually held on Saturday night, and

the next day, being Sunday, I missed Enriquez; but as he was a devout Catholic I remembered that he was at mass in the morning, and possibly at the bullfight at San Antonio in the afternoon. But I was somewhat surprised on the Monday morning following, as I was crossing the plaza, to have my arm taken by the Reverend Mr. Mannersley in the nearest approach to familiarity that was consistent with the reserve of this eminent divine. I looked at him inquiringly. Although scrupulously correct in attire, his features always had a sin- gular resemblance to the national caricature known as "Uncle Sam," but with the humorous expression left out. Softly stroking his goatee with three fingers, he began condescend- ingly:—

"You are, I think, more or less familiar with the charac- teristics and customs of the Spanish as exhibited by the set- tlers here."

A thrill of apprehension went through me. Had he heard of Enriquez's proceedings? Had Miss Mannersley cruelly betrayed him to her uncle?

"I have not given that attention myself to their language and social peculiarities," he continued, with a large wave of the hand, "being much occupied with a study of their re- ligious beliefs and superstitions,"—it struck me that this was apt to be a common fault of people of the Mannersley type,— "but I have refrained from a personal discussion of them; on the contrary, I have held somewhat broad views on the sub- ject of their remarkable missionary work, and have suggested a scheme of coöperation with them, quite independent of doctrinal teaching, to my brethren of other Protestant Chris- tian sects. These views I first incorporated in a sermon last Sunday week, which I am told has created considerable atten- tion." He stopped and coughed slightly. "I have not yet heard from any of the Roman clergy, but I am led to believe that

my remarks were not ungrateful to Catholics generally."
I was relieved, although still in some wonder why he
should address me on this topic. I had a vague remembrance
of having heard that he had said something on Sunday which
had offended some Puritans of his flock, but nothing more.

He continued: "I have just said that I was unacquainted
with the characteristics of the Spanish-American race. I presume, however, they have the impulsiveness of their Latin
origin. They gesticulate—eh? They express their gratitude,
their joy, their affection, their emotions generally, by spasmodic movements? They naturally dance—sing—eh?"

A horrible suspicion crossed my mind; I could only stare
helplessly at him.

"I see," he said graciously; "perhaps it is a somewhat general question. I will explain myself. A rather singular occurrence happened to me the other night. I had returned from
visiting a parishioner, and was alone in my study reviewing
my sermon for the next day. It must have been quite late before I concluded, for I distinctly remember my niece had returned with her servant fully an hour before. Presently I
heard the sounds of a musical instrument in the road, with
the accents of some one singing or rehearsing some metrical
composition in words that, although couched in a language
foreign to me, in expression and modulation gave me the
impression of being distinctly adulatory. For some little time,
in the greater preoccupation of my task, I paid little attention
to the performance; but its persistency at length drew me in
no mere idle curiosity to the window. From thence, standing
in my dressing-gown, and believing myself unperceived, I
noticed under the large oak in the roadside the figure of a
young man, who, by the imperfect light, appeared to be of
Spanish extraction. But I evidently miscalculated my own
invisibility; for he moved rapidly forward as I came to the

window, and in a series of the most extraordinary pantomimic gestures saluted me. Beyond my experience of a few
Greek plays in earlier days, I confess I am not an adept in
the understanding of gesticulation; but it struck me that the
various phases of gratitude, fervor, reverence, and exaltation
were successively portrayed. He placed his hands upon his
head, his heart, and even clasped them together in this
manner."

To my consternation the reverend gentleman here imitated
Enriquez's most extravagant pantomime.

"I am willing to confess," he continued, "that I was singularly moved by them, as well as by the highly creditable
and Christian interest that evidently produced them. At last
I opened the window. Leaning out, I told him that I regretted
that the lateness of the hour prevented any further response
from me than a grateful though hurried acknowledgment of
his praiseworthy emotion, but that I should be glad to see him
for a few moments in the vestry before service the next day,
or at early candlelight, before the meeting of the Bible class.
I told him that as my sole purpose had been the creation of
an evangelical brotherhood and the exclusion of merely doctrinal views, nothing could be more gratifying to me than this
spontaneous and unsolicited testimony to my motives. He
appeared for an instant to be deeply affected, and, indeed,
quite overcome with emotion, and then gracefully retired,
with some agility and a slight saltatory movement."

He paused. A sudden and overwhelming idea took possession of me, and I looked impulsively into his face. Was it
possible that for once Enriquez's ironical extravagance had
been understood, met, and vanquished by a master hand?
But the Reverend Mr. Mannersley's self-satisfied face betrayed no ambiguity or lurking humor. He was evidently in
earnest; he had complacently accepted for himself the aban-

doned Enriquez's serenade to his niece. I felt an hysterical desire to laugh, but it was checked by my companion's next words.

"I informed my niece of the occurrence in the morning at breakfast. She had not heard anything of the strange performance, but she agreed with me as to its undoubted origin in a grateful recognition of my liberal efforts toward his co-religionists. It was she, in fact, who suggested that your knowledge of these people might corroborate my impressions."

I was dumfounded. Had Miss Mannersley, who must have recognized Enriquez's hand in this, concealed the fact in a desire to shield him? But this was so inconsistent with her utter indifference to him, except as a grotesque study, that she would have been more likely to tell her uncle all about his previous performance. Nor could it be that she wished to conceal her visit to the fandango. She was far too independent for that, and it was even possible that the reverend gentleman, in his desire to know more of Enriquez's compatriots, would not have objected. In my confusion I meekly added my conviction to hers, congratulated him upon his evident success, and slipped away.

But I was burning with a desire to see Enriquez and know all. He was imaginative but not untruthful. Unfortunately, I learned that he was just then following one of his erratic impulses, and had gone to a rodeo at his cousin's, in the foothills, where he was alternately exercising his horsemanship in catching and breaking wild cattle, and delighting his relatives with his incomparable grasp of the American language and customs, and of the airs of a young man of fashion. Then my thoughts recurred to Miss Mannersley. Had she really been oblivious that night to Enriquez's serenade? I resolved to find out, if I could, without betraying Enriquez. Indeed, it was possible, after all, that it might not have been he.

Chance favored me. The next evening I was at a party where Miss Mannersley, by reason of her position and quality, was a distinguished—I had almost written a popular—guest. But, as I have formerly stated, although the youthful fair of the Encinal were flattered by her casual attentions, and secretly admired her superior style and aristocratic calm, they were more or less uneasy under the dominance of her intelligence and education, and were afraid to attempt either confidence or familiarity. They were also singularly jealous of her, for although the average young man was equally afraid of her cleverness and candor, he was not above paying a tremulous and timid court to her for its effect upon her humbler sisters. This evening she was surrounded by her usual satellites, including, of course, the local notables and special guests of distinction. She had been discussing, I think, the existence of glaciers on Mount Shasta with a spectacled geologist, and had participated with charming frankness in a conversation on anatomy with the local doctor and a learned professor, when she was asked to take a seat at the piano. She played with remarkable skill and wonderful precision, but coldly and brilliantly. As she sat there in her subdued but perfectly fitting evening dress, her regular profile and short but slender neck firmly set upon her high shoulders, exhaling an atmosphere of refined puritanism and provocative intelligence, the utter incongruity of Enriquez's extravagant attentions, if ironical, and their equal hopelessness if not, seemed to me plainer than ever. What had this well-poised, coldly observant spinster to do with that quaintly ironic ruffler, that romantic cynic, that rowdy Don Quixote, that impossible Enriquez? Presently she ceased playing. Her slim, narrow slipper, revealing her thin ankle, remained upon the pedal; her delicate fingers were resting idly on the keys;

her head was slightly thrown back, and her narrow eyebrows prettily knit toward the ceiling in an effort of memory.

"Something of Chopin's," suggested the geologist ardently.

"That exquisite sonata!" pleaded the doctor.

"Suthin' of Rubinstein. Heard him once," said a gentleman of Siskiyou. "He just made that pianner get up and howl. Play Rube."

She shook her head with parted lips and a slight touch of girlish coquetry in her manner. Then her fingers suddenly dropped upon the keys with a glassy tinkle; there were a few quick pizzicato chords, down went the low pedal with a monotonous strumming, and she presently began to hum to herself. I started,—as well I might,—for I recognized one of Enriquez's favorite and most extravagant guitar solos. It was audacious; it was barbaric; it was, I fear, vulgar. As I remembered it,—as he sang it,—it recounted the adventures of one Don Francisco, a provincial gallant and roisterer of the most objectionable type. It had one hundred and four verses, which Enriquez never spared me. I shuddered as in a pleasant, quiet voice the correct Miss Mannersley warbled in musical praise of the *pellejo,* or wine-skin, and a eulogy of the dice-box came caressingly from her thin red lips. But the company was far differently affected: the strange, wild air and wilder accompaniment were evidently catching; people moved towards the piano; somebody whistled the air from a distant corner; even the faces of the geologist and doctor brightened.

"A tarantella, I presume?" blandly suggested the doctor.

Miss Mannersley stopped, and rose carelessly from the piano.

"It is a Moorish gypsy song of the fifteenth century," she said dryly.

"It seemed sorter familiar, too," hesitated one of the young men timidly, "like as if—don't you know?—you had without knowing it, don't you know?"—he blushed slightly—"sorter picked it up somewhere."

"I 'picked it up,' as you call it, in the collection of mediæval manuscripts of the Harvard Library, and copied it," returned Miss Mannersley coldly, as she turned away.

But I was not inclined to let her off so easily. I presently made my way to her side.

"Your uncle was complimentary enough to consult me as to the meaning of the appearance of a certain exuberant Spanish visitor at his house the other night."

I looked into her brown eyes, but my own slipped off her velvety pupils without retaining anything.

Then she reinforced her gaze with a pince-nez, and said carelessly:—

"Oh, it's you? How are you? Well, could you give him any information?"

"Only generally," I returned, still looking into her eyes. "These people are impulsive. The Spanish blood is a mixture of gold and quicksilver."

She smiled slightly. "That reminds me of your volatile friend. He was mercurial enough, certainly. Is he still dancing?"

"And singing sometimes," I responded pointedly.

But she only added casually, "A singular creature," without exhibiting the least consciousness, and drifted away, leaving me none the wiser. I felt that Enriquez alone could enlighten me. I must see him.

I did, but not in the way I expected. There was a bull-fight at San Antonio the next Saturday afternoon, the usual Sunday performance being changed in deference to the Sabbatical habits of the Americans. An additional attraction was offered in the shape of a bull and bear fight, also a concession to American taste, which had voted the bullfight "slow," and had averred that the bull "did not get a fair show." I am glad that I am able to spare the reader the usual realistic horrors, for in the Californian performances there was very little of the brutality that distinguished this function in the mother country. The horses were not miserable, worn-out hacks, but young and alert mustangs; and the display of horsemanship by the picadors was not only wonderful, but secured an almost absolute safety to horse and rider. I never saw a horse gored; although unskillful riders were sometimes thrown in wheeling quickly to avoid the bull's charge, they generally regained their animals without injury.

The Plaza de Toros was reached through the decayed and tile-strewn outskirts of an old Spanish village. It was a rudely built, oval amphitheatre, with crumbling, white-washed adobe walls, and roofed only over portions of the gallery reserved for the provincial "notables," but now occupied by a few shopkeepers and their wives, with a sprinkling of American travelers and ranchmen. The impalpable adobe-dust of the arena was being whirled into the air by the strong onset of the afternoon trade-winds, which happily, however, helped also to dissipate a reek of garlic, and the acrid fumes of cheap tobacco rolled in corn-husk cigarettes. I was leaning over the second barrier, waiting for the meagre and circus-like procession to enter with the keys of the bull-pen, when my attention was attracted to a movement in the reserved gallery. A lady and gentleman of a quality that was evidently unfamiliar to the rest of the audience were picking their way along the rickety benches to a front seat. I recognized the geologist with some surprise, and the lady he was leading with still greater astonishment. For it was Miss Mannersley, in her precise, well-fitting walking-costume—a monotone of sober color among the parti-colored audience.

However, I was perhaps less surprised than the audience, for I was not only becoming as accustomed to the young girl's vagaries as I had been to Enriquez's extravagance, but I was also satisfied that her uncle might have given her permission to come, as a recognition of the Sunday concession of the management, as well as to conciliate his supposed Catholic friends. I watched her sitting there until the first bull had entered, and, after a rather brief play with the picadors and banderilleros, was dispatched. At the moment when the matador approached the bull with his lethal weapon I was not sorry for an excuse to glance at Miss Mannersley. Her hands were in her lap, her head slightly bent forward over her knees. I fancied that she, too, had dropped her eyes before the brutal situation; to my horror I saw that she had a drawing-book in her hand, and was actually sketching it. I turned my eyes in preference to the dying bull.

The second animal led out for this ingenious slaughter was, however, more sullen, uncertain, and discomposing to his butchers. He accepted the irony of a trial with gloomy, suspicious eyes, and he declined the challenge of whirling and insulting picadors. He bristled with banderillas like a hedgehog, but remained with his haunches backed against the barrier, at times almost hidden in the fine dust raised by the monotonous stroke of his sullenly pawing hoof—his one dull, heavy protest. A vague uneasiness had infected his adversaries; the picadors held aloof, the banderilleros skirmished at a safe distance. The audience resented only the indecision of the bull. Galling epithets were flung at him, followed by cries of "Espada!" and, curving his elbow under his short cloak, the matador, with his flashing blade in hand, advanced and—stopped. The bull remained motionless.

For at that moment a heavier gust of wind than usual swept down upon the arena, lifted a suffocating cloud of dust, and whirled it around the tiers of benches and the balcony, and for a moment seemed to stop the performance. I heard an exclamation from the geologist, who had risen to his feet. I fancied I heard even a faint cry from Miss Mannersley; but the next moment, as the dust was slowly settling, we saw a sheet of paper in the air, that had been caught up in this brief cyclone, dropping, dipping from side to side on uncertain wings, until it slowly descended in the very middle of the arena. It was a leaf from Miss Mannersley's sketch-book, the one on which she had been sketching.

In the pause that followed it seemed to be the one object that at last excited the bull's growing but tardy ire. He glanced at it with murky, distended eyes; he snorted at it with vague yet troubled fury. Whether he detected his own presentment in Miss Mannersley's sketch, or whether he recognized it as an unknown and unfamiliar treachery in his surroundings, I could not conjecture; for the next moment the matador, taking advantage of the bull's concentration, with a complacent leer at the audience, advanced toward the paper. But at that instant a young man cleared the barrier into the arena with a single bound, shoved the matador to one side, caught up the paper, turned toward the balcony and Miss Mannersley with a gesture of apology, dropped gayly before the bull, knelt down before him with an exaggerated humility, and held up the drawing as if for his inspection.

A roar of applause broke from the audience, a cry of warning and exasperation from the attendants, as the goaded bull suddenly charged the stranger. But he sprang to one side with great dexterity, made a courteous gesture to the matador as if passing the bull over to him, and still holding the paper in his hand, re-leaped the barrier, and rejoined the audience in safety. I did not wait to see the deadly, dominant thrust with which the matador received the charging bull; my eyes were following the figure now bounding up the steps to the balcony, where with an exaggerated salutation he laid the drawing in Miss Mannersley's lap, and vanished. There was no mistaking that thin lithe form, the narrow black mustache, and gravely dancing eyes. The audacity of conception, the extravagance of execution, the quaint irony of the sequel, could belong to no one but Enriquez.

I hurried up to her as the six yoked mules dragged the carcass of the bull away. She was placidly putting up her book, the unmoved focus of a hundred eager and curious eyes. She smiled slightly as she saw me.

"I was just telling Mr. Briggs what an extraordinary creature it was, and how you know him. He must have had great experience to do that sort of thing so cleverly and safely. Does he do it often? Of course, not just that. But does he pick up cigars and things that I see they throw to the matador? Does he belong to the management? Mr. Briggs thinks the whole thing was a feint to distract the bull," she added, with a wicked glance at the geologist, who, I fancied, looked disturbed.

"I am afraid," I said dryly, "that his act was as unpremeditated and genuine as it was unusual."

"Why afraid?"

It was a matter-of-fact question, but I instantly saw my mistake. What right had I to assume that Enriquez's attentions were any more genuine than her own easy indifference; and if I suspected that they were, was it fair in me to give my friend away to this heartless coquette?

"You are not very gallant," she said, with a slight laugh, as I was hesitating, and turned away with her escort before I could frame a reply.

But at least Enriquez was now accessible, and I should gain

some information from him. I knew where to find him, unless he were still lounging about the building, intent upon more extravagance; but I waited until I saw Miss Mannersley and Briggs depart without further interruption.

The hacienda of Ramon Saltello, Enriquez's cousin, was on the outskirts of the village. When I arrived there I found Enriquez's pinto mustang steaming in the corral, and although I was momentarily delayed by the servants at the gateway, I was surprised to find Enriquez himself lying languidly on his back in a hammock in the patio. His arms were hanging down listlessly on each side as if in the greatest prostration, yet I could not resist the impression that the rascal had only just got into the hammock when he heard of my arrival.

"You have arrived, friend Pancho, in time," he said, in accents of exaggerated weakness. "I am absolutely exhaust. I am bursted, caved in, kerflummoxed. I have behold you, my friend, at the barrier. I speak not, I make no sign at the first, because I was on fire; I speak not at the feenish—for I am exhaust."

"I see; the bull made it lively for you."

He instantly bounded up in the hammock.

"The bull! Caramba! Not a thousand bulls! And thees one, look you, was a craven. I snap my fingers over his horn; I roll my cigarette under his nose."

"Well, then—what was it?"

He instantly lay down again, pulling up the sides of the hammock. Presently his voice came from its depths, appealing in hollow tones to the sky.

"He asks me—thees friend of my soul, thees brother of my life, thees Pancho that I lofe—what it was? He would that I should tell him why I am game in the legs, why I shake in the hand, crack in the voice, and am generally wipe out!

And yet he, my pardner—thees Francisco—know that I have seen the mees from Boston! That I have gaze into the eye, touch the hand, and for the instant possess the picture that hand have drawn! It was a sublime picture, Pancho," he said, sitting up again suddenly, "and have kill the bull before our friend Pepe's sword have touch even the bone of hees back and make feenish of him."

"Look here, Enriquez," I said bluntly, "have you been sere-nading that girl?"

He shrugged his shoulders without the least embarrass-ment, and said:—

"Ah, yes. What would you? It is of a necessity."

"Well," I retorted, "then you ought to know that her uncle took it all to himself—thought you some grateful Catholic pleased with his religious tolerance."

He did not even smile. "Bueno," he said gravely. "That make something, too. In thees affair it is well to begin with the duenna. He is the duenna."

"And," I went on relentlessly, "her escort told her just now that your exploit in the bull-ring was only a trick to divert the bull, suggested by the management."

"Bah! her escort is a geologian. Naturally, she is to him as a stone."

I would have continued, but a peon interrupted us at this moment with a sign to Enriquez, who leaped briskly from the hammock, bidding me wait his return from a messenger in the gateway.

Still unsatisfied of mind I waited, and sat down in the hammock that Enriquez had quitted. A scrap of paper was lying in its meshes, which at first appeared to be of the kind from which Enriquez rolled his cigarettes; but as I picked it up to throw it away, I found it was of much firmer and stouter material. Looking at it more closely, I was surprised to recognize it as a piece of the tinted drawing-paper torn off the "block" that Miss Mannersley had used. It had been deeply creased at right angles as if it had been folded; it looked as if it might have been the outer half of a sheet used for a note.

It might have been a trifling circumstance, but it greatly excited my curiosity. I knew that he had returned the sketch to Miss Mannersley, for I had seen it in her hand. Had she given him another? And if so, why had it been folded to the destruction of the drawing? Or was it part of a note which he had destroyed? In the first impulse of discovery I walked quickly with it toward the gateway where Enriquez had disappeared, intending to restore it to him. He was just outside talking with a young girl. I started, for it was Jocasta—Miss Mannersley's maid.

With this added discovery came that sense of uneasiness and indignation with which we illogically are apt to resent the withholding of a friend's confidence, even in matters concerning only himself. It was no use for me to reason that it was no business of mine, that he was right in keeping a secret that concerned another—and a lady; but I was afraid I was even more meanly resentful because the discovery quite upset my theory of his conduct and of Miss Mannersley's attitude toward him.

I continued to walk on to the gateway, where I bade Enriquez a hurried good-by, alleging the sudden remembrance of another engagement, but without appearing to recognize the girl, who was moving away, when, to my further discomfiture, the rascal stopped me with an appealing wink, threw his arms around my neck, whispered hoarsely in my ear, "Ah! you see—you comprehend—but you are the mirror of discretion!" and returned to Jocasta. But whether this meant that he had received a message from Miss Mannersley, or that he was trying to suborn her maid to carry one, was still uncertain. He was capable of either.

During the next two or three weeks I saw him frequently; but as I had resolved to try the effect of ignoring Miss Mannersley in our conversation, I gathered little further of their relations, and, to my surprise, after one or two characteristic extravagances of allusion, Enriquez dropped the subject, too. Only one afternoon, as we were parting, he said carelessly:—

"My friend, you are going to the casa of Mannersley to-night. I too have the honor of the invitation. But you will be my Mercury—my Leporello—you will take of me a message to thees Mees Boston, that I am crushed, desolated, prostrate, and flabbergasted—that I cannot arrive, for I have of that night to sit up with the grand-aunt of my brother-in-law, who has a quinsy to the death. It is sad."

This was the first indication I had received of Miss Mannersley's advances. I was equally surprised at Enriquez's refusal.

"Nonsense!" I said bluntly. "Nothing keeps you from going."

"My friend," returned Enriquez, with a sudden lapse into languishment that seemed to make him absolutely infirm, "it is everything that shall restrain me. I am not strong. I shall become weak of the knee and tremble under the eye of Mees Boston. I shall precipitate myself to the geologian by the throat. Ask me another conundrum that shall be easy."

He seemed idiotically inflexible, and did not go. But I did. I found Miss Mannersley exquisitely dressed and looking singularly animated and pretty. The lambent glow of her inscrutable eye as she turned towards me might have been flattering but for my uneasiness in regard to Enriquez. I delivered his excuses as naturally as I could. She stiffened for an instant, and seemed an inch higher.

"I am so sorry," she said at last in a level voice. "I thought he would have been so amusing. Indeed, I had hoped we might try an old Moorish dance together which I have found and was practicing."

"He would have been delighted, I know. It's a great pity he didn't come with me," I said quickly; "but," I could not help adding, with emphasis on her words, "he is such an 'extraordinary creature,' you know."

"I see nothing extraordinary in his devotion to an aged relative," returned Miss Mannersley quietly, as she turned away, "except that it justifies my respect for his character."

I do not know why I did not relate this to him. Possibly I had given up trying to understand them; perhaps I was beginning to have an idea that he could take care of himself. But I was somewhat surprised a few days later when, after asking me to go with him to a rodeo at his uncle's he added composedly, "You will meet Mees Boston."

I stared, and but for his manner would have thought it part of his extravagance. For the rodeo—a yearly chase of wild cattle for the purpose of lassoing and branding them —was a rather brutal affair, and purely a man's function; it was also a family affair—a property stock-taking of the great Spanish cattle-owners—and strangers, particularly Americans, found it difficult to gain access to its mysteries and the festa that followed.

"But how did she get an invitation?" I asked. "You did not dare to ask"—I began.

"My friend," said Enriquez, with a singular deliberation, 'the great and respectable Boston herself, and her serene, venerable oncle, and other Boston magnificoes, have of a truth done me the inexpressible honor to solicit of my degraded, papistical oncle that she shall come—that she shall of her own superior eye behold the barbaric customs of our race."

His tone and manner were so peculiar that I stepped quickly before him, laid my hands on his shoulders, and looked down into his face. But the actual devil which I now for the first time saw in his eyes went out of them suddenly, and he relapsed again in affected languishment in his chair.

"I shall be there, friend Pancho," he said, with a preposterous gasp. "I shall nerve my arm to lasso the bull, and tumble him before her at her feet. I shall throw the 'buck-jump' mustang at the same sacred spot. I shall pluck for her the buried chicken at full speed from the ground, and present it to her. You shall see it, friend Pancho. I shall be there."

He was as good as his word. When Don Pedro Amador, his uncle, installed Miss Mannersley, with Spanish courtesy, on a raised platform in the long valley where the rodeo took place, the gallant Enriquez selected a bull from the frightened and galloping herd, and, cleverly isolating him from the band, lassoed his hind legs, and threw him exactly before the platform where Miss Mannersley was seated. It was Enriquez who caught the unbroken mustang, sprang from his own saddle to the bare back of his captive, and with only the lasso for a bridle, halted him on rigid haunches at Miss Mannersley's feet. It was Enriquez who, in the sports that followed, leaned from his saddle at full speed, caught up the chicken buried to its head in the sand without wringing its neck, and tossed it unharmed and fluttering toward his mistress. As for her, she wore the same look of animation that I had seen in her face at our previous meeting. Although she did not bring her sketch-book with her, as at the bullfight, she did not shrink from the branding of the cattle, which took place under her very eyes.

Yet I had never seen her and Enriquez together; they had never, to my actual knowledge, even exchanged words. And now, although she was the guest of his uncle, his duties seemed to keep him in the field, and apart from her. Nor, as far as I could detect, did either apparently make any effort to have it otherwise. The peculiar circumstance seemed to attract no attention from any one else. But for what I alone knew—or thought I knew—of their actual relations, I should have thought them strangers.

But I felt certain that the festa which took place in the broad patio of Don Pedro's casa would bring them together. And later in the evening, as we were all sitting on the veranda watching the dancing of the Mexican women, whose white-flounced sayas were monotonously rising and falling to the strains of two melancholy harps, Miss Mannersley rejoined us from the house. She seemed to be utterly absorbed and abstracted in the barbaric dances, and scarcely moved as she leaned over the railing with her cheek resting on her hand. Suddenly she arose with a little cry.

"What is it?" asked two or three.

"Nothing—only I have lost my fan."

She had risen, and was looking abstractedly on the floor.

Half a dozen men jumped to their feet. "Let me fetch it," they said.

"No, thank you. I think I know where it is, and will go for it myself." She was moving away.

But Don Pedro interposed with Spanish gravity. Such a thing was not to be heard of in his casa. If the señorita would not permit *him*—an old man—to go for it, it must be brought by Enriquez, her cavalier of the day.

But Enriquez was not to be found. I glanced at Miss Mannersley's somewhat disturbed face, and begged her to let me fetch it. I thought I saw a flush of relief come into her pale cheek, as she said, in a lower voice, "On the stone seat in the garden."

I hurried away, leaving Don Pedro still protesting. I

knew the gardens, and the stone seat at an angle of the wall, not a dozen yards from the casa. The moon shone full upon it. There, indeed, lay the little gray-feathered fan. But close beside it, also, lay the crumpled, black, gold-embroidered riding-gauntlet that Enriquez had worn at the rodeo.

I thrust it hurriedly into my pocket, and ran back. As I passed through the gateway I asked a peon to send Enri-quez to me. The man stared. Did I not know that Don Enriquez had ridden away two minutes ago?

When I reached the veranda, I handed the fan to Miss Mannersley without a word.

"Bueno," said Don Pedro gravely; "it is as well. There shall be no bones broken over the getting of it, for Enriquez, I hear, has had to return to the Encinal this very evening."

Miss Mannersley retired early. I did not inform her of my discovery, nor did I seek in any way to penetrate her secret. There was no doubt that she and Enriquez had been together, perhaps not for the first time; but what was the result of their interview? From the young girl's demeanor and Enriquez's hurried departure, I could only fear th worst for him. Had he been tempted into some further ex-travagance and been angrily rebuked, or had he avowed a real passion concealed under his exaggerated mask, and been deliberately rejected? I tossed uneasily half the night, fol-lowing in my dreams my poor friend's hurrying hoofbeats, and ever starting from my sleep at what I thought was the sound of galloping hoofs.

I rose early, and lounged into the patio; but others were there before me, and a small group of Don Pedro's family were excitedly discussing something, and I fancied they turned away awkwardly and consciously as I approached. There was an air of indefinite uneasiness everywhere. A strange fear came over me with the chill of the early morning air. Had anything happened to Enriquez? I had always looked upon his extravagance as part of his playful humor. Could it be possible that under the sting of rejection he had made his grotesque threat of languishing effacement real? Surely Miss Mannersley would know or suspect something, if it were the case.

I approached one of the Mexican women and asked if the señorita had risen. The woman started, and looked covertly round before she replied. Did not Don Pancho know that Miss Mannersley and her maid had not slept in their beds that night, but had gone, none knew where?

For an instant I felt an appalling sense of my own responsibility in this suddenly serious situation, and hurried after the retreating family group. But as I entered the corridor a vaquero touched me on the shoulder. He had evidently just dismounted, and was covered with the dust of the road. He handed me a note written in pencil on a leaf from Miss Mannersley's sketch-book. It was in Enriquez's hand, and his signature was followed by his most extravagant rubric.

FRIEND PANCHO.—When you read this line you shall of a possibility think I am no more. That is where you shall slip up, my little brother! I am much more—I am two times as much, for I have marry Miss Boston. At the mission church, at five of the morning, sharp! No cards shall be left! I kiss the hand of my venerable uncle-in-law. You shall say to him that we fly to the South wilderness as the combined evangelical missionary to the heathen! Miss Boston herself say this. Ta-ta! How are you now?

Your own

ENRIQUEZ.

The Best Short Stories by Bret Harte

A YELLOW DOG

I NEVER knew why in the Western States of America a yellow dog should be proverbially considered the acme of canine degradation and incompetency, nor why the possession of one should seriously affect the social standing of its possessor. But the fact being established, I think we accepted it at Rattlers Ridge without question. The matter of ownership was more difficult to settle; and although the dog I have in my mind at the present writing attached himself impartially and equally to every one in camp, no one ventured to exclusively claim him; while, after the perpetration of any canine atrocity, everybody repudiated him with indecent haste.

"Well, I can swear he hasn't been near our shanty for weeks," or the retort, "He was last seen comin' out of *your* cabin," expressed the eagerness with which Rattlers Ridge washed its hands of any responsibility. Yet he was by no means a common dog, nor even an unhandsome dog; and it was a singular fact that his severest critics vied with each other in narrating instances of his sagacity, insight, and agility which they themselves had witnessed.

He had been seen crossing the "flume" that spanned Grizzly Cañon, at a height of nine hundred feet, on a plank six inches wide. He had tumbled down the "shoot" to the South Fork, a thousand feet below, and was found sitting on the river bank "without a scratch, 'cept that he was lazily givin' himself with his off hind paw." He had been forgotten in a snowdrift on a Sierran shelf, and had come home in the early spring with the conceited complacency of an Alpine traveler and a plumpness alleged to have been the result of an exclusive diet of buried mail bags and their contents. He was generally believed to read the advance election posters, and disappear a day or two before the candidates and the brass band—which he hated—came to the Ridge. He was suspected of having overlooked Colonel Johnson's hand at poker, and of having conveyed to the Colonel's adversary, by a succession of barks, the danger of betting against four kings.

While these statements were supplied by wholly unsupported witnesses, it was a very human weakness of Rattlers Ridge that the responsibility of corroboration was passed to *the dog* himself, and *he* was looked upon as a consummate liar.

"Snoopin' round yere, and *callin'* yourself a poker sharp, are ye! Scoot, you yaller pizin!" was a common adjuration whenever the unfortunate animal intruded upon a card party. "Ef thar was a spark, an *atom* of truth in *that dog,* I'd believe my own eyes that I saw him sittin' up and trying to magnetize a jay bird off a tree. But wot are ye goin' to do with a yaller equivocator like that?"

I have said that he was yellow—or, to use the ordinary expression, "yaller." Indeed, I am inclined to believe that much of the ignominy attached to the epithet lay in this favorite pronunciation. Men who habitually spoke of a *"yellow* bird," a *"yellow* hammer," a *"yellow* leaf," always alluded to him as a *"yaller* dog."

He certainly *was* yellow. After a bath—usually compulsory—he presented a decided gamboge streak down his back, from the top of his forehead to the stump of his tail, fading in his sides and flank to a delicate straw color.

His breast, legs, and feet—when not reddened by "slum-gullion," in which he was fond of wading—were white. A few attempts at ornamental decoration from the India-ink pot of the storekeeper failed, partly through the yellow dog's excessive agility, which would never give the paint time to dry on him, and partly through his success in transferring his markings to the trousers and blankets of the camp.

The size and shape of his tail—which had been cut off before his introduction to Rattlers Ridge—were favorite sources of speculation to the miners, both as determining his breed and his moral responsibility in coming into camp in that defective condition. There was a general opinion that he couldn't have looked worse with a tail, and its removal was therefore a gratuitous effrontery.

His best feature was his eyes, which were a lustrous Vandyke brown, and sparkling with intelligence; but here again he suffered from evolution through environment, and their original trustful openness was marred by the experience of watching for flying stones, sods, and passing kicks from the rear, so that the pupils were continually reverting to the outer angle of the eyelid.

Nevertheless, none of these characteristics decided the vexed question of his *breed*. His speed and scent pointed to a "hound," and it is related that on one occasion he was laid on the trail of a wildcat with such success that he followed it apparently out of the State, returning at the end of two weeks, footsore, but blandly contented.

Attaching himself to a prospecting party, he was sent under the same belief "into the brush" to drive off a bear, who was supposed to be haunting the camp-fire. He returned in a few minutes *with* the bear, *driving it into* the unarmed circle and scattering the whole party. After this the theory of his being a hunting dog was abandoned. Yet it was said—on the usual uncorroborated evidence—that he had "put up" a quail; and his qualities as a retriever were for a long time accepted, until, during a shooting expedition for wild ducks, it was discovered that the one he had brought back had never been *shot,* and the party were obliged to compound damages with an adjacent settler.

His fondness for paddling in the ditches and "slumgullion" at one time suggested a water spaniel. He could swim, and would occasionally bring out of the river sticks and pieces of bark that had been thrown in; but as *he* always had to be thrown in with them, and was a good-sized dog, his aquatic reputation faded also. He remained simply "a yaller dog." What more could be said? His actual name was "Bones"—given to him, no doubt, through the provincial custom of confounding the occupation of the individual with his quality, for which it was pointed out precedent could be found in some old English family names.

But if Bones generally exhibited no preference for any particular individual in camp, he always made an exception in favor of drunkards. Even an ordinary roistering bacchanalian party brought him out from under a tree or a shed in the keenest satisfaction. He would accompany them through the long straggling street of the settlement, barking his delight at every step or mis-step of the revelers, and exhibiting none of that mistrust of eye which marked his attendance upon the sane and the respectable. He accepted even their uncouth play without a snarl or a yelp, hypocritically pretending even to like it; and I conscientiously believe would have allowed a tin can to be attached to his tail if the hand that tied it on were only unsteady, and the voice that bade him "lie still" were husky with liquor. He would "see" the party cheerfully into a saloon, wait outside the door—his tongue fairly lolling from his mouth in enjoyment—until they reappeared, permit them even to tumble over him with pleasure, and then gambol away before them, heedless of awkwardly projected stones and epithets. He would afterwards accompany them separately home, or lie with them at crossroads until they were assisted to their cabins. Then he would trot rakishly to his own haunt by the saloon stove, with the slightly conscious air of having been a bad dog, yet of having had a good time.

We never could satisfy ourselves whether his enjoyment arose from some merely selfish conviction that he was more *secure* with the physically and mentally incompetent, from some active sympathy with active wickedness, or from a grim sense of his own mental superiority at such moments. But the general belief leant towards his kindred sympathy as a "yaller dog" with all that was disreputable. And this was supported by another very singular canine manifestation— the "sincere flattery" of simulation or imitation.

"Uncle Billy" Riley for a short time enjoyed the position of being the camp drunkard, and at once became an object of Bones' greatest solicitude. He not only accompanied him everywhere, curled at his feet or head according to Uncle Billy's attitude at the moment, but, it was noticed, began presently to undergo a singular alteration in his own habits and appearance. From being an active, tireless scout and forager, a bold and unovertakable marauder, he became lazy and apathetic; allowed gophers to burrow under him without endeavoring to undermine the settlement in his frantic endeavors to dig them out, permitted squirrels to flash their tails at him a hundred yards away, forgot his usual *caches,* and let his favorite bones unburied and bleaching in the sun. His eyes grew dull, his coat lustreless, in proportion as his companion became blear-eyed and ragged; in running, his usual arrow-like directness began to deviate, and it was not unusual to meet the pair together, zig-zagging up the hill. Indeed, Uncle Billy's condition could be predetermined by Bones' appearance at times when his temporary master was invisible. "The old man must have an awful jag on to-day," was casually remarked when an extra fluffiness and imbecility was noticeable in the passing Bones. At first it was believed that he drank also, but when careful investigation proved this hypothesis untenable, he was freely called a "derned time-servin', yaller hypocrite." Not a few advanced the opinion that if Bones did not actually lead Uncle Billy astray, he at least "slavered him over and coddled him until the old man got conceited in his wickedness." This undoubtedly led to a compulsory divorce between them, and Uncle Billy was happily despatched to a neighboring town and a doctor.

Bones seemed to miss him greatly, ran away for two days, and was supposed to have visited him, to have been shocked at his convalescence, and to have been "cut" by Uncle Billy in his reformed character; and he returned to his old active life again, and buried his past with his forgotten bones. It was said that he was afterwards detected in trying to lead an intoxicated tramp into camp after the methods employed by a blind man's dog, but was discovered in time by the—of course—uncorroborated narrator.

I should be tempted to leave him thus in his original and picturesque sin, but the same veracity which compelled me to transcribe his faults and iniquities obliges me to describe his ultimate and somewhat monotonous reformation, which came from no fault of his own.

It was a joyous day at Rattlers Ridge that was equally the advent of his change of heart and the first stagecoach that had been induced to diverge from the highroad and stop regularly at our settlement. Flags were flying from the post office and Polka saloon—and Bones was flying before the brass band that he detested, when the sweetest girl in the county—Pinkey Preston—daughter of the county judge and hopelessly beloved by all Rattlers Ridge, stepped from the coach which she had glorified by occupying as an invited guest.

"What makes him run away?" she asked quickly, opening her lovely eyes in a possible innocent wonder that anything could be found to run away from her.

"He don't like the brass band," we explained eagerly.

"How funny," murmured the girl; "is it as out of tune as all that?"

This irresistible witticism alone would have been enough to satisfy us—we did nothing but repeat it to each other all the next day—but we were positively transported when we saw her suddenly gather her dainty skirts in one hand and trip off through the red dust towards Bones, who, with his eyes over his yellow shoulder, had halted in the road, and half turned in mingled disgust and rage at the spectacle of the descending trombone. We held our breath as she approached him. Would Bones evade her as he did us at such moments, or would he save our reputation, and consent, for the moment, to accept her as a new kind of inebriate? She came nearer; he saw her; he began to slowly quiver with excitement—his stump of a tail vibrating with such rapidity that the loss of the missing portion was scarcely noticeable. Suddenly she stopped before him, took his yellow head between her little hands, lifted it, and looked down in his handsome brown eyes with her two lovely blue ones. What passed between them in that magnetic glance no one ever knew. She returned with him; said to him casually: "We're not afraid of brass bands, are we?" to which he apparently acquiesced, at least stifling his disgust of them, while he was near her—which was nearly all the time.

During the speech-making her gloved hand and his yellow head were always near together, and at the crowning ceremony—her public checking of Yuba Bill's "waybill," on behalf of the township, with a gold pencil, presented to her by the Stage Company—Bones' joy, far from knowing no bounds, seemed to know nothing but them, and he witnessed it apparently in the air. No one dared to interfere. For the first time a local pride in Bones sprang up in our hearts— and we lied to each other in his praises openly and shamelessly.

Then the time came for parting. We were standing by the door of the coach, hats in hand, as Miss Pinkey was about to step into it; Bones was waiting by her side, confidently looking into the interior, and apparently selecting his own seat on the lap of Judge Preston in the corner, when Miss Pinkey held up the sweetest of admonitory fingers. Then, taking his head between her two hands, she again looked into his brimming eyes, and said, simply, "*Good* dog," with the gentlest of emphasis on the adjective, and popped into the coach.

The six bay horses started as one, the gorgeous green and gold vehicle bounded forward, the red dust rose behind, and the yellow dog danced in and out of it to the very outskirts of the settlement. And then he soberly returned.

A day or two later he was missed—but the fact was afterwards known that he was at Spring Valley, the county town where Miss Preston lived—and he was forgiven. A week afterwards he was missed again, but this time for a longer period, and then a pathetic letter arrived from Sacramento for the storekeeper's wife.

"Would you mind," wrote Miss Pinkey Preston, "asking some of your boys to come over here to Sacramento and bring back Bones? I don't mind having the dear dog walk out with me at Spring Valley, where every one knows me; but here he *does* make one so noticeable, on account of *his color*. I've got scarcely a frock that he agrees with. He don't go with my pink muslin, and that lovely buff tint he makes three shades lighter. You know yellow is *so* trying."

A consultation was quickly held by the whole settlement, and a deputation sent to Sacramento to relieve the unfortunate girl. We were all quite indignant with Bones—but, oddly enough, I think it was greatly tempered with our new pride in him. While he was with us alone, his peculiarities had been scarcely appreciated, but the recurrent phrase, "that yellow dog that they keep at the Rattlers," gave us a mysterious importance along the country side, as if we had secured a "mascot" in some zoölogical curiosity.

This was further indicated by a singular occurrence. A new church had been built at the crossroads, and an eminent divine had come from San Francisco to preach the opening sermon. After a careful examination of the camp's wardrobe, and some felicitous exchange of apparel, a few of us were deputed to represent "Rattlers" at the Sunday service. In our white ducks, straw hats, and flannel blouses, we were sufficiently picturesque and distinctive as "honest miners" to be shown off in one of the front pews.

Seated near the prettiest girls, who offered us their hymn-books—in the cleanly odor of fresh pine shavings, and ironed muslin, and blown over by the spices of our own woods through the open windows, a deep sense of the abiding peace of Christian communion settled upon us. At this supreme moment some one murmured in an awe-stricken whisper:—

"*Will* you look at Bones?"

We looked. Bones had entered the church and gone up in the gallery through a pardonable ignorance and modesty;

out, perceiving his mistake, was now calmly walking along the gallery rail before the astounded worshipers. Reaching the end, he paused for a moment, and carelessly looked down. It was about fifteen feet to the floor below—the simplest jump in the world for the mountain-bred Bones. Daintily, gingerly, lazily, and yet with a conceited airiness of manner, as if, humanly speaking, he had one leg in his pocket and were doing it on three, he cleared the distance, dropping just in front of the chancel, without a sound, turned himself around three times, and then lay comfortably down.

Three deacons were instantly in the aisle coming up before the eminent divine, who, we fancied, wore a restrained smile. We heard the hurried whispers: "Belongs to them." "Quite a local institution here, you know." "Don't like to offend sensibilities"; and the minister's prompt "By no means," as he went on with his service.

A short month ago we would have repudiated Bones; to-day we sat there in slightly supercilious attitudes, as if to indicate that any affront offered to Bones would be an insult to ourselves, and followed by our instantaneous withdrawal in a body.

All went well, however, until the minister, lifting the large Bible from the communion table and holding it in both hands before him, walked towards a reading-stand by the altar rails. Bones uttered a distinct growl. The minister stopped.

We, and we alone, comprehended in a flash the whole situation. The Bible was nearly the size and shape of one of those soft clods of sod which we were in the playful habit of launching at Bones when he lay half asleep in the sun, in order to see him cleverly evade it.

We held our breath. What was to be done? But the opportunity belonged to our leader, Jeff Briggs—a confoundedly good-looking fellow, with the golden mustache of a northern viking and the curls of an Apollo. Secure in his beauty and bland in his self-conceit, he rose from the pew, and stepped before the chancel rails.

"I would wait a moment, if I were you, sir," he said, respectfully, "and you will see that he will go out quietly."

"What is wrong?" whispered the minister in some concern.

"He thinks you are going to heave that book at him, sir, without giving him a fair show, as we do."

The minister looked perplexed, but remained motionless, with the book in his hands. Bones arose, walked half way down the aisle, and vanished like a yellow flash!

With this justification of his reputation, Bones disappeared for a week. At the end of that time we received a polite note from Judge Preston, saying that the dog had become quite domiciled in their house, and begged that the camp, without yielding up their valuable *property* in him, would allow him to remain at Spring Valley for an indefinite time; that both the judge and his daughter—with whom Bones was already an old friend—would be glad if the members of the camp would visit their old favorite whenever they desired, to assure themselves that he was well cared for.

I am afraid that the bait thus ingenuously thrown out had a good deal to do with our ultimate yielding. However, the reports of those who visited Bones were wonderful and marvelous. He was residing there in state, lying on rugs in the drawing-room, coiled up under the judicial desk in the judge's study, sleeping regularly on the mat outside Miss Pinkey's bedroom door, or lazily snapping at flies on the judge's lawn.

"He's as yallar as ever," said one of our informants, "but it don't somehow seem to be the same back that we used to break clods over in the old time, just to see him scoot out of the dust."

And now I must record a fact which I am aware all lovers of dogs will indignantly deny, and which will be furiously bayed at by every faithful hound since the days of Ulysses. Bones not only *forgot,* but absolutely *cut us!* Those who called upon the judge in "store clothes" he would perhaps casually notice, but he would sniff at them as if detecting and resenting them under their superficial exterior. The rest he simply paid no attention to. The more familiar term of "Bonesy"—formerly applied to him, as in our rare moments of endearment—produced no response. This pained, I think, some of the more youthful of us; but, through some strange human weakness, it also increased the camp's respect for him. Nevertheless, we spoke of him familiarly to strangers at the very moment he ignored us. I am afraid that we also took some pains to point out that he was getting fat and unwieldy, and losing his elasticity, implying covertly that his choice was a mistake and his life a failure.

A year after he died, in the odor of sanctity and respectability, being found one morning coiled up and stiff on the mat outside Miss Pinkey's door. When the news was conveyed to us, we asked permission, the camp being in a prosperous condition, to erect a stone over his grave. But when it came to the inscription we could only think of the two words murmured to him by Miss Pinkey, which we always believe effected his conversion:—

"Good Dog!"

ONLY one shot had been fired. It had gone wide of its mark, —the ringleader of the Vigilantes,—and had left Red Pete, who had fired it, covered by their rifles and at their mercy. For his hand had been cramped by hard riding, and his eye distracted by their sudden onset, and so the inevitable end had come. He submitted sullenly to his captors; his companion fugitive and horse-thief gave up the protracted struggle with a feeling not unlike relief. Even the hot and revengeful victors were content. They had taken their men alive. At any time during the long chase they could have brought them down by a rifle-shot, but it would have been unsportsmanlike, and have ended in a free fight, instead of an example. And, for the matter of that, their doom was already sealed. Their end, by a rope and a tree, although not sanctified by law, would have at least the deliberation of justice. It was the tribute paid by the Vigilantes to that order which they had themselves disregarded in the pursuit and capture. Yet this strange logic of the frontier sufficed them, and gave a certain dignity to the climax.

"Ef you've got anything to say to your folks, say it *now,* and say it quick," said the ringleader.

Red Pete glanced around him. He had been run to earth at his own cabin in the clearing, whence a few relations and friends, mostly women and children, non-combatants, had outflowed, gazing vacantly at the twenty Vigilantes who surrounded them. All were accustomed to scenes of violence, blood-feud, chase, and hardship; it was only the suddenness of the onset and its quick result that had surprised them. They looked on with dazed curiosity and some disappointment; there had been no fight to speak of—no spectacle! A boy, nephew of Red Pete, got upon the rain-barrel to view the proceedings more comfortably; a tall, handsome, lazy Kentucky girl, a visiting neighbor, leaned against the doorpost, chewing gum. Only a yellow hound was actively perplexed. He could not make out if a hunt were just over or beginning, and ran eagerly backwards and forwards, leaping alternately upon the captives and the captors.

The ringleader repeated his challenge. Red Pete gave a reckless laugh and looked at his wife.

At which Mrs. Red Pete came forward. It seemed that she had much to say, incoherently, furiously, vindictively, to the ringleader. His soul would roast in hell for that day's work! He called himself a man, skunkin' in the open and afraid to show himself except with a crowd of other "Kiyi's" around a house of women and children. Heaping insult upon insult, inveighing against his low blood, his ancestors, his dubious origin, she at last flung out a wild taunt of his invalid wife, the insult of a woman to a woman, until his white face grew rigid, and only that Western-American fetich of the sanctity of sex kept his twitching fingers from the lock of his rifle. Even her husband noticed it, and with a half-authoritative "Let up on that, old gal," and a pat of his freed left hand on her back, took his last parting. The ringleader, still white under the lash of the woman's tongue, turned abruptly to the second captive. "And if *you've* got anybody to say 'good-by' to, now's your chance."

The man looked up. Nobody stirred or spoke. He was a stranger there, being a chance confederate picked up by Red

Pete, and known to no one. Still young, but an outlaw from his abandoned boyhood, of which father and mother were only a forgotten dream, he loved horses and stole them, fully accepting the frontier penalty of life for the interference with that animal on which a man's life so often depended. But he understood the good points of a horse, as was shown by the one he bestrode—until a few days before the property of Judge Boompointer. This was his sole distinction.

The unexpected question stirred him for a moment out of the attitude of reckless indifference, for attitude it was, and a part of his profession. But it may have touched him that at that moment he was less than his companion and his virago wife. However, he only shook his head. As he did so his eye casually fell on the handsome girl by the doorpost, who was looking at him. The ringleader, too, may have been touched by his complete loneliness, for *he* hesitated. At the same moment he saw that the girl was looking at his friendless captive.

A grotesque idea struck him.

"Salomy Jane, ye might do worse than come yere and say 'good-by' to a dying man, and him a stranger," he said.

There seemed to be a subtle stroke of poetry and irony in this that equally struck the apathetic crowd. It was well known that Salomy Jane Clay thought no small potatoes of herself, and always held off the local swain with a lazy, nymph-like scorn. Nevertheless, she slowly disengaged herself from the doorpost, and, to everybody's astonishment, lounged with languid grace and outstretched hand towards the prisoner. The color came into the gray, reckless mask which the doomed man wore as her right hand grasped his left, just loosed by his captors. Then she paused; her shy, fawn-like eyes grew bold, and fixed themselves upon him. She took the chewing-gum from her mouth, wiped her red lips with the back of her hand, by a sudden lithe spring placed her foot on his stirrup, and, bounding to the saddle, threw her arms about his neck and pressed a kiss upon his lips.

They remained thus for a hushed moment—the man on the threshold of death, the young woman in the fullness of youth and beauty—linked together. Then the crowd laughed; in the audacious effrontery of the girl's act the ultimate fate of the two men was forgotten. She slipped languidly to the ground; *she* was the focus of all eyes,—she only! The ringleader saw it and his opportunity. He shouted: "Time's up! Forward!" urged his horse beside his captives, and the next moment the whole cavalcade was sweeping over the clearing into the darkening woods.

Their destination was Sawyer's Crossing, the headquarters of the committee, where the council was still sitting, and where both culprits were to expiate the offense of which that council had already found them guilty. They rode in great and breathless haste,—a haste in which, strangely enough, even the captives seemed to join. That haste possibly prevented them from noticing the singular change which had taken place in the second captive since the episode of the kiss. His high color remained, as if it had burned through his mask of indifference; his eyes were quick, alert, and keen, his mouth half open as if the girl's kiss still lingered there. And that haste had made them careless, for the horse of the man who led him slipped in a gopher-hole, rolled over, unseated his rider, and even dragged the bound and helpless second captive from Judge Boompointer's favorite mare. In an instant they were all on their feet again, but in that supreme moment the second captive felt the cords which bound his arms had slipped to his wrists. By keeping his elbows to his sides, and obliging the others to help him mount, it escaped their notice. By riding close to his captors, and keeping in the crush of the throng, he further concealed the accident, slowly working his hands downwards out of his bonds.

Their way lay through a sylvan wilderness, mid-leg deep in ferns, whose tall fronds brushed their horses' sides in their furious gallop and concealed the flapping of the captive's loosened cords. The peaceful vista, more suggestive of the offerings of nymph and shepherd than of human sacrifice, was in a strange contrast to this whirlwind rush of stern, armed men. The westering sun pierced the subdued light and the tremor of leaves with yellow lances; birds started into song on blue and dove-like wings, and on either side of the trail of this vengeful storm could be heard the murmur of hidden and tranquil waters. In a few moments they would be on the open ridge, whence sloped the common turnpike to "Sawyer's," a mile away. It was the custom of returning cavalcades to take this hill at headlong speed, with shouts and cries that heralded their coming. They withheld the latter that day, as inconsistent with their dignity; but, emerging from the wood, swept silently like an avalanche down the slope. They were well under way, looking only to their horses, when the second captive slipped his right arm from the bonds and succeeded in grasping the reins that lay trailing on the horse's neck. A sudden vaquero jerk, which the well-trained animal understood, threw him on his haunches with his forelegs firmly planted on the slope. The rest of the cavalcade swept on; the man who was leading the captive's horse by the riata, thinking only of another accident, dropped the line to save himself from being dragged backwards from his horse. The captive wheeled, and the next moment was galloping furiously up the slope.

It was the work of a moment; a trained horse and an experienced hand. The cavalcade had covered nearly fifty yards before they could pull up; the freed captive had covered half that distance uphill. The road was so narrow that only two shots could be fired, and these broke dust two yards ahead of the fugitive. They had not dared to fire low; the horse was the more valuable animal. The fugitive knew this in his extremity also, and would have gladly taken a shot in his own leg to spare that of his horse. Five men were detached to recapture or kill him. The latter seemed inevitable But he had calculated his chances; before they could reload he had reached the woods again; winding in and out between the pillared tree trunks, he offered no mark. They knew his horse was superior to their own; at the end of two hours they returned, for he had disappeared without track or trail. The end was briefly told in the "Sierra Record:"—

"Red Pete, the notorious horse-thief, who had so long eluded justice, was captured and hung by the Sawyer's Crossing Vigilantes last week; his confederate, unfortunately, escaped on a valuable horse belonging to Judge Boompointer. The judge had refused one thousand dollars for the horse only a week before. As the thief, who is still at large, would find it difficult to dispose of so valuable an animal without detection, the chances are against either of them turning up again."

Salomy Jane watched the cavalcade until it had disappeared. Then she became aware that her brief popularity had passed. Mrs. Red Pete, in stormy hysterics, had included her in a sweeping denunciation of the whole universe, possibly for simulating an emotion in which she herself was deficient. The other women hated her for her momentary exaltation above them; only the children still admired her as one who had undoubtedly "canoodled" with a man "a-going to be hung"—a daring flight beyond their wildest ambition. Salomy Jane accepted the change with charming unconcern She put on her yellow nankeen sunbonnet,—a hideous affair that would have ruined any other woman, but which only enhanced the piquancy of her fresh brunette skin,—tied the strings, letting the blue-black braids escape below its frilled curtain behind, jumped on her mustang with a casual display of agile ankles in shapely white stockings, whistled to the hound, and waving her hand with a "So long, sonny!" to the lately bereft but admiring nephew, flapped and fluttered away in her short brown holland gown.

Her father's house was four miles distant. Contrasted with the cabin she had just quitted, it was a superior dwelling, with a long "lean-to" at the rear, which brought the eaves almost to the ground and made it look like a low triangle. It had a long barn and cattle sheds, for Madison Clay was a "great" stock-raiser and the owner of a "quarter section." It had a sitting-room and a parlor organ, whose transportation thither had been a marvel of "packing." These things were supposed to give Salomy Jane an undue importance, but the girl's reserve and inaccessibility to local advances were rather the result of a cool, lazy temperament and the preoccupation of a large, protecting admiration for her father, for some years a widower. For Mr. Madison Clay's life had been threatened in one or two feuds,—it was said, not without cause,—and it is possible that the pathetic spectacle of her father doing his visiting with a shotgun may have touched her closely and somewhat prejudiced her against the neighboring masculinity. The thought that cattle, horses, and "quarter section" would one day be hers did not disturb her calm. As for Mr. Clay, he accepted her as housewifely, though somewhat "interfering," and, being one of "his own womankind," therefore not without some degree of merit.

"Wot's this yer I'm hearin' of your doin's over at Red Pete's? Honeyfoglin' with a horse-thief, eh?" said Mr. Clay two days later at breakfast.

"I reckon you heard about the straight thing, then," said Salomy Jane unconcernedly, without looking round.

"What do you kalkilate Rube will say to it? What are you goin' to tell *him*?" said Mr. Clay sarcastically.

"Rube," or Reuben Waters, was a swain supposed to be favored particularly by Mr. Clay. Salomy Jane looked up.

"I'll tell him that when *he's* on his way to be hung, I'll kiss him,—not till then," said the young lady brightly.

This delightful witticism suited the paternal humor, and Mr. Clay smiled; but, nevertheless, he frowned a moment afterwards.

"But this yer hoss-thief got away arter all, and that's a hoss of a different color," he said grimly.

Salomy Jane put down her knife and fork. This was certainly a new and different phase of the situation. She had never thought of it before, and, strangely enough, for the first time she became interested in the man. "Got away?" she repeated. "Did they let him off?"

"Not much," said her father briefly. "Slipped his cords, and going down the grade pulled up short, just like a vaquero agin a lassoed bull, almost draggin' the man leadin' him off his hoss, and then skyuted up the grade. For that matter, on that hoss o' Judge Boompointer's he mout have dragged the whole posse of 'em down on their knees ef he liked! Sarved 'em right, too. Instead of stringin' him up afore the door, or shootin' him on sight, they must allow to take him down afore the hull committee 'for an example.' 'Example' be blowed! Ther' 's example enough when some stranger comes unbeknownst slap onter a man hanged to a tree and plugged full of holes. *That's* an example, and *he* knows what it means.

Wot more do ye want? But then those Vigilantes is allus clingin' and hangin' onter some mere scrap o' the law they're pretendin' to despise. It makes me sick! Why, when Jake Myers shot your ole Aunt Viney's second husband, and I laid in wait for Jake afterwards in the Butternut Hollow, did *I* tie him to his hoss and fetch him down to your Aunt Viney's cabin 'for an example' before I plugged him? No!" in deep disgust. "No! Why, I just meandered through the woods, careless-like, till he comes out, and I just rode up to him, and I said"—

But Salomy Jane had heard her father's story before. Even one's dearest relatives are apt to become tiresome in narration. "I know, dad," she interrupted; "but this yer man,— this hoss-thief,—did *he* get clean away without gettin' hurt at all?"

"He did, and unless he's fool enough to sell the hoss, he kin keep away, too. So ye see, ye can't ladle out purp stuff about a 'dyin' stranger' to Rube. He won't swaller it."

"All the same, dad," returned the girl cheerfully, "I reckon to say it, and say *more;* I'll tell him that ef *he* manages to get away too, I'll marry him—there! But ye don't ketch Rube takin' any such risks in gettin' ketched, or in gettin' away arter!"

Madison Clay smiled grimly, pushed back his chair, rose, dropped a perfunctory kiss on his daughter's hair, and, taking his shotgun from the corner, departed on a peaceful Samaritan mission to a cow who had dropped a calf in the far pasture. Inclined as he was to Reuben's wooing from his eligibility as to property, he was conscious that he was sadly deficient in certain qualities inherent in the Clay family. It certainly would be a kind of *mésalliance*.

Left to herself, Salomy Jane stared a long while at the coffee-pot, and then called the two squaws who assisted her in her household duties, to clear away the things while she went up to her own room to make her bed. Here she was confronted with a possible prospect of that proverbial bed she might be making in her willfulness, and on which she must lie, in the photograph of a somewhat serious young man of refined features—Reuben Waters—stuck in her window-frame. Salomy Jane smiled over her last witticism regarding him and enjoyed it, like your true humorist, and then, catching sight of her own handsome face in the little mirror, smiled again. But wasn't it funny about that horse-thief getting off after all? Good Lordy! Fancy Reuben hearing he was alive and going round with that kiss of hers set on his lips! She laughed again, a little more abstractedly. And he had returned it like a man, holding her tight and almost breathless, and he going to be hung the next minute! Salomy Jane had been kissed at other times, by force, chance, or stratagem. In a certain ingenuous forfeit game of the locality, known as "I'm a-pinin'," many had "pined" for a "sweet kiss" from Salomy Jane, which she had yielded in a sense of honor and fair play. She had never been kissed like this before—she would never again; and yet the man was alive! And behold, she could see in the mirror that she was blushing!

She should hardly know him again. A young man with very bright eyes, a flushed and sunburnt cheek, a kind of fixed look in the face, and no beard; no, none that she could feel. Yet he was not at all like Reuben, not a bit. She took Reuben's picture from the window, and laid it on her work-box. And to think she did not even know this young man's name! That was queer. To be kissed by a man whom she might never know! Of course he knew hers. She wondered if he remembered it and her. But of course he was so glad to get off with his life that he never thought of anything else. Yet she did not give more than four or five minutes to these speculations, and, like a sensible girl, thought of something else. Once again, however, in opening the closet, she found the brown holland gown she had worn on the day before; thought it very unbecoming, and regretted that she had not worn her best gown on her visit to Red Pete's cottage. On such an occasion she really might have been more impressive.

When her father came home that night she asked him the news. No, they had *not* captured the second horse-thief, who was still at large. Judge Boompointer talked of invoking the aid of the despised law. It remained, then, to see whether the horse-thief was fool enough to try to get rid of the animal. Red Pete's body had been delivered to his widow. Perhaps it would only be neighborly for Salomy Jane to ride over to the funeral. But Salomy Jane did not take to the suggestion kindly, nor yet did she explain to her father that, as the other man was still living, she did not care to undergo a second disciplining at the widow's hands. Nevertheless, she contrasted her situation with that of the widow with a new and singular satisfaction. It might have been Red Pete who had escaped. But he had not the grit of the nameless one. She had already settled his heroic quality.

"Ye ain't harkenin' to me, Salomy."

Salomy Jane started.

"Here I'm askin' ye if ye've see that hound Phil Larrabee sneaking by yer to-day?"

Salomy Jane had not. But she became interested and self-reproachful, for she knew that Phil Larrabee was one of her father's enemies. "He wouldn't dare to go by here unless he knew you were out," she said quickly.

"That's what gets me," he said, scratching his grizzled head. "I've been kind o' thinkin' o' him all day, and one of them Chinamen said he saw him at Sawyer's Crossing. He was a kind of friend o' Pete's wife. That's why I thought yer might find out ef he'd been there." Salomy Jane grew more self-reproachful at her father's self-interest in her "neighborliness." "But that ain't all," continued Mr. Clay. "Thar was tracks over the far pasture that warn't mine. I followed them, and they went round and round the house two or three times, ez ef they mout hev bin prowlin', and then I lost 'em in the woods again. It's just like that sneakin' hound Larrabee to hev bin lyin' in wait for me and afraid to meet a man fair and square in the open."

"You just lie low, dad, for a day or two more, and let me do a little prowlin'," said the girl, with sympathetic indignation in her dark eyes. "Ef it's that skunk, I'll spot him soon enough and let you know whar he's hiding."

"You'll just stay where ye are, Salomy," said her father decisively. "This ain't no woman's work—though I ain't sayin' you haven't got more head for it than some men I know."

Nevertheless, that night, after her father had gone to bed, Salomy Jane sat by the open window of the sitting-room in an apparent attitude of languid contemplation, but alert and intent of eye and ear. It was a fine moonlit night. Two pines near the door, solitary pickets of the serried ranks of distant forest, cast long shadows like paths to the cottage, and sighed their spiced breath in the windows. For there was no frivolity of vine or flower round Salomy Jane's bower. The clearing was too recent, the life too practical, for vanities like these. But the moon added a vague elusiveness to everything, softened the rigid outlines of the sheds, gave shadows to the lidless windows, and touched with merciful indirectness the hideous débris of refuse gravel and the gaunt scars of burnt vegetation before the door. Even Salomy Jane was affected by it, and exhaled something between a sigh and a yawn with the breath of the pines. Then she suddenly sat upright. Her quick ear had caught a faint "click, click," in the direction of the wood; her quicker instinct and rustic training enabled her to determine that it was the ring of a horse's shoe on flinty ground; her knowledge of the locality told her it came from the spot where the trail passed over an outcrop of flint, scarcely a quarter of a mile from where she sat, and within the clearing. It was no errant "stock," for the foot was *shod* with iron; it was a mounted trespasser by night, and boded no good to a man like Clay.

She rose, threw her shawl over her head, more for disguise than shelter, and passed out of the door. A sudden impulse made her seize her father's shotgun from the corner where it stood,—not that she feared any danger to herself, but that it was an excuse. She made directly for the wood, keeping in the shadow of the pines as long as she could. At the fringe she halted; whoever was there must pass her before reaching the house.

Then there seemed to be a suspense of all nature. Every-thing was deadly still—even the moonbeams appeared no longer tremulous; soon there was a rustle as of some stealthy animal among the ferns, and then a dismounted man stepped into the moonlight. It was the horse-thief—the man she had kissed!

For a wild moment a strange fancy seized her usually sane intellect and stirred her temperate blood. The news they had told her was *not* true; he had been hung, and this was his ghost! He looked as white and spirit-like in the moonlight, dressed in the same clothes, as when she saw him last. He had evidently seen her approaching, and moved quickly to meet her. But in his haste he stumbled slightly; she reflected suddenly that ghosts did not stumble, and a feeling of relief came over her. And it was no assassin of her father that had been prowling around—only this unhappy fugitive. A mo-mentary color came into her cheek; her coolness and hardihood returned; it was with a tinge of sauciness in her voice that she said:—

"I reckoned you were a ghost."

"I mout have been," he said, looking at her fixedly; "but I reckon I'd have come back here all the same."

"It's a little riskier comin' back alive," she said, with a levity that died on her lips, for a singular nervousness, half fear and half expectation, was beginning to take the place of her relief of a moment ago. "Then it was *you* who was prowlin' round and makin' tracks in the far pasture?"

"Yes; I came straight here when I got away."

She felt his eyes were burning her, but did not dare to raise her own. "Why," she began, hesitated, and ended vaguely. "*How* did you get here?"

"You helped me!"

"I?"

"Yes. That kiss you gave me put life into me—gave me strength to get away. I swore to myself I'd come back and thank you, alive or dead."

Every word he said she could have anticipated, so plain the situation seemed to her now. And every word he said she knew was the truth. Yet her cool common sense struggled against it.

"What's the use of your escaping, ef you're comin' back here to be ketched again?" she said pertly.

He drew a little nearer to her, but seemed to her the more awkward as she resumed her self-possession. His voice, too, was broken, as if by exhaustion, as he said, catching his breath at intervals:—

"I'll tell you. You did more for me than you think. You made another man o' me. I never had a man, woman, or child do to me what you did. I never had a friend—only a pal like Red Pete, who picked me up 'on shares.' I want to quit this yer—what I'm doin'. I want to begin by doin' the square thing to you"— He stopped, breathed hard, and then said brokenly, "My hoss is over thar, staked out. I want to give him to you. Judge Boompointer will give you a thousand dollars for him. I ain't lyin'; it's God's truth! I saw it on the handbill agin a tree. Take him, and I'll get away afoot. Take him. It's the only thing I can do for you, and I know it don't half pay for what you did. Take it; your father can get a reward for you, if you can't."

Such were the ethics of this strange locality that neither the man who made the offer nor the girl to whom it was made was struck by anything that seemed illogical or indelicate, or at all inconsistent with justice or the horse-thief's real conversion. Salomy Jane nevertheless dissented, from another and weaker reason.

"I don't want your hoss, though I reckon dad might; but you're just starvin'. I'll get suthin'." She turned towards the house.

"Say you'll take the hoss first," he said, grasping her hand. At the touch she felt herself coloring and struggled, expecting perhaps another kiss. But he dropped her hand. She turned again with a saucy gesture, said, "Hol' on; I'll come right back," and slipped away, the mere shadow of a coy and flying nymph in the moonlight, until she reached the house.

Here she not only procured food and whiskey, but added a long dust-coat and hat of her father's to her burden. They would serve as a disguise for him and hide that heroic figure, which she thought everybody must now know as she did. Then she rejoined him breathlessly. But he put the food and whiskey aside.

"Listen," he said; "I've turned the hoss into your corral. You'll find him there in the morning, and no one will know but that he got lost and joined the other horses."

Then she burst out. "But you—*you*—what will become of you? You'll be ketched!"

"I'll manage to get away," he said in a low voice, "ef—ef"—

"Ef what?" she said tremblingly.

"Ef you'll put the heart in me again,—as you did!" he gasped.

She tried to laugh—to move away. She could do neither. Suddenly he caught her in his arms, with a long kiss, which she returned again and again. Then they stood embraced as they had embraced two days before, but no longer the same. For the cool, lazy Salomy Jane had been transformed into another woman—a passionate, clinging savage. Perhaps something of her father's blood had surged within her at that supreme moment. The man stood erect and determined.

"Wot's your name?" she whispered quickly. It was a woman's quickest way of defining her feelings.

"Dart."

"Yer first name?"

"Jack."

"Let me go now, Jack. Lie low in the woods till to-morrow sunup. I'll come again."

He released her. Yet she lingered a moment. "Put on those things," she said, with a sudden happy flash of eyes and teeth, "and lie close till I come." And then she sped away home.

But midway up the distance she felt her feet going slower, and something at her heartstrings seemed to be pulling her back. She stopped, turned, and glanced to where he had been standing. Had she seen him then, she might have returned. But he had disappeared. She gave her first sigh, and then ran quickly again. It must be nearly ten o'clock! It was not very long to morning!

She was within a few steps of her own door, when the

sleeping woods and silent air appeared to suddenly awake with a sharp "crack!"

She stopped, paralyzed. Another "crack!" followed, that echoed over to the far corral. She recalled herself instantly and dashed off wildly to the woods again.

As she ran she thought of one thing only. He had been "dogged" by one of his old pursuers and attacked. But there were two shots, and he was unarmed. Suddenly she remembered that she had left her father's gun standing against the tree where they were talking. Thank God! she may again have saved him. She ran to the tree; the gun was gone. She ran hither and thither, dreading at every step to fall upon his lifeless body. A new thought struck her; she ran to the corral. The horse was not there! He must have been able to regain it, and escaped, *after* the shots had been fired. She drew a long breath of relief, but it was caught up in an apprehension of alarm. Her father, awakened from his sleep by the shots, was hurriedly approaching her.

"What's up now, Salomy Jane?" he demanded excitedly.

"Nothin'," said the girl, with an effort. "Nothin', at least, that *I* can find." She was usually truthful because fearless, and a lie stuck in her throat; but she was no longer fearless, thinking of *him*. "I wasn't abed; so I ran out as soon as I heard the shots fired," she answered in return to his curious gaze.

"And you've hid my gun somewhere where it can't be found," he said reproachfully. "Ef it was that sneak Larrabee, and he fired them shots to lure me out, he might have potted me, without a show, a dozen times in the last five minutes."

She had not thought since of her father's enemy! It might indeed have been he who had attacked Jack. But she made a quick point of the suggestion. "Run in, dad, run in and find the gun; you've got no show out here without it." She seized him by the shoulders from behind, shielding him from the woods, and hurried him, half expostulating, half struggling, to the house.

But there no gun was to be found. It was strange; it must have been mislaid in some corner! Was he sure he had not left it in the barn? But no matter now. The danger was over; the Larrabee trick had failed; he must go to bed now, and in the morning they would make a search together. At the same time she had inwardly resolved to rise before him and make another search of the wood, and perhaps—fearful joy as she recalled her promise!—find Jack alive and well, awaiting her!

Salomy Jane slept little that night, nor did her father. But towards morning he fell into a tired man's slumber until the sun was well up the horizon. Far different was it with his daughter: she lay with her face to the window, her head half lifted to catch every sound, from the creaking of the sun-warped shingles above her head to the far-off moan of the rising wind in the pine-trees. Sometimes she fell into a breathless, half-ecstatic trance, living over every moment of the stolen interview; feeling the fugitive's arm still around her, his kisses on her lips; hearing his whispered voice in her ears—the birth of her new life! This was followed again by a period of agonizing dread—that he might even then be lying, his life ebbing away, in the woods, with her name on his lips, and she resting here inactive, until she half started from her bed to go to his succor. And this went on until a pale opal glow came into the sky, followed by a still paler pink on the summit of the white Sierras, when she rose and hurriedly began to dress. Still so sanguine was her hope of meeing him, that she lingered yet a moment to select the brown holland skirt and yellow sunbonnet she had worn when she first saw him. And she had only seen him twice! Only *twice*! It would be cruel, too cruel, not to see him again!

She crept softly down the stairs, listening to the long-drawn breathing of her father in his bedroom, and then, by the light of a guttering candle, scrawled a note to him, begging him not to trust himself out of the house until she returned from her search, and leaving the note open on the table, swiftly ran out into the growing day.

Three hours afterwards Mr. Madison Clay awoke to the sound of loud knocking. At first this forced itself upon his consciousness as his daughter's regular morning summons, and was responded to by a grunt of recognition and a nestling closer in the blankets. Then he awoke with a start and a muttered oath, remembering the events of last night, and his intention to get up early, and rolled out of bed. Becoming aware by this time that the knocking was at the outer door, and hearing the shout of a familiar voice, he hastily pulled on his boots, his jean trousers, and fastening a single suspender over his shoulder as he clattered downstairs, stood in the lower room. The door was open, and waiting upon the threshold was his kinsman, an old ally in many a blood-feud—Breckenridge Clay!

"You *are* a cool one, Mad!" said the latter in half-admiring indignation.

"What's up?" said the bewildered Madison.

"*You* ought to be, and scootin' out o' this," said Breckenridge grimly. "It's all very well to 'know nothin';' but here Phil Larrabee's friends hev just picked him up, drilled through with slugs and deader nor a crow, and now they're lettin' loose Larrabee's two half-brothers on you. And you must go like a derned fool and leave these yer things behind you in the bresh," he went on querulously, lifting Madison

Clay's dust-coat, hat, and shotgun from his horse, which stood saddled at the door. "Luckily I picked them up in the woods comin' here. Ye ain't got more than time to get over the state line and among your folks thar afore they'll be down on you. Hustle, old man! What are you gawkin' and starin' at?"

Madison Clay had stared amazed and bewildered—horror-stricken. The incidents of the past night for the first time flashed upon him clearly—hopelessly! The shots; his finding Salomy Jane alone in the woods; her confusion and anxiety to rid herself of him; the disappearance of the shotgun; and now this new discovery of the taking of his hat and coat for a disguise! *She* had killed Phil Larrabee in that disguise, after provoking his first harmless shot! She, his own child, Salomy Jane, had disgraced herself by a man's crime; had disgraced him by usurping his right, and taking a mean advantage, by deceit, of a foe!

"Gimme that gun," he said hoarsely.

Breckenridge handed him the gun in wonder and slowly gathering suspicion. Madison examined nipple and muzzle; one barrel had been discharged. It was true! The gun dropped from his hand.

"Look here, old man," said Breckenridge, with a darkening face, "there's bin no foul play here. Thar's bin no hiring of men, no deputy to do this job. *You* did it fair and square—yourself?"

"Yes, by God!" burst out Madison Clay, in a hoarse voice. "Who says I didn't?"

Reassured, yet believing that Madison Clay had nerved himself for the act by an over-draught of whiskey, which had affected his memory, Breckenridge said curtly, "Then wake up and 'lite' out, ef ye want me to stand by you."

"Go to the corral and pick me out a hoss," said Madison

slowly, yet not without a certain dignity of manner. "I've suthin' to say to Salomy Jane afore I go." He was holding her scribbled note, which he had just discovered, in his shaking hand.

Struck by his kinsman's manner, and knowing the dependent relations of father and daughter, Breckenridge nodded and hurried away. Left to himself, Madison Clay ran his fingers through his hair, and straightened out the paper on which Salomy Jane had scrawled her note, turned it over, and wrote on the back:—

You might have told me you did it, and not leave your ole father to find it out how you disgraced yourself with him, too, by a low-down, underhanded, woman's trick! I've said I done it, and took the blame myself, and all the sneakiness of it that folks suspect. If I get away alive—and I don't care much which—you needn't foller. The house and stock are yours; but you ain't any longer the daughter of your disgraced father,

MADISON CLAY.

He had scarcely finished the note when, with a clatter of hoofs and a led horse, Breckenridge reappeared at the door elate and triumphant. "You're in nigger luck, Mad! I found that stole hoss of Judge Boompointer's had got away and strayed among your stock in the corral. Take him and you're safe; he can't be outrun this side of the state line."

"I ain't no hoss-thief," said Madison grimly.

"Nobody sez ye are, but you'd be wuss—a fool—ef you didn't take him. I'm testimony that you found him among your hosses; I'll tell Judge Boompointer you've got him, and ye kin send him back when you're safe. The judge will be mighty glad to get him back, and call it quits. So ef you've writ to Salomy Jane, come."

Madison Clay no longer hesitated. Salomy Jane might return at any moment,—it would be part of her "fool womanishness,"—and he was in no mood to see her before a third party. He laid the note on the table, gave a hurried glance around the house, which he grimly believed he was leaving forever, and, striding to the door, leaped on the stolen horse, and swept away with his kinsman.

But that note lay for a week undisturbed on the table in full view of the open door. The house was invaded by leaves, pine cones, birds, and squirrels during the hot, silent, empty days, and at night by shy, stealthy creatures, but never again, day or night, by any of the Clay family. It was known in the district that Clay had flown across the state line, his daughter was believed to have joined him the next day, and the house was supposed to be locked up. It lay off the main road, and few passed that way. The starving cattle in the corral at last broke bounds and spread over the woods. And one night a stronger blast than usual swept through the house and carried the note from the table to the floor, where, whirled into a crack in the flooring, it slowly rotted.

But though the sting of her father's reproach was spared her, Salomy Jane had no need of the letter to know what had happened. For as she entered the woods in the dim light of that morning, she saw the figure of Dart gliding from the shadow of a pine towards her. The unaffected cry of joy that rose from her lips died there as she caught sight of his face in the open light.

"You are hurt," she said, clutching his arm passionately.

"No," he said. "But I wouldn't mind that if"—

"You're thinkin' I was afeard to come back last night when I heard the shootin', but I *did* come," she went on feverishly. "I ran back here when I heard the two shots, but you were gone. I went to the corral, but your hoss wasn't there, and I thought you'd got away."

"I *did* get away," said Dart gloomily. "I killed the man, thinkin' he was huntin' *me,* and forgettin' I was disguised. He thought I was your father."

"Yes," said the girl joyfully, "he was after dad, and *you* —you killed him." She again caught his hand admiringly.

But he did not respond. Possibly there were points of honor which this horse-thief felt vaguely with her father. "Listen," he said grimly. "Others think it was your father killed him. When *I* did it—for he fired at me first—I ran to the corral again and took my hoss, thinkin' I might be follered. I made a clear circuit of the house, and when I found he was the only one, and no one was follerin', I come back here and took off my disguise. Then I heard his friends find him in the wood, and I know they suspected your father. And then another man come through the woods while I was hidin' and found the clothes and took them away." He stopped and stared at her gloomily.

But all this was unintelligible to the girl. "Dad would have got the better of him ef you hadn't," she said eagerly, "so what's the difference?"

"All the same," he said gloomily, "I must take his place."

She did not understand, but turned her head to her master. "Then you'll go back with me and tell him *all*?" she said obediently.

"Yes," he said.

She put her hand in his, and they crept out of the wood together. She foresaw a thousand difficulties, but, chiefest of all, that he did not love as she did. *She* would not have taken these risks against their happiness.

But alas for ethics and heroism. As they were issuing from

the wood they heard the sound of galloping hoofs, and had barely time to hide themselves before Madison Clay, on the stolen horse of Judge Boompointer, swept past them with his kinsman.

Salomy Jane turned to her lover.

And here I might, as a moral romancer, pause, leaving the guilty, passionate girl eloped with her disreputable lover, destined to lifelong shame and misery, misunderstood to the last by a criminal, fastidious parent. But I am confronted by certain facts, on which this romance is based. A month later a handbill was posted on one of the sentinel pines, announcing that the property would be sold by auction to the highest bidder by Mrs. John Dart, daughter of Madison Clay, Esq., and it was sold accordingly. Still later—by ten years—the chronicler of these pages visited a certain "stock" or "breeding farm," in the "Blue Grass Country," famous for the popular racers it has produced. He was told that the owner was the "best judge of horseflesh in the country." "Small wonder," added his informant, "for they say as a young man out in California he was a horse-thief, and only saved himself by eloping with some rich farmer's daughter. But he's a straight-out and respectable man now, whose word about horses can't be bought; and as for his wife, *she's* a beauty! To see her at the 'Springs,' rigged out in the latest fashion, you'd never think she had ever lived out of New York or wasn't the wife of one of its millionaires."

UNCLE JIM
AND UNCLE BILLY

THEY were partners. The avuncular title was bestowed on them by Cedar Camp, possibly in recognition of a certain matured good humor, quite distinct from the spasmodic exuberant spirits of its other members, and possibly from what, to its youthful sense, seemed their advanced ages—which must have been at least forty! They had also set habits even in their improvidence, lost incalculable and unpayable sums to each other over euchre regularly every evening, and inspected their sluice-boxes punctually every Saturday for repairs—which they never made. They even got to resemble each other, after the fashion of old married couples, or, rather, as in matrimonial partnerships, were subject to the domination of the stronger character; although in their case it is to be feared that it was the feminine Uncle Billy—enthusiastic, imaginative, and loquacious—who swayed the masculine, steady-going, and practical Uncle Jim. They had lived in the camp since its foundation in 1849; there seemed to be no reason why they should not remain there until its inevitable evolution into a mining town. The younger members might leave through restless ambition or a desire for change or novelty; they were subject to no such trifling mutation. Yet Cedar Camp was surprised one day to hear that Uncle Billy was going away.

The rain was softly falling on the bark thatch of the cabin with a muffled murmur, like a sound heard through sleep.

The southwest trades were warm even at that altitude, as the open door testified, although a fire of pine bark was flickering on the adobe hearth and striking out answering fires from the freshly scoured culinary utensils on the rude sideboard, which Uncle Jim had cleaned that morning with his usual serious persistency. Their best clothes, which were interchangeable and worn alternately by each other on festal occasions, hung on the walls, which were covered with a coarse sailcloth canvas instead of lath-and-plaster, and were diversified by pictures from illustrated papers and stains from the exterior weather. Two "bunks," like ships' berths,—an upper and lower one,—occupied the gable-end of this single apartment, and on beds of coarse sacking, filled with dry moss, were carefully rolled their respective blankets and pillows. They were the only articles not used in common, and whose individuality was respected.

Uncle Jim, who had been sitting before the fire, rose as the square bulk of his partner appeared at the doorway with an armful of wood for the evening stove. By that sign he knew it was nine o'clock: for the last six years Uncle Billy had regularly brought in the wood at that hour, and Uncle Jim had as regularly closed the door after him, and set out their single table, containing a greasy pack of cards taken from its drawer, a bottle of whiskey, and two tin drinking-cups. To this was added a ragged memorandum-book and a stick of pencil. The two men drew their stools to the table.

"Hol' on a minit," said Uncle Billy.

His partner laid down the cards as Uncle Billy extracted from his pocket a pill-box, and, opening it, gravely took a pill. This was clearly an innovation on their regular proceedings, for Uncle Billy was always in perfect health.

"What's this for?" asked Uncle Jim half scornfully.

"Agin ager."

"You ain't got no ager," said Uncle Jim, with the assurance of intimate cognizance of his partner's physical condition.

"But it's a pow'ful preventive! Quinine! Saw this box at Riley's store, and laid out a quarter on it. We kin keep it here, comfortable, for evenings. It's mighty soothin' arter a man's done a hard day's work on the river-bar. Take one."

Uncle Jim gravely took a pill and swallowed it, and handed the box back to his partner.

"We'll leave it on the table, sociable like, in case any of the boys come in," said Uncle Billy, taking up the cards. "Well. How do we stand?"

Uncle Jim consulted the memorandum-book. "You were owin' me sixty-two thousand dollars on the last game, and the limit's seventy-five thousand!"

"Je whillikins!" ejaculated Uncle Billy. "Let me see."

He examined the book, feebly attempted to challenge the additions, but with no effect on the total. "We oughter hev made the limit a hundred thousand," he said seriously; "seventy-five thousand is only triflin' in a game like ours. And you've set down my claim at Angel's?" he continued.

"I allowed you ten thousand dollars for that," said Uncle Jim, with equal gravity, "and it's a fancy price too."

The claim in question being an unprospected hillside ten miles distant, which Uncle Jim had never seen, and Uncle Billy had not visited for years, the statement was probably true; nevertheless, Uncle Billy retorted:—

"Ye kin never tell how these things will pan out. Why, only this mornin' I was taking a turn round Shot Up Hill, that ye know is just rotten with quartz and gold, and I couldn't help thinkin' how much it was like my ole claim at Angel's. I must take a day off to go on there and strike a pick in it, if only for luck."

Suddenly he paused and said, "Strange, ain't it, you should speak of it to-night? Now I call that queer!"

He laid down his cards and gazed mysteriously at his companion. Uncle Jim knew perfectly that Uncle Billy had regularly once a week for many years declared his final determination to go over to Angel's and prospect his claim, yet nevertheless he half responded to his partner's suggestion of mystery, and a look of fatuous wonder crept into his eyes. But he contented himself by saying cautiously, "You spoke of it first."

"That's the more sing'lar," said Uncle Billy confidently. "And I've been thinking about it, and kinder seeing myself thar all day. It's mighty queer!" He got up and began to rummage among some torn and coverless books in the corner.

"Where's that 'Dream Book' gone to?"

"The Carson boys borrowed it," replied Uncle Jim. "Anyhow, yours wasn't no dream—only a kind o' vision, and the book don't take no stock in visions." Nevertheless, he watched his partner with some sympathy, and added, "That reminds me that I had a dream the other night of being in 'Frisco at a small hotel, with heaps o' money, and all the time being sort o' scared and bewildered over it."

"No?" queried his partner eagerly yet reproachfully. "You never let on anything about it to *me*! It's mighty queer you havin' these strange feelin's, for I've had 'em myself. And only to-night, comin' up from the spring, I saw two crows hopping in the trail, and I says, 'If I see another, it's luck, sure!' And you'll think I'm lyin', but when I went to the wood-pile just now there was the *third* one sittin' up on a log as plain as I see you. Tell 'e what, folks ken laugh—but that's just what Jim Filgee saw the night before he made the big strike!"

They were both smiling, yet with an underlying credulity

and seriousness as singularly pathetic as it seemed incongruous to their years and intelligence. Small wonder, however, that in their occupation and environment—living daily in an atmosphere of hope, expectation, and chance, looking forward each morning to the blind stroke of a pick that might bring fortune—they should see signs in nature and hear mystic voices in the trackless woods that surrounded them. Still less strange that they were peculiarly susceptible to the more recognized diversions of chance, and were gamblers on the turning of a card who trusted to the revelation of a shovelful of upturned earth.

It was quite natural, therefore, that they should return from their abstract form of divination to the table and their cards. But they were scarcely seated before they heard a crackling step in the brush outside, and the free latch of their door was lifted. A younger member of the camp entered. He uttered a peevish "Halloo!" which might have passed for a greeting, or might have been a slight protest at finding the door closed, drew the stool from which Uncle Jim had just risen before the fire, shook his wet clothes like a Newfoundland dog, and sat down. Yet he was by no means churlish nor coarse-looking, and this act was rather one of easy-going, selfish, youthful familiarity than of rudeness. The cabin of Uncles Billy and Jim was considered a public right or "common" of the camp. Conferences between individual miners were appointed there. "I'll meet you at Uncle Billy's" was a common tryst. Added to this was a tacit claim upon the partners' arbitrative powers, or the equal right to request them to step outside if the interviews were of a private nature. Yet there was never any objection on the part of the partners, and to-night there was not a shadow of resentment of this intrusion in the patient, good-humored, tolerant eyes of Uncles Jim and Billy as they gazed at their guest. Perhaps there was a slight gleam of relief in Uncle Jim's when he found that the guest was unaccompanied by any one, and that it was not a tryst. It would have been unpleasant for the two partners to have stayed out in the rain while their guests were exchanging private confidences in their cabin. While there might have been no limit to their good will, there might have been some to their capacity for exposure.

Uncle Jim drew a huge log from beside the hearth and sat on the driest end of it, while their guest occupied the stool. The young man, without turning away from his discontented, peevish brooding over the fire, vaguely reached backward for the whiskey bottle and Uncle Billy's tin cup, to which he was assisted by the latter's hospitable hand. But on setting down the cup his eye caught sight of the pill-box.

"Wot's that?" he said, with gloomy scorn. "Rat poison?"

"Quinine pills—agin ager," said Uncle Jim. "The newest thing out. Keeps out damp like Injin-rubber! Take one to follow yer whiskey. Me and Uncle Billy wouldn't think o' settin' down, quiet like, in the evening arter work, without 'em. Take one—ye'r' welcome! We keep 'em out here for the boys."

Accustomed as the partners were to adopt and wear each other's opinions before folks, as they did each other's clothing, Uncle Billy was, nevertheless, astonished and delighted at Uncle Jim's enthusiasm over *his* pills. The guest took one and swallowed it.

"Mighty bitter!" he said, glancing at his hosts with the quick Californian suspicion of some practical joke. But the honest faces of the partners reassured him.

"That bitterness ye taste," said Uncle Jim quickly, "is whar the thing's gittin' in its work. Sorter sickenin' the malaria —and kinder water-proofin' the insides all to onct and at the same lick! Don't yer see? Put another in yer vest pocket; you'll be cryin' for 'em like a child afore ye get home. Thar! Well, how's things agoin' on your claim, Dick? Boomin', eh?"

The guest raised his head and turned it sufficiently to fling his answer back over his shoulder at his hosts. "I don't know what *you'd* call 'boomin',' " he said gloomily; "I suppose you two men sitting here comfortably by the fire, without caring whether school keeps or not, would call two feet of backwater over one's claim 'boomin' '; I reckon *you'd* consider a hundred and fifty feet of sluicing carried away, and drifting to thunder down the South Fork, something in the way of advertising to your old camp! I suppose *you'd* think it was an inducement to investors! I shouldn't wonder," he added still more gloomily, as a sudden dash of rain down the wide-throated chimney dropped in his tin cup—"and it would be just like you two chaps, sittin' there gormandizing over your quinine—if yer said this rain that's lasted three weeks was something to be proud of!"

It was the cheerful and the satisfying custom of the rest of the camp, for no reason whatever, to hold Uncle Jim and Uncle Billy responsible for its present location, its vicissitudes, the weather, or any convulsion of nature; and it was equally the partners' habit, for no reason whatever, to accept these animadversions and apologize.

"It's a rain that's soft and mellowin'," said Uncle Billy gently, "and supplin' to the sinews and muscles. Did ye ever notice, Jim,"—ostentatiously to his partner,—"did ye ever notice that you get inter a kind o' sweaty lather workin' in it? Sorter openin' to the pores!"

"Fetches 'em every time," said Uncle Jim. "Better nor fancy soap."

Their guest laughed bitterly. "Well, I'm going to leave

it to you. I reckon to cut the whole concern to-morrow, and 'lite' out for something new. It can't be worse than this."

The two partners looked grieved, albeit they were accustomed to these outbursts. Everybody who thought of going away from Cedar Camp used it first as a threat to these patient men, after the fashion of runaway nephews, or made an exemplary scene of their going.

"Better think twice afore ye go," said Uncle Billy.

"I've seen worse weather afore ye came," said Uncle Jim slowly. "Water all over the Bar; the mud so deep ye couldn't get to Angel's for a sack o' flour, and we had to grub on pine nuts and jackass-rabbits. And yet—we stuck by the camp, and here we are!"

The mild answer apparently goaded their guest to fury. He rose from his seat, threw back his long, dripping hair from his handsome but querulous face, and scattered a few drops on the partners. "Yes, that's just it. That's what gets me! Here you stick, and here you are! And here you'll stick and rust until you starve or drown! Here you are,—two men who ought to be out in the world, playing your part as grown men,—stuck here like children 'playing house' in the woods; playing work in your wretched mud-pie ditches, and content. Two men not so old that you mightn't be taking your part in the fun of the world, going to balls or theatres, or paying attention to girls, and yet old enough to have married and have your families around you, content to stay in this God-forsaken place; old bachelors, pigging together like poor-house paupers. That's what gets me! Say you *like* it? Say you expect by hanging on to make a strike—and what does that amount to? What are *your* chances? How many of us have made, or are making, more than grub wages? Say you're willing to share and share alike as you do—have you got enough for two? Aren't you actually living off each other?

Aren't you grinding each other down, choking each other's struggles, as you sink together deeper and deeper in the mud of this cussed camp? And while you're doing this, aren't you, by your age and position here, holding out hopes to others that you know cannot be fulfilled?"

Accustomed as they were to the half-querulous, half-humorous, but always extravagant, criticism of the others, there was something so new in this arraignment of themselves that the partners for a moment sat silent. There was a slight flush on Uncle Billy's cheek, there was a slight paleness on Uncle Jim's. He was the first to reply. But he did so with a certain dignity which neither his partner nor their guest had ever seen on his face before.

"As it's *our* fire that's warmed ye up like this, Dick Bullen," he said, slowly rising, with his hand resting on Uncle Billy's shoulder, "and as it's *our* whiskey that's loosened your tongue, I reckon we must put up with what ye'r' saying, just as we've managed to put up with our own way o' living, and not quo'll with ye under our own roof."

The young fellow saw the change in Uncle Jim's face and quickly extended his hand, with an apologetic backward shake of his long hair. "Hang it all, old man," he said, with a laugh of mingled contrition and amusement, "you mustn't mind what I said just now. I've been so worried thinking of things about *myself,* and, maybe, a little about you, that I quite forgot I hadn't a call to preach to anybody—least of all to you. So we part friends, Uncle Jim, and you too, Uncle Billy, and you'll forget what I said. In fact, I don't know why I spoke at all—only I was passing your claim just now, and wondering how much longer your old sluice-boxes would hold out, and where in thunder you'd get others when they caved in! I reckon that sent me off. That's all, old chap!"

Uncle Billy's face broke into a beaming smile of relief,

and it was *his* hand that first grasped his guest's; Uncle Jim quickly followed with as honest a pressure, but with eyes that did not seem to be looking at Bullen, though all trace of resentment had died out of them. He walked to the door with him, again shook hands, but remained looking out in the darkness some time after Dick Bullen's tangled hair and broad shoulders had disappeared.

Meantime, Uncle Billy had resumed his seat, and was chuckling and reminiscent as he cleaned out his pipe.

"Kinder reminds me of Jo Sharp, when he was cleaned out at poker by his own partners in his own cabin, comin' up here and bedevilin' *us* about it! What was it you lint him?"

But Uncle Jim did not reply; and Uncle Billy, taking up the cards, began to shuffle them, smiling vaguely, yet at the same time somewhat painfully. "Arter all, Dick was mighty cut up about what he said, and I felt kinder sorry for him. And, you know, I rather cotton to a man that speaks his mind. Sorter clears him out, you know, of all the slumgullion that's in him. It's just like washin' out a pan o' prospecting: you pour in the water, and keep slushing it round and round, and out comes first the mud and dirt, and then the gravel, and then the black sand, and then—it's all out, and there's a speck o' gold glistenin' at the bottom!"

"Then you think there *was* suthin' in what he said?" said Uncle Jim, facing about slowly.

An odd tone in his voice made Uncle Billy look up. "No," he said quickly, shying with the instinct of an easy, pleasure-loving nature from a possible grave situation. "No, I don't think he ever got the color! But wot are ye moonin' about for? Ain't ye goin' to play? It's mor' 'n half past nine now."

Thus adjured, Uncle Jim moved up to the table and sat

down, while Uncle Billy dealt the cards, turning up the Jack or right bower—but *without* that exclamation of delight which always accompanied his good fortune, nor did Uncle Jim respond with the usual corresponding simulation of deep disgust. Such a circumstance had not occurred before in the history of their partnership. They both played in silence,— a silence only interrupted by a larger splash of raindrops down the chimney.

"We orter put a couple of stones on the chimney-top, edgewise, like Jack Curtis does. It keeps out the rain without interferin' with the draft," said Uncle Billy musingly.

"What's the use if"—

"If what?" said Uncle Billy quietly.

"If we don't make it broader," said Uncle Jim half wearily.

They both stared at the chimney, but Uncle Jim's eye followed the wall around to the bunks. There were many discolorations on the canvas, and a picture of the Goddess of Liberty from an illustrated paper had broken out in a kind of damp, measly eruption. "I'll stick that funny handbill of the 'Washin' Soda' I got at the grocery store the other day right over the Liberty gal. It's a mighty perty woman washin' with short sleeves," said Uncle Billy. "That's the comfort of them picters, you kin always get somethin' new, and it adds thickness to the wall."

Uncle Jim went back to the cards in silence. After a moment he rose again, and hung his overcoat against the door.

"Wind's comin' in," he said briefly.

"Yes," said Uncle Billy cheerfully, "but it wouldn't seem nat'ral if there wasn't that crack in the door to let the sunlight in o' mornin's. Makes a kind o' sundial, you know. When the streak o' light's in that corner, I say 'six o'clock!' when it's across the chimney I say 'seven!' and so 't is!"

It certainly had grown chilly, and the wind was rising.

The candle guttered and flickered; the embers on the hearth brightened occasionally, as if trying to dispel the gathering shadows, but always ineffectually. The game was frequently interrupted by the necessity of stirring the fire. After an interval of gloom, in which each partner successively drew the candle to his side to examine his cards, Uncle Jim said:—

"Say?"

"Well!" responded Uncle Billy.

"Are you sure you saw that third crow on the wood-pile?"

"Sure as I see you now—and a darned sight plainer. Why?"

"Nothin', I was just thinkin'. Look here! How do we stand now?"

Uncle Billy was still losing. "Nevertheless," he said cheerfully, "I'm owin' you a matter of sixty thousand dollars."

Uncle Jim examined the book abstractedly. "Suppose," he said slowly, but without looking at his partner,—"suppose, as it's gettin' late now, we play for my half share of the claim agin the limit—seventy thousand—to square up."

"Your half share!" repeated Uncle Billy, with amused incredulity.

"My half share of the claim,—of this yer house, you know, —one half of all that Dick Bullen calls our rotten starvation property," reiterated Uncle Jim, with a half smile.

Uncle Billy laughed. It was a novel idea; it was, of course, "all in the air," like the rest of their game, yet even then he had an odd feeling that he would have liked Dick Bullen to have known it. "Wade in, old pard," he said. "I'm on it."

Uncle Jim lit another candle to reinforce the fading light, and the deal fell to Uncle Billy. He turned up Jack of clubs. He also turned a little redder as he took up his cards, looked at them, and glanced hastily at his partner. "It's no use playing," he said. "Look here!" He laid down his cards on the table. They were the ace, king and queen of clubs, and Jack of spades,—or left bower,—which, with the turned-up Jack of clubs,—or right bower,—comprised *all* the winning cards!

"By jingo! If we'd been playin' four-handed, say you an' me agin some other ducks, we'd have made 'four' in that deal, and h'isted some money—eh?" and his eyes sparkled. Uncle Jim, also, had a slight tremulous light in his own.

"Oh, no! I didn't see no three crows this afternoon," added Uncle Billy gleefully, as his partner, in turn, began to shuffle the cards with laborious and conscientious exactitude. Then dealing, he turned up a heart for trumps.

Uncle Billy took up his cards one by one, but when he had finished his face had become as pale as it had been red before. "What's the matter?" said Uncle Jim quickly, his own face growing white.

Uncle Billy slowly and with breathless awe laid down his cards, face up on the table. It was exactly the same sequence *in hearts,* with the knave of a diamonds added. He could again take every trick.

They stared at each other with vacant faces and a half-drawn smile of fear. They could hear the wind moaning in the trees beyond; there was a sudden rattling at the door. Uncle Billy started to his feet, but Uncle Jim caught his arm. "*Don't leave the cards!* It's only the wind; sit down," he said in a low, awe-hushed voice, "it's your deal; you were two before, and two now, that makes your four; you've only one point to make to win the game. Go on."

They both poured out a cup of whiskey, smiling vaguely, yet with a certain terror in their eyes. Their hands were cold; the cards slipped from Uncle Billy's benumbed fingers; when he had shuffled them he passed them to his partner to shuffle them also, but did not speak. When Uncle Jim had shuffled them methodically he handed them back fatefully to his partner. Uncle Billy dealt them with a trembling hand. He turned up a club. "If you are sure of these tricks, you know you've won," said Uncle Jim in a voice that was scarcely audible. Uncle Billy did not reply, but tremulously laid down the ace and right and left bowers.

He had won!

A feeling of relief came over each, and they laughed hysterically and discordantly. Ridiculous and childish as their contest might have seemed to a looker-on, to each the tension had been as great as that of the greatest gambler, without the gambler's trained restraint, coolness, and composure. Uncle Billy nervously took up the cards again.

"Don't," said Uncle Jim gravely; "it's no use—the luck's gone now."

"Just one more deal," pleaded his partner.

Uncle Jim looked at the fire, Uncle Billy hastily dealt, and threw the two hands face up on the table. They were the ordinary average cards. He dealt again, with the same result. "I told you so," said Uncle Jim, without looking up.

It certainly seemed a tame performance after their wonderful hands, and after another trial Uncle Billy threw the cards aside and drew his stool before the fire. "Mighty queer, warn't it?" he said, with reminiscent awe. "Three times running. Do you know, I felt a kind o' creepy feelin' down my back all the time. Criky! what luck! None of the boys would believe if it we told 'em—least of all that Dick Bullen, who don't believe in luck, anyway. Wonder what he'd have said! and, Lord! how he'd have looked! Wall! what are you starin' so for?"

Uncle Jim had faced around, and was gazing at Uncle Billy's good-humored, simple face. "Nothin'!" he said briefly, and his eyes again sought the fire.

"Then don't look as if you was seein' suthin'—you give me the creeps," returned Uncle Billy a little petulantly. "Let's turn in, afore the fire goes out!"

The fateful cards were put back into the drawer, the table shoved against the wall. The operation of undressing was quickly got over, the clothes they wore being put on top of their blankets. Uncle Billy yawned, "I wonder what kind of a dream I'll have to-night—it oughter be suthin' to explain that luck." This was his "good-night" to his partner. In a few moments he was sound asleep.

Not so Uncle Jim. He heard the wind gradually go down, and in the oppressive silence that followed could detect the deep breathing of his companion and the far-off yelp of a coyote. His eyesight becoming accustomed to the semi-darkness, broken only by the scintillation of the dying embers of their fire, he could take in every detail of their sordid cabin and the rude environment in which they had lived so long. The dismal patches on the bark roof, the wretched make-shifts of each day, the dreary prolongation of discomfort, were all plain to him now, without the sanguine hope that had made them bearable. And when he shut his eyes upon them, it was only to travel in fancy down the steep mountain-side that he had trodden so often to the dreary claim on the overflowed river, to the heaps of "tailings" that encumbered it, like empty shells of the hollow, profitless days spent there, which they were always waiting for the stroke of good fortune to clear away. He saw again the rotten "sluicing," through whose hopeless rifts and holes even their scant daily earnings had become scantier. At last he arose, and with infinite gentleness let himself down from his berth without disturbing his sleeping partner, and wrapping himself in his blanket, went to the door, which he noiselessly opened. From the position of a few stars that were glittering in the northern sky he knew that it was yet scarcely midnight; there were still long, restless hours before the day! In the feverish state into which he had gradually worked himself it seemed to him impossible to wait the coming of the dawn.

But he was mistaken. For even as he stood there all nature seemed to invade his humble cabin with its free and fragrant breath, and invest him with its great companionship. He felt again, in that breath, that strange sense of freedom, that mystic touch of partnership with the birds and beasts, the shrubs and trees, in this greater home before him. It was this vague communion that had kept him there, that still held these world-sick, weary workers in their rude cabins on the slopes around him; and he felt upon his brow that balm that had nightly lulled him and them to sleep and forgetfulness. He closed the door, turned away, crept as noiselessly as before into his bunk again, and presently fell into a profound slumber.

But when Uncle Billy awoke the next morning he saw it was late; for the sun, piercing the crack of the closed door, was sending a pencil of light across the cold hearth, like a match to rekindle its dead embers. His first thought was of his strange luck the night before, and of disappointment that he had not had the dream of divination that he had looked for. He sprang to the floor, but as he stood upright his glance fell on Uncle Jim's bunk. It was empty. Not only that, but his *blankets*—Uncle Jim's own particular blankets —*were gone*!

A sudden revelation of his partner's manner the night before struck him now with the cruelty of a blow; a sudden intelligence, perhaps the very divination he had sought, flashed upon him like lightning! He glanced wildly around the cabin. The table was drawn out from the wall a little ostentatiously, as if to catch his eye. On it was lying the stained chamois-skin purse in which they had kept the few grains of gold remaining from their last week's "clean up." The grains had been carefully divided, and half had been taken! But near it lay the little memorandum-book, open, with the stick of pencil lying across it. A deep line was drawn across the page on which was recorded their imaginary extravagant gains and losses, even to the entry of Uncle Jim's half share of the claim which he had risked and lost! Underneath were hurriedly scrawled the words:—

"Settled by *your* luck, last night, old pard.—JAMES FOSTER."

It was nearly a month before Cedar Camp was convinced that Uncle Billy and Uncle Jim had dissolved partnership. Pride had prevented Uncle Billy from revealing his suspicions of the truth, or of relating the events that preceded Uncle Jim's clandestine flight, and Dick Bullen had gone to Sacramento by stagecoach the same morning. He briefly gave out that his partner had been called to San Francisco on important business of their own, that indeed might necessitate his own removal there later. In this he was singularly assisted by a letter from the absent Jim, dated at San Francisco, begging him not to be anxious about his success, as he had hopes of presently entering into a profitable business, but with no further allusions to his precipitate departure, nor any suggestion of a reason for it. For two or three days Uncle Billy was staggered and bewildered; in his profound simplicity he wondered if his extraordinary good fortune that night had made him deaf to some explanation of his partner's, or, more terrible, if he had shown some "low" and incredible intimation of taking his partner's extravagant bet as *real* and binding. In this distress he wrote to Uncle Jim an appealing and apologetic letter, albeit somewhat incoherent and inaccurate, and bristling with misspelling, camp slang, and old partnership jibes. But to this elaborate epistle he received only Uncle Jim's repeated assurances of his own bright prospects, and his hopes that his old partner would be more fortunate, single-handed, on the old claim. For a whole week or two Uncle Billy sulked, but his invincible optimism and good humor got the better of him, and he thought only of his old partner's good fortune. He wrote him regularly, but always to one address—a box at the San Francisco post-office, which to the simple-minded Uncle Billy suggested a certain official importance. To these letters Uncle Jim responded regularly but briefly.

From a certain intuitive pride in his partner and his affection, Uncle Billy did not show these letters openly to the camp, although he spoke freely of his former partner's promising future, and even read them short extracts. It is needless to say that the camp did not accept Uncle Billy's story with unsuspecting confidence. On the contrary, a hundred surmises, humorous or serious, but always extravagant, were afloat in Cedar Camp. The partners had quarreled over their clothes—Uncle Jim, who was taller than Uncle Billy, had refused to wear his partner's trousers. They had quarreled over cards—Uncle Jim had discovered that Uncle Billy was in possession of a "cold deck," or marked pack. They had quarreled over Uncle Billy's carelessness in grinding up half a box of "bilious pills" in the morning's coffee. A gloomily imaginative mule-driver had darkly suggested that, as no one had really seen Uncle Jim leave the camp, he was still there, and his bones would yet be found in one of the ditches; while a still more credulous miner averred that what he had thought was the cry of a screech-owl the night previous to Uncle Jim's disappearance, might have been the agonized utterance of that murdered man. It was highly characteristic of that camp—and, indeed, of others in California—that nobody, not even the ingenious theorists themselves, believed their story, and that no one took the slightest pains to verify or disprove it. Unhappily, Uncle Billy never knew it, and moved all unconsciously in this atmosphere of burlesque suspicion. And then a singular change took place in the attitude of the camp towards him and the disrupted partnership. Hitherto, for no reason whatever, all had agreed to put the blame upon Billy—possibly because he was present to receive it. As days passed that slight reticence and dejection in his manner, which they had at first attributed to remorse and a guilty conscience, now began to tell as absurdly in his favor. Here was poor Uncle Billy toiling through the ditches, while his selfish partner was lolling in the lap of luxury in San Francisco! Uncle Billy's glowing accounts of Uncle Jim's success only contributed to the sympathy now fully given in his behalf and their execration of the absconding partner. It was proposed at Biggs's store that a letter expressing the indignation of the camp over his heartless conduct to his late partner, William Fall, should be forwarded to him. Condolences were offered to Uncle Billy, and uncouth attempts were made to cheer his loneliness. A procession of half a dozen men twice a week to his cabin, carrying their own whiskey and winding up with a "stag dance" before the premises, was sufficient to lighten his eclipsed gayety and remind him of a happier past. "Surprise" working parties visited his claim with spasmodic essays towards helping him, and great good humor and hilarity prevailed. It was not an unusual thing for an honest miner to arise from an idle gathering in some cabin and excuse himself with the remark that he "reckoned he'd put in an hour's work in Uncle Billy's tailings!" And yet, as before, it was very improbable if any of these reckless benefactors *really* believed in their own earnestness or in the gravity of the situation. Indeed, a kind of hopeful cynicism ran through their performances. "Like as not, Uncle Billy is still in 'cahoots' [*i. e.,* shares] with his old pard, and is just laughin' at us as he's sendin' him accounts of our tomfoolin'."

And so the winter passed and the rains, and the days of cloudless skies and chill starlit nights began. There were still freshets from the snow reservoirs piled high in the Sierran passes, and the Bar was flooded, but that passed too, and only the sunshine remained. Monotonous as the seasons were, there was a faint movement in the camp with the stirring of the sap in the pines and cedars. And then, one day, there was a strange excitement on the Bar. Men were seen running hither and thither, but mainly gathering in a crowd on Uncle Billy's claim, that still retained the old partner's names in "The Fall and Foster." To add to the excitement, there was the quickly repeated report of a revolver, to all appearance aimlessly exploded in the air by some one on the outskirts of the assemblage. As the crowd opened, Uncle Billy appeared, pale, hysterical, breathless, and staggering a little under the back-slapping and hand-shaking of the whole camp. For Uncle Billy had "struck it rich"—had just discovered a "pocket," roughly estimated to be worth fifteen thousand dollars!

Although in that supreme moment he missed the face of his old partner, he could not help seeing the unaffected delight and happiness shining in the eyes of all who surrounded him. It was characteristic of that sanguine but uncertain life that success and good fortune brought no jealousy nor envy to the unfortunate, but was rather a promise and prophecy of the fulfillment of their own hopes. The gold was there— Nature but yielded up her secret. There was no prescribed limit to her bounty. So strong was this conviction that a long-suffering but still hopeful miner, in the enthusiasm of the moment, stooped down and patted a large boulder with the apostrophic "Good old gal!"

Then followed a night of jubilee, a next morning of hurried consultation with a mining expert and speculator lured to the camp by the good tidings; and then the very next night —to the utter astonishment of Cedar Camp—Uncle Billy, with a draft for twenty thousand dollars in his pocket, started for San Francisco, and took leave of his claim and the camp forever!

When Uncle Billy landed at the wharves of San Francisco he was a little bewildered. The Golden Gate beyond was obliterated by the incoming sea-fog, which had also roofed in the whole city, and lights already glittered along the gray streets that climbed the grayer sand-hills. As a Western man, brought up by inland rivers, he was fascinated and thrilled by the tall-masted sea-going ships, and he felt a strange sense of the remoter mysterious ocean, which he had never seen. But he was impressed and startled by smartly dressed men and women, the passing of carriages, and a sudden conviction that he was strange and foreign to what he saw. It had been his cherished intention to call upon his old partner in his working clothes, and then clap down on the table before him a draft for ten thousand dollars as *his* share of their old claim. But in the face of these brilliant strangers a sudden and unexpected timidity came upon him. He had heard of a cheap popular hotel, much frequented by the returning gold-miner, who entered its hospitable doors—which held an easy access to shops—and emerged in a few hours a gorgeous butterfly of fashion, leaving his old chrysalis behind him. Thence he inquired his way; hence he afterwards issued in garments glaringly new and ill fitting. But he had not sacrificed his beard, and there was still something fine and original in his handsome weak face that overcame the cheap convention of his clothes. Making his way to the post-office, he was again discomfited by the great size of the building, and bewildered by the array of little square letter-boxes behind glass which occupied one whole wall, and an equal number of opaque and locked wooden ones legibly numbered. His heart leaped; he remembered the number, and before him was a window with a clerk behind it. Uncle Billy leaned forward.

"Kin you tell me if the man that box 690 b'longs to is in?"

The clerk stared, made him repeat the question, and then turned away. But he returned almost instantly, with two or three grinning heads besides his own, apparently set behind his shoulders. Uncle Billy was again asked to repeat his question. He did so.

"Why don't you go and see if 690 is in his box?" said the first clerk, turning with affected asperity to one of the others.

The clerk went away, returned, and said with singular gravity, "He was there a moment ago, but he's gone out to stretch his legs. It's rather crampin' at first; and he can't stand it more than ten hours at a time, you know."

But simplicity has its limits. Uncle Billy had already guessed his real error in believing his partner was officially connected with the building; his cheek had flushed and then paled again. The pupils of his blue eyes had contracted into suggestive black points. "Ef you'll let me in at that winder, young fellers," he said, with equal gravity, "I'll show yer how I kin make *you* small enough to go in a box without crampin'! But I only wanted to know where Jim Foster *lived*."

At which the first clerk became perfunctory again, but civil. "A letter left in his box would get you that information," he said, "and here's paper and pencil to write it now."

Uncle Billy took the paper and began to write, "Just got

here. Come and see me at"—He paused. A brilliant idea had struck him; he could impress both his old partner and the upstarts at the window; he would put in the name of the latest "swell" hotel in San Francisco, said to be a fairy dream of opulence. He added "the Oriental," and without folding the paper shoved it in the window.

"Don't you want an envelope?" asked the clerk.

"Put a stamp on the corner of it," responded Uncle Billy, laying down a coin, "and she'll go through." The clerk smiled, but affixed the stamp, and Uncle Billy turned away.

But it was a short-lived triumph. The disappointment at finding Uncle Jim's address conveyed no idea of his habitation seemed to remove him farther away, and lose his identity in the great city. Besides, he must now make good his own address, and seek rooms at the Oriental. He went thither. The furniture and decorations, even in these early days of hotel-building in San Francisco, were extravagant and overstrained, and Uncle Billy felt lost and lonely in his strange surroundings. But he took a handsome suite of rooms, unhesitatingly paid for them in advance, and then, half frightened, walked out of them to ramble vaguely through the city in the feverish hope of meeting his old partner. At night his inquietude increased; he could not face the long row of tables in the pillared dining-room, filled with smartly dressed men and women; he evaded his bedroom, with its brocaded satin chairs and its gilt bedstead, and fled to his modest lodgings at the Good Cheer House, and appeased his hunger at its cheap restaurant, in the company of retired miners and freshly arrived Eastern emigrants. Two or three days passed thus in this quaint double existence. Three or four times a day he would enter the gorgeous Oriental with affected ease and carelessness, demand his key from the hotel-clerk, ask for the letter that did not come, go to his room, gaze vaguely from his window on the passing crowd below for the partner he could not find, and then return to the Good Cheer House for rest and sustenance. On the fourth day he received a short note from Uncle Jim; it was couched in his usual sanguine but brief and business-like style. He was very sorry, but important and profitable business took him out of town, but he trusted to return soon and welcome his old partner. He was also, for the first time, jocose, and hoped that Uncle Billy would not "see all the sights" before he, Uncle Jim, returned. Disappointing as this procrastination was to Uncle Billy, a gleam of hope irradiated it: the letter had bridged over that gulf which seemed to yawn between them at the post-office. His old partner had accepted his visit to San Francisco without question, and had alluded to a renewal of their old intimacy. For Uncle Billy, with all his trustful simplicity, had been tortured by two harrowing doubts: one, whether Uncle Jim in his new-fledged smartness as a "city" man—such as he saw in the streets—would care for his rough companionship; the other, whether he, Uncle Billy, ought not to tell him at once of his changed fortune. But, like all weak, unreasoning men, he clung desperately to a detail—he could not forego his old idea of astounding Uncle Jim by giving him his share of the "strike" as his first intimation of it, and he doubted, with more reason, perhaps, if Jim would see him after he had heard of his good fortune. For Uncle Billy had still a frightened recollection of Uncle Jim's sudden stroke for independence, and that rigid punctiliousness which had made him doggedly accept the responsibility of his extravagant stake at euchre.

With a view of educating himself for Uncle Jim's company, he "saw the sights" of San Francisco—as an overgrown and somewhat stupid child might have seen them —with great curiosity, but little contamination or corruption.

But I think he was chiefly pleased with watching the arrival of the Sacramento and Stockton steamers at the wharves, in the hope of discovering his old partner among the passengers on the gang-plank. Here, with his old superstitious tendency and gambler's instinct, he would augur great success in his search that day if any one of the passengers bore the least resemblance to Uncle Jim, if a man or woman stepped off first, or if he met a single person's questioning eye. Indeed, this got to be the real occupation of the day, which he would on no account have omitted, and to a certain extent revived each day in his mind the morning's work of their old partnership. He would say to himself, "It's time to go and look up Jim," and put off what he was pleased to think were his pleasures until this act of duty was accomplished.

In this singleness of purpose he made very few and no entangling acquaintances, nor did he impart to any one the secret of his fortune, loyally reserving it for his partner's first knowledge. To a man of his natural frankness and simplicity this was a great trial, and was, perhaps, a crucial test of his devotion. When he gave up his rooms at the Oriental—as not necessary after his partner's absence—he sent a letter, with his humble address, to the mysterious lock-box of his partner without fear or false shame. He would explain it all when they met. But he sometimes treated unlucky and returning miners to a dinner and a visit to the gallery of some theatre. Yet while he had an active sympathy with and understanding of the humblest, Uncle Billy, who for many years had done his own and his partner's washing, scrubbing, mending, and cooking, and saw no degradation in it, was somewhat inconsistently irritated by menial functions in men, and although he gave extravagantly to waiters, and threw a dollar to the crossing-sweeper, there was always a certain shy avoidance of them in his manner. Coming from the theatre one night

Uncle Billy was, however, seriously concerned by one of these crossing-sweepers turning hastily before them and being knocked down by a passing carriage. The man rose and limped hurriedly away; but Uncle Billy was amazed and still more irritated to hear from his companion that this kind of menial occupation was often profitable, and that at some of the principal crossings the sweepers were already rich men.

But a few days later brought a more notable event to Uncle Billy. One afternoon in Montgomery Street he recognized in one of its smartly dressed frequenters a man who had a few years before been a member of Cedar Camp. Uncle Billy's childish delight at this meeting, which seemed to bridge over his old partner's absence, was, however, only half responded to by the ex-miner, and then somewhat satirically. In the fullness of his emotion, Uncle Billy confided to him that he was seeking his old partner, Jim Foster, and, reticent of his own good fortune, spoke glowingly of his partner's brilliant expectations, but deplored his inability to find him. And just now he was away on important business. "I reckon he's got back," said the man dryly. "I didn't know he had a lock-box at the post-office, but I can give you his other address. He lives at the Presidio, at Washerwoman's Bay." He stopped and looked with a satirical smile at Uncle Billy. But the latter, familiar with California mining-camp nomenclature, saw nothing strange in it, and merely repeated his companion's words.

"You'll find him there! Good-by! So long! Sorry I'm in a hurry," said the ex-miner, and hurried away.

Uncle Billy was too delighted with the prospect of a speedy meeting with Uncle Jim to resent his former associate's supercilious haste, or even to wonder why Uncle Jim had not informed him that he had returned. It was not the first time that he had felt how wide was the gulf between himself and these others, and the thought drew him closer to his old partner, as well as his old idea, as it was now possible to surprise him with the draft. But as he was going to surprise him in his own boarding-house—probably a handsome one—Uncle Billy reflected that he would do so in a certain style.

He accordingly went to a livery stable and ordered a landau and pair, with a Negro coachman. Seated in it, in his best and most ill-fitting clothes, he asked the coachman to take him to the Presidio, and leaned back in the cushions as they drove through the streets with such an expression of beaming gratification on his good-humored face that the passers-by smiled at the equipage and its extravagant occupant. To them it seemed the not unusual sight of the successful miner "on a spree." To the unsophisticated Uncle Billy their smiling seemed only a natural and kindly recognition of his happiness, and he nodded and smiled back to them with unsuspecting candor and innocent playfulness. "These yer 'Frisco fellers ain't *all* slouches, you bet," he added to himself half aloud, at the back of the grinning coachman.

Their way led through well-built streets to the outskirts, or rather to that portion of the city which seemed to have been overwhelmed by shifting sand-dunes, from which half-submerged fences and even low houses barely marked the line of highway. The resistless trade-winds which had marked this change blew keenly in his face and slightly chilled his ardor. At a turn in the road the sea came in sight, and sloping towards it the great Cemetery of Lone Mountain, with white shafts and marbles that glittered in the sunlight like the sails of ships waiting to be launched down that slope into the Eternal Ocean. Uncle Billy shuddered. What if it had been his fate to seek Uncle Jim there!

"Dar's yar Presidio!" said the Negro coachman a few moments later, pointing with his whip, "and dar's yar Wash'-woman's Bay!"

Uncle Billy stared. A huge quadrangular fort of stone with a flag flying above its battlements stood at a little distance, pressed against the rocks, as if beating back the encroaching surges; between him and the fort but farther inland was a lagoon with a number of dilapidated, rudely patched cabins or cottages, like stranded driftwood around its shore. But there was no mansion, no block of houses, no street, not another habitation or dwelling to be seen!

Uncle Billy's first shock of astonishment was succeeded by a feeling of relief. He had secretly dreaded a meeting with his old partner in the "haunts of fashion"; whatever was the cause that made Uncle Jim seek this obscure retirement affected him but slightly; he even was thrilled with a vague memory of the old shiftless camp they had both abandoned. A certain instinct—he knew not why, or less still that it might be one of delicacy—made him alight before they reached the first house. Bidding the carriage wait, Uncle Billy entered, and was informed by a blowzy Irish laundress at a tub that Jim Foster, or "Arkansaw Jim," lived at the fourth shanty "beyant." He was at home, for "he'd shprained his fut." Uncle Billy hurried on, stopped before the door of a shanty scarcely less rude than their old cabin, and half timidly pushed it open. A growling voice from within, a figure that rose hurriedly, leaning on a stick, with an attempt to fly, but in the same moment sank back in a chair with an hysterical laugh —and Uncle Billy stood in the presence of his old partner! But as Uncle Billy darted forward, Uncle Jim rose again, and this time with outstretched hands. Uncle Billy caught them, and in one supreme pressure seemed to pour out and transfuse his whole simple soul into his partner's. There they swayed each other backwards and forwards and sideways by their still clasped hands, until Uncle Billy, with a glance at Uncle Jim's bandaged ankle, shoved him by sheer force down into his chair.

Uncle Jim was the first to speak. "Caught, b'gosh! I mighter known you'd be as big a fool as me! Look you, Billy Fall, do you know what you've done? You've druv me out er the streets whar I was makin' an honest livin', by day, on three crossin's! Yes," he laughed forgivingly, "you druv me out er it, by day, jest because I reckoned that some time I might run into your darned fool face,"—another laugh and a grasp of the hand,—"and then, b'gosh! not content with ruinin' my business *by day,* when I took to it at night, *you* took to goin' out at nights too, and so put a stopper on me there! Shall I tell you what else you did? Well, by the holy poker! I owe this sprained foot to your darned foolishness and my own, for it was getting away from *you* one night after the theatre that I got run into and run over!

"Ye see," he went on, unconscious of Uncle Billy's paling face, and with a naïveté, though perhaps not a delicacy, equal to Uncle Billy's own, "I had to play roots on you with that lock-box business and these letters, because I didn't want you to know what I was up to, for you mightn't like it, and might think it was lowerin' to the old firm, don't yer see? I wouldn't hev gone into it, but I was played out, and I don't mind tellin' you *now,* old man, that when I wrote you that first chipper letter from the lock-box I hedn't eat anythin' for two days. But it's all right *now,*" with a laugh. "Then I got into this business—thinkin' it nothin'—jest the very last thing—and do you know, old pard, I couldn't tell anybody but *you*—and, in fact, I kept it jest to tell you—I've made nine hundred and fifty-six dollars—Yes, sir, *nine hundred and fifty-six dollars!* solid money, in Adams and Co.'s Bank, just out er my trade."

"Wot trade?" asked Uncle Billy.

Uncle Jim pointed to the corner, where stood a large, heavy, crossing-sweeper's broom. "That trade."

"Certingly," said Uncle Billy, with a quick laugh.

"It's an outdoor trade," said Uncle Jim gravely, but with no suggestion of awkwardness or apology in his manner; "and thar ain't much difference between sweepin' a crossin' with a broom and rakin' over tailin' with a rake, *only—wot ye get* with a broom, *you have handed to ye,* and ye don't have to *pick it up and fish it out er* the wet rocks and sluice-gushin'; and it's a heap less tirin' to the back."

"Certingly, you bet!" said Uncle Billy enthusiastically, yet with a certain nervous abstraction.

"I'm glad ye say so; for yer see I didn't know at first how you'd tumble to my doing it, until I'd made my pile. And ef I hadn't made it, I wouldn't hev set eyes on ye again, old pard—never!"

"Do you mind my runnin' out a minit," said Uncle Billy, rising. "You see, I've got a friend waitin' for me outside—and I reckon"—he stammered—"I'll jest run out and send him off, so I kin talk comf'ble to ye."

"Ye ain't got anybody you're owin' money to," said Uncle Jim earnestly, "anybody follerin' you to get paid, eh? For I kin jest set down right here and write ye off a check on the bank!"

"No," said Uncle Billy. He slipped out of the door, and ran like a deer to the waiting carriage. Thrusting a twenty-dollar gold-piece into the coachman's hand, he said hoarsely, "I ain't wantin' that kerridge just now; ye ken drive around and hev a private jamboree all by yourself the rest of the afternoon, and then come and wait for me at the top o' the hill yonder."

Thus quit of his gorgeous equipage, he hurried back to Uncle Jim, grasping his ten-thousand dollar draft in his pocket. He was nervous, he was frightened, but he must get rid of the draft and his story, and have it over. But before he could speak, he was unexpectedly stopped by Uncle Jim.

"Now, look yer, Billy boy!" said Uncle Jim; "I got suthin' to say to ye—and I might as well clear it off my mind at once, and then we can start fair agin. Now," he went on, with a half laugh, "wasn't it enough for *me* to go on pretendin' I was rich and doing a big business, and gettin' up that lock-box dodge so as ye couldn't find out whar I hung out and what I was doin'—wasn't it enough for *me* to go on with all this play-actin', but *you,* you long-legged or'nary cuss! must get up and go to lyin' and play-actin', too!"

"*Me* play-actin'? *Me* lyin'?" gasped Uncle Billy.

Uncle Jim leaned back in his chair and laughed. "Do you think you could fool *me?* Do you think I didn't see through your little game o' going to that swell Oriental, jest as if ye'd made a big strike—and all the while ye wasn't sleepin' or eatin' there, but jest wrastlin' her hash and having a roll down at the Good Cheer! Do you think I didn't spy on ye and find that out? Oh, you long-eared jackass-rabbit!"

He laughed until the tears came into his eyes, and Uncle Billy laughed too, albeit until the laugh on his face became quite fixed, and he was fain to bury his head in his handkerchief.

"And yet," said Uncle Jim, with a deep breath, "gosh! I was frighted—jest for a minit! I thought, mebbe, you *had* made a big strike—when I got your first letter—and I made up my mind what I'd do! And then I remembered you was jest that kind of an open sluice that couldn't keep anythin' to yourself, and you'd have been sure to have yelled it out to *me* the first thing. So I waited. And I found you out, you old sinner!" He reached forward and dug Uncle Billy in the ribs.

"What *would* you hev done?" said Uncle Billy, after an hysterical collapse.

Uncle Jim's face grew grave again. "I'd hev—I'd—hev cl'ared out! Out er 'Frisco! out er Californy! out er Ameriky! I couldn't have stud it! Don't think I would hev begrudged ye yer luck! No man would have been gladder than me." He leaned forward again, and laid his hand caressingly upon his partner's arm—"Don't think I'd hev wanted to take a penny of it—but I—thar! I *couldn't* hev stood up under it! To hev had *you,* you that I left behind, comin' down here rollin' in wealth and new partners and friends, and arrive upon me—and this shanty—and"—he threw towards the corner of the room a terrible gesture, none the less terrible that it was illogical and inconsequent to all that had gone before—"and—and—*that broom!*"

There was a dead silence in the room. With it Uncle Billy seemed to feel himself again transported to the homely cabin at Cedar Camp and that fateful night, with his partner's strange, determined face before him as then. He even fancied that he heard the roaring of the pines without, and did not know that it was the distant sea.

But after a minute Uncle Jim resumed:—

"Of course you've made a little raise somehow, or you wouldn't be here?"

"Yes," said Uncle Billy eagerly. "Yes! I've got"—He stopped and stammered. "I've got—a—few hundreds."

"Oh, oh!" said Uncle Jim cheerfully. He paused, and then added earnestly, "I say! You ain't got left, over and above your d—d foolishness at the Oriental, as much as five hundred dollars?"

"I've got," said Uncle Billy, blushing a little over his first deliberate and affected lie,—"I've got at least five hundred and seventy-two dollars. Yes," he added tentatively, gazing anxiously at his partner, "I've got at least that."

"Je whillikins!" said Uncle Jim, with a laugh. Then eagerly, "Look here, pard! Then we're on velvet! I've got *nine* hundred; put your *five* with that, and I know a little ranch that we can get for twelve hundred. That's what I've been savin' up for—that's my little game! No more minin' for *me*. It's got a shanty twice as big as our old cabin, nigh on a hundred acres, and two mustangs. We can run it with two Chinamen and jest make it howl! Wot yer say—eh?" He extended his hand.

"I'm in," said Uncle Billy, radiantly grasping Uncle Jim's. But his smile faded, and his clear, simple brow wrinkled in two lines.

Happily Uncle Jim did not notice it. "Now, then, old pard," he said brightly, "we'll have a gay old time to-night—one of our jamborees! I've got some whiskey here and a deck o' cards, and we'll have a little game, you understand, but not for 'keeps' now! No, siree; we'll play for beans."

A sudden light illuminated Uncle Billy's face again, but he said, with a grim desperation, "Not to-night! I've got to go into town. That fren' o' mine expects me to go to the theayter, don't ye see? But I'll be out to-morrow at sun-up, and we'll fix up this thing o' the ranch."

"Seems to me you're kinder stuck on this fren'," grunted Uncle Jim.

Uncle Billy's heart bounded at his partner's jealousy. "No —but I *must*, you know," he returned, with a faint laugh.

"I say—it ain't a *her*, is it?" said Uncle Jim.

Uncle Billy achieved a diabolical wink and a creditable blush at his lie.

"Billy?"

"Jim!"

And under cover of this festive gallantry Uncle Billy escaped. He ran through the gathering darkness, and toiled up the shifting sands to the top of the hill, where he found the carriage waiting.

"Wot," said Uncle Billy in a low confidential tone to the coachman,—"wot do you 'Frisco fellers allow to be the best, biggest, and riskiest gamblin'-saloon here? Suthin' high-toned, you know?"

The Negro grinned. It was the usual case of the extravagant spendthrift miner, though perhaps he had expected a different question and order.

"Dey is de 'Polka,' de 'El Dorado,' and de 'Arcade' saloon, boss," he said, flicking his whip meditatively. "Most gents from de mines prefer de 'Polka,' for dey is dancing wid de gals frown in. But de real *prima facie* place for gents who go for buckin' agin de tiger and straight-out gamblin' is de 'Arcade.'"

"Drive there like thunder!" said Uncle Billy, leaping into the carriage.

True to his word, Uncle Billy was at his partner's shanty early the next morning. He looked a little tired, but happy, and had brought a draft with him for five hundred and seventy-five dollars, which he explained was the total of his capital. Uncle Jim was overjoyed. They would start for Napa that very day, and conclude the purchase of the ranch; Uncle Jim's sprained foot was a sufficient reason for his giving up his present vocation, which he could also sell at a small profit. His domestic arrangements were very simple; there was nothing to take with him—there was everything to leave behind. And that afternoon, at sunset, the two reunited partners were seated on the deck of the Napa boat as she swung into the stream.

Uncle Billy was gazing over the railing with a look of abstracted relief towards the Golden Gate, where the sinking sun seemed to be drawing towards him in the ocean a golden stream that was forever pouring from the Bay and the three-hilled city beside it. What Uncle Billy was thinking of, or what the picture suggested to him, did not transpire; for Uncle Jim, who, emboldened by his holiday, was luxuriating in an evening paper, suddenly uttered a long-drawn whistle, and moved closer to his abstracted partner. "Look yer," he said, pointing to a paragraph he had evidently jest read, "just you listen to this, and see if we ain't lucky, you and me, to be jest wot we air—trustin' to our own hard work—and not thinkin' o' 'strikes' and 'fortins.' Jest unbutton yer ears, Billy, while I reel off this yer thing I've jest struck in the paper, and see what d—d fools some men kin make o' themselves. And that theer reporter wot wrote it—must hev seed it reely!"

Uncle Jim cleared his throat, and holding the paper close to his eyes read aloud slowly:—

" 'A scene of excitement that recalled the palmy days of '49 was witnessed last night at the Arcade saloon. A stranger, who might have belonged to that reckless epoch, and who bore every evidence of being a successful Pike County miner out on a "spree," appeared at one of the tables with a negro coachman bearing two heavy bags of gold. Selecting a faro-bank as his base of operations, he began to bet heavily and with apparent recklessness, until his play excited the breathless attention of every one. In a few moments he had won a sum variously estimated at from eighty to a hundred thousand dollars. A rumor went round the room that it was a concerted attempt to "break the bank" rather than the

drunken freak of a Western miner, dazzled by some successful strike. To this theory the man's careless and indifferent
bearing towards his extraordinary gains lent great credence.
The attempt, if such it was, however, was unsuccessful. After
winning ten times in succession the luck turned, and the unfortunate "bucker" was cleared out not only of his gains, but
of his original investment, which may be placed roughly at
twenty thousand dollars. This extraordinary play was witnessed by a crowd of excited players, who were less impressed
by the magnitude of the stakes than by the perfect *sang-froid*
and recklessness of the player, who, it is said, at the close of
the game tossed a twenty-dollar gold-piece to the banker and
smilingly withdrew. The man was not recognized by any of
the *habitués* of the place.'

"There!" said Uncle Jim, as he hurriedly slurred over the
French substantive at the close, "did ye ever see such God-
forsaken foolishness?"

Uncle Billy lifted his abstracted eyes from the current, still
pouring its unreturning gold into the sinking sun, and said,
with a deprecatory smile, "Never!"

Nor even in the days of prosperity that visited the Great
Wheat Ranch of "Fall and Foster" did he ever tell his secret
to his partner.

DICK SPINDLER'S
FAMILY CHRISTMAS

THERE was surprise and sometimes disappointment in Rough and Ready, when it was known that Dick Spindler intended to give a "family" Christmas party at his own house. That he should take an early opportunity to cele-brate his good fortune and show hospitality was only ex-pected from the man who had just made a handsome "strike" on his claim; but that it should assume so conservative, old-fashioned, and respectable a form was quite unlooked-for by Rough and Ready, and was thought by some a trifle pretentious. There were not half-a-dozen families in Rough and Ready; nobody ever knew before that Spindler had any relations, and this "ringing in" of strangers to the settle-ment seemed to indicate at least a lack of public spirit. "He might," urged one of his critics, "hev given the boys,—that had worked alongside o' him in the ditches by day, and slung lies with him around the camp-fire by night,—he might hev given them a square 'blow out,' and kep' the leavin's for his old Spindler crew, just as other families do. Why, when old man Scudder had his house-raisin' last year, his family lived for a week on what was left over, arter the boys had waltzed through the house that night,—and the Scudders warn't strangers, either." It was also evident that there was an uneasy feeling that Spindler's action indicated an unhal-lowed leaning towards the minority of respectability and ex-clusiveness, and a desertion—without the excuse of matri mony—of the convivial and independent bachelor majority of Rough and Ready.

"Ef he was stuck after some gal and was kinder looking ahead, I'd hev understood it," argued another critic.

"Don't ye be too sure he ain't," said Uncle Jim Starbuck gloomily. "Ye'll find that some blamed woman is at the bottom of this yer 'family' gathering. That and trouble is almost all they're made for!"

There happened to be some truth in this dark prophecy, but none of the kind that the misogynist supposed. In fact, Spindler had called a few evenings before at the house of the Rev. Mr. Saltover, and Mrs. Saltover, having one of her "Saleratus headaches," had turned him over to her widow sister, Mrs. Huldy Price, who obediently bestowed upon him that practical and critical attention which she divided with the stocking she was darning. She was a woman of thirty-five, of singular nerve and practical wisdom, who had once smuggled her wounded husband home from a border affray, calmly made coffee for his deceived pursuers while he lay hidden in the loft, walked four miles for that medical assistance which arrived too late to save him, buried him secretly in his own "quarter section," with only one other witness and mourner, and so saved her position and property in that wild community, who believed he had fled. There was very little of this experience to be traced in her round, fresh-colored brunette cheek, her calm black eyes, set in a prickly hedge of stiff lashes, her plump figure, or her frank, courageous laugh. The latter appeared as a smile when she welcomed Mr. Spindler. "She hadn't seen him for a coon's age," but "reckon he was busy fixin' up his new house."

"Well, yes," said Spindler, with a slight hesitation, "ye see, I'm reckonin' to hev a kinder Christmas gatherin' of my"— he was about to say "folks," but dismissed it for "relations," and finally settled upon "relatives" as being more correct in a preacher's house.

Mrs. Price thought it a very good idea. Christmas was the natural season for the family to gather to "see who's here and who's there, who's gettin' on and who isn't, and who's dead and buried. It was lucky for them who were so placed that they could do so and be joyful." Her invincible philosophy probably carried her past any dangerous recollections of the lonely grave in Kansas, and holding up the stocking to the light, she glanced cheerfully along its level to Mr. Spindler's embarrassed face by the fire.

"Well, I can't say much ez to that," responded Spindler, still awkwardly, "for you see I don't know much about it anyway."

"How long since you've seen 'em?" asked Mrs. Price, apparently addressing herself to the stocking.

Spindler gave a weak laugh. "Well, you see, ef it comes to that, I've never seen 'em!"

Mrs. Price put the stocking in her lap and opened her direct eyes on Spindler. "Never seen 'em?" she repeated. "Then, they're not near relations?"

"There are three cousins," said Spindler, checking them off on his fingers, "a half-uncle, a kind of brother-in-law,— that is, the brother of my sister-in-law's second husband,— and a niece. That's six."

"But if you've not seen them, I suppose they've corresponded with you?" said Mrs. Price.

"They've nearly all of 'em written to me for money, seeing my name in the paper ez hevin' made a strike," returned Spindler simply; "and hevin' sent it, I jest know their addresses."

"Oh!" said Mrs. Price, returning to the stocking.

Something in the tone of her ejaculation increased Spindler's embarrassment, but it also made him desperate. "You see, Mrs. Price," he blurted out, "I oughter tell ye that I reckon they are the folks that 'hevn't got on,' don't you see, and so it seemed only the square thing for me, ez had 'got on,' to give them a sort o' Christmas festival. Suthin', don't ye know, like what your brother-in-law was sayin' last Sunday in the pulpit about this yer peace and goodwill 'twixt man and man."

Mrs. Price looked again at the man before her. His sallow, perplexed face exhibited some doubt, yet a certain determination, regarding the prospect the quotation had opened to him. "A very good idea, Mr. Spindler, and one that does you great credit," she said gravely.

"I'm mighty glad to hear you say so, Mrs. Price," he said, with an accent of great relief, "for I reckoned to ask you a great favor! You see," he fell into his former hesitation, "that is—the fact is—that this sort o' thing is rather suddent to me,—a little outer my line, don't you see, and I was goin' to ask ye ef you'd mind takin' the hull thing in hand and runnin' it for me."

"Runnin' it for you," said Mrs. Price, with a quick eyeshot from under the edge of her lashes. "Man alive! What are you thinking of?"

"Bossin' the whole job for me," hurried on Spindler, with nervous desperation. "Gettin' together all the things and makin' ready for 'em,—orderin' in everythin' that's wanted, and fixin' up the rooms,—I kin step out while you're doin' it,—and then helpin' me receivin' 'em, and sittin' at the head o' the table, you know,—like ez ef you was the mistress."

"But," said Mrs. Price, with her frank laugh, "that's the duty of one of your relations,—your niece, for instance,—or cousin, if one of them is a woman."

"But," persisted Spindler, "you see, they're strangers to

me; I don't know 'em, and I do you. You'd make it easy for
'em,—and for me,—don't you see? Kinder introduce 'em,—
don't you know? A woman of your gin'ral experience would
smooth down all them little difficulties," continued Spindler, with a vague recollection of the Kansas story, "and put
everybody on velvet. Don't say 'No,' Mrs. Price! I'm just
calkilatin' on you."

Sincerity and persistency in a man goes a great way with
even the best of women. Mrs. Price, who had at first received
Spindler's request as an amusing originality, now began to
incline secretly towards it. And, of course, began to suggest
objections.

"I'm afraid it won't do," she said thoughtfully, awakening to the fact that it would do and could be done. "You
see, I've promised to spend Christmas at Sacramento with my
nieces from Baltimore. And then there's Mr. Saltover and
my sister to consult."

But here Spindler's simple face showed such signs of distress that the widow declared she would "think it over,"—a
process which the sanguine Spindler seemed to consider so
nearly akin to talking it over that Mrs. Price began to believe
it herself, as he hopefully departed.

She "thought it over" sufficiently to go to Sacramento and
excuse herself to her nieces. But here she permitted herself
to "talk it over," to the infinite delight of those Baltimore
girls, who thought this extravaganza of Spindler's "so Californian and eccentric!" So that it was not strange that presently the news came back to Rough and Ready, and his old
associates learned for the first time that he had never seen
his relatives, and that they would be doubly strangers. This
did not increase his popularity; neither, I grieve to say, did
the intelligence that his relatives were probably poor, and
that the Reverend Mr. Saltover had approved of his course,

and had likened it to the rich man's feast, to which the halt and blind were invited. Indeed, the allusion was supposed to add hypocrisy and a bid for popularity to Spindler's defection, for it was argued that he might have feasted "Wall-eyed Joe" or "Tanglefoot Billy,"—who had once been "chawed" by a bear while prospecting,—if he had been sincere. Howbeit, Spindler's faith was oblivious to these criticisms, in his joy at Mr. Saltover's adhesion to his plans and the loan of Mrs. Price as a hostess. In fact, he proposed to her that the invitations should also convey that information in the expression, "by the kind permission of the Rev. Mr. Saltover," as a guarantee of good faith, but the widow would have none of it. The invitations were duly written and dispatched.

"Suppose," suggested Spindler, with a sudden lugubrious apprehension,—"suppose they shouldn't come?"

"Have no fear of that," said Mrs. Price, with a frank laugh.

"Or ef they was dead," continued Spindler.

"They couldn't all be dead," said the widow cheerfully.

"I've written to another cousin by marriage," said Spindler dubiously, "in case of accident; I didn't think of him before, because he was rich."

"And have you ever seen him either, Mr. Spindler?" asked the widow, with a slight mischievousness.

"Lordy! No!" he responded, with unaffected concern.

Only one mistake was made by Mrs. Price in her arrangements for the party. She had noticed what the simple-minded Spindler could never have conceived,—the feeling towards him held by his old associates, and had tactfully suggested that a general invitation should be extended to them in the evening.

"You can have refreshments, you know, too, after the dinner, and games and music."

"But," said the unsophisticated host, "won't the boys think
I'm playing it rather low down on them, so to speak, givin'
'em a kind o' second table, as ef it was the tailings after
a strike?"

"Nonsense," said Mrs. Price, with decision. "It's quite
fashionable in San Francisco, and just the thing to do."

To this decision Spindler, in his blind faith in the widow's
management, weakly yielded. An announcement in the
"Weekly Banner" that, "On Christmas evening Richard
Spindler, Esq., proposed to entertain his friends and fellow
citizens at an 'at home,' in his own residence," not only
widened the breach between him and the "boys," but awakened an active resentment that only waited for an outlet.
It was understood that they were all coming; but that they
should have "some fun out of it" which might not coincide
with Spindler's nor his relatives' sense of humor seemed a
foregone conclusion.

Unfortunately, too, subsequent events lent themselves to
this irony of the situation. A few mornings after the invitations were dispatched, Spindler, at one of his daily conferences with Mrs. Price, took a newspaper from his pocket.
"It seems," he said, looking at her with an embarrassed
gravity, "that we will have to take one o' them names off
that list,—the name o' Sam Spindler,—and calkilate upon
only six relations coming."

"Ah," said Mrs. Price interestedly, "then you have had
an answer, and he has declined?"

"Not that exactly," said Spindler slowly, "but from remarks in this yer paper, he was hung last week by the
Vigilance Committee of Yolo."

Mrs. Price opened her eyes on Spindler's face as she took the paper from his hand. "But," she said quickly, "this may be all a mistake, some other Spindler! You know, you say you've never seen them!"

"I reckon it's no mistake," said Spindler, with patient gravity, "for the Committee sent me back my invitation, with the kinder disparagin' remark that they've 'sent him where it ain't bin the habit to keep Christmas!'"

Mrs. Price gasped, but a glance at Spindler's patient, wistful, inquiring eyes brought back her old courage. "Well," she said cheerfully, "perhaps it's just as well he didn't come."

"Are ye sure o' that, Mrs. Price?" said Spindler, with a slightly troubled expression. "Seems to me, now, that he was the sort as might hev bin gathered in at the feast, and kinder snatched like a brand from the burnin', accordin' to Scripter. But ye know best."

"Mr. Spindler," said Mrs. Price suddenly, with a slight snap in her black eyes, "are your—are the others like this? Or"—here her eyes softened again, and her laugh returned, albeit slightly hysterical—"is this kind of thing likely to happen again?"

"I think we're pretty sartin o' hevin' six to dinner," returned Spindler simply. Then, as if noticing some other significance in her speech, he added wistfully, "But you won't go back on me, Mrs. Price, ef things ain't pannin' out exackly as I reckoned? You see, I never really knew these yer relations."

He was so obviously sincere in his intent, and, above all, seemed to place such a pathetic reliance on her judgment, that she hesitated to let him know the shock his revelation had given her. And what might his other relations prove to be? Good Lord! Yet, oddly enough, she was so prepossessed by him, and so fascinated by his very Quixotism, that it was perhaps for these complex reasons that she said a little stiffly:—

"One of these cousins, I see, is a lady, and then there is your niece. Do you know anything about them, Mr. Spindler?"

His face grew serious. "No more than I know of the others," he said apologetically. After a moment's hesitation he went on: "Now you speak of it, it seems to me I've heard that my niece was di-vorced. But," he added, brightening up, "I've heard that she was popular."

Mrs. Price gave a short laugh, and was silent for a few minutes. Then this sublime little woman looked up at him. What he might have seen in her eyes was more than he expected, or, I fear, deserved. "Cheer up, Mr. Spindler," she said manfully. "I'll see you through this thing, don't you mind! But don't you say anything about—about—this Vigilance Committee business to anybody. Nor about your niece —it was your niece, wasn't it?—being divorced. Charley [the late Mr. Price] had a queer sort of sister, who—but that's neither here nor there! And your niece mayn't come, you know; or if she does, you ain't bound to bring her out to the general company."

At parting, Spindler, in sheer gratefulness, pressed her hand, and lingered so long over it that a little color sprang into the widow's brown cheek. Perhaps a fresh courage sprang into her heart, too, for she went to Sacramento the next day, previously enjoining Spindler on no account to show any answers he might receive. At Sacramento her nieces flew to her with confidences.

"We so wanted to see you, Aunt Huldy, for we've heard something so delightful about your funny Christmas Party!" Mrs. Price's heart sank, but her eyes snapped. "Only think cf it! One of Mr. Spindler's long-lost relatives—a Mr. Wragg

—lives in this hotel, and papa knows him. He's a sort of half-uncle, I believe, and he's just furious that Spindler should have invited him. He showed papa the letter; said it was the greatest piece of insolence in the world; that Spindler was an ostentatious fool, who had made a little money and wanted to use him to get into society; and the fun of the whole thing was that this half-uncle and whole brute is himself a parvenu, —a vulgar, ostentatious creature, who was only a"—

"Never mind what he was, Kate," interrupted Mrs. Price hastily. "I call his conduct a shame."

"So do we," said both girls eagerly. After a pause Kate clasped her knees with her locked fingers, and rocking backwards and forwards said, "Milly and I have got an idea, and don't you say 'No' to it. We've had it ever since that brute talked in that way. Now, through him we know more about this Mr. Spindler's family connections than you do; and we know all the trouble you and he'll have in getting up this party. You understand? Now, we first want to know what Spindler's like. Is he a savage, bearded creature, like the miners we saw on the boat?"

Mrs. Price said that, on the contrary, he was very gentle, soft-spoken, and rather good-looking.

"Young or old?"

"Young,—in fact, a mere boy, as you may judge from his actions," returned Mrs. Price, with a suggestive matronly air.

Kate here put up a long-handled eyeglass to her fine gray eyes, fitted it ostentatiously over her aquiline nose, and then said, in a voice of simulated horror, "Aunt Huldy,—this revelation is shocking!"

Mrs. Price laughed her usual frank laugh, albeit her brown cheek took upon it a faint tint of Indian red. "If that's the wonderful idea you girls have got, I don't see how it's going to help matters," she said dryly.

"No, that's not it! We really have an idea. Now look here."

Mrs. Price "looked here." This process seemed to the superficial observer to be merely submitting her waist and shoulders to the arms of her nieces, and her ears to their confidential and coaxing voices.

Twice she said "it couldn't be thought of," and "it was impossible"; once addressed Kate as "You limb!" and finally said that she "wouldn't promise, but might write!"

It was two days before Christmas. There was nothing in the air, sky, or landscape of that Sierran slope to suggest the season to the Eastern stranger. A soft rain had been dropping for a week on laurel, pine, and buckeye, and the blades of springing grasses and shyly opening flowers. Sedate and silent hillsides that had grown dumb and parched towards the end of the dry season became gently articulate again; there were murmurs in hushed and forgotten cañons, the leap and laugh of water among the dry bones of dusty creeks, and the full song of the larger forks and rivers. Southwest winds brought the warm odor of the pine sap swelling in the forest, or the faint, far-off spice of wild mustard springing in the lower valleys. But, as if by some irony of Nature, this gentle invasion of spring in the wild wood brought only disturbance and discomfort to the haunts and works of man. The ditches were overflowed, the fords of the Fork impassable, the sluicing adrift, and the trails and wagon roads to Rough and Ready knee-deep in mud. The stagecoach from Sacramento, entering the settlement by the mountain highway, its wheels and panels clogged and crusted with an unctuous pigment like mud and blood, passed out of it through the overflowed and dangerous ford, and emerged in spotless purity, leaving its stains behind with Rough and Ready. A week of enforced idleness on the river "Bar" had driven the miners to the more comfortable recreation of the saloon bar, its mirrors, its florid paintings, its armchairs, and its stove. The steam of their wet boots and the smoke of their pipes hung over the latter like the sacrificial incense from an altar. But the attitude of the men was more critical and censorious than contented, and showed little of the gentleness of the weather or season.

"Did you hear if the stage brought down any more relations of Spindler's?"

The bar-keeper, to whom this question was addressed, shifted his lounging position against the bar and said, "I reckon not, ez far ez I know."

"And that old bloat of a second cousin—that crimson beak—what kem down yesterday,—he ain't bin hangin' round here to-day for his reg'lar pizon?"

"No," said the bar-keeper thoughtfully, "I reckon Spindler's got him locked up, and is settin' on him to keep him sober till after Christmas, and prevent you boys gettin' at him."

"He'll have the jimjams before that," returned the first speaker; "and how about that dead beat of a half-nephew who borrowed twenty dollars of Yuba Bill on the way down, and then wanted to get off at Shootersville, but Bill wouldn't let him, and scooted him down to Spindler's and collected the money from Spindler himself afore he'd give him up?"

"He's up thar with the rest of the menagerie," said the bar-keeper, "but I reckon that Mrs. Price hez bin feedin' him up. And ye know the old woman—that fifty-fifty cousin by marriage—whom Joe Chandler swears he remembers ez an old cook for a Chinese restaurant in Stockton,—darn my skin ef that Mrs. Price hasn't rigged her out in some fancy duds of her own, and made her look quite decent."

A deep groan here broke from Uncle Jim Starbuck.

"Didn't I tell ye?" he said, turning appealingly to the others. "It's that darned widow that's at the bottom of it all! She first put Spindler up to givin' the party, and now, darn my skin, ef she ain't goin' to fix up these ragamuffins and drill 'em so we can't get any fun outer 'em after all! And it's bein' a woman that's bossin' the job, and not Spindler, we've got to draw things mighty fine and not cut up too rough, or some of the boys will kick."

"You bet," said a surly but decided voice in the crowd.

"And," said another voice, "Mrs. Price didn't live in 'Bleeding Kansas' for nothing."

"Wot's the programme you've settled on, Uncle Jim?" said the bar-keeper lightly, to check what seemed to promise a dangerous discussion.

"Well," said Starbuck, "we calkilate to gather early Christmas night in Hooper's Hollow and rig ourselves up Injun fashion, and then start for Spindler's with pitch-pine torches, and have a 'torchlight dance' around the house; them who does the dancin' and yellin' outside takin' their turn at goin' in and hevin' refreshment. Jake Cooledge, of Boston, sez if anybody objects to it, we've only got to say we're 'Mummers of the Olden Times,' sabe? Then, later, we'll have 'Them Sabbath Evening Bells' performed on prospectin' pans by the band. Then, at the finish, Jake Cooledge is goin' to give one of his surkastic speeches,—kinder welcomin' Spindler's family to the Free Openin' o' Spindler's Almshouse and Reformatory." He paused, possibly for that approbation which, however, did not seem to come spontaneously. "It ain't much," he added apologetically, "for we're hampered by women; but we'll add to the programme ez we see how things pan out. Ye see, from what we can hear, all of Spindler's relations ain't on hand yet! We've got to wait, like in elekshun times, for 'returns from the back counties.' Hello! What's that?"

It was the swish and splutter of hoofs on the road before the door. The Sacramento coach! In an instant every man was expectant, and Starbuck darted outside on the platform. Then there was the usual greeting and bustle, the hurried ingress of thirsty passengers into the saloon, and a pause. Uncle Jim returned, excitedly and pantingly. "Look yer, boys! Ef this ain't the richest thing out! They say there's two more relations o' Spindler's on the coach, come down as express freight, consigned,—d' ye hear?—consigned to Spindler!"

"Stiffs, in coffins?" suggested an eager voice.

"I didn't get to hear more. But here they are."

There was the sudden irruption of a laughing, curious crowd into the bar-room, led by Yuba Bill, the driver. Then the crowd parted, and out of their midst stepped two children, a boy and a girl, the oldest apparently of not more than six years, holding each other's hands. They were coarsely yet cleanly dressed, and with a certain uniform precision that suggested formal charity. But more remarkable than all, around the neck of each was a little steel chain, from which depended the regular check and label of the powerful Express Company, Wells, Fargo & Co., and the words: "To Richard Spindler." "Fragile." "With great care." "Collect on delivery." Occasionally their little hands went up automatically and touched their labels, as if to show them. They surveyed the crowd, the floor, the gilded bar, and Yuba Bill without fear and without wonder. There was a pathetic suggestion that they were accustomed to this observation.

"Now, Bobby," said Yuba Bill, leaning back against the bar, with an air half paternal, half managerial, "tell these gents how you came here."

"By Wellth, Fargoth Expreth," lisped Bobby.

"Whar from?"

"Wed Hill, Owegon."

"Red Hill, Oregon? Why, it's a thousand miles from here," said a bystander.

"I reckon," said Yuba Bill coolly, "they kem by stage to Portland, by steamer to 'Frisco, steamer again to Stockton, and then by stage over the whole line. Allers by Wells, Fargo & Co.'s Express, from agent to agent, and from messenger to messenger. Fact! They ain't bin tetched or handled by any one but the Kempany's agents; they ain't had a line or direction except them checks around their necks! And they've wanted for nothin' else. Why, I've carried heaps o' treasure before, gentlemen, and once a hundred thousand dollars in greenbacks, but I never carried anythin' that was watched and guarded as them kids! Why, the division inspector at Stockton wanted to go with 'em over the line; but Jim Bracy, the messenger, said he'd call it a reflection on himself and resign, ef they didn't give 'em to him with the other packages! Ye had a pretty good time, Bobby, didn't ye? Plenty to eat and drink, eh?"

The two children laughed a little weak laugh, turned each other bashfully around, and then looked up shyly at Yuba Bill and said, "Yeth."

"Do you know where you are goin'?" asked Starbuck, in a constrained voice.

It was the little girl who answered quickly and eagerly:—

"Yes, to Krissmass and Sandy Claus."

"To what?" asked Starbuck.

Here the boy interposed with a superior air:—

"Thee meanth Couthin Dick. He 'th got Krithmath."

"Where's your mother?"

"Dead."

"And your father?"

"In orthpittal."

There was a laugh somewhere on the outskirts of the crowd. Every one faced angrily in that direction, but the laughter had disappeared. Yuba Bill, however, sent his voice after him. "Yes, in hospital! Funny, ain't it?—amoosin' place! Try it. Step over here, and in five minutes, by the living Hoky, I'll qualify you for admission, and not charge you a cent!" He stopped, gave a sweeping glance of dissatisfaction around him, and then, leaning back against the bar, beckoned to some one near the door, and said in a disgusted tone, "You tell these galoots how it happened, Bracy. They make me sick!"

Thus appealed to, Bracy, the express messenger, stepped forward in Yuba Bill's place.

"It's nothing particular, gentlemen," he said, with a laugh, "only it seems that some man called Spindler, who lives about here, sent an invitation to the father of these children to bring his family to a Christmas party. It wasn't a bad sort of thing for Spindler to do, considering that they were his poor relations, though they didn't know him from Adam,—was it?" He paused; several of the bystanders cleared their throats, but said nothing. "At least," resumed Bracy, "that's what the boys up at Red Hill, Oregon, thought, when they heard of it. Well, as the father was in hospital with a broken leg, and the mother only a few weeks dead, the boys thought it mighty rough on these poor kids if they were done out of their fun because they had no one to bring them. The boys couldn't afford to go themselves, but they got a little money together, and then got the idea of sendin' 'em by express. Our agent at Red Hill tumbled to the idea at once; but he wouldn't take any money in advance, and said he would send 'em 'C. O. D.' like any other package. And he did, and here they are! That's all! And now, gentlemen, as I've got to deliver them personally to this Spindler, and get his receipt and take off their checks, I reckon we must toddle. Come, Bill, help take 'em up!"

"Hold on!" said a dozen voices. A dozen hands were thrust into a dozen pockets; I grieve to say some were regretfully withdrawn empty, for it was a hard season in Rough and Ready. But the expressman stepped before them, with warning, uplifted hand.

"Not a cent, boys,—not a cent! Wells, Fargo's Express Company don't undertake to carry bullion with those kids, at least on the same contract!" He laughed, and then, looking around him, said confidentially in a lower voice, which, however, was quite audible to the children, "There's as much as three bags of silver in quarter and half dollars in my treasure box in the coach that has been poured, yes, just showered upon them, ever since they started, and has been passed over from agent to agent and messenger to messenger,—enough to pay their passage from here to China! It's time to say quits now. But bet your life, they are not going to that Christmas party poor!"

He caught up the boy, as Yuba Bill lifted the little girl to his shoulder, and both passed out. Then one by one the loungers in the bar-room silently and awkwardly followed, and when the bar-keeper turned back from putting away his decanters and glasses, to his astonishment the room was empty.

Spindler's house, or "Spindler's Splurge," as Rough and Ready chose to call it, stood above the settlement, on a deforested hillside, which, however, revenged itself by producing not enough vegetation to cover even the few stumps that were ineradicable. A large wooden structure in the pseudo-classic style affected by Westerners, with an incongruous cupola, it was oddly enough relieved by a still more incongruous veranda extending around its four sides, upheld by wooden Doric columns, which were already picturesquely covered with flowering vines and sun-loving roses. Mr. Spindler had trusted the furnishing of its interior to the same contractor who had upholstered the gilded bar-room of the Eureka Saloon, and who had apparently bestowed the same design and material, impartially, on each. There were gilded mirrors all over the house and chilly marble-topped tables, gilt plaster Cupids in the corners, and stuccoed lions "in the way" everywhere. The tactful hands of Mrs. Price had screened some of these with seasonable laurels, fir boughs, and berries, and had imparted a slight Christmas flavor to the house. But the greater part of her time had been employed in trying to subdue the eccentricities of Spindler's amazing relations; in tranquilizing Mrs. "Aunt" Martha Spindler,— the elderly cook before alluded to,—who was inclined to regard the gilded splendors of the house as indicative of dangerous immorality; in restraining "Cousin" Morley Hewlett from considering the dining-room buffet as a bar for "intermittent refreshment"; and in keeping the weak-minded nephew, Phinney Spindler, from shooting at bottles from the veranda, wearing his uncle's clothes, or running up an account in his uncle's name for various articles at the general stores. Yet the unlooked-for arrival of the two children had been the one great compensation and diversion for her. She wrote at once to her nieces a brief account of her miraculous deliverance. "I think these poor children dropped from the skies here to make our Christmas party possible, to say nothing of the sympathy they have created in Rough and Ready for Spindler. He is going to keep them as long as he can, and is writing to the father. Think of the poor little tots traveling a thousand miles to 'Krissmass,' as they call it!—though they were so well cared for by the messengers that their little bodies were positively stuffed like quails. So you see, dear, we will be able to get along without airing your famous idea. I'm sorry, for I know you're just dying to see it all."

Whatever Kate's "idea" might have been, there certainly seemed now no need of any extraneous aid to Mrs. Price's management. Christmas came at last, and the dinner passed off without serious disaster. But the ordeal of the reception of Rough and Ready was still to come. For Mrs. Price well knew that although "the boys" were more subdued, and, indeed, inclined to sympathize with their host's uncouth endeavor, there was still much in the aspect of Spindler's relations to excite their sense of the ludicrous.

But here Fortune again favored the house of Spindler with a dramatic surprise, even greater than the advent of the children had been. In the change that had come over Rough and Ready, "the boys" had decided, out of deference to the women and children, to omit the first part of their programme, and had approached and entered the house as soberly and quietly as ordinary guests. But before they had shaken hands with the host and hostess, and seen the relations, the clatter of wheels was heard before the open door, and its lights flashed upon a carriage and pair,—an actual private carriage,—the like of which had not been seen since the governor of the State had come down to open the new ditch! Then there was a pause, the flash of the carriage lamp.

upon white silk, the light tread of a satin foot on the veranda and in the hall, and the entrance of a vision of loveliness! Middle-aged men and old dwellers of cities remembered their youth; younger men bethought themselves of Cinderella and the Prince! There was a thrill and a hush as this last guest—a beautiful girl, radiant with youth and adornment—put a dainty glass to her sparkling eye and advanced familiarly, with outstretched hand, to Dick Spindler. Mrs. Price gave a single gasp, and drew back speechless.

"Uncle Dick," said a laughing contralto voice, which, indeed, somewhat recalled Mrs. Price's own, in its courageous frankness, "I am so delighted to come, even if a little late, and so sorry that Mr. M'Kenna could not come on account of business."

Everybody listened eagerly, but none more eagerly and surprisingly than the host himself. M'Kenna! The rich cousin who had never answered the invitation! And Uncle Dick! This, then, was his divorced niece! Yet even in his astonishment he remembered that of course no one but himself and Mrs. Price knew it,—and that lady had glanced discreetly away.

"Yes," continued the half-niece brightly. "I came from Sacramento with some friends to Shootersville, and from thence I drove here; and though I must return tonight, I could not forego the pleasure of coming, if it was only for an hour or two, to answer the invitation of the uncle I have not seen for years." She paused, and, raising her glasses, turned a politely questioning eye towards Mrs. Price. "One of our relations?" she said smilingly to Spindler.

"No," said Spindler, with some embarrassment, "a—a friend!"

The half-niece extended her hand. Mrs. Price took it.

But the fair stranger,—what she did and said were the only

things remembered in Rough and Ready on that festive occasion; no one thought of the other relations; no one recalled them nor their eccentricities; Spindler himself was forgotten. People only recollected how Spindler's lovely niece lavished her smiles and courtesies on every one, and brought to her feet particularly the misogynist Starbuck and the sarcastic Cooledge, oblivious of his previous speech; how she sat at the piano and sang like an angel, hushing the most hilarious and excited into sentimental and even maudlin silence; how, graceful as a nymph, she led with "Uncle Dick" a Virginia reel until the whole assembly joined, eager for a passing touch of her dainty hand in its changes; how, when two hours had passed,—all too swiftly for the guests,—they stood with bared heads and glistening eyes on the veranda to see the fairy coach whirl the fairy princess away! How—but this incident was never known to Rough and Ready.

It happened in the sacred dressing-room, where Mrs. Price was cloaking with her own hands the departing half-niece of Mr. Spindler. Taking that opportunity to seize the lovely relative by the shoulders and shake her violently, she said: "Oh, yes, and it's all very well for you, Kate, you limb! For you're going away, and will never see Rough and Ready and poor Spindler again. But what am I to do, miss? How am I to face it out? For you know I've got to tell him at least that you're no half-niece of his!"

"Have you?" said the young lady.

"Have I?" repeated the widow impatiently. "Have I? Of course I have! What are you thinking of?"

"I was thinking, aunty," said the girl audaciously, "that from what I've seen and heard to-night, if I'm not his half-niece now, it's only a question of time! So you'd better wait. Good-night, dear."

And, really,—it turned out that she was right!

IT is to be feared that the hero of this chronicle began life as an impostor. He was offered to the credulous and sympathetic family of a San Francisco citizen as a lamb who, unless bought as a playmate for the children, would inevitably pass into the butcher's hands. A combination of refined sensibility and urban ignorance of nature prevented them from discerning certain glaring facts that betrayed his caprid origin. So a ribbon was duly tied round his neck, and in pleasing emulation of the legendary "Mary," he was taken to school by the confiding children. Here, alas! the fraud was discovered, and history was reversed by his being turned out by the teacher, because he was *not* "a lamb at school." Nevertheless, the kindhearted mother of the family persisted in retaining him, on the plea that he might yet become "useful." To her husband's feeble suggestion of "gloves," she returned a scornful negative, and spoke of the weakly infant of a neighbor, who might later receive nourishment from this providential animal. But even this hope was destroyed by the eventual discovery of his sex. Nothing remained now but to accept him as an ordinary kid, and to find amusement in his accomplishments,—eating, climbing, and butting. It must be confessed that these were of a superior quality; a capacity to eat everything from a cambric handkerchief to an election poster, an agility which brought him even to the roofs of houses, and a power of overturning by a single push the chubbiest child who opposed him, made him a fearful joy to the nursery. This last quality was incautiously developed in him by a negro boy-servant, who, later, was hurriedly propelled down a flight of stairs by his too proficient scholar. Having once tasted victory, "Billy" needed no further incitement to his performances. The small wagon he sometimes consented to draw for the benefit of the children never hindered his attempts to butt the passer-by. On the contrary, on well-known scientific principles he added the impact of the bodies of the children projected over his head in his charge, and the infelicitous pedestrian found himself not only knocked off his legs by Billy, but bombarded by the whole nursery.

Delightful as was this recreation to juvenile limbs, it was felt to be dangerous to the adult public. Indignant protestations were made, and as Billy could not be kept in the house, he may be said to have at last butted himself out of that sympathetic family and into a hard and unfeeling world. One morning he broke his tether in the small back yard. For several days thereafter he displayed himself in guilty freedom on the tops of adjacent walls and outhouses. The San Francisco suburb where his credulous protectors lived was still in a volcanic state of disruption, caused by the grading of new streets through rocks and sandhills. In consequence the roofs of some houses were on the level of the doorsteps of others, and were especially adapted to Billy's performances. One afternoon, to the admiring and perplexed eyes of the nursery, he was discovered standing on the apex of a neighbor's new Elizabethan chimney, on a space scarcely larger than the crown of a hat, calmly surveying the world beneath him. High infantile voices appealed to him in vain; baby arms were outstretched to him in hopeless invitation; he remained exalted and obdurate, like Milton's hero, probably by his own merit "raised to that bad eminence." Indeed, there was already something Satanic in his budding horns and pointed mask as the smoke curled softly around him. Then he appropriately vanished, and San Francisco knew him no more. At the same time, however, one Owen M'Ginnis, a neighboring sandhill squatter, also disappeared, leaving San Francisco for the southern mines, and he was said to have taken Billy with him,—for no conceivable reason except for companionship. Howbeit, it was the turning-point of Billy's career; such restraint as kindness, civilization, or even policemen had exercised upon his nature was gone. He retained, I fear, a certain wicked intelligence, picked up in San Francisco with the newspapers and theatrical and election posters he had consumed. He reappeared at Rocky Cañon among the miners as an exceedingly agile chamois, with the low cunning of a satyr. That was all that civilization had done for him!

If Mr. M'Ginnis had fondly conceived that he would make Billy "useful," as well as companionable, he was singularly mistaken. Horses and mules were scarce in Rocky Cañon, and he attempted to utilize Billy by making him draw a small cart, laden with auriferous earth, from his claim to the river. Billy, rapidly gaining strength, was quite equal to the task, but alas! not his inborn propensity. An incautious gesture from the first passing miner Billy chose to construe into the usual challenge. Lowering his head, from which his budding horns had been already pruned by his master, he instantly went for his challenger, cart and all. Again the scientific law already pointed out prevailed. With the shock of the onset the entire contents of the cart arose and poured over the astonished miner, burying him from sight. In any other but a Californian mining-camp such a propensity in a draught animal would have been condemned, on account of the damage and suffering it entailed, but in Rocky Cañon it proved unprofitable to the owner from the very amusement and interest it excited. Miners lay in wait for Billy with a "greenhorn," or new-comer, whom they would put up to challenge the animal by some indiscreet gesture. In this way hardly a cartload of "pay-gravel" ever arrived safely at its destination, and the unfortunate M'Ginnis was compelled to withdraw Billy as a beast of burden. It was whispered that so great had his propensity become, under repeated provocation, that M'Ginnis himself was no longer safe. Going ahead of his cart one day to remove a fallen bough from the trail, Billy construed the act of stooping into a playful challenge from his master,—with the inevitable result.

The next day M'Ginnis appeared with a wheelbarrow, but without Billy. From that day he was relegated to the rocky crags above the camp, from whence he was only lured occasionally by the mischievous miners, who wished to exhibit his peculiar performances. For although Billy had ample food and sustenance among the crags, he had still a civilized longing for posters; and whenever a circus, a concert, or a political meeting was "billed" in the settlement, he was on hand while the paste was yet fresh and succulent. In this way it was averred that he once removed a gigantic theatre bill setting forth the charms of the "Sacramento Pet," and being caught in the act by the advance agent, was pursued through the main street, carrying the damp bill on his horns, eventually affixing it, after his own peculiar fashion, on the back of Judge Boompointer, who was standing in front of his own court-house.

In connection with the visits of this young lady another story concerning Billy survives in the legends of Rocky Cañon. Colonel Starbottle was at that time passing through the settlement on election business, and it was part of his chivalrous admiration for the sex to pay a visit to the pretty actress. The single waiting-room of the little hotel gave upon the veranda, which was also level with the street. After a brief yet gallant interview, in which he oratorically expressed the gratitude of the settlement with old-fashioned Southern courtesy, Colonel Starbottle lifted the chubby little hand of the "Pet" to his lips, and, with a low bow, backed out upon the veranda. But the Pet was astounded by his instant reappearance, and by his apparently casting himself passionately and hurriedly at her feet! It is needless to say that he was followed closely by Billy, who from the street had casually noticed him, and construed his novel exit into an ungentlemanly challenge.

Billy's visits, however, became less frequent, and as Rocky Cañon underwent the changes incidental to mining settlements, he was presently forgotten in the invasion of a few Southwestern families, and the adoption of amusements less practical and turbulent than he had afforded. It was alleged that he was still seen in the more secluded fastnesses of the mountains, having reverted to a wild state, and it was suggested by one or two of the more adventurous that he might yet become edible, and a fair object of chase. A traveler through the Upper Pass of the cañon related how he had seen a savage-looking, hairy animal like a small elk perched upon inaccessible rocks, but always out of gunshot. But these and other legends were set at naught and overthrown by an unexpected incident.

The Pioneer Coach was toiling up the long grade towards Skinners Pass when Yuba Bill suddenly pulled up, with his feet on the brake.

"Jiminy!" he ejaculated, drawing a deep breath.

The startled passenger beside him on the box followed the direction of his eyes. Through an opening in the wayside pines he could see, a few hundred yards away, a cup-like hollow in the hillside of the vividest green. In the centre a young girl of fifteen or sixteen was dancing and keeping step to the castanet "click" of a pair of "bones," such as Negro minstrels use, held in her hands above her head. But, more singular still, a few paces before her a large goat, with its neck roughly wreathed with flowers and vines, was taking ungainly bounds and leaps in imitation of its companion. The wild background of the Sierras, the pastoral hollow, the incongruousness of the figures, and the vivid color of the girl's red flannel petticoat showing beneath her calico skirt, that had been pinned around her waist, made a striking picture, which by this time had attracted all eyes. Perhaps the dancing of the girl suggested a Negro "break-down" rather than any known sylvan measure; but all this, and even the clatter of the bones, was made gracious by the distance.

"Esmeralda! by the living Harry!" shouted the excited passenger on the box.

Yuba Bill took his feet off the brake, and turned a look of deep scorn upon his companion as he gathered the reins again.

"It's that blanked goat, outer Rocky Cañon beyond, and Polly Harkness! How did she ever come to take up with *him?*"

Nevertheless, as soon as the coach reached Rocky Cañon, the story was quickly told by the passengers, corroborated by Yuba Bill, and highly colored by the observer on the box-seat. Harkness was known to be a new-comer who lived with his wife and only daughter on the other side of Skinners Pass. He was a "logger" and charcoal-burner, who had eaten his way into the serried ranks of pines below the pass, and established in these efforts an almost insurmountable cordon of fallen trees, stripped bark, and charcoal pits around the clearing where his rude log hut stood,—which kept his seclusion unbroken. He was said to be a half-savage mountaineer from Georgia, in whose rude fastnesses he had distilled unlawful whiskey, and that his tastes and habits unfitted him for civilization. His wife chewed and smoked; he was believed to make a fiery brew of his own from acorns and pine nuts; he seldom came to Rocky Cañon except for provisions; his logs were slipped down a "shoot" or slide to the river, where they voyaged once a month to a distant mill, but *he* did not accompany them. The daughter, seldom seen at Rocky Cañon, was a half-grown girl, brown as autumn fern, wild-eyed, disheveled, in a homespun skirt, sunbonnet, and boy's brogans. Such were the plain facts which skeptical Rocky Cañon opposed to the passengers' legends. Nevertheless, some of the younger miners found it not out of their way to go over Skinners Pass on the journey to the river, but with what success was not told. It was said, however, that a celebrated New York artist, making a tour of California, was on the coach one day going through the pass, and preserved the memory of what he saw there in a well-known picture entitled "Dancing Nymph and Satyr," said by competent critics to be "replete with the study of Greek life." This did not affect Rocky Cañon, where the study of mythology was presumably displaced by an experience of more wonderful flesh-and-blood people, but later it was remembered with some significance.

Among the improvements already noted, a zinc and wooden chapel had been erected in the main street, where a certain popular revivalist preacher of a peculiar Southwestern sect regularly held exhortatory services. His rude emotional power over his ignorant fellow-sectarians was well known, while curiosity drew others. His effect upon the females of his flock was hysterical and sensational. Women prematurely aged by frontier drudgery and child-bearing, girls who had known only the rigors and pains of a half-equipped, ill-nourished youth in their battling with the hard realities of nature around them, all found a strange fascination in the extravagant glories and privileges of the unseen world he pictured to them, which they might have found in the fairy tales and nursery legends of civilized children had they known them. Personally he was not attractive; his thin, pointed face, and bushy hair rising on either side of his square forehead in two rounded knots, and his long, straggling, wiry beard dropping from a strong neck and shoulders were indeed of a common Southwestern type; yet in him they suggested something more. This was voiced by a miner who attended his first service, and as the Reverend Mr. Withholder rose in the pulpit, the former was heard to audibly ejaculate, "Dod blasted!—if it ain't Billy!" But when on the following Sunday, to everybody's astonishment, Polly Harkness, in a new white muslin frock and broad-brimmed Leghorn hat, appeared before the church door with the real Billy, and exchanged conversation with the preacher, the likeness was appalling.

I grieve to say that the goat was at once christened by Rocky Cañon as "The Reverend Billy," and the minister himself was Billy's "brother." More than that, when an attempt was made by outsiders, during the service, to inveigle the tethered goat into his old butting performances, and he took not the least notice of their insults and challenges, the epithet "blanked hypocrite" was added to his title.

Had he really reformed? Had his pastoral life with his nymph-like mistress completely cured him of his pugnacious propensity, or had he simply found it was inconsistent with his dancing, and seriously interfered with his "fancy steps"? Had he found tracts and hymn-books were as edible as theatre posters? These were questions that Rocky Cañon discussed lightly, although there was always the more serious mystery of the relations of the Reverend Mr. Withholder, Polly Harkness, and the goat towards each other. The appearance of Polly at church was no doubt due to the minister's active canvass of the districts. But had he ever heard of Polly's dancing with the goat? And where in this plain, angular, badly dressed Polly was hidden that beautiful vision of the dancing nymph which had enthralled so many? And when had Billy ever given any suggestion of his Terpsichorean abilities—before or since? Were there any "points" of the kind to be discerned in him now? None! Was it not more probable that the Reverend Mr. Withholder had himself been dancing with Polly, and been mistaken for the goat? Passengers who could have been so deceived with regard to Polly's beauty might have as easily mistaken the minister for Billy. About this time another incident occurred which increased the mystery.

The only male in the settlement who apparently dissented from the popular opinion regarding Polly was a new-comer, Jack Filgee. While discrediting her performance with the goat,—which he had never seen,—he was evidently greatly prepossessed with the girl herself. Unfortunately, he was equally addicted to drinking, and as he was exceedingly shy and timid when sober, and quite unpresentable at other times, his wooing, if it could be so called, progressed but slowly. Yet when he found that Polly went to church, he listened so far to the exhortations of the Reverend Mr. Withholder as to promise to come to "Bible class" immediately after the Sunday service. It was a hot afternoon, and Jack, who had kept sober for two days, incautiously fortified himself for the ordeal by taking a drink before arriving. He was nervously early, and immediately took a seat in the empty church near the open door. The quiet of the building, the drowsy buzzing of flies, and perhaps the soporific effect of the liquor caused his eyes to close and his head to fall forward on his breast repeatedly. He was recovering himself for the fourth time when he suddenly received a violent cuff on the ear, and was knocked backward off the bench on which he was sitting. That was all he knew.

He picked himself up with a certain dignity, partly new to him, and partly the result of his condition, and staggered, somewhat bruised and disheveled, to the nearest saloon. Here a few frequenters who had seen him pass, who knew his errand and the devotion to Polly which had induced it, exhibited a natural concern.

"How's things down at the gospel shop?" said one. "Look as ef you'd been wrastlin' with the Sperit, Jack!"

"Old man must hev exhorted pow'ful," said another, glancing at his disordered Sunday attire.

"Ain't be'n hevin' a row with Polly? I'm told she slings an awful left."

Jack, instead of replying, poured out a dram of whiskey, drank it, and putting down his glass, leaned heavily against the counter as he surveyed his questioners with a sorrow chastened by reproachful dignity.

"I'm a stranger here, gentlemen," he said slowly; "ye've known me only a little; but ez ye've seen me both blind drunk and sober, I reckon ye've caught on to my gin'ral gait! Now I wanter put it to you, ez fair-minded men, ef you ever saw me strike a parson?"

"No," said a chorus of sympathetic voices. The bar-keeper, however, with a swift recollection of Polly and the Reverend Withholder, and some possible contingent jealousy in Jack, added prudently, "Not yet."

The chorus instantly added reflectively, "Well, no; not yet."

"Did ye ever," continued Jack solemnly, "know me to cuss, sass, bully-rag, or say anything agin parsons, or the church?"

"No," said the crowd, overthrowing prudence in curiosity, "ye never did,—we swear it! And now, what's up?"

"I ain't what you call 'a member in good standin','" he went on, artistically protracting his climax. "I ain't be'n convicted o' sin; I ain't 'a meek an' lowly follower'; I ain't be'n exactly what I orter be'n; I hevn't lived anywhere up to my lights; but is thet a reason why a parson should strike me?"

"Why? What? When did he? Who did?" asked the eager crowd, with one voice.

Jack then painfully related how he had been invited by the Reverend Mr. Withholder to attend the Bible class. How he had arrived early, and found the church empty. How he had taken a seat near the door to be handy when the parson came. How he just felt "kinder kam and good," listenin' to the flies buzzing, and must have fallen asleep,—only he pulled himself up every time,—though, after all, it warn't no crime to fall asleep in an empty church! How "all of a suddent" the parson came in, "give him a clip side o' the head," and knocked him off the bench, and left him there!

"But what did he *say*?" queried the crowd.

"Nuthin'. Afore I could get up, he got away."

"Are you sure it was him?" they asked. "You know you *say* you was asleep."

"Am I sure?" repeated Jack scornfully. "Don't I know thet face and beard? Didn't I feel it hangin' over me?"

"What are you going to do about it?" continued the crowd eagerly.

"Wait till he comes out—and you'll see," said Jack, with dignity.

This was enough for the crowd; they gathered excitedly at the door, where Jack was already standing, looking towards the church. The moments dragged slowly; it might be a long meeting. Suddenly the church door opened and a figure appeared, looking up and down the street. Jack colored—he recognized Polly—and stepped out into the road. The crowd delicately, but somewhat disappointedly, drew back in the saloon. They did not care to interfere in *that* sort of thing.

Polly saw him, and came hurriedly towards him. She was holding something in her hand.

"I picked this up on the church floor," she said shyly, "so I reckoned you *had* be'n there,—though the parson said you hadn't,—and I just excused myself and ran out to give it ye. It's yourn, ain't it?" She held up a gold specimen pin, which he had put on in honor of the occasion. "I had a harder time, though, to git this yer,—it's yourn too,—for Billy was laying down in the yard, back o' the church, and just comf'bly swallerin' it."

"Who?" said Jack quickly.

"Billy,—my goat."

Jack drew a long breath, and glanced back at the saloon. "Ye ain't goin' back to class now, are ye?" he said hurriedly. "Ef you ain't, I'll—I'll see ye home."

"I don't mind," said Polly demurely, "if it ain't takin' ye outer y'ur way."

Jack offered his arm, and hurrying past the saloon, the happy pair were soon on the road to Skinners Pass.

Jack did not, I regret to say, confess his blunder, but left the Reverend Mr. Withholder to remain under suspicion of having committed an unprovoked assault and battery. It was characteristic of Rocky Cañon, however, that this suspicion, far from injuring his clerical reputation, incited a respect that had been hitherto denied him. A man who could hit out straight from the shoulder had, in the language of the critics, "suthin' in him." Oddly enough, the crowd that had at first sympathized with Jack now began to admit provocations. His subsequent silence, a disposition when questioned on the subject to smile inanely, and, later, when insidiously asked if he had ever seen Polly dancing with the goat, his bursting into uproarious laughter completely turned the current of opinion against him. The public mind, however, soon became engrossed by a more interesting incident.

The Reverend Mr. Withholder had organized a series of Biblical tableaux at Skinnerstown for the benefit of his church. Illustrations were to be given of "Rebecca at the Well," "The Finding of Moses," "Joseph and his Brethren"; but Rocky Cañon was more particularly excited by the announcement that Polly Harkness would personate "Jephthah's Daughter." On the evening of the performance, however, it was found that this tableau had been withdrawn and another substituted, for reasons not given. Rocky Cañon, naturally indignant at this omission to represent native talent, indulged in a hundred wild surmises. But it was generally believed that Jack Filgee's revengeful animosity to the Reverend Mr. Withholder was at the bottom of it. Jack, as usual, smiled inanely, but nothing was to be got from him. It was not until a few days later, when another incident crowned the climax of these mysteries, that a full disclosure came from his lips.

One morning a flaming poster was displayed at Rocky Cañon, with a charming picture of the "Sacramento Pet" in the briefest of skirts, disporting with a tambourine before a goat garlanded with flowers, who bore, however, an undoubted likeness to Billy. The text in enormous letters, and bristling with points of admiration, stated that the "Pet" would appear as "Esmeralda," assisted by a performing goat, especially trained by the gifted actress. The goat would dance, play cards, and perform those tricks of magic familiar to the readers of Victor Hugo's beautiful story of the "Hunchback of Notre Dame," and finally knock down and overthrow the designing seducer, Captain Phœbus. The marvelous spectacle would be produced under the patronage of the Hon. Colonel Starbottle and the Mayor of Skinnerstown.

As all Rocky Cañon gathered open-mouthed around the poster, Jack demurely joined the group. Every eye was turned upon him.

"It don't look as if yer Polly was in *this* show, any more that she was in the tablows," said one, trying to conceal his curiosity under a slight sneer. "She don't seem to be doin' any dancin'!"

"She never *did* any dancin'," said Jack, with a smile.

"Never *did*! Then what was all these yarns about her dancin' up at the pass?"

"It was the Sacramento Pet who did all the dancin'; Polly only *lent* the goat. Ye see, the Pet kinder took a shine to Billy arter he bowled Starbottle over thet day at the hotel, and she thought she might teach him tricks. So she *did*, doing all her teachin' and stage-rehearsin' up there at the pass, so's to be outer sight, and keep this thing dark. She bribed Polly to lend her the goat and keep her secret, and Polly never let on a word to anybody but me."

"Then it was the Pet that Yuba Bill saw dancin' from the coach?"

"Yes."

"And that yer artist from New York painted as an 'Imp and Satire'?"

"Yes."

"Then that's how Polly didn't show up in them tablows at Skinnerstown? It was Withholder who kinder smelt a rat, eh? and found out it was only a theayter gal all along that did the dancin'?"

"Well, you see," said Jack, with affected hesitation, "thet's another yarn. I don't know mebbe ez I oughter tell it. Et ain't got anything to do with this advertisement o' the Pet, and might be rough on old man Withholder! Ye mustn't ask me, boys."

But there was that in his eye, and above all in this lazy procrastination of the true humorist when he is approaching his climax, which rendered the crowd clamorous and unappeasable. They *would* have the story!

Seeing which, Jack leaned back against a rock with great gravity, put his hands in his pockets, looked discontentedly at the ground, and began: "You see, boys, old Parson Withholder had heard all these yarns about Polly and thet trickgoat, and he kinder reckoned that she might do for some one of his tablows. So he axed her if she'd mind standin' with the goat and a tambourine for Jephthah's Daughter, at about the time when old Jeph comes home, sailin' in and vowin' he'll kill the first thing he sees,—jest as it is in the Bible story. Well, Polly didn't like to say it wasn't *her* that performed with the goat, but the Pet, for thet would give the Pet dead away; so Polly agrees to come thar with the goat and rehearse the tablow. Well, Polly's thar, a little shy; and Billy,—you bet *he's* all thar and ready for the fun; but the darned fool who plays Jephthah ain't worth shucks, and when *he* comes in he does nothin' but grin at Polly and seem skeert at the goat. This makes old Withholder jest wild, and at last he goes on the platform hisself to show them how the thing oughter be done. So he comes bustlin' and prancin' in, and ketches sight o' Polly dancin' in with the goat to welcome him; and then he clasps his hands—so—and drops on his knees, and hangs down his head—so—and sez, 'Me chyld! me vow! Oh, heavens!' But jest then Billy—who's gettin' rather tired o' all this foolishness—kinder slues round on his hind legs, and ketches sight o' the parson!" Jack paused a moment, and thrusting his hands still deeper in his pockets said lazily, "I don't know if you fellers have noticed how much old Withholder looks like Billy?"

There was a rapid and impatient chorus of "Yes! yes!" and "Go on!"

"Well," continued Jack, "when Billy sees Withholder kneelin' thar with his head down, he gives a kind o' joyous leap and claps his hoofs together, ez much ez to say, 'I'm on in this scene,' drops his own head, and jest lights out for the parson!"

"And butts him clean through the side scenes into the street," interrupted a delighted auditor.

But Jack's face never changed. "Ye think so?" he said gravely. "But thet's jest whar ye slip up; and thet's jest whar Billy slipped up!" he added slowly. "Mebbe ye've noticed, too, thet the parson's built kinder solid about the head and shoulders. It mought hev be'n thet, or thet Billy didn't get a fair start, but thet goat went down on his fore legs like a shot, and the parson gave one heave, and jest scooted him off the platform! Then the parson reckoned thet this yer 'tablow' had better be left out, as thar didn't seem to be any other man who could play Jephthah, and it wasn't dignified for *him* to take the part. But the parson allowed thet it might be a great moral lesson to Billy!"

And it *was*, for from that moment Billy never attempted to butt again. He performed with great docility later on in the Pet's engagement at Skinnerstown; he played a distinguished rôle throughout the provinces; he had had the advantages of Art from "the Pet," and of Simplicity from Polly, but only Rocky Cañon knew that his real education had come with his first rehearsal with the Reverend Mr. Withholder.

THE BOOM IN THE
"CALAVERAS
CLARION"

THE editorial sanctum of the "Calaveras Clarion" opened upon the "composing-room" of that paper on the one side, and gave apparently upon the rest of Calaveras County upon the other. For, situated on the very outskirts of the settlement and the summit of a very steep hill, the pines sloped away from the editorial windows to the long valley of the South Fork and—infinity. The little wooden building had invaded Nature without subduing it. It was filled night and day with the murmur of pines and their fragrance. Squirrels scampered over its roof when it was not preoccupied by woodpeckers, and a printer's devil had once seen a nest-building blue jay enter a window in the composing-room, flutter before one of the slanting type-cases with an air of deliberate selection, and then fly off with a vowel in its bill.

Amidst these sylvan surroundings the temporary editor of the "Clarion" sat at his sanctum, reading the proofs of an editorial. As he was occupying that position during a six weeks' absence of the *bona fide* editor and proprietor, he was consequently reading the proof with some anxiety and responsibility. It had been suggested to him by certain citizens that the "Clarion" needed a firmer and more aggressive policy towards the Bill before the Legislature for the wagon road to the South Fork. Several Assembly men had been "got at" by the rival settlement of Liberty Hill, and a scathing exposure and denunciation of such methods was necessary.

The interests of their own township were also to be "whooped up." All this had been vigorously explained to him, and he had grasped the spirit, if not always the facts, of his informants. It is to be feared, therefore, that he was perusing his article more with reference to its vigor than his own convictions. And yet he was not so greatly absorbed as to be unmindful of the murmur of the pines without, his half-savage environment, and the lazy talk of his sole companions, —the foreman and printer in the adjoining room.

"Bet your life! I've always said that a man *inside* a news-paper office could hold his own agin any outsider that wanted to play rough or tried to raid the office! Thar's the press, and thar's the printin' ink and roller! Folks talk a heap o' the power o' the Press!—I tell ye, ye don't half know it. Why, when old Kernel Fish was editin' the 'Sierra Banner,' one o' them bullies that he'd lampooned in the 'Banner' fought his way past the Kernel in the office, into the composin'-room, to wreck everythin' and 'pye' all the types. Spoffrel—ye don't remember Spoffrel?—little red-haired man?—was foreman. Spoffrel fended him off with the roller and got one good dab inter his eyes that blinded him, and then Spoffrel sorter skirmished him over to the press,—a plain lever just like ours,— whar the locked-up form of the inside was still a-lyin'! Then, quick as lightnin', Spoffrel tilts him over agin it, and *he* throws out his hand and ketches hold o' the form to steady himself, when Spoffrel just runs the form and the hand under the press and down with the lever! And that held the feller fast as grim death! And when at last he begs off, and Spoff lets him loose, the hull o' that 'ere lampooning article he objected to was printed right onto the skin o' his hand! Fact, and it wouldn't come off, either."

"Gosh, but I'd like to hev seen it," said the printer. "There ain't any chance, I reckon, o' such a sight here. The boss don't take no risks lampoonin', and he" (the editor knew he was being indicated by some unseen gesture of the unseen workman) "ain't that style."

"Ye never kin tell," said the foreman didactically, "what might happen! I've known editors to get into a fight jest for a little innercent bedevilin' o' the opposite party. Sometimes for a misprint. Old man Pritchard of the 'Argus' oncet had a hole blown through his arm because his proof-reader had called Colonel Starbottle's speech an 'ignominious' defense, when the old man hed written 'ingenuous' defense."

The editor paused in his proof-reading. He had just come upon the sentence: "We cannot congratulate Liberty Hill—in its superior elevation—upon the ignominious silence of the representative of all Calaveras when this infamous Bill was introduced." He referred to his copy. Yes! He had certainly written "ignominious,"—that was what his informants had suggested. But was he sure they were right? He had a vague recollection, also, that the representative alluded to—Senator Bradley—had fought two duels, and was a "good" though somewhat impulsive shot! He might alter the word to "ingenuous" or "ingenious," either would be finely sarcastic, but then—there was his foreman, who would detect it! He would wait until he had finished the entire article. In that occupation he became oblivious of the next room, of a silence, a whispered conversation, which ended with a rapping at the door and the appearance of the foreman in the doorway.

"There's a man in the office who wants to see the editor," he said.

"Show him in," replied the editor briefly. He was, however, conscious that there was a singular significance in his foreman's manner, and an eager apparition of the other printer over the foreman's shoulder.

"He's carryin' a shot-gun, and is a man twice as big as you be," said the foreman gravely.

The editor quickly recalled his own brief and as yet blameless record in the "Clarion." "Perhaps," he said tentatively, with a gentle smile, "he's looking for Captain Brush" (the absent editor).

"I told him all that," said the foreman grimly, "and he said he wanted to see the man in charge."

In proportion as the editor's heart sank his outward crest arose. "Show him in," he said loftily.

"We *kin* keep him out," suggested the foreman, lingering a moment; "me and him," indicating the expectant printer behind him, "is enough for that."

"Show him up," repeated the editor firmly.

The foreman withdrew; the editor seated himself and again took up his proof. The doubtful word "ignominious" seemed to stand out of the paragraph before him; it certainly *was* a strong expression! He was about to run his pencil through it when he heard the heavy step of his visitor approaching. A sudden instinct of belligerency took possession of him, and he wrathfully threw the pencil down.

The burly form of the stranger blocked the doorway. He was dressed like a miner, but his build and general physiognomy were quite distinct from the local variety. His upper lip and chin were clean-shaven, still showing the blue-black roots of the beard which covered the rest of his face and depended in a thick fleece under his throat. He carried a small bundle tied up in a silk handkerchief in one hand, and a "shot-gun" in the other, perilously at half-cock. Entering the sanctum, he put down his bundle and quietly closed the door behind him. He then drew an empty chair towards him and dropped heavily into it with his gun on his knees. The editor's heart dropped almost as heavily, although he quite composedly held out his hand.

"Shall I relieve you of your gun?"

"Thank ye, lad—noa. It's moor coomfortable wi' me, and it's main dangersome to handle on the half-cock. That's why I didn't leave 'im on the horse outside!"

At the sound of his voice and occasional accent a flash of intelligence relieved the editor's mind. He remembered that twenty miles away, in the illimitable vista from his windows, lay a settlement of English north-country miners, who, while faithfully adopting the methods, customs, and even slang of the Californians, retained many of their native peculiarities. The gun he carried on his knee, however, was evidently part of the Californian imitation.

"Can I do anything for you?" said the editor blandly.

"Ay! I've coom here to bill ma woife."

"I—don't think I understand," hesitated the editor, with a smile.

"I've coom here to get ye to put into your paper a warnin', a notiss, that onless she returns to my house in four weeks, I'll have nowt to do wi' her again."

"Oh!" said the editor, now perfectly reassured, "you want an advertisement? That's the business of the foreman; I'll call him." He was rising from his seat when the stranger laid a heavy hand on his shoulder and gently forced him down again.

"Noa, lad! I don't want noa foreman nor understrappers to take this job, I want to talk it over wi' you. *Sabe?* My woife she bin up and awaa these six months. We had a bit of difference, that ain't here nor there, but she skedaddled outer my house. I want to give her fair warning, and let her know I ain't payin' any debts o' hers arter this notiss, and I ain't takin' her back arter four weeks from date."

"I see," said the editor glibly. "What's your wife's name?"

"Eliza Jane Dimmidge."

"Good," continued the editor, scribbling on the paper before him; "something like this will do: 'Whereas my wife, Eliza Jane Dimmidge, having left my bed and board without just cause or provocation, this is to give notice that I shall not be responsible for any debts of her contracting on or after this date.'"

"Ye must be a lawyer," said Mr. Dimmidge admiringly.

It was an old enough form of advertisement, and the remark showed incontestably that Mr. Dimmidge was not a native; but the editor smiled patronizingly and went on: "'And I further give notice that if she does not return within the period of four weeks from this date, I shall take such proceedings for relief as the law affords.'"

"Coom, lad, I didn't say *that*."

"But you said you wouldn't take her back."

"Ay."

"And you can't prevent her without legal proceedings. She's your wife. But you needn't take proceedings, you know. It's only a warning."

Mr. Dimmidge nodded approvingly. "That's so."

"You'll want it published for four weeks, until date?" asked the editor.

"Mebbe longer, lad."

The editor wrote "till forbid" in the margin of the paper and smiled.

"How big will it be?" said Mr. Dimmidge.

The editor took up a copy of the "Clarion" and indicated about an inch of space. Mr. Dimmidge's face fell.

"I want it bigger,—in large letters, like a play-card," he said. "That's no good for a warning."

"You can have half a column or a whole column if you like," said the editor airily.

"I'll take a whole one," said Mr. Dimmidge simply.

The editor laughed. "Why! it would cost you a hundred dollars."

"I'll take it," repeated Mr. Dimmidge.

"But," said the editor gravely, "the same notice in a small space will serve your purpose and be quite legal."

"Never you mind that, lad! It's the looks of the thing I'm arter, and not the expense. I'll take that column."

The editor called in the foreman and showed him the copy. "Can you display that so as to fill a column?"

The foreman grasped the situation promptly. It would be big business for the paper. "Yes," he said meditatively, "that bold-faced election type will do it."

Mr. Dimmidge's face brightened. The expression "bold-faced" pleased him. "That's it! I told you. I want to bill her in a portion of the paper."

"I might put in a cut," said the foreman suggestively; "something like this." He took a venerable woodcut from the case. I grieve to say it was one which, until the middle of the present century, was common enough in the newspaper offices in the Southwest. It showed the running figure of a Negro woman carrying her personal property in a knotted handkerchief slung from a stick over her shoulder, and was supposed to represent "a fugitive slave."

Mr. Dimmidge's eyes brightened. "I'll take that, too. It's a little dark-complected for Mrs. D., but it will do. Now roon away, lad," he said to the foreman, as he quietly pushed him into the outer office again and closed the door. Then, facing the surprised editor, he said, "Theer's another notiss I want ye to put in your paper; but that's atween *us*. Not a word to *them*," he indicated the banished foreman with a jerk of his thumb. "*Sabe?* I want you to put this in another part o' your paper, quite innocent-like, ye know." He drew from his pocket a gray wallet, and taking out a slip of paper read from it gravely, " 'If this should meet the eye of R. B., look out for M. J. D. He is on your track. When this you see write a line to E. J. D., Elktown Post Office.' I want this to go in as 'Personal and Private'—*sabe?* like them notisses in the big 'Frisco papers."

"I see," said the editor, laying it aside. "It shall go in the same issue in another column."

Apparently Mr. Dimmidge expected something more than this reply, for after a moment's hesitation he said with an odd smile:—

"Ye ain't seein' the meanin' o' that, lad?"

"No," said the editor lightly; "but I suppose R. B. does, and it isn't intended that any one else should."

"Mebbe it is, and mebbe it isn't," said Mr. Dimmidge, with a self-satisfied air. "I don't mind saying atween us that R. B. is the man as I've suspicioned as havin' something to do with my wife goin' away; and ye see, if he writes to E. J. D.— that's my wife's initials—at Elktown, *I'll* get that letter and so make sure."

"But suppose your wife goes there first, or sends?"

"Then I'll ketch her or her messenger. Ye see?"

The editor did not see fit to oppose any argument to this phenomenal simplicity, and Mr. Dimmidge, after settling his bill with the foreman, and enjoining the editor to the strictest secrecy regarding the origin of the "personal notice," took up his gun and departed, leaving the treasury of the "Clarion" unprecedentedly enriched, and the editor to his proofs.

The paper duly appeared the next morning with the column advertisement, the personal notice, and the weighty editorial on the wagon road. There was a singular demand for the paper, the edition was speedily exhausted, and the editor was proportionately flattered, although he was surprised to receive neither praise nor criticism from his subscribers. Before evening, however, he learned to his astonishment that the excitement was caused by the column advertisement. Nobody knew Mr. Dimmidge, nor his domestic infelicities, and the editor and foreman, being equally in the dark, took refuge in a mysterious and impressive evasion of all inquiry. Never since the last San Francisco Vigilance Committee had the office been so besieged. The editor, foreman, and even the apprentice were buttonholed and "treated" at the bar, but to no effect. All that could be learned was that it was a *bona fide* advertisement, for which one hundred dollars had been received! There were great discussions and conflicting theories as to whether the value of the wife, or the husband's anxiety to get rid of her, justified the enormous expense and ostentatious display. She was supposed to be an exceedingly beautiful woman by some, by others a perfect Sycorax; in one breath Mr. Dimmidge was a weak, uxorious spouse, wasting his substance on a creature who did not care for him, and in another a maddened, distracted, henpecked man, content to purchase peace and rest at any price. Certainly, never was advertisement more effective in its publicity, or cheaper in proportion to the circulation it commanded. It was copied throughout the whole Pacific slope; mighty San Francisco papers described its size and setting under the attractive headline, "How they Advertise a Wife in the Mountains!" It reappeared in the Eastern journals, under the title of "Whimsicalities of the Western Press." It was believed to have crossed to England as a specimen of "Transatlantic Savagery." The real editor of the "Clarion" awoke one morning, in San Francisco, to find his paper famous. Its advertising columns were eagerly sought for; he at once advanced the rates. People bought successive issues to gaze upon this monumental record of extravagance. A singular idea, which, however, brought further fortune to the paper, was advanced by an astute critic at the Eureka Saloon. "My opinion, gentlemen, is that the whole blamed thing is a bluff! There ain't no Mr. Dimmidge; there ain't no Mrs. Dimmidge; there ain't no desertion! The whole rotten thing is an *advertisement* o' suthin'! Ye'll find afore ye get through with it that that there wife won't come back until that blamed husband buys Somebody's Soap, or treats her to Somebody's particular Starch or Patent Medicine! Ye jest watch and see!" The idea was startling, and seized upon the mercantile mind. The principal merchant of the town, and purveyor to the mining settlements beyond, appeared the next morning at the office of the "Clarion." "Ye wouldn't mind puttin' this 'ad' in a column alongside o' the Dimmidge one, would ye?" The young editor glanced at it, and then, with a serpent-like sagacity, veiled, however, by the suavity of the dove, pointed out that the original advertiser might think it called his *bona fides* into question and withdraw his advertisement. "But if we secured you by an offer of double the amount per column?" urged the merchant. "That," responded the *locum tenens*, "was for the actual editor and proprietor in San Francisco to determine. He would telegraph." He did so. The response was, "Put it in." Whereupon in the next issue, side by side with Mr. Dimmidge's protracted warning, appeared a column with the announcement, in large letters, "*WE* HAVEN'T LOST ANY WIFE, but WE are prepared to furnish the following goods at a lower rate than any other advertiser in the county," followed by the usual price list of the merchant's wares. There was an unprecedented demand for that issue. The reputation of the "Clarion," both as a shrewd advertising medium and a comic paper, was established at once. For a few days the editor waited with some apprehension for a remonstrance from the absent Dimmidge, but none came. Whether Mr. Dimmidge recognized that this new advertisement gave extra publicity to his own, or that he was already on the track of the fugitive, the editor did not know. The few curious citizens who had, early in the excitement, penetrated the settlement of the English miners twenty miles away in search of information, found that Mr. Dimmidge had gone away, and that Mrs. Dimmidge had *never* resided there with him!

Six weeks passed. The limit of Mr. Dimmidge's advertisement had been reached, and, as it was not renewed, it had passed out of the pages of the "Clarion," and with it the merchant's advertisement in the next column. The excitement had subsided, although its influence was still felt in the circulation of the paper and its advertising popularity. The temporary editor was also nearing the limit of his incumbency, but had so far participated in the good fortune of the "Clarion" as to receive an offer from one of the San Francisco dailies.

It was a warm night, and he was alone in his sanctum. The rest of the building was dark and deserted, and his solitary light, flashing out through the open window, fell upon the nearer pines and was lost in the dark, indefinable slope below. He had reached the sanctum by the rear, and a door which he also left open to enjoy the freshness of the aromatic air. Nor did it in the least mar his privacy. Rather the solitude of the great woods without seemed to enter through that door and encompassed him with its protecting loneliness. There was occasionally a faint "peep" in the scant eaves, or a "pat-pat," ending in a frightened scurry across the roof, or the slow flap of a heavy wing in the darkness below. These gentle disturbances did not, however, interrupt his work or

"The True Functions of the County Newspaper," the editorial on which he was engaged.

Presently a more distinct rustling against the straggling blackberry bushes beside the door attracted his attention. It was followed by a light tapping against the side of the house. The editor started and turned quickly towards the open door. Two outside steps led to the ground. Standing upon the lower one was a woman. The upper part of her figure, illuminated by the light from the door, was thrown into greater relief by the dark background of the pines. Her face was unknown to him, but it was a pleasant one, marked by a certain good-humored determination.

"May I come in?" she said confidently.

"Certainly," said the editor. "I am working here alone because it is so quiet." He thought he would precipitate some explanation from her by excusing himself.

"That's the reason why I came," she said, with a quiet smile.

She came up the next step and entered the room. She was plainly but neatly dressed, and now that her figure was revealed he saw that she was wearing a linsey-woolsey riding-skirt, and carried a serviceable raw-hide whip in her cotton-gauntleted hand. She took the chair he offered her and sat down sideways on it, her whip hand now also holding up her skirt, and permitting a hem of clean white petticoat and a smart, well-shaped boot to be seen.

"I don't remember to have had the pleasure of seeing you in Calaveras before," said the editor tentatively.

"No. I never was here before," she said composedly, "but you've heard enough of me, I reckon. I'm Mrs. Dimmidge." She threw one hand over the back of the chair, and with the other tapped her riding-whip on the floor.

The editor started. Mrs. Dimmidge! Then she was not a

myth. An absurd similarity between her attitude with the whip and her husband's entrance with his gun six weeks before forced itself upon him and made her an invincible presence.

"Then you have returned to your husband?" he said hesitatingly.

"Not much!" she returned, with a slight curl of her lip.

"But you read his advertisement?"

"I saw that column of fool nonsense he put in your paper —ef that's what you mean," she said with decision, "but I didn't come here to see *him*—but *you*."

The editor looked at her with a forced smile, but a vague misgiving. He was alone at night in a deserted part of the settlement, with a plump, self-possessed woman who had a contralto voice, a horsewhip, and—he could not help feeling —an evident grievance.

"To see me?" he repeated, with a faint attempt at gallantry. "You are paying me a great compliment, but really"—

"When I tell you I've come three thousand miles from Kansas straight here without stopping, ye kin reckon it's so," she replied firmly.

"Three thousand miles!" echoed the editor wonderingly.

"Yes. Three thousand miles from my own folks' home in Kansas, where six years ago I married Mr. Dimmidge,—a British furriner as could scarcely make himself understood in any Christian language! Well, he got round me and dad, allowin' he was a reg'lar out-and-out profeshnal miner,—had lived in mines ever since he was a boy; and so, not knowin' what kind o' mines, and dad just bilin' over with the gold fever, we were married and kem across the plains to Californy. He was a good enough man to look at, but it warn't three months before I discovered that he allowed a wife was no better nor a nigger slave, and he the master. That made me open my eyes; but then, as he didn't drink, and didn't gamble, and didn't swear, and was a good provider and laid by money, why, I shifted along with him as best I could. We drifted down the first year to Sonora, at Red Dog, where there wasn't another woman. Well, I did the nigger slave business,—never stirring out o' the settlement, never seein' a town or a crowd o' decent people,—and he did the lord and master! We played that game for two years, and I got tired. But when at last he allowed he'd go up to Elktown Hill, where there was a passel o' his countrymen at work, with never a sign o' any other folks, and leave me alone at Red Dog until he fixed up a place for me at Elktown Hill,—I kicked! I gave him fair warning! I did as other nigger slaves did,—I ran away!"

A recollection of the wretched woodcut which Mr. Dimmidge had selected to personify his wife flashed upon the editor with a new meaning. Yet perhaps she had not seen it, and had only read a copy of the advertisement. What could she want? The "Calaveras Clarion," although a "Palladium" and a "Sentinel upon the Heights of Freedom" in reference to wagon roads, was not a redresser of domestic wrongs,— except through its advertising columns! Her next words intensified that suggestion.

"I've come here to put an advertisement in your paper."

The editor heaved a sigh of relief, as once before. "Certainly," he said briskly. "But that's another department of the paper, and the printers have gone home. Come to-morrow morning early."

"To-morrow morning I shall be miles away," she said decisively, "and what I want done has got to be done *now*! I don't want to see no printers; I don't want *anybody* to know I've been here but you. That's why I kem here at night, and rode all the way from Sawyer's Station, and wouldn't take the stagecoach. And when we've settled about the advertisement, I'm going to mount my horse, out thar in the bushes, and scoot outer the settlement."

"Very good," said the editor resignedly. "Of course I can deliver your instructions to the foreman. And now—let me see—I suppose you wish to intimate in a personal notice to your husband that you've returned."

"Nothin' o' the kind!" said Mrs. Dimmidge coolly. "I want to placard him as he did me. I've got it all written out here. *Sabe?*"

She took from her pocket a folded paper, and spreading it out on the editor's desk, with a certain pride of authorship, read as follows:—

"Whereas my husband, Micah J. Dimmidge, having given out that I have left his bed and board,—the same being a bunk in a log cabin and pork and molasses three times a day, —and having advertised that he'd pay no debts of *my* contractin',—which, as thar ain't any, might be easier collected than debts of his own contractin',—this is to certify that unless he returns from Elktown Hill to his only home in Sonora in one week from date, payin' the cost of this advertisement, I'll know the reason why.—Eliza Jane Dimmidge."

"Thar," she added, drawing a long breath, "put that in a column of the 'Clarion,' same size as the last, and let it work, and that's all I want of you."

"A column?" repeated the editor. "Do you know the cost is very expensive, and I *could* put it in a single paragraph?"

"I reckon I kin pay the same as Mr. Dimmidge did for *his*," said the lady complacently. "I didn't see your paper myself, but the paper as copied it—one of them big New York dailies—said that it took up a whole column."

The editor breathed more freely; she had not seen the

infamous woodcut which her husband had selected. At the same moment he was struck with a sense of retribution, justice, and compensation.

"Would you," he asked hesitatingly,—"would you like it illustrated—by a cut?"

"With which?"

"Wait a moment; I'll show you."

He went into the dark composing-room, lit a candle, and rummaging in a drawer sacred to weather-beaten, old-fashioned electrotyped advertising symbols of various trades, finally selected one and brought it to Mrs. Dimmidge. It represented a bare and exceedingly stalwart arm wielding a large hammer.

"Your husband being a miner,—a quartz miner,—would that do?" he asked. (It had been previously used to advertise a blacksmith, a gold-beater, and a stone-mason.)

The lady examined it critically.

"It does look a little like Micah's arm," she said meditatively. "Well—you kin put it in."

The editor was so well pleased with his success that he must needs make another suggestion. "I suppose," he said ingenuously, "that you don't want to answer the 'Personal'?"

"'Personal'?" she repeated quickly, "what's that? I ain't seen no 'Personal.'"

The editor saw his blunder. She, of course, had never seen Mr. Dimmidge's artful "Personal"; *that* the big dailies naturally had not noticed nor copied. But it was too late to withdraw now. He brought out a file of the "Clarion," and snipping out the paragraph with his scissors, laid it before the lady.

She stared at it with wrinkled brows and a darkening face.

"And *this* was in the same paper?—put in by Mr. Dimmidge?" she asked breathlessly.

The editor, somewhat alarmed, stammered "Yes." But the next moment he was reassured. The wrinkles disappeared, a dozen dimples broke out where they had been, and the determined, matter-of-fact Mrs. Dimmidge burst into a fit of rosy merriment. Again and again she laughed, shaking the building, startling the sedate, melancholy woods beyond, until the editor himself laughed in sheer vacant sympathy.

"Lordy!" she said at last, gasping, and wiping the laughter from her wet eyes. "I never thought of *that*."

"No," explained the editor smilingly; "of course you didn't. Don't you see, the papers that copied the big advertisement never saw that little paragraph, or if they did, they never connected the two together."

"Oh, it ain't that," said Mrs. Dimmidge, trying to regain her composure and holding her sides. "It's that blessed *dear* old dunderhead of a Dimmidge I'm thinking of. That gets me. I see it all now. Only, sakes alive! I never thought *that* of him. Oh, it's just too much!" and she again relapsed behind her handkerchief.

"Then I suppose you don't want to reply to it," said the editor.

Her laughter instantly ceased. "Don't I?" she said, wiping her face into its previous complacent determination. "Well, young man, I reckon that's just what I *want* to do! Now, wait a moment; let's see what he said," she went on, taking up and reperusing the "Personal" paragraph. "Well, then," she went on, after a moment's silent composition with moving lips, "you just put these lines in."

The editor took up his pencil.

"To Mr. M. J. Dimmidge.—Hope you're still on R. B.'s tracks. Keep there!—E. J. D."

The editor wrote down the line, and then, remembering Mr. Dimmidge's voluntary explanation of *his* "Personal," waited with some confidence for a like frankness from Mrs. Dimmidge. But he was mistaken.

"You think that he—R. B.—or Mr. Dimmidge—will understand this?" he at last asked tentatively. "Is it enough?"

"Quite enough," said Mrs. Dimmidge emphatically. She took a roll of greenbacks from her pocket, selected a hundred-dollar bill and then a five, and laid them before the editor. "Young man," she said, with a certain demure gravity, "you've done me a heap o' good. I never spent money with more satisfaction than this. I never thought much o' the 'power o' the Press,' as you call it, afore. But this has been a right comfortable visit, and I'm glad I ketched you alone. But you understand one thing: this yer visit, and *who* I am, is betwixt you and me only."

"Of course I must say that the advertisement was *authorized*," returned the editor. "I'm only the temporary editor. The proprietor is away."

"So much the better," said the lady complacently. "You just say you found it on your desk with the money; but don't you give me away."

"I can promise you that the secret of your personal visit is safe with me," said the young man, with a bow, as Mrs. Dimmidge rose. "Let me see you to your horse," he added. "It's quite dark in the woods."

"I can see well enough alone, and it's just as well you shouldn't know *how* I kem or *how* I went away. Enough for you to know that I'll be miles away before that paper comes out. So stay where you are."

She pressed his hand frankly and firmly, gathered up her riding-skirt, slipped backwards to the door, and the next moment rustled away into the darkness.

Early the next morning the editor handed Mrs. Dimmidge's advertisement, and the woodcut he had selected, to his foreman. He was purposely brief in his directions, so as to avoid inquiry, and retired to his sanctum. In the space of a few moments the foreman entered with a slight embarrassment of manner.

"You'll excuse my speaking to you, sir," he said, with a singular mixture of humility and cunning. "It's no business of mine, I know; but I thought I ought to tell you that this yer kind o' thing won't pay any more,—it's about played out!"

"I don't think I understand you," said the editor loftily, but with an inward misgiving. "You don't mean to say that a regular, actual advertisement"—

"Of course, I know all that," said the foreman, with a peculiar smile; "and I'm ready to back you up in it, and so's the boy; but it won't pay."

"It *has* paid a hundred and five dollars," said the editor, taking the notes from his pocket; "so I'd advise you to simply attend to your duty and set it up."

A look of surprise, followed, however, by a kind of pitying smile, passed over the foreman's face. "Of course, sir, *that's* all right, and you know your own business; but if you think that the new advertisement will pay this time as the other one did, and whoop up another column from an advertiser, I'm afraid you'll slip up. It's a little 'off color' now,—not 'up to date,'—if it ain't a regular 'back number,' as you'll see."

"Meantime I'll dispense with your advice," said the editor curtly, "and I think you had better let our subscribers and advertisers do the same, or the 'Clarion' might also be obliged to dispense with your *services*."

"I ain't no blab," said the foreman, in an aggrieved manner, "and I don't intend to give the show away even if it don't *pay*. But I thought I'd tell you, because I know the folks round here better than you do."

He was right. No sooner had the advertisement appeared than the editor found that everybody believed it to be a sheer invention of his own to "once more boom" the "Clarion." If they had doubted *Mr.* Dimmidge, they utterly rejected *Mrs.* Dimmidge as an advertiser! It was a stale joke that nobody would follow up; and on the heels of this came a letter from the editor-in-chief.

My DEAR BOY,—You meant well, I know, but the second Dimmidge "ad" was a mistake. Still, it was a big bluff of yours to show the money, and I send you back your hundred dollars, hoping you won't "do it again." Of course you'll have to keep the advertisement in the paper for two issues, just as if it were a real thing, and it's lucky that there's just now no pressure in our columns. You might have told a better story than that hogwash about your finding the "ad" and a hundred dollars lying loose on your desk one morning. It was rather thin, and I don't wonder the foreman kicked.

The young editor was in despair. At first he thought of writing to Mrs. Dimmidge at the Elktown Post-Office, asking her to relieve him of his vow of secrecy; but his pride forbade. There was a humorous concern, not without a touch of pity, in the faces of his contributors as he passed; a few affected to believe in the new advertisement, and asked him vague, perfunctory questions about it. His position was trying, and he was not sorry when the term of his engagement expired the next week, and he left Calaveras to take his new position on the San Francisco paper.

He was standing in the saloon of the Sacramento boat when he felt a sudden heavy pressure on his shoulder, and looking round sharply, beheld not only the black-bearded face of Mr. Dimmidge, lit up by a smile, but beside it the beaming, buxom face of Mrs. Dimmidge, overflowing with good-humor. Still a little sore from his past experience, he was about to address them abruptly, when he was utterly vanquished by the hearty pressure of their hands and the unmistakable look of gratitude in their eyes.

"I was just saying to 'Lizy Jane," began Mr. Dimmidge breathlessly, "if I could only meet that young man o' the 'Clarion' what brought us together again"—

"You'd be willin' to pay four times the amount we both paid him," interpolated the laughing Mrs. Dimmidge.

"But I didn't bring you together," burst out the dazed young man, "and I'd like to know, in the name of Heaven, what brought you together now?"

"Don't you see, lad," said the imperturbable Mr. Dimmidge, " 'Lizy Jane and myself had qua'led, and we just unpacked our fool nonsense in your paper and let the hull world know it! And we both felt kinder skeert and shamed like, and it looked such small hogwash, and of so little account, for all the talk it made, that we kinder felt lonely as two separated fools that really ought to share their foolishness together."

"And that ain't all," said Mrs. Dimmidge, with a sly glance at her spouse, "for I found out from that 'Personal' you showed me that this particular old fool was actooally jealous!—*jealous*!"

"And then?" said the editor impatiently.

"And then I *knew* he loved me all the time."

THE YOUNGEST
MISS PIPER

I do not think that any of us who enjoyed the acquaintance of the Piper girls or the hospitality of Judge Piper, their father, ever cared for the youngest sister. Not on account of her extreme youth, for the eldest Miss Piper confessed to twenty-six—and the youth of the youngest sister was established solely, I think, by one big braid down her back. Neither was it because she was the plainest, for the beauty of the Piper girls was a recognized general distinction, and the youngest Miss Piper was not entirely devoid of the family charms. Nor was it from any lack of intelligence, nor from any defective social quality; for her precocity was astounding, and her good-humored frankness alarming. Neither do I think it could be said that a slight deafness, which might impart an embarrassing publicity to any statement—the reverse of our general feeling—that might be confided by any one to her private ear, was a sufficient reason; for it was pointed out that she always understood everything that Tom Sparrell told her in his ordinary tone of voice. Briefly, it was very possible that Delaware—the youngest Miss Piper—did not like us.

Yet it was fondly believed by us that the other sisters failed to show that indifference to our existence shown by Miss Delaware, although the heartburnings, misunderstandings, jealousies, hopes, and fears, and finally the chivalrous resignation with which we at last accepted the long foregone conclusion that they were not for us, and far beyond our reach, is not a part of this veracious chronicle. Enough that none of the flirtations of her elder sisters affected or were shared by the youngest Miss Piper. She moved in this heart-breaking atmosphere with sublime indifference, treating her sisters' affairs with what we considered rank simplicity or appalling frankness. Their few admirers who were weak enough to attempt to gain her mediation or confidence had reason to regret it.

"It's no kind o' use givin' me goodies," she said to a helpless suitor of Louisiana Piper's who had offered to bring her some sweets, "for I ain't got no influence with Lu, and if I don't give 'em up to her when she hears of it, she'll nag me and hate you like pizen. Unless," she added thoughtfully, "it was wintergreen lozenges; Lu can't stand them, or anybody who eats them within a mile." It is needless to add that the miserable man, thus put upon his gallantry, was obliged in honor to provide Del with the wintergreen lozenges that kept him in disfavor and at a distance. Unfortunately, too, any predilection or pity for any particular suitor of her sister's was attended by even more disastrous consequences. It was reported that while acting as "gooseberry"—a rôle usually assigned to her—between Virginia Piper and an exceptionally timid young surveyor, during a ramble she conceived a rare sentiment of humanity towards the unhappy man. After once or twice lingering behind in the ostentatious picking of a wayside flower, or "running on ahead" to look at a mountain view, without any apparent effect on the shy and speechless youth, she decoyed him aside while her elder sister rambled indifferently and somewhat scornfully on. The youngest Miss Piper leaped upon the rail of a fence, and with the stalk of a thimbleberry in her mouth swung her small feet to and fro and surveyed him dispassionately.

"Ye don't seem to be ketchin' on?" she said tentatively.

The young man smiled feebly and interrogatively.

"Don't seem to be either follerin' suit nor trumpin'," continued Del bluntly.

"I suppose so—that is, I fear that Miss Virginia"—he stammered.

"Speak up! I'm a little deaf. Say it again!" said Del, screwing up her eyes and eyebrows.

The young man was obliged to admit in stentorian tones that his progress had been scarcely satisfactory.

"You're goin' on too slow—that's it," said Del critically. "Why, when Captain Savage meandered along here with Jinny" (Virginia) "last week, afore we got as far as this he'd reeled off a heap of Byron and Jamieson" (Tennyson), "and sich; and only yesterday Jinny and Doctor Beveridge was blowin' thistletops to know which was a flirt all along the trail past the crossroads. Why, ye ain't picked ez much as a single berry for Jinny, let along Lad's Love or Johnny Jumpups and Kissme's, and ye keep talkin' across me, you two, till I'm tired. Now look here," she burst out with sudden decision, "Jinny's gone on ahead in a kind o' huff; but I reckon she's done that afore too, and you'll find her, jest as Spinner did, on the rise of the hill, sittin' on a pine stump and lookin' like this." (Here the youngest Miss Piper locked her fingers over her left knee, and drew it slightly up,—with a sublime indifference to the exposure of considerable small-ankled red stocking,—and with a far-off, plaintive stare, achieved a colorable imitation of her elder sister's probable attitude.) "Then you jest go up softly, like as you was a bear, and clap your hands on her eyes, and say in a disguised voice like this" (here Del turned on a high falsetto beyond any masculine compass), " 'Who's who?' jest like in forfeits."

"But she'll be sure to know me," said the surveyor timidly.

"She won't," said Del in scornful skepticism.

"I hardly think"—stammered the young man, with an awkward smile, "that I—in fact—she'll discover me—before I can get beside her."

"Not if you go softly, for she'll be sittin' back to the road, so—gazing away, so"—the youngest Miss Piper again stared dreamily in the distance, "and you'll creep up just behind, like this."

"But won't she be angry? I haven't known her long—that is—don't you see?" He stopped embarrassedly.

"Can't hear a word you say," said Del, shaking her head decisively. "You've got my deaf ear. Speak louder, or come closer."

But here the instruction suddenly ended, once and for all time! For whether the young man was seriously anxious to perfect himself; whether he was truly grateful to the young girl and tried to show it; whether he was emboldened by the childish appeal of the long brown distinguishing braid down her back, or whether he suddenly found something peculiarly provocative in the reddish brown eyes between their thick-set hedge of lashes, and with the trim figure and piquant pose, and was seized with that hysteric desperation which sometimes attacks timidity itself, I cannot say! Enough that he suddenly put his arm around her waist and his lips to her soft satin cheek, peppered and salted as it was by sun-freckles and mountain air, and received a sound box on the ear for his pains. The incident was closed. He did not repeat the experiment on either sister. The disclosure of his rebuff seemed, however, to give a singular satisfaction to Red Gulch.

While it may be gathered from this that the youngest Miss Piper was impervious to general masculine advances, it was not until later that Red Gulch was thrown into skeptical astonishment by the rumors that all this time she really had a lover! Allusion has been made to the charge that her deafness did not prevent her from perfectly understanding the ordinary tone of voice of a certain Mr. Thomas Sparrell.

No undue significance was attached to this fact through the very insignificance and "impossibility" of that individual, —a lanky, red-haired youth, incapacitated for manual labor through lameness,—a clerk in a general store at the crossroads! He had never been the recipient of Judge Piper's hospitality; he had never visited the house even with parcels; apparently his only interviews with her or any of the family had been over the counter. To do him justice he certainly had never seemed to seek any nearer acquaintance; he was not at the church door when her sisters, beautiful in their Sunday gowns, filed into the aisle, with little Delaware bringing up the rear; he was not at the Democratic barbecue, that we attended without reference to our personal politics, and solely for the sake of Judge Piper and the girls; nor did he go to the Agricultural Fair Ball—open to all. His abstention we believed to be owing to his lameness; to a wholesome consciousness of his own social defects; or an inordinate passion for reading cheap scientific textbooks, which did not, however, add fluency nor conviction to his speech. Neither had he the abstraction of a student, for his accounts were kept with an accuracy which struck us, who dealt at the store, as ignobly practical, and even malignant. Possibly we might have expressed this opinion more strongly but for a certain rude vigor of repartee which he possessed, and a suggestion that he might have a temper on occasion. "Them red-haired chaps is like to be tetchy and to kinder see blood through their eyelashes," had been suggested by an observing customer.

In short, little as we knew of the youngest Miss Piper,

he was the last man we should have suspected her to select as an admirer. What we did know of their public relations, purely commercial ones, implied the reverse of any cordial understanding. The provisioning of the Piper household was entrusted to Del, with other practical odds and ends of housekeeping, not ornamental, and the following is said to be a truthful record of one of their overheard interviews at the store:—

The youngest Miss Piper, entering, displacing a quantity of goods in the centre to make a sideways seat for herself, and looking around loftily as she took a memorandum-book and pencil from her pocket.

"Ahem! If I ain't taking you away from your studies, Mr. Sparrell, maybe you'll be good enough to look here a minit;—but" (in affected politeness) "if I'm disturbing you I can come another time."

Sparrell, placing the book he had been reading carefully under the counter, and advancing to Miss Delaware with a complete ignoring of her irony: "What can we do for you to-day, Miss Piper?"

Miss Delaware, with great suavity of manner, examining her memorandum-book: "I suppose it wouldn't be shocking your delicate feelings too much to inform you that the canned lobster and oysters you sent us yesterday wasn't fit for hogs?"

Sparrell (blandly): "They weren't intended for them, Miss Piper. If we had known you were having company over from Red Gulch to dinner, we might have provided something more suitable for them. We have a fair quality of oil-cake and corncobs in stock, at reduced figures. But the canned provisions were for your own family."

Miss Delaware (secretly pleased at this sarcastic allusion to her sister's friends, but concealing her delight): "I admire to hear you talk that way, Mr. Sparrell; it's better than minstrels or a circus. I suppose you get it outer that book," indicating the concealed volume. "What do you call it?"

Sparrell (politely): "'The First Principles of Geology.'"

Miss Delaware, leaning sideways and curling her little fingers around her pink ear: "Did you say the first principles of 'geology' or 'politeness'? You know I am so deaf; but, of course, it couldn't be that."

Sparrell (easily): "Oh, no, you seem to have that in your hand"—pointing to Miss Delaware's memorandum-book "you were quoting from it when you came in."

Miss Delaware, after an affected silence of deep resignation: "Well! it's too bad folks can't just spend their lives listenin' to such elegant talk; I'd admire to do nothing else! But there's my family up at Cottonwood—and they must eat. They're that low that they expect me to waste my time getting food for 'em here, instead of drinking in the 'First Principles of the Grocery.'"

"Geology," suggested Sparrell blandly. "The history of rock formation."

"Geology," accepted Miss Delaware apologetically; "the history of rocks, which is so necessary for knowing just how much sand you can put in the sugar. So I reckon I'll leave my list here, and you can have the things toted to Cottonwood when you've got through with your 'First Principles.'"

She tore out a list of her commissions from a page of her memorandum-book, leaped lightly from the counter, threw her brown braid from her left shoulder to its proper place down her back, shook out her skirts deliberately, and saying, "Thank you for a most improvin' afternoon, Mr. Sparrell," sailed demurely out of the store.

A few auditors of this narrative thought it inconsistent

that a daughter of Judge Piper and a sister of the angelic host should put up with a mere clerk's familiarity, but it was pointed out that "she gave him as good as he sent," and the story was generally credited. But certainly no one ever dreamed that it pointed to any more precious confidences between them.

I think the secret burst upon the family, with other things, at the big picnic at Reservoir Cañon. This festivity had been arranged for weeks previously, and was undertaken chiefly by the "Red Gulch Contingent," as we were called, as a slight return to the Piper family for their frequent hospitality. The Piper sisters were expected to bring nothing but their own personal graces and attend to the ministration of such viands and delicacies as the boys had profusely supplied.

The site selected was Reservoir Cañon, a beautiful, triangular valley with very steep sides, one of which was crowned by the immense reservoir of the Pioneer Ditch Company. The sheer flanks of the cañon descended in furrowed lines of vines and clinging bushes, like folds of falling skirts, until they broke again into flounces of spangled shrubbery over a broad level carpet of monkshood, mariposas, lupines, poppies, and daisies. Tempered and secluded from the sun's rays by its lofty shadows, the delicious obscurity of the cañon was in sharp contrast to the fiery mountain trail that in the full glare of the noonday sky made its tortuous way down the hillside, like a stream of lava, to plunge suddenly into the valley and extinguish itself in its coolness as in a lake. The heavy odors of wild honeysuckle, syringa, and ceanothus that hung over it were lightened and freshened by the sharp spicing of pine and bay. The mountain breeze which sometimes shook the serrated tops of the large redwoods above with a chill from the remote snow peaks even in the heart of summer, never reached the little valley.

It seemed an ideal place for a picnic. Everybody was therefore astonished to hear that an objection was suddenly raised to this perfect site. They were still more astonished to know that the objector was the youngest Miss Piper! Pressed to give her reasons, she had replied that the locality was dangerous; that the reservoir placed upon the mountain, notoriously old and worn out, had been rendered more unsafe by false economy in unskillful and hasty repairs to satisfy speculating stockbrokers, and that it had lately shown signs of leakage and sapping of its outer walls; that, in the event of an outbreak, the little triangular valley, from which there was no outlet, would be instantly flooded. Asked still more pressingly to give her authority for these details, she at first hesitated, and then gave the name of Tom Sparrell.

The derision with which this statement was received by us all, as the opinion of a sedentary clerk, was quite natural and obvious, but not the anger which it excited in the breast of Judge Piper; for it was not generally known that the judge was the holder of a considerable number of shares in the Pioneer Ditch Company, and that large dividends had been lately kept up by a false economy of expenditure, to expedite a "sharp deal" in the stock, by which the judge and others could sell out of a failing company. Rather, it was believed, that the judge's anger was due only to the discovery of Sparrell's influence over his daughter and his interference with the social affairs of Cottonwood. It was said that there was a sharp scene between the youngest Miss Piper and the combined forces of the judge and the elder sisters, which ended in the former's resolute refusal to attend the picnic at all if that site was selected.

As Delaware was known to be fearless even to the point of recklessness, and fond of gayety, her refusal only intensified the belief that she was merely "stickin' up for Sparrell's judgment" without any reference to her own personal safety or that of her sisters. The warning was laughed away; the opinion of Sparrell treated with ridicule as the dyspeptic and envious expression of an impractical man. It was pointed out that the reservoir had lasted a long time even in its alleged ruinous state; that only a miracle of co-incidence could make it break down that particular afternoon of the picnic; that even if it did happen, there was no direct proof that it would seriously flood the valley, or at best add more than a spice of excitement to the affair. The "Red Gulch Contingent," who *would* be there, was quite as capable of taking care of the ladies, in case of any accident, as any lame crank who wouldn't, but could only croak a warning to them from a distance. A few even wished something might happen that they might have an opportunity of showing their superior devotion; indeed, the prospect of carrying the half-submerged sisters, in a condition of helpless loveliness, in their arms to a place of safety was a fascinating possibility. The warning was conspicuously ineffective; everybody looked eagerly forward to the day and the unchanged locality; to the greatest hopefulness and anticipation was added the stirring of defiance, and when at last the appointed hour had arrived, the picnic party passed down the twisting mountain trail through the heat and glare in a fever of enthusiasm.

It was a pretty sight to view this sparkling procession—the girls cool and radiant in their white, blue, and yellow muslins and flying ribbons, the "Contingent" in its cleanest ducks, and blue and red flannel shirts, the judge white-waistcoated and panama-hatted, with a new dignity borrowed from the previous circumstances, and three or four impressive Chinamen bringing up the rear with hampers—as it at last debouched into Reservoir Cañon.

Here they dispersed themselves over the limited area,

scarcely half an acre, with the freedom of escaped school
children. They were secure in their woodland privacy.
They were overlooked by no high road and its passing
teams; they were safe from accidental intrusion from the
settlement; indeed, they went so far as to effect the exclu-
siveness of "clique." At first they amused themselves by
casting humorously defiant eyes at the long, low Ditch
Reservoir, which peeped over the green wall of the ridge,
six hundred feet above them; at times they even simulated an
exaggerated terror of it, and one recognized humorist declaimed a grotesque appeal to its forbearance, with delightful local allusions. Others pretended to discover near a
woodman's hut, among the belt of pines at the top of the
descending trail, the peeping figure of the ridiculous and
envious Sparrell. But all this was presently forgotten in
the actual festivity. Small as was the range of the valley,
it still allowed retreats during the dances for waiting couples
among the convenient laurel and manzanita bushes which
flounced the mountainside. After the dancing, old-fashioned
children's games were revived with great laughter and half-
hearted and coy protests from the ladies; notably one pastime
known as "I'm a-pinin'," in which ingenious performance
the victim was obliged to stand in the centre of a circle
and publicly "pine" for a member of the opposite sex. Some
hilarity was occasioned by the mischievous Miss "Georgy"
Piper declaring, when it came to her turn, that she was
"pinin'" for a look at the face of Tom Sparrell just now!

In this local trifling two hours passed, until the party sat
down to the long-looked-for repast. It was here that the
health of Judge Piper was neatly proposed by the editor of
the "Argus." The judge responded with great dignity and
some emotion. He reminded them that it had been his
humble endeavor to promote harmony—that harmony so

characteristic of American principles—in social as he had in political circles, and particularly among the strangely constituted yet purely American elements of frontier life. He accepted the present festivity with its overflowing hospitalities, not in recognition of himself—("yes! yes!")—nor of his family—(enthusiastic protests)—but of that American principle! If at one time it seemed probable that these festivities might be marred by the machinations of envy—(groans)—or that harmony interrupted by the importation of low-toned material interests—(groans)—he could say that, looking around him, he had never before felt—er—that— Here the judge stopped short, reeled slightly forward, caught at a camp-stool, recovered himself with an apologetic smile, and turned inquiringly to his neighbor.

A light laugh—instantly suppressed—at what was at first supposed to be the effect of the "overflowing hospitality" upon the speaker himself, went around the male circle until it suddenly appeared that half a dozen others had started to their feet at the same time, with white faces, and that one of the ladies had screamed.

"What is it?" everybody was asking with interrogatory smiles.

It was Judge Piper who replied.

"A little shock of earthquake," he said blandly; "a mere thrill! I think," he added with a faint smile, "we may say that Nature herself has applauded our efforts in good old Californian fashion, and signified her assent. What are you saying, Fludder?"

"I was thinking, sir," said Fludder deferentially, in a lower voice, "that if anything was wrong in the reservoir, this shock, you know, might"—

He was interrupted by a faint crashing and crackling sound, and looking up, beheld a good-sized boulder, evidently detached from some greater height, strike the upland plateau at the left of the trail and bound into the fringe of forest beside it. A slight cloud of dust marked its course, and then lazily floated away in mid air. But it had been watched agitatedly, and it was evident that that singular loss of nervous balance which is apt to affect all those who go through the slightest earthquake experience was felt by all. But some sense of humor, however, remained.

"Looks as if the water risks we took ain't goin' to cover earthquakes," drawled Dick Frisney; "still that wasn't a bad shot, if we only knew what they were aiming at."

"Do be quiet," said Virginia Piper, her cheeks pink with excitement. "Listen, can't you? What's that funny murmuring you hear now and then up there?"

"It's only the snow-wind playin' with the pines on the summit. You girls won't allow anybody any fun but yourselves."

But here a scream from "Georgy," who, assisted by Captain Fairfax, had mounted a camp-stool at the mouth of the valley, attracted everybody's attention. She was standing upright, with dilated eyes, staring at the top of the trail. "Look!" she said excitedly, "if the trail isn't moving!"

Everybody faced in that direction. At the first glance it seemed indeed as if the trail was actually moving; wriggling and undulating its tortuous way down the mountain like a huge snake, only swollen to twice its usual size. But the second glance showed it to be no longer a trail but a channel of water, whose stream, lifted in a bore-like wall four or five feet high, was plunging down into the devoted valley.

For an instant they were unable to comprehend even the nature of the catastrophe. The reservoir was directly over their heads; the bursting of its wall they had imagined would naturally bring down the water in a dozen trickling streams or falls over the cliff above them and along the flanks of the mountain. But that its suddenly liberated volume should overflow the upland beyond and then descend in a pent-up flood by their own trail and their only avenue of escape, had been beyond their wildest fancy.

They met this smiting truth with that characteristic short laugh with which the American usually receives the blow of Fate or the unexpected—as if he recognized only the absurdity of the situation. Then they ran to the women, collected them together, and dragged them to vantages of fancied security among the bushes which flounced the long skirts of the mountain walls. But I leave this part of the description to the characteristic language of one of the party:—

"When the flood struck us, it did not seem to take any stock of us in particular, but laid itself out to 'go for' that picnic for all it was worth! It wiped it off the face of the earth in about twenty-five seconds! It first made a clean break from stem to stern, carrying everything along with it. The first thing I saw was old Judge Piper, puttin' on his best licks to get away from a big can of strawberry ice cream that was trundling after him and trying to empty itself on his collar, whenever a bigger wave lifted it. He was followed by what was left of the brass band; the big drum just humpin' itself to keep abreast o' the ice cream, mixed up with camp-stools, music-stands, a few Chinamen, and then what they call in them big San Francisco processions 'citizens generally.' The hull thing swept up the cañon inside o' thirty seconds. Then, what Captain Fairfax called 'the reflex action in the laws o' motion' happened, and darned if the hull blamed procession didn't sweep back again—this time all the heavy artillery, such as camp-kettles, lager beer kegs, bottles, glasses, and crockery that was left behind takin' the lead now, and Jedge Piper and that ice cream can bringin' up the rear. As the jedge passed us the second time, we noticed that that ice cream can—hevin' swallowed water—was kinder losing its wind, and we encouraged the old man by shoutin' out, 'Five to one on him!' And then, you wouldn't believe what followed. Why, darn my skin, when that 'reflex' met the current at the other end, it just swirled around again in what Captain Fairfax called the 'centrifugal curve,' and just went round and round the cañon like ez when yer washin' the dirt out o' a prospectin' pan—every now and then washin' some one of the boys that was in it, like scum, up ag'in the banks.

"We managed in this way to snake out the jedge, jest ez he was sailin 'round on the home stretch, passin' the quarter post two lengths ahead o' the can. A good deal o' the ice cream had washed away, but it took us ten minutes to shake the cracked ice and powdered salt out o' the old man's clothes, and warm him up again in the laurel bush where he was clinging. This sort o' 'Here we go round the mulberry bush' kep' on until most o' the humans was got out, and only the furniture o' the picnic was left in the race. Then it got kinder mixed up, and went sloshin' round here and there, ez the water kep' comin' down by the trail. Then Lulu Piper, what I was holdin' up all the time in a laurel bush, gets an idea, for all she was wet and draggled; and ez the things went bobbin' round, she calls out the figures o' a cotillon to 'em. 'Two camp-stools forward.' 'Sashay and back to your places.' 'Change partners.' 'Hands all round.'

"She was clear grit, you bet! And the joke caught on and the other girls jined in, and it kinder cheered 'em, for they was wantin' it. Then Fludder allowed to pacify 'em by sayin' he just figured up the size o' the reservoir and the size o' the cañon, and he kalkilated that the cube was about ekal, and the cañon couldn't flood any more. And then Lulu—who was peart as a jay and couldn't be fooled —speaks up and says, 'What's the matter with the ditch, Dick?'

"Lord! then we knew that she knew the worst; for of course all the water in the ditch itself—fifty miles of it!— was drainin' now into that reservoir and was bound to come down to the cañon."

It was at this point that the situation became really desperate, for they had now crawled up the steep sides as far as the bushes afforded foothold, and the water was still rising. The chatter of the girls ceased, there were long silences, in which the men discussed the wildest plans, and proposed to tear their shirts into strips to make ropes to support the girls by sticks driven into the mountainside. It was in one of those intervals that the distinct strokes of a woodman's axe were heard high on the upland at the point where the trail descended to the cañon. Every ear was alert, but only those on one side of the cañon could get a fair view of the spot. This was the good fortune of Captain Fairfax and Georgy Piper, who had climbed to the highest bush on that side, and were now standing up, gazing excitedly in that direction.

"Some one is cutting down a tree at the head of the trail," shouted Fairfax. The response and joyful explanation, "for a dam across the trail," was on everybody's lips at the same time.

But the strokes of the axe were slow and painfully intermittent. Impatience burst out.

"Yell to him to hurry up! Why haven't they brought two men?"

"It's only one man," shouted the captain, "and he seems to be a cripple. By Jiminy!—it is—yes!—it's Tom Sparrell!"

There was a dead silence. Then, I grieve to say, shame

and its twin brother rage took possession of their weak humanity. Oh, yes! It was all of a piece! Why in the name of Folly hadn't he sent for an able-bodied man? Were they to be drowned through his cranky obstinacy?

The blows still went on slowly. Presently, however, they seemed to alternate with other blows—but alas! they were slower, and if possible feebler!

"Have they got another cripple to work?" roared the Contingent in one furious voice.

"No—it's a woman—a little one—yes! a girl. Hello! Why, sure as you live, it's Delaware!"

A spontaneous cheer burst from the Contingent, partly as a rebuke to Sparrell, I think, partly from some shame over their previous rage. He could take it as he liked.

Still the blows went on distressingly slow. The girls were hoisted on the men's shoulders; the men were half submerged. Then there was a painful pause; then a crumbling crash. Another cheer went up from the cañon.

"It's down! straight across the trail," shouted Fairfax, "and a part of the bank on the top of it."

There was another moment of suspense. Would it hold or be carried away by the momentum of the flood? It held! In a few moments Fairfax again gave voice to the cheering news that the flow had stopped and the submerged trail was reappearing. In twenty minutes it was clear—a muddy river bed, but possible of ascent! Of course there was no diminution of the water in the cañon, which had no outlet, yet it now was possible for the party to swing from bush to bush along the mountainside until the foot of the trail—no longer an opposing one—was reached. There were some missteps and mishaps,—flounderings in the water, and some dangerous rescues,—but in half an hour the whole concourse stood upon the trail and commenced the ascent. It was a slow, difficult, and lugubrious procession—I fear not the best-tempered one, now that the stimulus of danger and chivalry was past. When they reached the dam made by the fallen tree, although they were obliged to make a long detour to avoid its steep sides, they could see how successfully it had diverted the current to a declivity on the other side.

But strangely enough they were greeted by nothing else! Sparrell and the youngest Miss Piper were gone; and when they at last reached the high road, they were astounded to hear from a passing teamster that no one in the settlement knew anything of the disaster!

This was the last drop in their cup of bitterness! They who had expected that the settlement was waiting breathlessly for their rescue, who anticipated that they would be welcomed as heroes, were obliged to meet the ill-concealed amusement of passengers and friends at their disheveled and bedraggled appearance, which suggested only the blundering mishaps of an ordinary summer outing! "Boatin' in the reservoir, and fell in?" "Playing at canal-boat in the ditch?" were some of the cheerful hypotheses. The fleeting sense of gratitude they had felt for their deliverers was dissipated by the time they had reached their homes, and their rancor increased by the information that when the earthquake occurred Mr. Tom Sparrell and Miss Delaware were enjoying a "pasear" in the forest—he having a half holiday by virtue of the festival—and that the earthquake had revived his fears of a catastrophe. The two had procured axes in the woodman's hut and did what they thought was necessary to relieve the situation of the picnickers. But the very modesty of this account of their own performance had the effect of belittling the catastrophe itself, and the picnickers' report of their exceeding peril was received with incredulous laughter.

For the first time in the history of Red Gulch there was

a serious division between the Piper family, supported by the Contingent and the rest of the settlement. Tom Sparrell's warning was remembered by the latter, and the ingratitude of the picnickers to their rescuers commented upon; the actual calamity to the reservoir was more or less attributed to the imprudent and reckless contiguity of the revelers on that day, and there were not wanting those who referred the accident itself to the machinations of the scheming Ditch Director Piper!

It was said that there was a stormy scene in the Piper household that evening. The judge had demanded that Delaware should break off her acquaintance with Sparrell, and she had refused; the judge had demanded of Sparrell's employer that he should discharge him, and had been met with the astounding information that Sparrell was already a silent partner in the concern. At this revelation Judge Piper was alarmed; while he might object to a clerk who could not support a wife, as a consistent democrat he could not oppose a fairly prosperous tradesman. A final appeal was made to Delaware; she was implored to consider the situation of her sisters, who had all made more ambitious marriages or were about to make them. Why should she now degrade the family by marrying a country storekeeper?

It was said that here the youngest Miss Piper made a memorable reply, and a revelation the truth of which was never gainsaid:—

"You all wanter know why I'm going to marry Tom Sparrell?" she queried, standing up and facing the whole family circle.

"Yes."

"Why I prefer him to the hull caboodle that you girls have married or are going to marry?" she continued, meditatively biting the end of her braid.

"Yes."

"Well, he's the only man of the whole lot that hasn't proposed to me first."

It is presumed that Sparrell made good the omission, or that the family were glad to get rid of her, for they were married that autumn. And really a later comparison of the family records shows that while Captain Fairfax remained "Captain Fairfax," and the other sons-in-law did not advance proportionately in standing or riches, the lame storekeeper of Red Gulch became the Hon. Senator Tom Sparrell.

```
┌─────────────────────────────────┐
│        C O L O N E L            │
│      S T A R B O T T L E        │
│    F O R  T H E  P L A I N T I F F │
└─────────────────────────────────┘
```

It had been a day of triumph for Colonel Starbottle. First, for his personality, as it would have been difficult to separate the Colonel's achievements from his individuality; second, for his oratorical abilities as a sympathetic pleader; and third, for his functions as the leading legal counsel for the Eureka Ditch Company *versus* the State of California. On his strictly legal performances in this issue I prefer not to speak; there were those who denied them, although the jury had accepted them in the face of the ruling of the half-amused, half-cynical Judge himself. For an hour they had laughed with the Colonel, wept with him, been stirred to personal indignation or patriotic exaltation by his passionate and lofty periods,—what else could they do than give him their verdict? If it was alleged by some that the American eagle, Thomas Jefferson, and the Resolutions of '98 had nothing whatever to do with the contest of a ditch company over a doubtfully worded legislative document; that whole-sale abuse of the State Attorney and his political motives had not the sligthest connection with the legal question raised— it was, nevertheless, generally accepted that the losing party would have been only too glad to have the Colonel on their side. And Colonel Starbottle knew this, as, perspiring, florid, and panting, he rebuttoned the lower buttons of his blue frock-coat, which had become loosed in an oratorical spasm, and readjusted his old-fashioned, spotless shirt frill above it as he strutted from the court-room amidst the hand-shakings and acclamations of his friends.

And here an unprecedented thing occurred. The Colonel absolutely declined spirituous refreshment at the neighboring Palmetto Saloon, and declared his intention of proceeding directly to his office in the adjoining square. Nevertheless, the Colonel quitted the building alone, and apparently unarmed, except for his faithful gold-headed stick, which hung as usual from his forearm. The crowd gazed after him with undisguised admiration of this new evidence of his pluck. It was remembered also that a mysterious note had been handed to him at the conclusion of his speech,—evidently a challenge from the State Attorney. It was quite plain that the Colonel—a practiced duelist—was hastening home to answer it.

But herein they were wrong. The note was in a female hand, and simply requested the Colonel to accord an interview with the writer at the Colonel's office as soon as he left the court. But it was an engagement that the Colonel—as devoted to the fair sex as he was to the "code"—was no less prompt in accepting. He flicked away the dust from his spotless white trousers and varnished boots with his handkerchief, and settled his black cravat under his Byron collar as he neared his office. He was surprised, however, on opening the door of his private office, to find his visitor already there; he was still more startled to find her somewhat past middle age and plainly attired. But the Colonel was brought up in a school of Southern politeness, already antique in the republic, and his bow of courtesy belonged to the epoch of his shirt frill and strapped trousers. No one could have detected his disappointment in his manner, albeit his sentences were short and incomplete. But the Colonel's colloquial speech was apt to be fragmentary incoherencies of his larger oratorical utterances.

"A thousand pardons—for—er—having kept a lady waiting—er! But—er—congratulations of friends—and—er—courtesy due to them—er—interfered with—though perhaps only heightened—by procrastination—the pleasure of—ha!" And the Colonel completed his sentence with a gallant wave of his fat but white and well-kept hand.

"Yes! I came to see you along o' that speech of yours. I was in court. When I heard you gettin' it off on that jury, I says to myself, 'That's the kind o' lawyer *I* want. A man that's flowery and convincin'! Just the man to take up our case.' "

"Ah! It's a matter of business, I see," said the Colonel, inwardly relieved, but externally careless. "And—er—may I ask the nature of the case?"

"Well! it's a breach-o'-promise suit," said the visitor calmly.

If the Colonel had been surprised before, he was now really startled, and with an added horror that required all his politeness to conceal. Breach-of-promise cases were his peculiar aversion. He had always held them to be a kind of litigation which could have been obviated by the prompt killing of the masculine offender—in which case he would have gladly defended the killer. But a suit for damages,—*damages*!—with the reading of love-letters before a hilarious jury and court, was against all his instincts. His chivalry was outraged; his sense of humor was small, and in the course of his career he had lost one or two important cases through an unexpected development of this quality in a jury.

The woman had evidently noticed his hesitation, but mistook its cause. "It ain't me—but my darter."

The Colonel recovered his politeness. "Ah! I am relieved, my dear madam! I could hardly conceive a man ignorant

enough to—er—er—throw away such evident good fortune—or base enough to deceive the trustfulness of womanhood—matured and experienced only in the chivalry of our
sex, ha!"

The woman smiled grimly. "Yes!—it's my darter, Zaidee
Hooker—so ye might spare some of them pretty speeches
for *her*—before the jury."

The Colonel winced slightly before this doubtful prospect,
but smiled. "Ha! Yes!—certainly—the jury. But—er—my
dear lady, need we go as far as that? Cannot this affair be
settled—er—out of court? Could not this—er—individual—
be admonished—told that he must give satisfaction—personal
satisfaction—for his dastardly conduct—to—er—near relative
—or even valued personal friend? The—er—arrangements
necessary for that purpose I myself would undertake."

He was quite sincere; indeed, his small black eyes shone
with that fire which a pretty woman or an "affair of honor"
could alone kindle. The visitor stared vacantly at him, and
said slowly, "And what good is that goin' to do *us*?"

"Compel him to—er—perform his promise," said the
Colonel, leaning back in his chair.

"Ketch him doin' it!" she exclaimed scornfully. "No—that
ain't wot we're after. We must make him *pay*! Damages—
and nothin' short o' *that*."

The Colonel bit his lip. "I suppose," he said gloomily, "you
have documentary evidence—written promises and protestations—er—er—love-letters, in fact?"

"No—nary a letter! Ye see, that's jest it—and that's where
you come in. You've got to convince that jury yourself. You've
got to show what it is—tell the whole story your own way.
Lord! to a man like you that's nothin'."

Startling as this admission might have been to any other
lawyer, Starbottle was absolutely relieved by it. The absence

of any mirth-provoking correspondence, and the appeal solely to his own powers of persuasion, actually struck his fancy. He lightly put aside the compliment with a wave of his white hand.

"Of course," he said confidently, "there is strongly presumptive and corroborative evidence? Perhaps you can give me—er—a brief outline of the affair?"

"Zaidee kin do that straight enough, I reckon," said the woman; "what I want to know first is, kin you take the case?"

The Colonel did not hesitate; his curiosity was piqued. "I certainly can. I have no doubt your daughter will put me in possession of sufficient facts and details—to constitute what we call—er—a brief."

"She kin be brief enough—or long enough—for the matter of that," said the woman, rising. The Colonel accepted this implied witticism with a smile.

"And when may I have the pleasure of seeing her?" he asked politely.

"Well, I reckon as soon as I can trot out and call her. She's just outside, meanderin' in the road—kinder shy, ye know, at first."

She walked to the door. The astounded Colonel nevertheless gallantly accompanied her as she stepped out into the street and called shrilly, "You Zaidee!"

A young girl here apparently detached herself from a tree and the ostentatious perusal of an old election poster, and sauntered down towards the office door. Like her mother, she was plainly dressed; unlike her, she had a pale, rather refined face, with a demure mouth and downcast eyes. This was all the Colonel saw as he bowed profoundly and led the way into his office, for she accepted his salutations without lifting her head. He helped her gallantly to a chair, on which she seated herself sideways, somewhat ceremoniously, with her eyes following the point of her parasol as she traced a pattern on the carpet. A second chair offered to the mother, that lady, however, declined. "I reckon to leave you and Zaidee together to talk it out," she said; turning to her daughter, she added, "Jest you tell him all, Zaidee," and before the Colonel could rise again, disappeared from the room. In spite of his professional experience, Starbottle was for a moment embarrassed. The young girl, however, broke the silence without looking up.

"Adoniram K. Hotchkiss," she began, in a monotonous voice, as if it were a recitation addressed to the public, "first began to take notice of me a year ago. Arter that—off and on"—

"One moment," interrupted the astounded Colonel; "do you mean Hotchkiss the President of the Ditch Company?" He had recognized the name of a prominent citizen—a rigid, ascetic, taciturn, middle-aged man—a deacon—and more than that, the head of the company he had just defended. It seemed inconceivable.

"That's him," she continued, with eyes still fixed on the parasol and without changing her monotonous tone—"off and on ever since. Most of the time at the Free-Will Baptist Church—at morning service, prayer-meetings, and such. And at home—outside—er—in the road."

"Is it this gentleman—Mr. Adoniram K. Hotchkiss—who—er—promised marriage?" stammered the Colonel.

"Yes."

The Colonel shifted uneasily in his chair. "Most extraordinary! for—you see—my dear young lady—this becomes—a—er—most delicate affair."

"That's what maw said," returned the young woman

simply, yet with the faintest smile playing around her demure lips and downcast cheek.

"I mean," said the Colonel, with a pained yet courteous smile, "that this—er—gentleman—is in fact—er—one of my clients."

"That's what maw said too, and of course your knowing him will make it all the easier for you."

A slight flush crossed the Colonel's cheek as he returned quickly and a little stiffly, "On the contrary—er—it may make it impossible for me to—er—act in this matter."

The girl lifted her eyes. The Colonel held his breath as the long lashes were raised to his level. Even to an ordinary observer that sudden revelation of her eyes seemed to transform her face with subtle witchery. They were large, brown, and soft, yet filled with an extraordinary penetration and prescience. They were the eyes of an experienced woman of thirty fixed in the face of a child. What else the Colonel saw there Heaven only knows! He felt his inmost secrets plucked from him—his whole soul laid bare—his vanity, belligerency, gallantry—even his mediæval chivalry, penetrated, and yet illuminated, in that single glance. And when the eyelids fell again, he felt that a greater part of himself had been swallowed up in them.

"I beg your pardon," he said hurriedly. "I mean—this matter may be arranged—er—amicably. My interest with—and as you wisely say—my—er—knowledge of my client—er—Mr. Hotchkiss—may effect—a compromise."

"And *damages*," said the young girl, readdressing her parasol, as if she had never looked up.

The Colonel winced. "And—er—undoubtedly *compensation*—if you do not press a fulfillment of the promise. Unless," he said, with an attempted return to his former easy gallantry, which, however, the recollection of her eyes made difficult, "it is a question of—er—the affections."

"Which?" asked his fair client softly.

"If you still love him?" explained the Colonel, actually blushing.

Zaidee again looked up; again taking the Colonel's breath away with eyes that expressed not only the fullest perception of what he had *said,* but of what he thought and had not said, and with an added subtle suggestion of what he might have thought. "That's tellin'," she said, dropping her long lashes again.

The Colonel laughed vacantly. Then feeling himself growing imbecile, he forced an equally weak gravity. "Pardon me —I understand there are no letters; may I know the way in which he formulated his declaration and promises?"

"Hymn-books."

"I beg your pardon," said the mystified lawyer.

"Hymn-books—marked words in them with pencil—and passed 'em on to me," repeated Zaidee. "Like 'love,' 'dear,' 'precious,' 'sweet,' and 'blessed,'" she added, accenting each word with a push of her parasol on the carpet. "Sometimes a whole line outer Tate and Brady—and Solomon's Song, you know, and sich."

"I believe," said the Colonel loftily, "that the—er—phrases of sacred psalmody lend themselves to the language of the affections. But in regard to the distinct promise of marriage —was there—er—no *other* expression?"

"Marriage Service in the prayer-book—lines and words outer that—all marked," Zaidee replied.

The Colonel nodded naturally and approvingly. "Very good. Were others cognizant of this? Were there any witnesses?"

"Of course not," said the girl. "Only me and him. It was

generally at church-time—or prayer-meeting. Once, in passing the plate, he slipped one o' them peppermint lozenges with the letters stamped on it 'I love you' for me to take."

The Colonel coughed slightly. "And you have the lozenge?"

"I ate it."

"Ah," said the Colonel. After a pause he added delicately, "But were these attentions—er—confined to—er—sacred precincts? Did he meet you elsewhere?"

"Useter pass our house on the road," returned the girl, dropping into her monotonous recital, "and useter signal."

"Ah, signal?" repeated the Colonel approvingly.

"Yes! He'd say 'Keerow,' and I'd say 'Keeree.' Suthing like a bird, you know."

Indeed, as she lifted her voice in imitation of the call, the Colonel thought it certainly very sweet and birdlike. At least as *she* gave it. With his remembrance of the grim deacon he had doubts as to the melodiousness of *his* utterance. He gravely made her repeat it.

"And after that signal?" he added suggestively.

"He'd pass on."

The Colonel again coughed slightly, and tapped his desk with his penholder.

"Were there any endearments—er—caresses—er—such as taking your hand—er—clasping your waist?" he suggested, with a gallant yet respectful sweep of his white hand and bowing of his head; "er—slight pressure of your fingers in the changes of a dance—I mean," he corrected himself, with an apologetic cough—"in the passing of the plate?"

"No; he was not what you'd call 'fond,'" returned the girl.

"Ah! Adoniram K. Hotchkiss was not 'fond' in the ordinary acceptance of the word," noted the Colonel, with professional gravity.

She lifted her disturbing eyes, and again absorbed his in her own. She also said "Yes," although her eyes in their mysterious prescience of all he was thinking disclaimed the necessity of any answer at all. He smiled vacantly. There was a long pause; on which she slowly disengaged her parasol from the carpet pattern, and stood up.

"I reckon that's about all," she said.

"Er—yes—but one moment," began the Colonel vaguely. He would have liked to keep her longer, but with her strange premonition of him he felt powerless to detain her, or explain his reason for doing so. He instinctively knew she had told him all; his professional judgment told him that a more hopeless case had never come to his knowledge. Yet he was not daunted, only embarrassed. "No matter," he said. "Of course I shall have to consult with you again."

Her eyes again answered that she expected he would, and she added simply, "When?"

"In the course of a day or two," he replied quickly. "I will send you word."

She turned to go. In his eagerness to open the door for her, he upset his chair, and with some confusion, that was actually youthful, he almost impeded her movements in the hall, and knocked his broad-brimmed Panama hat from his bowing hand in a final gallant sweep. Yet as her small, trim, youthful figure, with its simple Leghorn straw hat confined by a blue bow under her round chin, passed away before him, she looked more like a child than ever.

The Colonel spent that afternoon in making diplomatic inquiries. He found his youthful client was the daughter of a widow who had a small ranch on the crossroads, near the new Free-Will Baptist Church—the evident theatre of this pastoral. They led a secluded life, the girl being little known in the town, and her beauty and fascination apparently not yet being a recognized fact. The Colonel felt a pleasurable relief at this, and a general satisfaction he could not account for. His few inquiries concerning Mr. Hotchkiss only confirmed his own impressions of the alleged lover,— a serious-minded, practically abstracted man, abstentive of youthful society, and the last man apparently capable of levity of the affections or serious flirtation. The Colonel was mystified, but determined of purpose, whatever that purpose might have been.

The next day he was at his office at the same hour. He was alone—as usual—the Colonel's office being really his private lodgings, disposed in connecting rooms, a single apartment reserved for consultation. He had no clerk, his papers and briefs being taken by his faithful body-servant and ex-slave "Jim" to another firm who did his office work since the death of Major Stryker, the Colonel's only law partner, who fell in a duel some years previous. With a fine constancy the Colonel still retained his partner's name on his doorplate, and, it was alleged by the superstitious, kept a certain invincibility also through the *manes* of that lamented and somewhat feared man.

The Colonel consulted his watch, whose heavy gold case still showed the marks of a providential interference with a bullet destined for its owner, and replaced it with some difficulty and shortness of breath in his fob. At the same moment he heard a step in the passage, and the door opened to Adoniram K. Hotchkiss. The Colonel was impressed; he had a duelist's respect for punctuality.

The man entered with a nod and the expectant inquiring look of a busy man. As his feet crossed that sacred threshold the Colonel became all courtesy; he placed a chair for his visitor, and took his hat from his half-reluctant hand. He then opened a cupboard and brought out a bottle of whiskey and two glasses.

"A—er—slight refreshment, Mr. Hotchkiss," he suggested politely.

"I never drink," replied Hotchkiss, with the severe attitude of a total abstainer.

"Ah—er—not the finest Bourbon whiskey, selected by a Kentucky friend? No? Pardon me! A cigar, then—the mildest Havana."

"I do not use tobacco nor alcohol in any form," repeated Hotchkiss ascetically. "I have no foolish weaknesses."

The Colonel's moist, beady eyes swept silently over his client's sallow face. He leaned back comfortably in his chair, and half closing his eyes as in dreamy reminiscence, said slowly: "Your reply, Mr. Hotchkiss, reminds me of—er—sing'lar circumstance that—er—occurred, in point of fact—at the St. Charles Hotel, New Orleans. Pinkey Hornblower—personal friend—invited Senator Doolittle to join him in social glass. Received, sing'larly enough, reply similar to yours. 'Don't drink nor smoke?' said Pinkey. 'Gad, sir, you must be mighty sweet on the ladies.' Ha!" The Colonel paused long enough to allow the faint flush to pass from Hotchkiss's cheek, and went on, half closing his eyes: "'I allow no man, sir, to discuss my personal habits,' declared Doolittle, over his shirt collar. 'Then I reckon shootin' must be one of those habits,' said Pinkey coolly. Both men drove out on the Shell Road back of cemetery next morning. Pinkey put bullet at twelve paces through Doolittle's temple. Poor Doo never spoke again. Left three wives and seven children, they say—two of 'em black."

"I got a note from you this morning," said Hotchkiss,

with badly concealed impatience. "I suppose in reference to our case. You have taken judgment, I believe."

The Colonel, without replying, slowly filled a glass of whiskey and water. For a moment he held it dreamily before him, as if still engaged in gentle reminiscences called up by the act. Then tossing it off, he wiped his lips with a large white handkerchief, and leaning back comfortably in his chair, said, with a wave of his hand, "The interview I requested, Mr. Hotchkiss, concerns a subject—which I may say is—er—er—at present *not* of a public or business nature —although *later* it might become—er—er—both. It is an affair of some—er—delicacy."

The Colonel paused, and Mr. Hotchkiss regarded him with increased impatience. The Colonel, however, continued, with unchanged deliberation: "It concerns—er—er—a young lady—a beautiful, high-souled creature, sir, who, apart from her personal loveliness—er—er—I may say is of one of the first families of Missouri, and—er—not remotely connected by marriage with one of—er—er—my boyhood's dearest friends." The latter, I grieve to say, was a pure invention of the Colonel's—an oratorical addition to the scanty information he had obtained the previous day. "The young lady," he continued blandly, "enjoys the further distinction of being the object of such attention from you as would make this interview—really—a confidential matter—er—er—among friends and—er—er—relations in present and future. I need not say that the lady I refer to is Miss Zaidee Juno Hooker, only daughter of Almira Ann Hooker, relict of Jefferson Brown Hooker, formerly of Boone County, Kentucky, and latterly of—er—Pike County, Missouri."

The sallow, ascetic hue of Mr. Hotchkiss's face had passed through a livid and then a greenish shade, and finally settled into a sullen red. "What's all this about?" he demanded roughly.

The least touch of belligerent fire came into Starbottle's eye, but his bland courtesy did not change. "I believe," he said politely, "I have made myself clear as between—er—gentlemen, though perhaps not as clear as I should to—er—er—jury."

Mr. Hotchkiss was apparently struck with some significance in the lawyer's reply. "I don't know," he said, in a lower and more cautious voice, "what you mean by what you call 'my attentions' to—any one—or how it concerns you. I have not exchanged half a dozen words with—the person you name—have never written her a line—nor even called at her house."

He rose with an assumption of ease, pulled down his waistcoat, buttoned his coat, and took up his hat. The Colonel did not move.

"I believe I have already indicated my meaning in what I have called 'your attentions,'" said the Colonel blandly, "and given you my 'concern' for speaking as—er—er—mutual friend. As to *your* statement of your relations with Miss Hooker, I may state that it is fully corroborated by the statement of the young lady herself in this very office yesterday."

"Then what does this impertinent nonsense mean? Why am I summoned here?" demanded Hotchkiss furiously.

"Because," said the Colonel deliberately, "that statement is infamously—yes, damnably to your discredit, sir!"

Mr. Hotchkiss was here seized by one of those impotent and inconsistent rages which occasionally betray the habitually cautious and timid man. He caught up the Colonel's stick, which was lying on the table. At the same moment the Colonel, without any apparent effort, grasped it by the handle. To Mr. Hotchkiss's astonishment, the stick separated in two pieces, leaving the handle and about two feet of narrow glittering steel in the Colonel's hand. The man recoiled, dropping the useless fragment. The Colonel picked it up, fitted the shining blade in it, clicked the spring, and then rising with a face of courtesy yet of unmistakably genuine pain, and with even a slight tremor in his voice, said gravely,—

"Mr. Hotchkiss, I owe you a thousand apologies, sir, that—er—a weapon should be drawn by me—even through your own inadvertence—under the sacred protection of my roof, and upon an unarmed man. I beg your pardon, sir, and I even withdraw the expressions which provoked that inadvertence. Nor does this apology prevent you from holding me responsible—personally responsible—*elsewhere* for an indiscretion committed in behalf of a lady—my—er—client."

"Your client? Do you mean you have taken her case? You, the counsel for the Ditch Company?" asked Mr. Hotchkiss, in trembling indignation.

"Having won *your* case, sir," replied the Colonel coolly, "the—er—usages of advocacy do not prevent me from espousing the cause of the weak and unprotected."

"We shall see, sir," said Hotchkiss, grasping the handle of the door and backing into the passage. "There are other lawyers who"—

"Permit me to see you out," interrupted the Colonel, rising politely.

—"will be ready to resist the attacks of blackmail," continued Hotchkiss, retreating along the passage.

"And then you will be able to repeat your remarks to me *in the street*," continued the Colonel, bowing, as he persisted in following his visitor to the door.

But here Mr. Hotchkiss quickly slammed it behind him,

and hurried away. The Colonel returned to his office, and sitting down, took a sheet of letter-paper bearing the inscription "Starbottle and Stryker, Attorneys and Counselors," and wrote the following lines:—

Hooker *versus* Hotchkiss.

Dear Madam,—Having had a visit from the defendant in above, we should be pleased to have an interview with you at two p. m. to-morrow.

Your obedient servants,
Starbottle and Stryker.

This he sealed and dispatched by his trusted servant Jim, and then devoted a few moments to reflection. It was the custom of the Colonel to act first, and justify the action by reason afterwards.

He knew that Hotchkiss would at once lay the matter before rival counsel. He knew that they would advise him that Miss Hooker had "no case"—that she would be nonsuited on her own evidence, and he ought not to compromise, but be ready to stand trial. He believed, however, that Hotchkiss feared such exposure, and although his own instincts had been at first against this remedy, he was now instinctively in favor of it. He remembered his own power with a jury; his vanity and his chivalry alike approved of this heroic method; he was bound by no prosaic facts—he had his own theory of the case, which no mere evidence could gainsay. In fact, Mrs. Hooker's admission that he was to "tell the story in his own way" actually appeared to him an inspiration and a prophecy.

Perhaps there was something else, due possibly to the lady's wonderful eyes, of which he had thought much. Yet it was not her simplicity that affected him solely; on the contrary, it was her apparent intelligent reading of the character of her recreant lover—and of his own! Of all the Colonel's previous "light" or "serious" loves, none had ever before flattered him in that way. And it was this, combined with the respect which he had held for their professional relations, that precluded his having a more familiar knowledge of his client, through serious questioning or playful gallantry. I am not sure it was not part of the charm to have a rustic *femme incomprise* as a client.

Nothing could exceed the respect with which he greeted her as she entered his office the next day. He even affected not to notice that she had put on her best clothes, and, he made no doubt, appeared as when she had first attracted the mature yet faithless attentions of Deacon Hotchkiss at church. A white virginal muslin was belted around her slim figure by a blue ribbon, and her Leghorn hat was drawn around her oval cheek by a bow of the same color. She had a Southern girl's narrow feet, encased in white stockings and kid slippers, which were crossed primly before her as she sat in a chair, supporting her arm by her faithful parasol planted firmly on the floor. A faint odor of southernwood exhaled from her, and, oddly enough, stirred the Colonel with a far-off recollection of a pine-shaded Sunday-school on a Georgia hillside, and of his first love, aged ten, in a short starched frock. Possibly it was the same recollection that revived something of the awkwardness he had felt then.

He, however, smiled vaguely, and sitting down, coughed slightly, and placed his finger-tips together. "I have had an —er—interview with Mr. Hotchkiss, but—I—er—regret to say there seems to be no prospect of—er—compromise."

He paused, and to his surprise her listless "company" face lit up with an adorable smile. "Of course!—ketch him!"

she said. "Was he mad when you told him?" She put her knees comfortably together and leaned forward for a reply.

For all that, wild horses could not have torn from the Colonel a word about Hotchkiss's anger. "He expressed his intention of employing counsel—and defending a suit," returned the Colonel, affably basking in her smile.

She dragged her chair nearer his desk. "Then you'll fight him tooth and nail?" she asked eagerly; "you'll show him up? You'll tell the whole story your own way? You'll give him fits?—and you'll make him pay? Sure?" she went on breathlessly.

"I—er—will," said the Colonel almost as breathlessly.

She caught his fat white hand, which was lying on the table, between her own and lifted it to her lips. He felt her soft young fingers even through the lisle-thread gloves that encased them, and the warm moisture of her lips upon his skin. He felt himself flushing—but was unable to break the silence or change his position. The next moment she had scuttled back with her chair to her old position.

"I—er—certainly shall do my best," stammered the Colonel, in an attempt to recover his dignity and composure.

"That's enough! You'll *do* it," said she enthusiastically. "Lordy! Just you talk for *me* as ye did for *his* old Ditch Company, and you'll fetch it—every time! Why, when you made that jury sit up the other day—when you got that off about the Merrikan flag waving equally over the rights of honest citizens banded together in peaceful commercial pursuits, as well as over the fortress of official proflig—"

"Oligarchy," murmured the Colonel courteously.

—"oligarchy," repeated the girl quickly, "my breath was just took away. I said to maw, 'Ain't he too sweet for anything!' I did, honest Injin! And when you rolled it all off at the end—never missing a word (you didn't need to mark

'em in a lesson-book, but had 'em all ready on your tongue)—
and walked out— Well! I didn't know you nor the Ditch
Company from Adam, but I could have just run over and
kissed you there before the whole court!"

She laughed, with her face glowing, although her strange
eyes were cast down. Alack! the Colonel's face was equally
flushed, and his own beady eyes were on his desk. To any
other woman he would have voiced the banal gallantry that
he should now, himself, look forward to that reward, but
the words never reached his lips. He laughed, coughed
slightly, and when he looked up again she had fallen into
the same attitude as on her first visit, with her parasol point
on the floor.

"I must ask you to—er—direct your memory to—er—
another point: the breaking off of the—er—er—er—engagement. Did he—er—give any reason for it? Or show any
cause?"

"No; he never said anything," returned the girl.

"Not in his usual way?—er—no reproaches out of the
hymn-book?—or the sacred writings?"

"No; he just *quit*."

"Er—ceased his attentions," said the Colonel gravely. "And
naturally you—er—were not conscious of any cause for his
doing so."

The girl raised her wonderful eyes so suddenly and so
penetratingly without replying in any other way that the
Colonel could only hurriedly say: "I see! None, of course!"

At which she rose, the Colonel rising also. "We—shall
begin proceedings at once. I must, however, caution you
to answer no questions, nor say anything about this case to
any one until you are in court."

She answered his request with another intelligent look
and a nod. He accompanied her to the door. As he took

her proffered hand, he raised the lisle-thread fingers to his lips with old-fashioned gallantry. As if that act had condoned for his first omissions and awkwardness, he became his old-fashioned self again, buttoned his coat, pulled out his shirt frill, and strutted back to his desk.

A day or two later it was known throughout the town that Zaidee Hooker had sued Adoniram Hotchkiss for breach of promise, and that the damages were laid at five thousand dollars. As in those bucolic days the Western press was under the secure censorship of a revolver, a cautious tone of criticism prevailed, and any gossip was confined to personal expression, and even then at the risk of the gossiper. Nevertheless, the situation provoked the intensest curiosity. The Colonel was approached—until his statement that he should consider any attempt to overcome his professional secrecy a personal reflection withheld further advances. The community were left to the more ostentatious information of the defendant's counsel, Messrs. Kitcham and Bilser, that the case was "ridiculous" and "rotten," that the plaintiff would be nonsuited, and the fire-eating Starbottle would be taught a lesson that he could not "bully" the law, and there were some dark hints of a conspiracy. It was even hinted that the "case" was the revengeful and preposterous outcome of the refusal of Hotchkiss to pay Starbottle an extravagant fee for his late services to the Ditch Company. It is unnecessary to say that these words were not reported to the Colonel. It was, however, an unfortunate circumstance for the calmer, ethical consideration of the subject that the Church sided with Hotchkiss, as this provoked an equal adherence to the plaintiff and Starbottle on the part of the larger body of non-church-goers, who were delighted at a possible exposure of the weakness of religious rectitude. "I've allus had my suspicions o' them early candle-light meetings down at that

gospel shop," said one critic, "and I reckon Deacon Hotch-kiss didn't rope in the gals to attend jest for psalm-singing."
"Then for him to get up and leave the board afore the game's finished and try to sneak out of it," said another,—"I suppose that's what they call *religious*."

It was therefore not remarkable that the court-house three weeks later was crowded with an excited multitude of the curious and sympathizing. The fair plaintiff, with her mother, was early in attendance, and under the Colonel's advice appeared in the same modest garb in which she had first visited his office. This and her downcast, modest demeanor were perhaps at first disappointing to the crowd, who had evidently expected a paragon of loveliness in this Circe of that grim, ascetic defendant, who sat beside his counsel. But presently all eyes were fixed on the Colonel, who certainly made up in *his* appearance any deficiency of his fair client. His portly figure was clothed in a blue dress coat with brass buttons, a buff waistcoat which permitted his frilled shirt-front to become erectile above it, a black satin stock which confined a boyish turned-down collar around his full neck, and immaculate drill trousers, strapped over varnished boots. A murmur ran round the court. "Old 'Personally Responsible' has got his war-paint on"; "The Old War-Horse is smelling powder," were whispered comments. Yet for all that, the most irreverent among them recognized vaguely, in this bizarre figure, something of an honored past in their country's history, and possibly felt the spell of old deeds and old names that had once thrilled their boyish pulses. The new District Judge returned Colonel Starbottle's profoundly punctilious bow. The Colonel was followed by his Negro servant, carrying a parcel of hymn-books and Bibles, who, with a courtesy evidently imitated from his master, placed one before the opposite counsel. This, after a first curious glance, the lawyer somewhat superciliously tossed aside. But when Jim, proceeding to the jury-box, placed with equal politeness the remaining copies before the jury, the opposite counsel sprang to his feet.

"I want to direct the attention of the Court to this unprecedented tampering with the jury, by this gratuitous exhibition of matter impertinent and irrelevant to the issue."

The Judge cast an inquiring look at Colonel Starbottle.

"May it please the Court," returned Colonel Starbottle with dignity, ignoring the counsel, "the defendant's counsel will observe that he is already furnished with the matter—which I regret to say he has treated—in the presence of the Court—and of his client, a deacon of the church—with—er—great superciliousness. When I state to Your Honor that the books in question are hymn-books and copies of the Holy Scriptures, and that they are for the instruction of the jury, to whom I shall have to refer them in the course of my opening, I believe I am within my rights."

"The act is certainly unprecedented," said the Judge dryly, "but unless the counsel for the plaintiff expects the jury to *sing* from these hymn-books, their introduction is not improper, and I cannot admit the objection. As defendant's counsel are furnished with copies also, they cannot plead 'surprise,' as in the introduction of new matter, and as plaintiff's counsel relies evidently upon the jury's attention to his opening, he would not be the first person to distract it." After a pause he added, addressing the Colonel, who remained standing, "The Court is with you, sir; proceed."

But the Colonel remained motionless and statuesque, with folded arms.

"I have overruled the objection," repeated the Judge; "you may go on."

"I am waiting, Your Honor, for the—er—withdrawal by

the defendant's counsel of the word 'tampering,' as refers to myself, and of 'impertinent,' as refers to the sacred volumes."

"The request is a proper one, and I have no doubt will be acceded to," returned the Judge quietly. The defendant's counsel rose and mumbled a few words of apology, and the incident closed. There was, however, a general feeling that the Colonel had in some way "scored," and if his object had been to excite the greatest curiosity about the books, he had made his point.

But impassive of his victory, he inflated his chest, with his right hand in the breast of his buttoned coat, and began. His usual high color had paled slightly, but the small pupils of his prominent eyes glittered like steel. The young girl leaned forward in her chair with an attention so breathless, a sympathy so quick, and an admiration so artless and unconscious that in an instant she divided with the speaker the attention of the whole assemblage. It was very hot; the court was crowded to suffocation; even the open windows revealed a crowd of faces outside the building, eagerly following the Colonel's words.

He would remind the jury that only a few weeks ago he stood there as the advocate of a powerful Company, then represented by the present defendant. He spoke then as the champion of strict justice against legal oppression; no less should he to-day champion the cause of the unprotected and the comparatively defenseless—save for that paramount power which surrounds beauty and innocence—even though the plaintiff of yesterday was the defendant of to-day. As he approached the court a moment ago he had raised his eyes and beheld the starry flag flying from its dome, and he knew that glorious banner was a symbol of the perfect equality, under the Constitution, of the rich and the poor, the strong and the weak—an equality which made the simple citizen taken from the plough in the field, the pick in the gulch, or from behind the counter in the mining town, who served on that jury, the equal arbiters of justice with that highest legal luminary whom they were proud to welcome on the bench to-day. The Colonel paused, with a stately bow to the impassive Judge. It was this, he continued, which lifted his heart as he approached the building. And yet—he had entered it with an uncertain—he might almost say—a timid step. And why? He knew, gentlemen, he was about to confront a profound—ay! a sacred responsibility! Those hymn-books and holy writings handed to the jury were *not*, as His Honor had surmised, for the purpose of enabling the jury to indulge in—er—preliminary choral exercise! He might, indeed, say, "Alas, not!" They were the damning, incontrovertible proofs of the perfidy of the defendant. And they would prove as terrible a warning to him as the fatal characters upon Belshazzar's wall. There was a strong sensation. Hotchkiss turned a sallow green. His lawyers assumed a careless smile.

It was his duty to tell them that this was not one of those ordinary "breach-of-promise" cases which were too often the occasion of ruthless mirth and indecent levity in the court-room. The jury would find nothing of that here. There were no love-letters with the epithets of endearment, nor those mystic crosses and ciphers which, he had been credibly informed, chastely hid the exchange of those mutual caresses known as "kisses." There was no cruel tearing of the veil from those sacred privacies of the human affection; there was no forensic shouting out of those fond confidences meant only for *one*. But there was, he was shocked to say, a new sacrilegious intrusion. The weak pipings of Cupid were mingled with the chorus of the saints,—the sanctity of the temple known as the "meeting house" was desecrated by proceedings more in keeping with the shrine of Venus; and the inspired writings themselves were used as the medium of amatory and wanton flirtation by the defendant in his sacred capacity as deacon.

The Colonel artistically paused after this thunderous denunciation. The jury turned eagerly to the leaves of the hymn-books, but the larger gaze of the audience remained fixed upon the speaker and the girl, who sat in rapt admiration of his periods. After the hush, the Colonel continued in a lower and sadder voice: "There are, perhaps, few of us here, gentlemen,—with the exception of the defendant,— who can arrogate to themselves the title of regular church-goers, or to whom these humbler functions of the prayer-meeting, the Sunday-school, and the Bible-class are habitually familiar. Yet"—more solemnly—"down in our hearts is the deep conviction of our shortcomings and failings, and a laudable desire that others, at least, should profit by the teachings we neglect. Perhaps," he continued, closing his eyes dreamily, "there is not a man here who does not recall the happy days of his boyhood, the rustic village spire, the lessons shared with some artless village maiden, with whom he later sauntered, hand in hand, through the woods, as the simple rhyme rose upon their lips,—

> *'Always make it a point to have it a rule,*
> *Never to be late at the Sabbath-school.'*

He would recall the strawberry feasts, the welcome annual picnic, redolent with hunks of gingerbread and sarsaparilla. How would they feel to know that these sacred recollections were now forever profaned in their memory by the knowledge that the defendant was capable of using such occasions to make love to the larger girls and teachers, whilst his artless companions were innocently—the Court will pardon me for introducing what I am credibly informed is the local expression—'doing gooseberry'?" The tremulous flicker of a smile passed over the faces of the listening crowd, and the Colonel slightly winced. But he recovered himself instantly, and continued,—

"My client, the only daughter of a widowed mother—who has for years stemmed the varying tides of adversity, in the western precincts of this town—stands before you to-day invested only in her own innocence. She wears no —er—rich gifts of her faithless admirer—is panoplied in no jewels, rings, nor mementos of affection such as lovers delight to hang upon the shrine of their affections; hers is not the glory with which Solomon decorated the Queen of Sheba, though the defendant, as I shall show later, clothed her in the less expensive flowers of the king's poetry. No, gentlemen! The defendant exhibited in this affair a certain frugality of—er—pecuniary investment, which I am willing to admit may be commendable in his class. His only gift was characteristic alike of his methods and his economy. There is, I understand, a certain not unimportant feature of religious exercise known as 'taking a collection.' The defendant, on this occasion, by the mute presentation of a tin plate covered with baize, solicited the pecuniary contributions of the faithful. On approaching the plaintiff, however, he himself slipped a love-token upon the plate and pushed it towards her. That love-token was a lozenge—a small disk, I have reason to believe, concocted of peppermint and sugar, bearing upon its reverse surface the simple words, 'I love you!' I have since ascertained that these disks may be bought for five cents a dozen—or at considerably less than one half cent for the single lozenge. Yes, gentlemen, the words 'I love you!'—the oldest legend of all; the refrain 'when the morning stars sang together'—were presented to the plaintiff by a medium so insignificant that there is, happily, no coin in the republic low enough to represent its value.

"I shall prove to you, gentlemen of the jury," said the Colonel solemnly, drawing a Bible from his coat-tail pocket, "that the defendant for the last twelve months conducted an amatory correspondence with the plaintiff by means of underlined words of Sacred Writ and church psalmody, such as 'beloved,' 'precious,' and 'dearest,' occasionally appropriating whole passages which seemed apposite to his tender passion. I shall call your attention to one of them. The defendant, while professing to be a total abstainer,— a man who, in my own knowledge, has refused spirituous refreshment as an inordinate weakness of the flesh,—with shameless hypocrisy underscores with his pencil the following passage, and presents it to the plaintiff. The gentlemen of the jury will find it in the Song of Solomon, page 548, chapter ii., verse 5." After a pause, in which the rapid rustling of leaves was heard in the jury-box, Colonel Starbottle declaimed in a pleading, stentorian voice, "'Stay me with—er—*flagons,* comfort me with—er—apples—for I am— er—sick of love.' Yes, gentlemen!—yes, you may well turn from those accusing pages and look at the double-faced defendant. He desires—to—er—be—'stayed with flagons'! I am not aware at present what kind of liquor is habitually dispensed at these meetings, and for which the defendant so urgently clamored; but it will be my duty, before this trial is over, to discover it, if I have to summon every barkeeper in this district. For the moment I will simply call your attention to the *quantity*. It is not a single drink that the defendant asks for—not a glass of light and generous wine, to be shared with his inamorata, but a number of flagons or vessels, each possibly holding a pint measure—*for himself!*"

The smile of the audience had become a laugh. The Judge looked up warningly, when his eye caught the fact that the Colonel had again winced at this mirth. He regarded him seriously. Mr. Hotchkiss's counsel had joined in the laugh affectedly, but Hotchkiss himself sat ashy pale. There was also a commotion in the jury-box, a hurried turning over of leaves, and an excited discussion.

"The gentlemen of the jury," said the Judge, with official gravity, "will please keep order and attend only to the speeches of counsel. Any discussion *here* is irregular and premature, and must be reserved for the jury-room after they have retired."

The foreman of the jury struggled to his feet. He was a powerful man, with a good-humored face, and, in spite of his unfelicitous nickname of "The Bone-Breaker," had a kindly, simple, but somewhat emotional nature. Nevertheless, it appeared as if he were laboring under some powerful indignation.

"Can we ask a question, Judge?" he said respectfully, although his voice had the unmistakable Western American ring in it, as of one who was unconscious that he could be addressing any but his peers.

"Yes," said the Judge good-humoredly.

"We're finding in this yere piece, out o' which the Kernel hes just bin a-quotin', some language that me and my pardners allow hadn't orter be read out afore a young lady in court, and we want to know of you—ez a fa'r-minded and impartial man—ef this is the reg'lar kind o' book given to gals and babies down at the meetin'-house."

"The jury will please follow the counsel's speech without comment," said the Judge briefly, fully aware that the defendant's counsel would spring to his feet, as he did promptly.

"The Court will allow us to explain to the gentlemen that the language they seem to object to has been accepted by the best theologians for the last thousand years as being purely mystic. As I will explain later, those are merely symbols of the Church"—

"Of wot?" interrupted the foreman, in deep scorn.

"Of the Church!"

"We ain't askin' any questions o' *you,* and we ain't takin' any answers," said the foreman, sitting down abruptly.

"I must insist," said the Judge sternly, "that the plaintiff's counsel be allowed to continue his opening without interruption. You" (to defendant's counsel) "will have your opportunity to reply later."

The counsel sank down in his seat with the bitter conviction that the jury was manifestly against him, and the case as good as lost. But his face was scarcely as disturbed as his client's, who, in great agitation, had begun to argue with him wildly, and was apparently pressing some point against the lawyer's vehement opposal. The Colonel's murky eyes brightened as he still stood erect, with his hand thrust in his breast.

"It will be put to you, gentlemen, when the counsel on the other side refrains from mere interruption and confines himself to reply, that my unfortunate client has no action —no remedy at law—because there were no spoken words of endearment. But, gentlemen, it will depend upon *you* to say what are and what are not articulate expressions of love. We all know that among the lower animals, with whom you may possibly be called upon to classify the defendant, there are certain signals more or less harmonious, as the case may be. The ass brays, the horse neighs, the sheep bleats—the feathered denizens of the grove call to their mates in more musical roundelays. These are recognized facts, gentlemen, which you yourselves, as dwellers among nature in this beautiful land, are all cognizant of. They are facts that no one would deny—and we should have a poor opinion of the ass who, at—er—such a supreme moment, would attempt to suggest that his call was unthinking and without significance. But, gentlemen, I shall prove to you that such was the foolish, self-convicting custom of the defendant. With the greatest reluctance, and the—er—greatest pain, I succeeded in wresting from the maidenly modesty of my fair client the innocent confession that the defendant had induced her to correspond with him in these methods. Picture to yourself, gentlemen, the lonely moonlight road beside the widow's humble cottage. It is a beautiful night, sanctified to the affections, and the innocent girl is leaning from her casement. Presently there appears upon the road a slinking, stealthy figure, the defendant on his way to church. True to the instruction she has received from him, her lips part in the musical utterance" (the Colonel lowered his voice in a faint falsetto, presumably in fond imitation of his fair client), " 'Keeree!' Instantly the night becomes resonant with the impassioned reply" (the Colonel here lifted his voice in stentorian tones), " 'Keerow.' Again, as he passes, rises the soft 'Keeree'; again, as his form is lost in the distance, comes back the deep 'Keerow.' "

A burst of laughter, long, loud, and irrepressible, struck the whole court-room, and before the Judge could lift his half-composed face and take his handkerchief from his mouth, a faint "Keeree" from some unrecognized obscurity of the court-room was followed by a loud "Keerow" from some opposite locality. "The Sheriff will clear the court," said the Judge sternly; but, alas! as the embarrassed and choking officials rushed hither and thither, a soft "Keeree" from the spectators at the window, *outside* the court-house, was answered by a loud chorus of "Keerows" from the opposite windows, filled with onlookers. Again the laughter arose everywhere,—even the fair plaintiff herself sat convulsed behind her handkerchief.

The figure of Colonel Starbottle alone remained erect— white and rigid. And then the Judge, looking up, saw— what no one else in the court had seen—that the Colonel was sincere and in earnest; that what he had conceived to be the pleader's most perfect acting and most elaborate irony were the deep, serious, mirthless *convictions* of a man without the least sense of humor. There was the respect of this conviction in the Judge's voice as he said to him gently, "You may proceed, Colonel Starbottle."

"I thank Your Honor," said the Colonel slowly, "for recognizing and doing all in your power to prevent an interruption that, during my thirty years' experience at the bar, I have never been subjected to without the privilege of holding the instigators thereof responsible—*personally* responsible. It is possibly my fault that I have failed, oratorically, to convey to the gentlemen of the jury the full force and significance of the defendant's signals. I am aware that my voice is singularly deficient in producing either the dulcet tones of my fair client or the impassioned vehemence of the defendant's response. I will," continued the Colonel, with a fatigued but blind fatuity that ignored the hurriedly knit brows and warning eyes of the Judge, "try again. The note uttered by my client" (lowering his voice to the faintest of falsettos) "was 'Keeree'; the response was 'Keerow-ow.' " And the Colonel's voice fairly shook the dome above him.

Another uproar of laughter followed this apparently audacious repetition, but was interrupted by an unlooked-for incident. The defendant rose abruptly, and tearing himself away from the withholding hand and pleading protestations of his counsel, absolutely fled from the court-room, his appearance outside being recognized by a prolonged "Kee-row" from the bystanders, which again and again followed him in the distance.

In the momentary silence which followed, the Colonel's voice was heard saying, "We rest here, Your Honor," and he sat down. No less white, but more agitated, was the face of the defendant's counsel, who instantly rose.

"For some unexplained reason, Your Honor, my client desires to suspend further proceedings, with a view to effect a peaceable compromise with the plaintiff. As he is a man of wealth and position, he is able and willing to pay liberally for that privilege. While I, as his counsel, am still convinced of his legal irresponsibility, as he has chosen publicly to abandon his rights here, I can only ask Your Honor's permission to suspend further proceedings until I can confer with Colonel Starbottle."

"As far as I can follow the pleadings," said the Judge gravely, "the case seems to be hardly one for litigation, and I approve of the defendant's course, while I strongly urge the plaintiff to accept it."

Colonel Starbottle bent over his fair client. Presently he rose, unchanged in look or demeanor. "I yield, Your Honor, to the wishes of my client, and—er—lady. We accept."

Before the court adjourned that day it was known throughout the town that Adoniram K. Hotchkiss had compromised the suit for four thousand dollars and costs.

Colonel Starbottle had so far recovered his equanimity as to strut jauntily towards his office, where he was to meet his fair client. He was surprised, however, to find her already there, and in company with a somewhat sheepish-looking young man—a stranger. If the Colonel had any disappointment in meeting a third party to the interview, his old-fashioned courtesy did not permit him to show it. He bowed graciously, and politely motioned them each to a seat.

"I reckoned I'd bring Hiram round with me," said the young lady, lifting her searching eyes, after a pause, to the Colonel's, "though he *was* awful shy, and allowed that you didn't know him from Adam, or even suspect his existence. But I said, 'That's just where you slip up, Hiram; a pow'ful man like the Colonel knows everything—and I've seen it in his eye.' Lordy!" she continued, with a laugh, leaning forward over her parasol, as her eyes again sought the Colonel's, "don't you remember when you asked me if I loved that old Hotchkiss, and I told you, 'That's tellin',' and you looked at me—Lordy! I knew *then* you suspected there was a Hiram *somewhere,* as good as if I'd told you. Now you jest get up, Hiram, and give the Colonel a good handshake. For if it wasn't for *him* and *his* searchin' ways, and *his* awful power of language, I wouldn't hev got that four thousand dollars out o' that flirty fool Hotchkiss—enough to buy a farm, so as you and me could get married! That's what you owe to *him.* Don't stand there like a stuck fool starin' at him. He won't eat you—though he's killed many a better man. Come, have *I* got to do *all* the kissin'?"

It is of record that the Colonel bowed so courteously and so profoundly that he managed not merely to evade the proffered hand of the shy Hiram, but to only lightly touch the franker and more impulsive finger-tips of the gentle Zaidee. "I—er—offer my sincerest congratulations—though I think you—er—overestimate—my—er—powers of penetration. Unfortunately, a pressing engagement, which may oblige me also to leave town to-night, forbids my saying more. I have

—er—left the—er—business settlement of this—er—case in the hands of the lawyers who do my office work, and who will show you every attention. And now let me wish you a very good afternoon."

Nevertheless, the Colonel returned to his private room, and it was nearly twilight when the faithful Jim entered, to find him sitting meditatively before his desk. " 'Fo' God! Kernel, I hope dey ain't nuffin de matter, but you's lookin' mighty solemn! I ain't seen you look dat way, Kernel, since de day pooh Massa Stryker was fetched home shot froo de head."

"Hand me down the whiskey, Jim," said the Colonel, rising slowly.

The Negro flew to the closet joyfully, and brought out the bottle. The Colonel poured out a glass of the spirit and drank it with his old deliberation.

"You're quite right, Jim," he said, putting down his glass, "but I'm—er—getting old—and—somehow—I am missing poor Stryker damnably!"

LANTY FOSTER'S
MISTAKE

Lᴀɴᴛʏ Fᴏsᴛᴇʀ was crouching on a low stool before the dying kitchen fire, the better to get its fading radiance on the book she was reading. Beyond, through the open window and door, the fire was also slowly fading from the sky and the mountain ridge whence the sun had dropped half an hour before. The view was uphill, and the sky-line of the hill was marked by two or three gibbet-like poles from which, on a now invisible line between them, depended certain objects—mere black silhouettes against the sky— which bore weird likeness to human figures. Absorbed as she was in her book, she nevertheless occasionally cast an impatient glance in that direction, as the sunlight faded more quickly than her fire. For the fluttering objects were the "week's wash" which had to be brought in before night fell and the mountain wind arose. It was strong at that altitude, and before this had ravished the clothes from the line, and scattered them along the highroad leading over the ridge, once even lashing the shy schoolmaster with a pair of Lanty's own stockings, and blinding the parson with a really tempestuous petticoat.

A whiff of wind down the big-throated chimney stirred the long embers on the hearth, and the girl jumped to her feet, closing the book with an impatient snap. She knew her mother's voice would follow. It was hard to leave her heroine at the crucial moment of receiving an explanation from a presumed faithless lover, just to climb a hill and take in a lot of soulless washing, but such are the infelicities of stolen romance reading. She threw the clothes-basket over her head like a hood, the handle resting across her bosom and shoulders, and with both her hands free started out of the cabin. But the darkness had come up from the valley in one stride after its mountain fashion, had outstripped her, and she was instantly plunged in it. Still the outline of the ridge above her was visible, with the white, steadfast stars that were not there a moment ago, and by that sign she knew she was late. She had to battle against the rushing wind now, which sung through the inverted basket over her head and held her back, but with bent shoulders she at last reached the top of the ridge and the level. Yet here, owing to the shifting of the lighter background above her, she now found herself again encompassed with the darkness. The outlines of the poles had disappeared, the white fluttering garments were distinct apparitions waving in the wind, like dancing ghosts. But there certainly was a queer misshapen bulk moving beyond, which she did not recognize, and as she at last reached one of the poles, a shock was communicated to it, through the clothes-line and the bulk beyond. Then she heard a voice say impatiently,—

"What in h——ll am I running into now?"

It was a man's voice, and, from its elevation, the voice of a man on horseback. She answered without fear and with slow deliberation,—

"Inter our clothes-line, I reckon."

"Oh!" said the man in a half-apologetic tone. Then in brisker accents, "The very thing I want! I say, can you give me a bit of it? The ring of my saddle girth has fetched loose. I can fasten it with that."

"I reckon," replied Lanty, with the same unconcern,

moving nearer the bulk, which now separated into two parts as the man dismounted. "How much do you want?"

"A foot or two will do."

They were now in front of each other, although their faces were not distinguishable to either. Lanty, who had been following the lines with her hand, here came upon the end knotted around the last pole. This she began to untie.

"What a place to hang clothes," he said curiously.

"Mighty dryin', though," returned Lanty laconically.

"And your house? Is it near by?" he continued.

"Just down the ridge—ye kin see from the edge. Got a knife?" She had untied the knot.

"No—yes—wait." He had hesitated a moment and then produced something from his breast pocket, which he however kept in his hand. As he did not offer it to her she simply held out a section of the rope between her hands, which he divided with a single cut. She saw only that the instrument was long and keen. Then she lifted the flap of the saddle for him as he attempted to fasten the loose ring with the rope, but the darkness made it impossible. With an ejaculation, he fumbled in his pockets. "My last match!" he said, striking it, as he crouched over it to protect it from the wind. Lanty leaned over also, with her apron raised between it and the blast. The flame for an instant lit up the ring, the man's dark face, mustache, and white teeth set together as he tugged at the girth, and Lanty's brown, velvet eyes and soft, round cheek framed in the basket. Then it went out, but the ring was secured.

"Thank you," said the man, with a short laugh, "but I thought you were a hump-backed witch in the dark there."

"And I couldn't make out whether you was a cow or a b'ar," returned the young girl simply.

Here, however, he quickly mounted his horse, but in the

action something slipped from his clothes, struck a stone, and bounded away into the darkness.

"My knife," he said hurriedly. "Please hand it to me." But although the girl dropped on her knees and searched the ground diligently, it could not be found. The man with a restrained ejaculation again dismounted, and joined in the search.

"Haven't you got another match?" suggested Lanty.

"No—it was my last!" he said impatiently.

"Just you hol' on here," she said suddenly, "and I'll run down to the kitchen and fetch you a light. I won't be long."

"No! no!" said the man quickly; "don't! I couldn't wait. I've been here too long now. Look here. You come in daylight and find it, and—just keep it for me, will you?" He laughed. "I'll come for it. And now, if you'll only help to set me on that road again, for it's so infernal black I can't see the mare's ears ahead of me, I won't bother you any more. Thank you."

Lanty had quietly moved to his horse's head and taken the bridle in her hand, and at once seemed to be lost in the gloom. But in a few moments he felt the muffled thud of his horse's hoof on the thick dust of the highway, and its still hot, impalpable powder rising to his nostrils.

"Thank you," he said again, "I'm all right now," and in the pause that followed it seemed to Lanty that he had extended a parting hand to her in the darkness. She put up her own to meet it, but missed his, which had blundered onto her shoulder. Before she could grasp it, she felt him stooping over her, the light brush of his soft mustache on her cheek, and then the starting forward of his horse. But the retaliating box on the ear she had promptly aimed at him spent itself in the black space which seemed suddenly to have swallowed up the man, and even his light laugh.

For an instant she stood still, and then, swinging the basket indignantly from her shoulder, took up her suspended task. It was no light one in the increasing wind, and the unfastened clothes-line had precipitated a part of its burden to the ground through the loosening of the rope. But on picking up the trailing garments her hand struck an unfamiliar object. The stranger's lost knife! She thrust it hastily into the bottom of the basket and completed her work. As she began to descend with her burden she saw that the light of the kitchen fire, seen through the windows, was augmented by a candle. Her mother was evidently awaiting her.

"Pretty time to be fetchin' in the wash," said Mrs. Foster querulously. "But what can you expect when folks stand gossipin' and philanderin' on the ridge instead o' tendin' to their work?"

Now Lanty knew that she had *not* been "gossipin'" nor "philanderin'," yet as the parting salute might have been open to that imputation, and as she surmised that her mother might have overheard their voices, she briefly said, to prevent further questioning, that she had shown a stranger the road. But for her mother's unjust accusation she would have been more communicative. As Mrs. Foster went back grumblingly into the sitting-room Lanty resolved to keep the knife at present a secret from her mother, and to that purpose removed it from the basket. But in the light of the candle she saw it for the first time plainly—and started.

For it was really a dagger! jeweled-handled and richly wrought—such as Lanty had never looked upon before. The hilt was studded with gems, and the blade, which had a cutting edge, was damascened in blue and gold. Her soft eyes reflected the brilliant setting, her lips parted breathlessly; then, as her mother's voice arose in the other room, she thrust it back into its velvet sheath and clapped it into her pocket.

Its rare beauty had confirmed her resolution of absolute secrecy. To have shown it now would have made "no end of talk." And she was not sure but that her parents would have demanded its custody! And it was given to *her* by *him* to keep. This settled the question of moral ethics. She took the first opportunity to run up to her bedroom and hide it under the mattress.

Yet the thought of it filled the rest of her evening. When her household duties were done she took up her novel again, partly from force of habit and partly as an attitude in which she could think of *It* undisturbed. For what was fiction to her now? True, it possessed a certain reminiscent value. A "dagger" had appeared in several romances she had devoured, but she never had a clear idea of one before. "The Count sprang back, and, drawing from his belt a richly jeweled dagger, hissed between his teeth," or, more to the purpose: "'Take this,' said Orlando, handing her the ruby-hilted poniard which had gleamed upon his thigh, 'and should the caitiff attempt thy unguarded innocence—'"

"Did ye hear what your father was sayin'?" Lanty started. It was her mother's voice in the doorway, and she had been vaguely conscious of another voice pitched in the same querulous key, which, indeed, was the dominant expression of the small ranchers of that fertile neighborhood. Possibly a too complaisant and unaggressive Nature had spoiled them.

"Yes!—no!" said Lanty abstractedly, "what did he say?"

"If you wasn't taken up with that fool book," said Mrs. Foster, glancing at her daughter's slightly conscious color, "ye'd know! He allowed ye'd better not leave yer filly in the far pasture nights. That gang o' Mexican horse-thieves is out again, and raided McKinnon's stock last night."

This touched Lanty closely. The filly was her own property, and she was breaking it for her own riding. But her distrust of her parents' interference was greater than any fear of horse-stealers. "She's mighty uneasy in the barn; and," she added, with a proud consciousness of that beautiful yet carnal weapon upstairs, "I reckon I ken protect her and myself agin any Mexican horse-thieves."

"My! but we're gettin' high and mighty," responded Mrs. Foster, with deep irony. "Did you git all that outer your fool book?"

"Mebbe," said Lanty curtly.

Nevertheless, her thoughts that night were not entirely based on written romance. She wondered if the stranger knew that she had really tried to box his ears in the darkness, also if he had been able to see her face. *His* she remembered, at least the flash of his white teeth against his dark face and darker mustache, which was quite as soft as her own hair. But if he thought "for a minnit" that she was "goin' to allow an entire stranger to kiss her—he was mighty mistaken." She should let him know it "pretty quick"! She should hand him back the dagger "quite careless like," and never let on that she'd thought anything of it. Perhaps that was the reason why, before she went to bed, she took a good look at it, and after taking off her straight, beltless, calico gown she even tried the effect of it, thrust in the stiff waistband of her petticoat, with the jeweled hilt displayed, and thought it looked charming—as indeed it did. And then, having said her prayers like a good girl, and supplicated that she should be less "tetchy" with her parents, she went to sleep and dreamed that she had gone out to take in the wash again, but that the clothes had all changed to the queerest lot of folks, who were all fighting and struggling with each other until she, Lanty, drawing her dagger, rushed up single-handed among them, crying, "Disperse, ye craven curs,—disperse, I say!" And they dispersed.

Yet even Lanty was obliged to admit the next morning that all this was somewhat incongruous with the baking of "corn dodgers," the frying of fish, the making of beds, and her other household duties, and dismissed the stranger from her mind until he should "happen along." In her freer and more acceptable outdoor duties she even tolerated the advances of neighboring swains who made a point of passing by "Foster's Ranch," and who were quite aware that Atalanta Foster, *alias* "Lanty," was one of the prettiest girls in the country. But Lanty's toleration consisted in that singular performance known to herself as "giving them as good as they sent," being a lazy traversing, qualified with scorn, of all that they advanced. How long they would have put up with this from a plain girl I do not know, but Lanty's short upper lip seemed framed for indolent and fascinating scorn, and her dreamy eyes usually looked beyond the questioner, or blunted his bolder glances in their velvety surfaces. The libretto of these scenes was not exhaustive, *e. g.*:—

The Swain (with bold, bad gayety). "Saw that shy schoolmaster hangin' round your ridge yesterday! Orter know by this time that shyness with a gal don't pay."

Lanty (decisively). "Mebbe he allows it don't get left as often as impudence."

The Swain (ignoring the reply and his previous attitude and becoming more direct). "I was calkilatin' to say that with these yer hoss-thieves about, yer filly ain't safe in the pasture. I took a turn round there two or three times last evening to see if she was all right."

Lanty (with a flattering show of interest). "No! *did* ye, now? I was jest wonderin'—"

The Swain (eagerly). "I did—quite late, too! Why, that's nothin', Miss Atalanty, to what I'd do for you."

Lanty (musing, with far-off eyes). "Then that's why she

was so awful skeerd and frightened! Just jumpin' outer her skin with horror. I reckoned it was a b'ar or panther or a spook! You ought to have waited till she got accustomed to your looks."

Nevertheless, despite this elegant raillery, Lanty was enough concerned in the safety of her horse to visit it the next day with a view of bringing it nearer home. She had just stepped into the alder fringe of a dry "run" when she came suddenly upon the figure of a horseman in the "run," who had been hidden by the alders from the plain beyond and who seemed to be engaged in examining the hoof marks in the dust of the old ford. Something about his figure struck her recollection, and as he looked up quickly she saw it was the owner of the dagger. But he appeared to be lighter of hair and complexion, and was dressed differently, and more like a *vaquero*. Yet there was the same flash of his teeth as he recognized her, and she knew it was the same man.

Alas for her preparation! Without the knife she could not make that haughty return of it which she had contemplated. And more than that, she was conscious she was blushing! Nevertheless she managed to level her pretty brown eyebrows at him, and said sharply that if he followed her to her home she would return his property at once.

"But I'm in no hurry for it," he said with a laugh,—the same light laugh and pleasant voice she remembered,—"and I'd rather not come to the house just now. The knife is in good hands, I know, and I'll call for it when I want it! And until then—if it's all the same to you—keep it to yourself,— keep it dark, as dark as the night I lost it!"

"I don't go about blabbing my affairs," said Lanty indignantly. "and if it hadn't *been* dark that night you'd have had your ears boxed—you know why!"

The stranger laughed again, waved his hand to Lanty, and galloped away.

Lanty was a little disappointed. The daylight had taken away some of her illusions. He was certainly very good-looking, but not quite as picturesque, mysterious, and thrilling as in the dark! And it was very queer—he certainly did look darker that night! Who was he? And why was he lingering near her? He was different from her neighbors—her admirers. He might be one of those locaters, from the big towns, who prospect the lands, with a view of settling government warrants on them,—they were always so secret until they had found what they wanted. She did not dare to seek information of her friends, for the same reason that she had concealed his existence from her mother,—it would provoke awkward questions; and it was evident that he was trusting to her secrecy, too. The thought thrilled her with a new pride, and was some compensation for the loss of her more intangible romance. It would be mighty fine, when he did call openly for his beautiful knife and declared himself, to have them all know that *she* knew about it all along.

When she reached home, to guard against another such surprise she determined to keep the weapon with her, and, distrusting her pocket, confided it to the cheap little country-made corset which only for the last year had confined her budding figure, and which now, perhaps, heaved with an additional pride. She was quite abstracted during the rest of the day, and paid but little attention to the gossip of the farm lads, who were full of a daring raid, two nights before, by the Mexican gang on the large stock farm of a neighbor. The Vigilance Committee had been baffled; it was even alleged that some of the smaller ranchmen and herders were in league with the gang. It was also believed to be a widespread con-

spiracy; to have a political complexion in its combination of
an alien race with Southwestern filibusters. The legal authori-
ties had been reinforced by special detectives from San Francisco. Lanty seldom troubled herself with these matters; she
knew the exaggeration, she suspected the ignorance of her
rural neighbors. She roughly referred it, in her own vocabu-
lary, to "jaw," a peculiarly masculine quality. But later in the
evening, when the domestic circle in the sitting-room had
been augmented by a neighbor, and Lanty had taken refuge
behind her novel as an excuse for silence, Zob Hopper, the
enamored swain of the previous evening, burst in with more
astounding news. A posse of the sheriff had just passed along
the ridge; they had "corraled" part of the gang, and rescued
some of the stock. The leader of the gang had escaped, but
his capture was inevitable, as the roads were stopped. "All the
same, I'm glad to see ye took my advice, Miss Atalanty, and
brought in your filly," he concluded, with an insinuating
glance at the young girl.

But "Miss Atalanty," curling a quarter of an inch of scarlet
lip above the edge of her novel, here "allowed" that if his
advice or the filly had to be "took," she didn't know which
was worse.

"I wonder ye kin talk to sech peartness, Mr. Hopper," said
Mrs. Foster severely; "she ain't got eyes nor senses for anythin' but that book."

"Talkin' o' what's to be 'took,'" put in the diplomatic
neighbor, "you bet it ain't that Mexican leader! No, sir! he's
been 'stopped' before this—and then got clean away all the
same! One o' them detectives got him once and disarmed him
—but he managed to give them the slip, after all. Why, he's
that full o' shifts and disguises thar ain't no spottin' him. He
walked right under the constable's nose oncet, and took a

drink with the sheriff that was arter him—and the blamed fool never knew it. He kin change even the color of his hair quick as winkin'."

"Is he a real Mexican,—a regular Greaser?" asked the paternal Foster. "Cos I never heard that they wuz smart."

"No! They say he comes o' old Spanish stock, a bad egg they threw outer the nest, I reckon," put in Hopper eagerly, seeing a strange animated interest dilating Lanty's eyes, and hoping to share in it; "but he's reg'lar high-toned, you bet! Why, I knew a man who seed him in his own camp—prinked out in a velvet jacket and silk sash, with gold chains and buttons down his wide pants and a dagger stuck in his sash, with a handle just blazin' with jew'ls. Yes! Miss Atalanty, they say that one stone at the top—a green stone, what they call an 'em'ral'—was worth the price o' a 'Frisco house-lot. True ez you live! Eh—what's up now?"

Lanty's book had fallen on the floor as she was rising to her feet with a white face, still more strange and distorted in an affected yawn behind her little hand. "Yer makin' me that sick and nervous with yer fool yarns," she said hysterically, "that I'm goin' to get a little fresh air. It's just stifling here with lies and terbacker!" With another high laugh, she brushed past him into the kitchen, opened the door, and then paused, and, turning, ran rapidly up to her bedroom. Here she locked herself in, tore open the bosom of her dress, plucked out the dagger, threw it on the bed, where the green stone gleamed for an instant in the candle-light, and then dropped on her knees beside the bed with her whirling head buried in her cold red hands.

It had all come to her in a flash, like a blaze of lightning,—the black, haunting figure on the ridge, the broken saddle girth, the abandonment of the dagger in the exigencies of flight and concealment; the second meeting, the skulking in the dry, alder-hidden "run," the changed dress, the lighter-colored hair, but always the same voice and laugh,—the leader, the fugitive, the Mexican horse-thief! And she, the God-forsaken fool, the chuckle-headed nigger baby, with not half the sense of her own filly or that sop-headed Hopper—had never seen it! She—*she* who would be the laughing-stock of them all—she had thought him a "locater," a "towny" from 'Frisco! And she had consented to keep his knife until he would call for it,—yes, call for it, with fire and flame perhaps, the trampling of hoofs, pistol shots—and—yet—

Yet!—he had *trusted* her. Yes! trusted her when he knew a word from her lips would have brought the whole district down on him! when the mere exposure of that dagger would have identified and damned him! Trusted her a second time, when she was within cry of her house! When he might have taken her filly without her knowing it! And now she remembered vaguely that the neighbors had said how strange it was that her father's stock had not suffered as theirs had. *He* had protected them—he who was now a fugitive—and their men pursuing him! She rose suddenly with a single stamp of her narrow foot, and as suddenly became cool and sane. And then, quite her old self again, she lazily picked up the dagger and restored it to its place in her bosom. That done, with her color back and her eyes a little brighter, she deliberately went downstairs again, stuck her little brown head into the sitting-room, said cheerfully, "Still yawpin', you folks," and quietly passed out into the darkness.

She ran swiftly up to the ridge, impelled by the blind memory of having met him there at night and the one vague thought to give him warning. But it was dark and empty, with no sound but the rushing wind. And then an idea seized her. If he were haunting the vicinity still, he might see the fluttering of the clothes upon the line and believe she was there. She stooped quickly, and in the merciful and exonerating darkness stripped off her only white petticoat and pinned it on the line. It flapped, fluttered, and streamed in the mountain wind. She lingered and listened. But there came a sound she had not counted on,—the clattering hoofs of not *one*, but many, horses on the lower road. She ran back to the house to find its inmates already hastening towards the road for news. She took that chance to slip in quietly, go to her room, whose window commanded a view of the ridge, and crouching low behind it, she listened. She could hear the sound of voices, and the dull trampling of heavy boots on the dusty path towards the barnyard on the other side of the house—a pause, and then the return of the trampling boots, and the final clattering of hoofs on the road again. Then there was a tap on her door and her mother's querulous voice.

"Oh! yer there, are ye? Well—it's the best place fer a girl—with all these man's doin's goin' on! They've got that Mexican horse-thief and have tied him up in your filly's stall in the barn—till the 'Frisco deputy gets back from rounding up the others. So ye jest stay where ye are till they've come and gone, and we're shut o' all that cattle. Are ye mindin'?"

"All right, maw; 'tain't no call o' mine, anyhow," returned Lanty through the half-open door.

At another time her mother might have been startled at her passive obedience. Still more would she have been startled had she seen her daughter's face now, behind the closed door—with her little mouth set over her clinched teeth. And yet it was her own child, and Lanty was her mother's real daughter; the same pioneer blood filled their veins, the blood that had never nourished cravens or degenerates, but had given itself to sprinkle and fertilize desert solitudes where man might follow. Small wonder, then, that this frontier-born Lanty, whose first infant cry had been answered by the yelp of wolf and scream of panther; whose father's rifle had been leveled across her cradle to cover the stealthy Indian who prowled outside—small wonder that she should feel herself equal to these "man's doin's," and prompt to take a part. For even in the first shock of the news of the capture she recalled the fact that the barn was old and rotten, that only that day the filly had kicked a board loose from behind her stall, which she, Lanty, had lightly returned to avoid "making a fuss." If his captors had not noticed it, or trusted only to their guards, she might make the opening wide enough to free him!

Two hours later the guard nearest the now sleeping house, a farm hand of the Fosters', saw his employer's daughter slip out and cautiously approach him. A devoted slave of Lanty's, and familiar with her impulses, he guessed her curiosity, and was not averse to satisfy it and the sense of his own importance. To her whispers of affected, half-terrified interest, he responded in whispers that the captive was really in the filly's stall, securely bound by his wrists behind his back, and his feet "hobbled" to a post. That Lanty couldn't see him, for it was dark inside, and he was sitting with his back to the wall, as he couldn't sleep comf'ble lyin' down. Lanty's eyes glowed, but her face was turned aside.

"And ye ain't reckonin' his friends will come and rescue him?" said Lanty, gazing with affected fearfulness in the darkness.

"Not much! There's two other guards down in the corral, and I'd fire my gun and bring 'em up."

But Lanty was gazing open-mouthed towards the ridge. "What's that wavin' on the ridge?" she said in awe-stricken tones.

She was pointing to the petticoat,—a vague, distant, moving object against the horizon.

"Why, that's some o' the wash on the line, ain't it?"

"Wash—*two days in the week*!" said Lanty sharply. "Wot's gone of you?"

"Thet's so," muttered the man, "and it wa'n't there at sundown, I'll swear! P'r'aps I'd better call the guard," and he raised his rifle.

"Don't," said Lanty, catching his arm. "Suppose it's nothin', they'll laugh at ye. Creep up softly and see; ye ain't afraid, are ye? If ye are, give me yer gun, and *I*'ll go."

This settled the question, as Lanty expected. The man cocked his piece, and bending low began cautiously to mount the acclivity. Lanty waited until his figure began to fade, and then ran like fire to the barn.

She had arranged every detail of her plan beforehand. Crouching beside the wall of the stall she hissed through a crack in thrilling whispers, "Don't move! Don't speak for your life's sake! Wait till I hand you back your knife, then do the best you can." Then slipping aside the loosened board she saw dimly the black outline of curling hair, back, shoulders, and tied wrists of the captive. Drawing the knife from her pocket, with two strokes of its keen cutting edge she severed the cords, threw the knife into the opening, and darted away. Yet in that moment she knew that the man was instinctively turning towards her. But it was one thing to free a horse-thief, and another to stop and "philander" with him.

She ran halfway up the ridge, and met the farm hand returning. It was only a bit of washing after all, and he was glad he hadn't fired his gun. On the other hand, Lanty confessed she had got "so skeert" being alone, that she came to seek him. She had the shivers; wasn't her hand cold? It was, but thrilling even in its coldness to the bashfully admiring man. And she was that weak and dizzy, he must let her lean on his arm going down; and they must go *slow*. She was sure he was cold too, and if he would wait at the back door she would give him a drink of whiskey. Thus Lanty, with her brain afire, her eyes and ears straining into the darkness, and the vague outline of the barn beyond. Another moment was protracted over the drink of whiskey, and then Lanty, with a faint archness, made him promise not to tell her mother of her escapade, and she promised on her part not to say anything about his "stalking a petticoat on the clothes-line," and then shyly closed the door and regained her room. *He* must have got away by this time, or have been discovered; she believed they would not open the barn door until the return of the posse.

She was right. It was near daybreak when they returned, and, again crouching low beside her window, she heard, with a fierce joy, the sudden outcry, the oaths, the wrangling voices, the summoning of her father to the front door, and then the tumultuous sweeping away again of the whole posse, and a blessed silence falling over the rancho. And then Lanty went quietly to bed, and slept like a three-year child!

Perhaps that was the reason why she was able at breakfast to listen with lazy and even rosy indifference to the startling events of the night; to the sneers of the farm hands at the posse who had overlooked the knife when they searched their prisoner, as well as the stupidity of the corral guard who had never heard him make a hole "the size of a house" in the barn side! Once she glanced demurely at Silas Briggs—the farm hand—and the poor fellow felt consoled in his shame at the remembrance of their confidences.

But Lanty's tranquillity was not destined to last long. There was again the irruption of exciting news from the highroad; the Mexican leader had been recaptured, and was now safely lodged in Brownsville jail! Those who were previously loud in their praises of the successful horse-thief who had baffled the vigilance of his pursuers were now equally keen in their admiration of the new San Francisco deputy who, in turn, had outwitted the whole gang. It was *he* who was fertile in expedients; *he* who had studied the whole country, and even risked his life among the gang, and *he* who had again closed the meshes of the net around the escaped outlaw. He was already returning by way of the rancho, and might stop there a moment,—so that they could all see the hero. Such was the power of success on the country-side! Outwardly indifferent, inwardly bitter, Lanty turned away. She should not grace his triumph, if she kept in her room all day! And when there was a clatter of hoofs on the road again, Lanty slipped upstairs.

But in a few moments she was summoned. Captain Lance Wetherby, Assistant Chief of Police of San Francisco, Deputy Sheriff and ex-United States scout, had requested to see Miss Foster a few moments alone. Lanty knew what it meant,—her secret had been discovered; but she was not the girl to shirk the responsibility! She lifted her little brown head proudly, and with the same resolute step with which she had left the house the night before, descended the stairs and entered the sitting-room. At first she saw nothing. Then a remembered voice struck her ear; she started, looked up, and gasping, fell back against the door. It was the stranger who had given her the dagger, the stranger she had met in the run!—the horse-thief himself! No! no! she saw it all now— she had cut loose the wrong man!

He looked at her with a smile of sadness—as he drew from his breast-pocket that dreadful dagger, the very sight of which Lanty now loathed! "This is the *second* time, Miss Foster," he said gently, "that I have taken this knife from Murietta, the Mexican bandit: once when I disarmed him three weeks ago, and he escaped, and last night, when he had again escaped and I recaptured him. After I lost it that night I understood from you that you had found it and were keeping it for me." He paused a moment and went on: "I don't ask you what happened last night. I don't condemn you for it; I can believe what a girl of your courage and sympathy might rightly do if her pity were excited; I only ask—why did you give *him* back that knife *I* trusted you with?"

"Why? Why did I?" burst out Lanty in a daring gush of truth, scorn, and temper. *"Because I thought you were that horse-thief.* There!"

He drew back astonished, and then suddenly came that laugh that Lanty remembered and now hailed with joy. "I believe you, by Jove!" he gasped. "That first night I wore the disguise in which I have tracked him and mingled with his gang. Yes! I see it all now—and more. I see that to *you* I owe his recapture!"

"To me!" echoed the bewildered girl. "How?"

"Why, instead of making for his cave he lingered here in the confines of the ranch! He thought you were in love with him, because you freed him and gave him his knife, and stayed to see you!"

But Lanty had her apron to her eyes, whose first tears were filling their velvet depths. And her voice was broken as she said,—

"Then he—cared—a—good deal more for me—than some people!"

But there is every reason to believe that Lanty was wrong! At least later events that are part of the history of Foster's Rancho and the Foster family pointed distinctly to the contrary.

THE FOUR
GUARDIANS
OF LAGRANGE

PART ONE

THE TRUST

It certainly was a matter of serious import that so gravely interested the four most experienced and self-contained citizens of Lagrange. For nearly half an hour they had been sitting in the private room of Riker's grocery without exchanging a word. Even the silent communion of libation was wanting; their liquor stood untasted before them, a fact that aroused the serious concern of the barkeeper and the free comment of the outside bar. "Mebbe it's some new 'skin' game imported from 'Frisco, and they want to keep their heads level," was suggested by a cautious gossiper.

The barkeeper shook his head. "Nary deck o' keerds thar— onless they plays 'm under the table, and that ain't their style."

"Ye didn't notice no lumps o' sugar, sorter lyin' round, keerless like, before each man," insinuated another, "and them chaps lyin' low and quiet, waitin' for some d——d fly to light and rake down the pile. I've heerd," the speaker continued cautiously, "that heaps o' good money hez been lost in thet onchristian-like way."

"Yes," interpolated a third, "and *trained* flies, ez knew jest when to light, hez been rung in on greenhorns. Thar was a man down at French Camp, et they say picked up about seven thousand dollars outer ther camp with an innocent lookin' hoss fly, and et wuzent ontil one o' the boys accidently sot his glass down on thet harmless inseck thet the boys smelt a mice."

"'Tain't no game, I tell ye," reiterated the barkeeper stoutly. "Thar's suthin' more'n flies and sugar on their minds. My belief is they're reck'nin' to revive the old vigilants of '52. Thar's a lot o' dead beats in this yer camp," he continued darkly, with an aggressive recollection of certain unsettled scores, "ez mebbe will find out soon enough wot's up."

Unfortunately, none of these surmises, however ingenious or reasonable, were correct. The simple fact was that a lately deceased miner had on his death-bed called to his side the above-mentioned four citizens of Lagrange, and solemnly confided to them the care of his only child in the "States," with the little property he possessed in trust for her maintenance. This trust was further burdened with the fact that the dying man had withheld from the child the news of the death of her mother, a year previous, and it now devolved upon the guardians to inform the orphan of her double bereavement. This was the first meeting of the guardians since they had last looked upon the face of their dead comrade. Hence their grave silence and perplexity.

At last the spell was broken. One of the party, a tall, thin, rickety man, who had been softly pacing the room with a certain deprecatory manner and a smile of imbecile acquiescence in everything and anything that shone out at the slightest expression, even of vexation or anxiety on the part of his companions, gradually neared the door, and laid a large, bony, good-humored hand on the lock. The act was instantly detected by one of the party, who coolly locked the door and put the key on the table. "Ye can't slip outer this, Rats," he said; "ye must sit down here with the rest of us, and see what's to he done."

Captain Rats weakly succumbed, and began to apologize. "I warn't goin' back on ye, Horton," he began. "I only reckoned as ye all seemed to be gitting along famous a-thinking, I'd jest slip out and 'tend to some business, and allow ye to make up yer mind without me—countin' me out, and yourselves as my proxies. Fer wot's agreeable to you is agreeable to me. I'm no sharp at this game."

"You're a guardian," responded Horton decisively.

"In course. Thet's so. But I allow it ain't no valid app'intment. The very fact thet the old man app'inted a d——d fool like me shows he warn't in his right mind."

"That's so, boys," ejaculated the eldest of the four, with a sudden gleam of hopefulness. "The old man was sorter flighty just afore he went off, and we can slip our heads outer this lasso he flung over us by allowin' insanity, you know."

"We can't slouch out of *this* kind of a trust though, Colonel," said Joe Fleet, the youngest of the party, yet with a leader's peremptoriness. "It ain't white to do it!"

The gleam faded from the Colonel's face.

"Thet's so, it wouldn't be the squar' thing," he said dejectedly; "kick me, boys."

"Couldn't we sorter club together and app'int a kind of sub-guardian to take care o' the whole thing on a high salary. I'll come down heavy," suggested Horton.

"If you could get a chap to do your feelin' for you at the same figure I don't know but it might suit," said Fleet with decided sarcasm. "As for me I ain't rich enough to buy up any chap's conscience."

"Ye may as well quit this foolin'," broke in the Colonel, with a groan. "The game's made, and we're goin' to wade in like men. Mebbe suthin' may turn up. Afore long some one of us may get shot or buried in a tunnel, and so get excused on the squar'. But just now we must wade in."

"Oh, yes, 'wade in'!" said Horton derisively. "Do you know the first thing we've got to do? Why, write to that gal, and tell her thet her father was a d——d old liar, and thet her mother's been dead a year, and thet now he's dead too, and thet the d——d old fool's property won't bring five hundred dollars, and that we're goin' to give her five thousand dollars for charity, and adopt her, and if she's a loving sort of gal, and a high-spirited gal, she'll like it, and like us all the better. Oh, yes!" he continued with sardonic shrillness, "it's easy enough to do that, of course. Wade in! Yes! Wade in—drop right out o' the ford into deep water over yer head the first thing."

The men looked aghast at each other, and there was another ominous silence. "Couldn't ye let it on easy?" suggested the Colonel despairingly, "sorter begin to-day with the mother, and next month, when she's feelin' better and more able to bear it, kinder light gently down on her with the decease of her father, and so on ontil, in the course of a year or so, she'll take the charity business quite peaceful?"

But Joe Fleet dismissed the idea fiercely. "Ef she's got any pluck she'll take it in a lump. You go to work driftin' into her feelin's like that instead of sinking your shaft straight down, and you'll hev her crazy here on your hands in a week!"

The latter idea was so awful as to compel another gloomy silence for its stern contemplation. "Couldn't ye drop it on her all in a lump,—money, deceased parients, et cettery," suggested Captain Rats, with vague and imbecile good humor, "kinder brisk and business like."

"It's a gal," said the Colonel, shaking his head, "over fourteen."

"Hold on, and give Cap'n Rats a show," interrupted Fleet.

"Ef there's a man ez can do it, it's him. Didn't he edit the 'Record' up at Murphy's? Wade in and give us a specimen."

The suggestion met with unanimous favor. Captain Rats was shamelessly pleased with this compliment to his literary abilities, and at once began: " 'Honored Miss,—Not knowin' what a day may bring forth, we beg to inform you'— No," reflected the Captain slowly, feeling some unfavorable criticism in the air, "no, that won't do. Let's see! Ah! 'The death of your mother, followed by the illness of your father, resulting in his decease, and the entire loss'—"

"Ain't them bricks follerin' each other rather close?" suggested the Colonel faintly. The Captain stopped, rubbed his long chin thoughtfully, and looked at the others. It was evident that this was the prevailing impression.

"Well, yes; I was rather thinkin' so myself," he assented vaguely.

"And its bein' a gal, don't you want to heave in here and thar a little sentiment," said Horton, "and sorter touch her up gently? They say when you make 'em cry easy, they kinder like it, and get over it quicker."

"Jess so," returned Captain Rats cheerfully. "I was thinkin' that very thing, only jist now I was sorter samplin' it; showin' ye what *could* be done. A good way," he added, now completely lost in the fascinations of condoling composition,—"a very good, takin' sort of way is to tell it, and yet seem not to tell it; to kinder ring in a cold deck of information, and never let her see ye shuffle the keerds. Suthin' like this, ye know: 'Honored Miss,—Enclosed please find draft for five thousand dollars; same would have been sent before but for Wells-Fargo's office being closed the day of your father's funeral. The weather here is fine, but we suppose is fur different with you in the East, as your deceased mother often remarked to the writer. Business is dull, and ores are running light, most o' the claims on the North Fork sharing the fate of your late father's property.' Ye see," continued Captain Rats, with the glow of successful authorship mantling his cheek, "that kind of letter mout be written so that by the time she got through with it, it would seem as if she'd knew it all before, and she couldn't get nary soul to sympathize with her, and help her take on." The feeling of the majority was so strongly in favor of the last composition that they all turned impatiently to the only dissenter, Joe Fleet. But at this moment a knock on the door checked further discussion.

It was Jack Foster, expressman,—alert, vigilant, familiar, and fateful,—holding a letter.

"For John Meritoe," said the Sierran Mercury crisply. "As we don't have no office nor agent at his present address, we deliver at his last residence." He tossed the letter on the table, winked, and was gone.

It was for the dead man, the great first cause of their perplexity. For a few moments it lay there undisturbed, while the men looked at each other in silence. Then Captain Rats, with a decision and independence new to him, took it up. "Ther's no one, boys, hez a better right to it than we has," he said. "I propose that we open it here afore each other and read it."

"As to opening it, I second the motion," said Joe Fleet's voice, "but we'll see who it's from before we read it," added that honorable man.

The letter was opened. It was signed "Fanny Meritoe."

"The girl herself," said Fleet promptly. "Read it."

With a hesitating voice, that at last seemed to almost simulate what might have been the hesitating youthful accents of the writer, Captain Rats began.

How shall I describe it? It was simple, it was girlish, it was affectionate, it was real. Against its candid frankness and simplicity poor Rats's previous rhetoric assumed the appearance of the most monstrous duplicity and deceitful sophistry. It was evident that the writer had seen but little of her real father, and that the rather commonplace, homely, often somewhat despicable figure known to the men who now listened to her yearnings was not the ideal parent of her dreams. At last Captain Rats finished. There was a slight huskiness in the Captain's voice, a slight dimness in his eyesight as he ended, and a blur upon the fair page that was not there when he began.

The Colonel had dropped his head between his hands. Horton had never taken his eyes from the paper. Fleet, who had walked to the window and had been apparently absorbed in staring at the staring sunlight without, suddenly turned, advanced to the table, and held out both his hands. In another moment they were locked in his companions', and the four men, holding hands, closed round the table and the letter that lay in its centre.

"We don't want no letter of condolence, Captain Rats," said Joe Fleet sturdily, "for there ain't anythin' to condole for. I don't see just how it is, or how we can fix it, but I *know* that girl's parents *ain't* dead, ez long, please God, as we are living!"

The men pressed each other's hands in silence, until Captain Rats, with a burst of revelation, disengaged his, and suddenly brought it against his right leg with resounding emphasis.

"That's it—and it makes the whole thing clar. We don't write no letters of condolence—for why? We goes straight on and writes ez if we was the old man. He's let on enough to me about hisself and his affairs to make it as easy as fallin' off a log. We'll just chip in whar he let off. We'll take his hand as it is, play out his little game, win or lose; and if four sharps like us can't make it easy for that child and rake in the pot every time, we'll leave the board. Yes, gentlemen," continued Rats, taking up the letter, "I'll answer this to-night myself, I, Captain Rats, late Meritoe, deceased."

PART TWO

HOW THE TRUST WAS FULFILLED

When the combined guardians of Lagrange first practiced to deceive, they did not forecast the tangled web whose pleasant intricacies and sinuosities they were presently to weave. And when Captain Rats calmly announced to his gentle confederates his intention of writing his first letter—*in loco parentis*—to the orphaned girl with his left hand, explaining to her the thereby changed chirography through the ingenious fiction of an accident that had happened to his right, it was accepted with acclamation. "You see," said the Captain sententiously, "every man slings ink with his left hand at about the same gait. The style ain't pretty nor plain, but she'll never find out it ain't the old man's."

The possibility of detection thus obviated,—and, indeed, it afterwards appeared that the simple-minded girl dwelt more anxiously upon the discomforts of the accident to her father than on his changed and almost illegible hand,—various other gentle frauds and deceits were introduced in the correspondence. A certain emulation of the Captain's skill and importance as a correspondent grew up among the other guardians. They began to make suggestions of their own, until at last steamer day brought them generally together, in conclave, in the back room of the saloon, where the fortnightly epistle was dictated finally by all. Captain

Rats's pride, which at first resented this interference, was finally placated by the compromise that the composition or "wording" of the letter should be his own, although the subject matter might be a various contribution.

The result of this unhallowed collaboration was a series of the most extraordinary letters ever inflicted on a single correspondent. It was not long before their fame reached beyond the horizon of their fair recipient. "Do you know, papa dear," wrote the simple girl from the seclusion of Madame Brimborion's academy, "do you know, your letters are so very, *very* interesting, I could not help showing them to some of the girls here! Your account [the Colonel's] of the fight with the bear was so *real* that I almost saw it. I laughed till I cried over the funny story of the Chinaman mending your clothes [a characteristic contribution from Horton], but then I did cry, really, too, papa, over what you [Fleet] said about your feeling that Sunday you saw the sunset from the poor little forlorn cemetery on the hill. Oh, papa! it was just lovely— and so sad—so very sad! Mary Ricketts said it was just like Shakespeare, and she knows, oh, so much, and is considered very, very smart! They all think I ought to be so fond of my dear papa, as if I wanted anything to make me love him! She, Mary, asked me if you were very old, and I said you couldn't be very—are you? Then that was very good about the mines that you [the Colonel] wrote. Mme. Brimborion asked permission to copy that part where you [the Colonel] describe the manner of reducing ores; she said it was so instructive and valuable. Dear papa, how much you do know! But I think I like you better when you're a little, just a little— sad, and say such sweet things about the landscape and your longings. I'm sure you're a real poet, papa, ain't you?"

It is scarcely necessary to say that when this letter was read Fleet coughed slightly. colored perceptibly, muttered something vaguely about "really having forgotten it all," but remembered only that he had dictated to Captain Rats some suggestions that he "thought might please the young thing," etc.; nor that a slight feeling of jealousy crept into the breasts of all but the complacent Captain. Indeed, the Colonel is said to have afterward remarked aside to Horton that he was of the opinion that Fleet's "flapdoodle" and "purp stuff" wasn't exactly the thing "to ladle out" to a young girl that was already "overdosed with chewing gum and licorice"; and Fleet is reported to have cautioned Captain Rats against the freedom of some of the Colonel's stories. "Ez fur as the wordin' goes," explained Captain Rats, "I plays my own cards; so don't you get skeert. On'y the other day, tellin' that story about the coon hunt, the Kernel allowed the dogs was 'hell bent' on gettin' the coon. Lord love ye! do ye think I set that down for that little gal's eye? Not much! I jist sat down sorter keerless and quiet like, and sling her this: 'Meanwhile, the noble hounds, justly emulating the feverish impatience and ambitious spirit of their master!' Lord, it's easy enough to turn the Kernel into decent English—ef you've got the *sabe*! Why, it's jist wonderful how keerless men is in their composition. Why, even *you*, Fleet, I hed to take *you* down last letter. Don't ye mind ye was lettin' on about Night walkin' in her scant robes on the hill? Did ye think I was goin' to hand that over to that child? No, sir. I stopped it! How? Why, I jest said, 'suitably appareled.' That's all. It's easy when you know how."

Another unlooked-for result naturally followed the baleful excellence of this correspondence. Miss Fanny grew more and more anxious to behold again the author of her being and of these extraordinary letters. One or two vague hints to that effect, thrown out in her correspondence, were received with alarm by her guardians, and it was finally resolved that the next letter should be composed in such a manner as to effectually check this wanton desire. For this purpose all the guardians assembled. Considerable excitement was manifested. I grieve to record the fact that much liquor was drunk, and that Captain Rats was somewhat exalted and discursive. But your true gentleman is never more fastidious and refined than in his cups; and the gentle Captain Rats, during the whole letter (save an occasional slip), held his rhetorical hat deferentially in his hand. A copy of this epistle has been preserved, and runs as follows:—

My Own Darling Child,—Your esteemed and precious favor came promptly to hand, and contents noted. We—that is, your sainted mother and myself—are glad to hear that the draft for two hundred and fifty dollars came promptly to hand, and trust that the balance of one hundred and fifty dollars, which you retained after paying Mme. Brimborion's bill, will be sufficient for you to purchase laces, furbelows, bonnets, shoe-ties, and hosiery suitable to the season and the fashions. We (that is, your mother—who is still unable to write by reason of a sore finger—and myself) hope you will not spare any expense to clothe yourself equal to your schoolmates. We note what you say about Mary Rickett's new silk dress, that cost seventy-five dollars. You are to see that seventy-five, and go her fifty or one hundred better, drawing on us for the balance, if short. Raise the Rickett girl or bust. We trust you are careful of your health, and do not partake too frequently of confectionery, and that your French and music lessons are the same. We trust that you wrap up warmly when you go out, and are careful about your flannels in that dreadful Eastern climate, and always wear your rubbers. The wheat crop this year will average nearly forty bushels to the acre, or supply each inhabitant of the State with forty-four barrels of flour, and still leave one hundred thousand bushels for exportation. With the Pacific Railroad finished, and the effete nations of Europe and Asia knocking at the Golden Gate for bread-stuffs, the time is not far distant when the State will be entirely self-producing. We often picture you, dear child, sitting at your tasks, your bright eyes occasionally dropping in reverie as you think of your parents so far away. Do you ever wander with us through these dim woods—God's first temples—and breathe with us the infinite peace of solitude, or reflect that long before we had our being or existence these grand old monarchs looked down on others as they do on us? Do you? We hope—that is, your mother and myself trust you do, although we earnestly beg and implore you not to dream of visiting us here. For the society is quite unfitted for a person of your age and sex. Murder not unfrequently stalks abroad, and sluice robbing is as common as the red hand of the assassin. Scarcely a day passes that we do not consign some victim to the silent tomb. Consumption is epidemic, and smallpox, too, often has marked the loveliest of your sex for his prey. The face of beauty fades quickly through a pestilential fever now quite common, and the exquisite daughter of one of the first families has been taken for an Indian squaw by reason of the same. Freckles are paramount. The hair withers and falls out,—the teeth likewise the same. Much as we hope to once more behold that darling face, we could not expose you to such certain ruin. Your mother fainted on reading your request to visit her. I fear, in her present state of health, a visit from you would be fatal! If you value your parents' love, banish this idea from your mind. In a few years, probably, we will be able to once more clasp you in our arms by the Atlantic shores.

YOUR AFFECTIONATE PARENTS.

Six weeks had elapsed, and the dutiful answer to the above, confidently looked for by the guardians, was due. Nevertheless, as the time approached, some nervousness on the part of Fleet was manifested by that gentleman's unrest, and his frequent visits to Captain Rats, to whom all letters addressed to their deceased friend were delivered. "Nothing from the young lady yet, I suppose?" Fleet would say indifferently. "No," the Captain would respond quietly. "I reckon it'll take her about two weeks to get over her disappointment. Then she'll write sassy—like as not—or mebbe not at all." Fleet turned pale, then red, and then bit his mustache. "You don't think, Captain," he asked with an affected laugh, "that we were a little—just a little too hard?" "Not too much for peace and quietness," replied the Captain gravely. "Women don't take a halfway 'no'; they can't believe a man means it," he added, "any more than *they* do." Nevertheless, the Captain himself grew a little anxious, and having to visit Sacramento, left strict orders with his comrades that he was to be recalled promptly on the arrival of Miss Fanny's reply.

But his visit was not interrupted, and it was nearly three weeks later that he mounted the box seat of the Pioneer stagecoach to return to Lagrange. As he settled himself beside the driver, after the interchange of a few complimentary epithets, his eye glanced down toward the wheels, and was attracted by an open letter and part of a female head obtruded from the coach. The fair reader had evidently thus sought to evade the gloom of the coach's interior and possibly the prying eyes of her fellow passengers, while she perused it. But why did the Captain's withered cheeks instantly change color, and why did he convulsively clasp the railing by his side? The letter was in his own handwriting, and had been mailed to Miss Fanny nine weeks before!

It was impossible, even by the utmost craning, and at the risk of his life, to see anything more than a bit of lace, some artificial flowers, a front of blonde hair, and the fatal letter. Yet his guilty conscience instantly recognized in these scant facts the formidable presentment of the deceived orphan. Had she discovered their trick, and was she now on their trail, with this terrible indictment in her hand? Or was she still in ignorance—an ignorance which a single chance question and answer now might dispel, amid faintings, shrieks, tears, and wailing? Captain Rats grew apoplectic with bewilderment; he dared not even ask a question of the driver, who was already beginning to survey him with a sardonic leer, and had audibly sought information if he, the Captain, called this kind of conduct proper at "his time o' life." "Let the gal alone, Rats! Don't you see it ain't a love letter from you she's porin' over?" he added, a statement that again covered the Captain with guilty blushes. But a sudden jolt of the vehicle, a little shriek, and the fluttering of the letter to the road, jarred from the reader's fingers, gave the Captain a providential opportunity. To jump from the box to the road and seize the truant epistle was the work of a moment. When he approached the coach to restore it to its fair owner, another passenger had appropriated his own seat on the box, and thus gave color and reason for his exchange to the "inside." The young lady thanked him, the coach again started forward, and Captain Rats fell into the seat beside her. Here was the supreme moment! With a profuse apology, the Captain drew his knees together, slipped into a respectfully diagonal position, so as to oppose the narrowest point of contact with her, and carefully dusted his knees and her dress softly with his handkerchief. The shyest nymph would scarcely have been startled, the coldest and most antiquated of duennas would not have been discomposed by the submissive respect of the Captain. The young lady, who evidently was neither, turned a pair of calm large gray eyes on her neighbor, and sat expectant. But how the Captain improved his chances I must refer the reader to his own account of the interview, delivered gravely the same evening to his brother guardians.

"When I saw we was in for it, boys," he said, rubbing his knees upward softly, "I kinder measured the gal afore I commenced, to see what sort of a hand she might hold. But you couldn't hev told anything by her looks. And short of axing her a downright saucy question, you couldn't get a word out of her about her own business, nor what she war up to. And then—well," continued the Captain, with a languid smile of conscious success, "I calkilated that this was one o' them peculiar cases that wanted skill and science, and I jist applied 'em, and in course I won. Thet's all. Yes," said the Captain, with a yawn of stifled indifference, "it's all right now, boys. Everything's explained."

"But how?" queried the others eagerly.

"Well," said the Captain lazily, "I sorter slipped into a gineral conversation about the opery, the fashions, and po'try, and sich. Speakin' o' literatoor, I told her of a yarn I'd read t' other day in a magazine, and then, kinder keerless and easy, I jist up and told her the whole story about her father and us and herself, giving her the name o' Seraphina, calling you and Horton 'Oscar' and 'Roderigo,' and Fleet 'Gustavus,' and myself 'Rodentio,' which is Latin for 'Rats.' Well, if I do say it myself, it wasn't no slouch of a story, fur I was kinder clipper and fresh, and the other passengers was jist about as much interested as she was. Then I sorter looked in her eye, you know, this way," and Captain Rats here achieved a peculiar leer, "and said that I allowed it wasn't true, and asked her what she thought about it as a story. And she said it might be true and it might not, but it was quite interesting. Them's her very words, gentlemen."

"Well, go on," said the Colonel eagerly.

"That's all!"

"All! All!" shrieked the guardians together. "Didn't she say anything else? Didn't you"—

"Nary," said the Captain coolly. "But it's all right, boys! You'll see."

Horton seized Captain Rats by one shoulder, and the Colonel grappled the other. For a few seconds they shook him furiously.

"Where is she now, you blank, blank mule? Answer us!"

"Why, I reckon she's over at the Union Hotel with Fleet. I forgot to say that he happened accidental to be there when the stage kem in. She seemed to be kinder easy and nat'ral with him, and I"—

But before Captain Rats had finished his speech the two men rose furiously and dashed out of the room bareheaded. And even as the Captain sat there, mute and astonished, yet with his usual vague smile of acquiescence lingering around his mouth, Horton returned, shook his fist fiercely at the Captain, seized his hat, and vanished. In another moment the Colonel also reëntered hastily, grasped his hat, kicked Captain Rats, and dashed out again.

As the door slammed on the last of his fellow guardians, Captain Rats slowly emptied his glass, thoughtfully placed one knee on a chair, and rubbed it in silence. Presently a more decided smile came into his eye, and crept to his mouth as his lips slowly fashioned this astounding reflection:—

"That's so—that's *it*! Fleet was allers kinder soft on the gal! Like as not—like as not—he's up and writ to her on the sly."

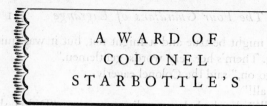

A WARD OF
COLONEL
STARBOTTLE'S

THE kernel seems a little off color to-day," said the bar-keeper as he replaced the whiskey decanter, and gazed reflectively after the departing figure of Colonel Starbottle.

"I didn't notice anything," said a bystander; "he passed the time o' day civil enough to me."

"Oh, he's allus polite enough to strangers and wimmin folk even when he is that way; it's only his old chums, or them ez like to be thought so, that he's peppery with. Why, ez to that, after he'd had that quo'll with his old partner, Judge Pratt, in one o' them spells, I saw him the next minit go half a block out of his way to direct an entire stranger; and ez for wimmin!—well, I reckon if he'd just got a bead drawn on a man, and a woman spoke to him, he'd drop his battery and take off his hat to her. No—ye can't judge by that!"

And perhaps in his larger experience the barkeeper was right. He might have added, too, that the colonel, in his general outward bearing and jauntiness, gave no indication of his internal irritation. Yet he was undoubtedly in one of his "spells," suffering from a moody cynicism which made him as susceptible of affront as he was dangerous in resentment.

Luckily, on this particular morning he reached his office and entered his private room without any serious *rencontre*. Here he opened his desk, and arranging his papers, he at once set to work with grim persistency. He had not been occupied for many minutes before the door opened to Mr. Pyecroft—one of a firm of attorneys who undertook the colonel's office work.

"I see you are early to work, Colonel," said Mr. Pyecroft cheerfully.

"You see, sir," said the colonel, correcting him with a slow deliberation that boded no good—"you see a Southern gentleman—blank it!—who has stood at the head of his profession for thirty-five years, obliged to work like a blank nigger, sir, in the dirty squabbles of psalm-singing Yankee traders, instead of—er—attending to the affairs of—er—legislation!"

"But you manage to get pretty good fees out of it—eh, Colonel?" continued Pyecroft, with a laugh.

"Fees, sir! Filthy shekels! and barely enough to satisfy a debt of honor with one hand, and wipe out a tavern score for the entertainment of—er—a few lady friends with the other!"

This allusion to his losses at poker, as well as an oyster supper given to the two principal actresses of the "North Star Troupe," then performing in the town, convinced Mr. Pyecroft that the colonel was in one of his "moods," and he changed the subject.

"That reminds me of a little joke that happened in Sacramento last week. You remember Dick Stannard, who died a year ago—one of your friends?"

"I have yet to learn," interrupted the colonel, with the same deadly deliberation, "what right *he*—or *anybody*—had to intimate that he held such a relationship with me. Am I to understand, sir, that he—er—publicly boasted of it?"

"Don't know!" resumed Pyecroft hastily; "but it don't matter, for if he wasn't a friend it only makes the joke bigger. Well, his widow didn't survive him long, but died in the States t' other day, leavin' the property in Sacramento —worth about three thousand dollars—to her little girl, who is at school at Santa Clara. The question of guardianship came up, and it appears that the widow—who only knew you through her husband—had, some time before her death, mentioned *your* name in that connection! He! he!"

"What!" said Colonel Starbottle, starting up.

"Hold on!" said Pyecroft hilariously. "That isn't all! Neither the executors nor the probate judge knew you from Adam, and the Sacramento bar, scenting a good joke, lay low and said nothing. Then the old fool judge said that 'as you appeared to be a lawyer, a man of mature years, and a friend of the family, you were an eminently fit person, and ought to be communicated with'—you know his hi-falutin' style. Nobody says anything. So that the next thing you'll know you'll get a letter from that executor asking you to look after that kid. Ha! ha! The boys said they could fancy they saw you trotting around with a ten year old girl holding on to your hand, and the Señorita Dolores or Miss Ballamont looking on! Or your being called away from a poker deal some night by the infant, singing, 'Gardy, dear gardy, come home with me now, the clock in the steeple strikes one!' And think of that old fool judge not knowing you! Ha! ha!"

A study of Colonel Starbottle's face during this speech would have puzzled a better physiognomist than Mr. Pyecroft. His first look of astonishment gave way to an empurpled confusion, from which a single short Silenus-like chuckle escaped, but this quickly changed again into a dull coppery indignation, and, as Pyecroft's laugh continued, faded out into a sallow rigidity in which his murky eyes alone seemed to keep what was left of his previous high color. But what was more singular, in spite of his enforced calm, something of his habitual old-fashioned loftiness and oratorical exaltation appeared to be returning to him as he placed his hand on his inflated breast and faced Pyecroft.

"The ignorance of the executor of Mrs. Stannard and the —er—probate judge," he began slowly, "may be pardonable, Mr. Pyecroft, since His Honor would imply that, although unknown to *him* personally, I am at least *amicus curiæ* in this question of—er—guardianship. But I am grieved—indeed I may say shocked—Mr. Pyecroft, that the—er—last sacred trust of a dying widow—perhaps the holiest trust that can be conceived by man—the care and welfare of her helpless orphaned girl—should be made the subject of mirth, sir, by yourself and the members of the Sacramento bar! I shall not allude, sir, to my own feelings in regard to Dick Stannard, one of my most cherished friends," continued the colonel, in a voice charged with emotion, "but I can conceive of no nobler trust laid upon the altar of friendship than the care and guidance of his orphaned girl! And if, as you tell me, the utterly inadequate sum of three thousand dollars is all that is left for her maintenance through life, the selection of a guardian sufficiently devoted to the family to be willing to augment that pittance out of his own means from time to time would seem to be most important."

Before the astounded Pyecroft could recover himself, Colonel Starbottle leaned back in his chair, half closing his eyes, and abandoned himself, quite after his old manner, to one of his dreamy reminiscences.

"Poor Dick Stannard! I have a vivid recollection, sir, of driving out with him on the Shell Road at New Orleans in '54, and of his saying, 'Star'—the only man, sir, who ever abbreviated my name—'Star, if anything happens to me or her, look after our child!' It was during that **very** drive, sir, that, through his incautious neglect to fortify himself against the swampy malaria by a glass of straight bourbon with a pinch of bark in it, he caught that fever which undermined his constitution. Thank you, Mr. Pyecroft, for—er—recalling the circumstance. I shall," continued the colonel, suddenly abandoning reminiscence, sitting up, and arranging his papers, "look forward with great interest to—er—letter from the executor."

The next day it was universally understood that Colonel Starbottle had been appointed guardian by Pansy Stannard by the probate judge of Sacramento.

There are of record two distinct accounts of Colonel Starbottle's first meeting with his ward after his appointment as her guardian. One, given by himself, varying slightly at times, but always bearing unvarying compliment to the grace, beauty, and singular accomplishments of this apparently gifted child, was nevertheless characterized more by vague, dreamy reminiscences of the departed parents than by any personal experience of the daughter.

"I found the young lady, sir," he remarked to Mr. Pyecroft, "recalling my cherished friend Stannard in—er—form and features, and—although—er—personally unacquainted with her deceased mother—who belonged, sir, to one of the first families of Virginia—I am told that she is—er—remarkably like her. Miss Stannard is at present a pupil in one of the best educational establishments in Santa Clara, where she is receiving tuition in—er—the English classics, foreign belles lettres, embroidery, the harp, and—er—the use of the —er—globes, and—er—blackboard—under the most fastidious care, and my own personal supervision. The principal of the school, Miss Eudoxia Tish—associated with—er—er— Miss Prinkwell—is—er—remarkably gifted woman; and as

I was present at one of the school exercises, I had the opportunity of testifying to her excellence in—er—short address I made to the young ladies." From such glittering but unsatisfying generalities as these I prefer to turn to the real interview, gathered from contemporary witnesses.

It was the usual cloudless, dazzling, Californian summer day, tempered with the asperity of the northwest trades, that Miss Tish, looking through her window towards the rose-embowered gateway of the seminary, saw an extraordinary figure advancing up the avenue. It was that of a man slightly past middle age, yet erect and jaunty, whose costume recalled the early water-color portraits of her own youthful days. His tightly buttoned blue frock coat with gilt buttons was opened far enough across the chest to allow the expanding of a frilled shirt, black stock, and nankeen waistcoat, and his immaculate white trousers were smartly strapped over his smart varnished boots. A white bell-crowned hat, carried in his hand to permit the wiping of his forehead with a silk handkerchief, and a gold-headed walking stick hooked over his arm, completed this singular equipment. He was followed, a few paces in the rear, by a Negro carrying an enormous bouquet, and a number of small boxes and parcels tied up with ribbons. As the figure paused before the door, Miss Tish gasped, and cast a quick restraining glance around the classroom. But it was too late; a dozen pairs of blue, black, round, inquiring, or mischievous eyes were already dancing and gloating over the bizarre stranger through the window.

"A cirkiss—or nigger minstrels—sure as you're born!" said Mary Frost, aged nine, in a fierce whisper.

"No!—a agent from 'The Emporium,' with samples," returned Miss Briggs, aged fourteen.

"Young ladies, attend to your studies," said Miss Tish,

as the servant brought in a card. Miss Tish glanced at it with some nervousness, and read to herself, "Colonel Culpeper Starbottle," engraved in script, and below it in pencil, "To see Miss Pansy Stannard, under favor of Miss Tish." Rising with some perturbation, Miss Tish hurriedly intrusted the class to an assistant, and descended to the reception room. She had never seen Pansy's guardian before (the executor had brought the child); and this extraordinary creature, whose visit she could not deny, might be ruinous to school discipline. It was therefore with an extra degree of frigidity of demeanor that she threw open the door of the reception room, and entered majestically. But to her utter astonishment, the colonel met her with a bow so stately, so ceremonious, and so commanding that she stopped, disarmed and speechless.

"I need not ask if I am addressing Miss Tish," said the colonel loftily, "for without having the pleasure of—er—previous acquaintance, I can at once recognize the—er—Lady Superior and—er—châtelaine of this—er—establishment." Miss Tish here gave way to a slight cough and an embarrassed curtsy, as the colonel, with a wave of his white hand towards the burden carried by his follower, resumed more lightly: "I have brought—er—few trifles and gewgaws for my ward—subject, of course, to your rules and discretion. They include some—er—dainties, free from any deleterious substance, as I am informed—a sash—a ribbon or two for the hair, gloves, mittens, and a nosegay—from which, I trust, it will be *her* pleasure, as it is my own, to invite you to cull such blossoms as may suit your taste. Boy, you may set them down and retire!"

"At the present moment," stammered Miss Tish, "Miss Stannard is engaged on her lessons. But"— She stopped again, hopelessly.

"I see," said the colonel, with an air of playful, poetical reminiscence—"her lessons! Certainly!

> *'We will—er—go to our places,*
> *With smiles on our faces,*
> *And say all our lessons distinctly and slow.'*

Certainly! Not for worlds would I interrupt them; until they are done, we will—er—walk through the classrooms and inspect"—

"No! no!" interrupted the horrified principal, with a dreadful presentiment of the appalling effect of the colonel's entry upon the class. "No!—that is—I mean—our rules exclude—except on days of public examination"—

"Say no more, my dear madam," said the colonel politely. "Until she is free I will stroll outside, through—er—the groves of the Academus"—

But Miss Tish, equally alarmed at the diversion this would create at the classroom windows, recalled herself with an effort. "Please wait here a moment," she said hurriedly; "I will bring her down"; and before the colonel could politely open the door for her, she had fled.

Happily unconscious of the sensation he had caused, Colonel Starbottle seated himself on the sofa, his white hands resting easily on the gold-headed cane. Once or twice the door behind him opened and closed quietly, scarcely disturbing him; or again opened more ostentatiously to the words, "Oh, excuse, please," and the brief glimpse of a flaxen braid, or a black curly head—to all of which the colonel nodded politely—even rising later to the apparition of a taller, demure young lady—and her more affected, "Really, I beg your pardon!" The only result of this evident curiosity was slightly to change the colonel's attitude, so as to enable him to put his other hand in his breast in his favorite pose.

But presently he was conscious of a more active movement in the hall, of the sounds of scuffling, of a high youthful voice saying "I won't" and "I shan't!" of the door opening to a momentary apparition of Miss Tish dragging a small hand and half of a small black-ribboned arm into the room, and her rapid disappearance again, apparently pulled back by the little hand and arm; of another and longer pause, of a whispered conference outside, and then the reappearance of Miss Tish majestically, reinforced and supported by the grim presence of her partner, Miss Prinkwell.

"This—er—unexpected visit," began Miss Tish—"not previously arranged by letter"—

"Which is an invariable rule of our establishment," supplemented Miss Prinkwell—

"And the fact that you are personally unknown to us," continued Miss Tish—

"An ignorance shared by the child, who exhibits a distaste for an interview," interpolated Miss Prinkwell, in a kind of antiphonal response—

"For which we have had no time to prepare her," continued Miss Tish—

"Compels us most reluctantly"— But here she stopped short. Colonel Starbottle, who had risen with a deep bow at their entrance and remained standing, here walked quietly towards them. His usually high color had faded except from his eyes, but his exalted manner was still more pronounced, with a dreadful deliberation superadded.

"I believe—er—I had—the honah—to send up my kyard!" (In his supreme moments the colonel's Southern accent was always in evidence.) "I may—er—be mistaken—but—er—that is my impression." The colonel paused, and placed his right hand statuesquely on his heart.

The two women trembled—Miss Tish fancied the very shirt frill of the colonel was majestically erecting itself—as they stammered in one voice,—

"Ye-e-es!"

"That kyard contained my full name—with a request to see my ward—Miss Stannard," continued the colonel slowly. "I believe that is the fact."

"Certainly! certainly!" gasped the women feebly.

"Then may I—er—point out to you that I *am*—er—*waiting*?"

Although nothing could exceed the laborious simplicity and husky sweetness of the colonel's utterance, it appeared to demoralize utterly his two hearers—Miss Prinkwell seemed to fade into the pattern of the wall paper, Miss Tish to droop submissively forward like a pink wax candle in the rays of the burning sun.

"We will bring her instantly. A thousand pardons, sir," they uttered in the same breath, backing towards the door.

But here the unexpected intervened. Unnoticed by the three during the colloquy, a little figure in a black dress had peeped through the door, and then glided into the room. It was a girl of about ten, who, in all candor, could scarcely be called pretty, although the awkward change of adolescence had not destroyed the delicate proportions of her hands and feet nor the beauty of her brown eyes. These were, just then, round and wondering, and fixed alternately on the colonel and the two women. But like many other round and wondering eyes, they had taken in the full meaning of the situation, with a quickness the adult mind is not apt to give them credit for. They saw the complete and utter subjugation of the two supreme autocrats of the school, and,

I grieve to say, they were filled with a secret and "fearful joy." But the casual spectator saw none of this; the round and wondering eyes, still rimmed with recent and recalcitrant tears, only looked big and innocently shining.

The relief of the two women was sudden and unaffected. "Oh, here you are, dearest, at last!" said Miss Tish eagerly. "This is your guardian, Colonel Starbottle. Come to him, dear!"

She took the hand of the child, who hung back with an odd mingling of shamefacedness and resentment of the interference, when the voice of Colonel Starbottle, in the same deadly calm deliberation, said,—

"I—er—will speak with her—alone."

The round eyes again saw the complete collapse of authority, as the two women shrank back from the voice, and said hurriedly,—

"Certainly, Colonel Starbottle; perhaps it would be better," and ingloriously quitted the room.

But the colonel's triumph left him helpless. He was alone with a simple child, an unprecedented, unheard-of situation, which left him embarrassed and—speechless. Even his vanity was conscious that his oratorical periods, his methods, his very attitude, were powerless here. The perspiration stood out on his forehead; he looked at her vaguely, and essayed a feeble smile. The child saw his embarrassment, even as she had seen and understood his triumph, and the small woman within her exulted. She put her little hands on her waist, and with the fingers turned downwards and outwards pressed them down her hips to her bended knees until they had forced her skirts into an egregious fullness before and behind, as if she were making a curtsy, and then jumped up and laughed.

"You did it! Hooray!"

"Did what?" said the colonel, pleased yet mystified.

"Frightened 'em!—the two old cats! Frightened 'em outen their slippers! Oh, jiminy! Never, *never*, NEVER before was they so skeert! Never since school kept did they have to crawl like that! They was skeert enough *first* when you come, but just now!— Lordy! They wasn't a-goin' to let you see me—but they had to! *had to!* HAD TO!" and she emphasized each repetition with a skip.

"I believe—er," said the colonel blandly, "that I—er—intimated with some firmness"—

"That's it—just it!" interrupted the child delightedly. "You —you—overdid 'em!"

"What?"

"*Overdid 'em!* Don't you know? They're always so high and mighty! Kinder 'Don't tech me. My mother's an angel; my father's a king'—all that sort of thing. They did *this*"— she drew herself up in a presumable imitation of the two women's majestic entrance—"and then," she continued, "you —*you* jest did this"—here she lifted her chin, and puffing out her small chest, strode towards the colonel in evident simulation of his grandest manner.

A short, deep chuckle escaped him—although the next moment his face became serious again. But Pansy in the mean time had taken possession of his coat sleeve and was rubbing her cheek against it like a young colt. At which the colonel succumbed feebly and sat down on the sofa, the child standing beside him, leaning over and transferring her little hands to the lapels of his frock coat, which she essayed to button over his chest as she looked into his murky eyes.

"The other girls said," she began, tugging at the button, "that you was a 'cirkiss' "—another tug—" 'a nigger minstrel' "—and a third tug—" 'a agent with samples'—but that showed all they knew!"

"Ah," said the colonel with exaggerated blandness, "and —er—what did *you*—er say?"

The child smiled. "I said you was a Stuffed Donkey— but that was *before* I knew you. I was a little skeert too; but *now*"—she succeeded in buttoning the coat and making the colonel quite apopletic,—"*now* I ain't frightened one bit— no, not one *tiny* bit! But," she added, after a pause, unbutton- ing the coat again and smoothing down the lapels between her fingers, "you're to keep on frightening the old cats— mind! Never mind about the *girls*. I'll tell them."

The colonel would have given worlds to be able to strug- gle up into an upright position with suitable oral expression. Not that his vanity was at all wounded by these irrespon- sible epithets, which only excited an amused wonder, but he was conscious of an embarrassed pleasure in the child's caressing familiarity, and her perfect trustfulness in him touched his extravagant chivalry. He ought to protect her, and yet correct her. In the consciousness of these duties he laid his white hand upon her head. Alas! she lifted her arm and instantly transferred his hand and part of his arm around her neck and shoulders, and comfortably snuggled against him. The colonel gasped. Nevertheless, something must be said, and he began, albeit somewhat crippled in delivery:—

"The—er—use of elegant and precise language by—er— young ladies cannot be too sedulously cultivated"—

But here the child laughed, and snuggling still closer, gurgled: "That's right! Give it to her when she comes down! That's the style!" and the colonel stopped, discom- fited. Nevertheless, there was a certain wholesome glow in the contact of this nestling little figure.

Presently he resumed tentatively: "I have—er—brought you a few dainties."

"Yes," said Pansy, "I see; but they're from the wrong shop, you dear old silly! They're from Tomkins's, and we girls just abominate his things. You oughter have gone to Emmons's. Never mind. I'll show you when we go out. We're going out, aren't we?" she said suddenly, lifting her head anxiously. "You know it's allowed, and it's *rights* 'to parents and guardians!'"

"Certainly, certainly," said the colonel. He knew he would feel a little less contrained in the open air.

"Then we'll go now," said Pansy, jumping up. "I'll just run upstairs and put on my things. I'll say it's 'orders' from you. And I'll wear my new frock—it's longer." (The colonel was slightly relieved at this; it had seemed to him, as a guardian, that there was perhaps an abnormal display of Pansy's black stockings.) "You wait; I won't be long."

She darted to the door, but reaching it, suddenly stopped, returned to the sofa, where the colonel still sat, imprinted a swift kiss on his mottled cheek, and fled, leaving him invested with a mingled flavor of freshly ironed muslin, wintergreen lozenges, and recent bread and butter. He sat still for some time, staring out of the window. It was very quiet in the room; a bumblebee blundered from the jasmine outside into the open window, and snored loudly at the panes. But the colonel heeded it not, and remained abstracted and silent until the door opened to Miss Tish and Pansy—in her best frock and sash, at which the colonel started and became erect again and courtly.

"I am about to take my ward out," he said deliberately, "to—er—taste the air in the Alameda, and—er—view the shops. We may—er—also—indulge in—er—slight suitable refreshment;—er—seed cake—or—bread and butter—and—a dish of tea."

Miss Tish, now thoroughly subdued, was delighted to

grant Miss Stannard the half holiday permitted on such occasions. She begged the colonel to suit his own pleasure, and intrusted "the dear child" to her guardian "with the greatest confidence."

The colonel made a low bow, and Pansy, demurely slipping her hand into his, passed with him into the hall; there was a slight rustle of vanishing skirts, and Pansy pressed his hand significantly. When they were well outside, she said, in a lower voice:—

"Don't look up until we're under the gymnasium windows." The colonel, mystified but obedient, strutted on. "Now!" said Pansy. He looked up, beheld the windows aglow with bright young faces, and bewildering with many handkerchiefs and clapping hands, stopped, and then taking off his hat, acknowledged the salute with a sweeping bow. Pansy was delighted. "I knew they'd be there; I'd already fixed 'em. They're just dyin' to know you."

The colonel felt a certain glow of pleasure. "I—er—had already intimated a—er—willingness to—er—inspect the classes; but—I—er—understood that the rules"—

"They're sick old rules," interrupted the child. "Tish and Prinkwell are the rules! You say just right out that you *will*! Just overdo her!"

The colonel had a vague sense that he ought to correct both the spirit and language of this insurrectionary speech, but Pansy pulled him along, and then swept him quite away with a torrent of prattle of the school, of her friends, of the teachers, of her life and its infinitely small miseries and pleasures. Pansy was voluble; never before had the colonel found himself relegated to the place of a passive listener. Nevertheless, he liked it, and as they passed on, under the shade of the Alameda, with Pansy alternately swinging from his hand and skipping beside him, there was a vague smile of satisfaction on his face. Passers-by turned to look after the strangely assorted pair, or smiled, accepting them, as the colonel fancied, as father and daughter. An odd feeling, half of pain and half of pleasure, gripped at the heart of the empty and childless man.

And now, as they approached the more crowded thoroughfares, the instinct of chivalrous protection was keen in his breast. He piloted her skillfully; he jauntily suited his own to her skipping step; he lifted her with scrupulous politeness over obstacles; strutting beside her on crowded pavements, he made way for her with his swinging stick. All the while, too, he had taken note of the easy carriage of her head and shoulders, and most of all of her small, slim feet and hands, that, to his fastidious taste, betokened her race. "Ged, sir," he muttered to himself, "she's 'Blue Grass' stock, all through." To admiration succeeded pride, with a slight touch of ownership. When they went into a shop, which, thanks to the ingenuous Pansy, they did pretty often, he would introduce her with a wave of the hand and the remark, "*I* am—er—seeking nothing to-day, but if you will kindly—er—serve my *ward*—Miss Stannard!" Later, when they went into the confectioner's for refreshment, and Pansy frankly declared for "ice cream and cream cakes," instead of the "dish of tea and bread and butter" he had ordered in pursuance of his promise, he heroically took it himself—to satisfy his honor. Indeed, I know of no more sublime figure than Colonel Starbottle—rising superior to a long-withstood craving for a "cocktail," morbidly conscious also of the ridiculousness of his appearance to any of his old associates who might see him—drinking lukewarm tea and pecking feebly at his bread and butter at a small table, beside his little tyrant.

And this domination of the helpless continued on their

way home. Although Miss Pansy no longer talked of herself, she was equally voluble in inquiry as to the colonel's habits, ways of life, friends and acquaintances, happily restricting her interrogations, in regard to those of her own sex, to "any *little* girls that he knew." Saved by this exonerating adjective, the colonel saw here a chance to indulge his postponed monitorial duty, as well as his vivid imagination. He accordingly drew elaborate pictures of impossible children he had known—creatures precise in language and dress, abstinent of play and confectionery, devoted to lessons and duties, and otherwise, in Pansy's own words, "loathsome to the last degree!" As "daughters of oldest and most cherished friends," they might perhaps have excited Pansy's childish jealousy but for the singular fact that they had all long ago been rewarded by marriage with senators, judges, and generals—also associates of the colonel. This remoteness of presence somewhat marred their effect as an example, and the colonel was mortified, though not entirely displeased, to observe that their surprising virtues did not destroy Pansy's voracity for sweets, the recklessness of her skipping, nor the freedom of her language. The colonel was remorseful—but happy.

When they reached the seminary again, Pansy retired with her various purchases, but reappeared after an interval with Miss Tish.

"I remember," hesitated that lady, trembling under the fascination of the colonel's profound bow, "that you were anxious to look over the school, and although it was not possible then, I shall be glad to show you now through one of the classrooms."

The colonel, glancing at Pansy, was momentarily shocked by a distortion of one side of her face, which seemed, however, to end in a wink of her innocent brown eyes, but recovering himself, gallantly expressed his gratitude. The next moment he was ascending the stairs, side by side with Miss Tish, and had a distinct impression that he had been pinched in the calf by Pansy, who was following close behind.

It was recess, but the large classroom was quite filled with pupils, many of them older and prettier girls, inveigled there, as it afterwards appeared, by Pansy, in some precocious presentiment of her guardian's taste. The colonel's apologetic yet gallant bow on entering, and his erect, old-fashioned elegance, instantly took their delighted attention. Indeed, all would have gone well had not Miss Prinkwell, with the view of impressing the colonel as well as her pupils, majestically introduced him as "a distinguished jurist deeply interested in the cause of education, as well as guardian of their fellow pupil." That opportunity was not thrown away on Colonel Starbottle.

Stepping up to the desk of the astounded principal, he laid the points of his fingers delicately upon it, and, with a preparatory inclination of his head towards her, placed his other hand in his breast, and with an invocatory glance at the ceiling, began.

It was the colonel's habit at such moments to state at first, with great care and precision, the things that he "would not say," that he "*need* not say," and apparently that it was absolutely unnecessary even to allude to. It was therefore not strange that the colonel informed them that he need not say that he counted his present privilege among the highest that had been granted him; for besides the privilege of beholding the galaxy of youthful talent and excellence before him, besides the privilege of being surrounded by a garland of the blossoms of the school in all their freshness and beauty, it was well understood that he had the greater privilege of—er—standing *in loco parentis* to one of these blossoms. It was not for him to allude to the high trust imposed upon him by—er—deceased and cherished friend, and daughter of one of the first families of Virginia, by the side of one who must feel that she was the recipient of trusts equally supreme (here the colonel paused, and statuesquely regarded the alarmed Miss Prinkwell as if he were in doubt of it), but he would say that it should be *his* devoted mission to champion the rights of the orphaned and innocent whenever and wherever the occasion arose, against all odds, and even in the face of misguided authority. (Having left the impression that Miss Prinkwell contemplated an invasion of those rights, the colonel became more lenient and genial.) He fully recognized her high and noble office; he saw in her the worthy successor of those two famous instructresses of Athens—those Greek ladies—er—whose names had escaped his memory, but which—er—no doubt Miss Prinkwell would be glad to recall to her pupils, with some account of their lives. (Miss Prinkwell colored; she had never heard of them before, and even the delight of the class in the colonel's triumph was a little dampened by this prospect of hearing more about them.) But the colonel was only too content with seeing before him these bright and beautiful faces, destined, as he firmly believed, in after years to lend their charm and effulgence to the highest places as the happy helpmeets of the greatest in the land. He was—er—leaving a —er—slight testimonial of his regard in the form of some—er —innocent refreshments in the hands of his ward, who would —er—act as—er—his proxy in their distribution; and the colonel sat down to the flutter of handkerchiefs, an applause only half restrained, and the utter demoralization of Miss Prinkwell.

But the time of his departure had come by this time, and

he was too experienced a public man to risk the possibility of an anticlimax by protracting his leave-taking. And in an ominous shining of Pansy's big eyes as the time approached he felt an embarrassment as perplexing as the odd presentiment of loneliness that was creeping over him. But with an elaborate caution as to the dangers of self-indulgence, and the private bestowal of a large gold piece slipped into her hand, a promise to come again soon, and an exaction that she would write to him often, the colonel received in return a wet kiss, a great deal of wet cheek pressed against his own, and a momentary tender clinging, like that which attends the pulling up of some small flower, as he passed out into the porch. In the hall, on the landing above him, there was a close packing of brief skirts against the railing, and a voice, apparently proceeding from a pair of very small mottled legs protruding through the balusters, said distinctly, "Free cheers for Ternel Tarbottle!" And to this benediction the colonel, hat in hand, passed out of this Eden into the world again.

The colonel's next visit to the seminary did not produce the same sensation as the first, although it was accompanied with equal disturbance to the fair principals. Had he been a less conceited man he might have noticed that their antagonism, although held in restraint by their wholesome fear of him, was in danger of becoming more a conviction than a mere suspicion. He was made aware of it through Pansy's resentment towards them, and her revelation of a certain inquisition that she had been subjected to in regard to his occupation, habits, and acquaintances. Naturally of these things Pansy knew very little, but this had not prevented her from saying a great deal. There had been enough in her questioners' manner to make her suspect that her guardian was being attacked, and to his defense she brought the mendacity and imagination of a clever child. What she had really said did not transpire except through her own comments to the colonel: "And of course you've killed people— for you're a kernel, you know!" (Here the colonel admitted, as a point of fact, that he had served in the Mexican war.) "And you kin *preach,* for they heard you do it when you was here before," she added confidently; "and of course you own niggers—for there's 'Jim.' " (The colonel here attempted to explain that Jim, being in a free State, was now a free man, but Pansy swept away such fine distinctions.) "And you're rich, you know, for you gave me that ten-dollar gold piece all for myself. So I jest gave 'em as good as they sent —the old spies and curiosity shops!"

The colonel, more pleased at Pansy's devotion than concerned over the incident itself, accepted this interpretation of his character as a munificent, militant priest with a smiling protest. But a later incident caused him to remember it more seriously.

They had taken their usual stroll through the Alameda, and had made the round of the shops, where the colonel had exhibited his usual liberality of purchase and his exalted parental protection, and so had passed on to their usual refreshment at the confectioner's, the usual ices and cakes for Pansy, but this time—a concession also to the tyrant Pansy —a glass of lemon soda and a biscuit for the colonel. He was coughing over his unaccustomed beverage, and Pansy, her equanimity and volubility restored by sweets, was chirruping at his side; the large saloon was filling up with customers—mainly ladies and children, embarrassing to him as the only man present, when suddenly Pansy's attention was diverted by another arrival. It was a good-looking young woman, overdressed, striking, and self-conscious, who, with an air of one who was in the habit of challenging attention, affectedly seated herself with a male companion at an empty table, and began to pull off an overtight glove.

"My!" said Pansy in admiring wonder, "ain't she fine?"

Colonel Starbottle looked up abstractedly, but at the first glance his face flushed redly, deepened to a purple, and then became gray and stern. He had recognized in the garish fair one Miss Flora Montague, the "Western Star of Terpsichore and Song," with whom he had supped a few days before at Sacramento. The lady was "on tour" with her "Combination Troupe."

The colonel leaned over and fixed his murky eyes on Pansy. "The room is filling up; the place is stifling; I must —er—request you to—er—hurry."

There was a change in the colonel's manner, which the quick-witted child heeded. But she had not associated it with the entrance of the strangers, and as she obediently gulped down her ice, she went on innocently,—

"That fine lady's smilin' and lookin' over here. Seems to know you; so does the man with her."

"I—er—must request you," said the colonel, with husky precision, "*not* to look that way, but finish your—er—repast."

His tone was so decided that the child's lips pouted, but before she could speak a shadow leaned over their table. It was the companion of the "fine lady."

"Don't seem to see us, Colonel," he said with coarse familiarity, laying his hand on the colonel's shoulder. "Florry wants to know what's up."

The colonel rose at the touch. "Tell her, sir," he said huskily, but with slow deliberation, "that *I* 'am up' and leaving this place with my ward, Miss Stannard. Good-morning."

He lifted Pansy with infinite courtesy from her chair, took

her hand, strolled to the counter, threw down a gold piece, and passing the table of the astonished fair one with an inflated breast, swept with Pansy out of the shop. In the street he paused, bidding the child go on; and then, finding he was not followed by the woman's escort, rejoined his little companion.

For a few moments they walked silently side by side. Then Pansy's curiosity, getting the better of her pout, demanded information. She had applied a child's swift logic to the scene. The colonel was angry, and had punished the woman for something. She drew closer to his side, and looking up with her big eyes, said confidentially,—

"What had she been a-doing?"

The colonel was amazed, embarrassed, and speechless. He was totally unprepared for the question, and as unable to answer it. His abrupt departure from the shop had been to evade the very truth now demanded of him. Only a supreme effort of mendacity was left him. He wiped his brow with his handkerchief, coughed, and began deliberately:—

"The—er—lady in question is in the habit of using a scent called—er—patchouli, a—er—perfume exceedingly distressing to me. I detected it instantly on her entrance. I wished to avoid it—without further contact. It is—er—singular but accepted fact that some people are—er—peculiarly affected by odors. I had—er—old cherished friend who always—er—fainted at the odor of jasmine; and I was intimately acquainted with General Bludyer, who—er—dropped like a shot on the presentation of a simple violet. The—er—habit of using such perfumes excessively in public," continued the colonel, looking down upon the innocent Pansy, and speaking in tones of deadly deliberation, "cannot be too greatly condemned, as well as the habit of—er—frequenting places of public resort in extravagant costumes, with—er—individuals who—er—intrude upon domestic privacy. I trust you will eschew such perfumes, places, costumes, and—er—companions *forever* and—*on all occasions*!" The colonel had raised his voice to his forensic emphasis, and Pansy, somewhat alarmed, assented. Whether she entirely accepted the colonel's explanation was another matter.

The incident, although not again alluded to, seemed to shadow the rest of their brief afternoon holiday, and the colonel's manner was unmistakably graver. But it seemed to the child more affectionate and thoughtful. He had previously at parting submitted to be kissed by Pansy with stately tolerance and an immediate resumption of his loftiest manner. On this present leave-taking he laid his straight closely shaven lips on the crown of her dark head, and as her small arms clipped his neck, drew her closely to his side. The child uttered a slight cry; the colonel hurriedly put his hand to his breast. Her round cheek had come in contact with his derringer—a small weapon of beauty and precision —which invariably nestled also at his side, in his waistcoat pocket. The child laughed; so did the colonel, but his cheek flushed mightily.

It was four months later, and a turbulent night. The early rains, driven by a strong southwester against the upper windows of the Magnolia Restaurant, sometimes blurred the radiance of the bright lights within, and the roar of the encompassing pines at times drowned the sounds of song and laughter that rose from a private supper room. Even the clattering arrival and departure of the Sacramento stagecoach, which disturbed the depths below, did not affect these upper revelers. For Colonel Starbottle, Jack Hamlin, Judge Beeswinger, and Jo Wynyard, assisted by Mesdames Montague, Montmorency, Bellefield, and "Tinky" Clifford, of the "Western Star Combination Troupe," then performing "on tour," were holding "high jinks" in the supper room. The colonel had been of late moody, irritable, and easily upset. In the words of a friend and admirer, "he was kam only at twelve paces."

In a lull in the general tumult a Chinese waiter was seen at the door vainly endeavoring to attract the attention of the colonel by signs and interjections. Mr. Hamlin's quick eye first caught sight of the intruder. "Come in, Confucious," said Jack pleasantly; "you're a trifle late for a regular turn, but any little thing in the way of knife swallowing"—

"Lill missee to see connle! Waitee waitee, bottom side housee," interrupted the Chinaman, dividing his speech between Jack and the colonel.

"What! *Another* lady? This is no place for me!" said Jack, rising with finely simulated decorum.

"Ask her up," chirped "Tinky" Clifford.

But at this moment the door opened against the Chinaman, and a small figure in a cloak and hat, dripping with raindrops, glided swiftly in. After a moment's half-frightened, half-admiring glance at the party, she darted forward with a little cry and threw her wet arms round the colonel. The rest of the company, arrested in their festivity, gasped with vague and smiling wonder; the colonel became purple and gasped. But only for a moment. The next instant he was on his legs, holding the child with one hand, while with the other he described a stately sweep of the table.

"My ward—Miss Pansy Stannard," he said with husky brevity. But drawing the child aside, he whispered quickly, "What has happened? Why are you here?"

But Pansy, child-like, already diverted by the lights, the table piled with delicacies, the gayly dressed women, and the air of festivity, answered half abstractedly, and as much, perhaps, to the curious eyes about her as to the colonel's voice,—

"I runned away!"

"Hush!" whispered the colonel, aghast.

But Pansy, responding again to the company rather than her guardian's counsel, and as if appealing to them, went on half poutingly: "Yes! I runned away because they teased me! Because they didn't like you and said horrid things. Because they told awful, dreadful lies! Because they said I wasn't no orphan!—that my name wasn't Stannard, and that you'd made it all up. Because they said I was a liar—and *you was my father*!"

A sudden outbreak of laughter here shook the room, and even drowned the storm outside; again and again it rose, as the colonel staggered gaspingly to his feet. For an instant it seemed as if his struggles to restrain himself would end in an apoplectic fit. Perhaps it was for this reason that Jack Hamlin checked his own light laugh and became alert and grave. Yet the next moment Colonel Starbottle went as suddenly dead white, as leaning over the table he said huskily, but deliberately, "I must request the ladies present to withdraw."

"Don't mind *us,* Colonel," said Judge Beeswinger, "it's all in the family here, you know! And—now I look at the girl—hang it all! she *does* favor you, old man. Ha! ha!"

"And as for the ladies," said Wynyard with a weak, vinous laugh, "unless any of 'em is inclined to take the matter as *personal*—eh?"

"Stop!" roared the colonel.

There was no mistaking his voice nor his intent now. The two men, insulted and instantly sobered, were silent. Mr. Hamlin rose, playfully but determinedly tapped his fair companions on the shoulders, saying, "Run away and play, girls," actually bundled them, giggling and protesting, from the room, closed the door, and stood with his back against it. Then it was seen that the colonel, still very white, was holding the child by the hand, as she shrank back wonderingly and a little frightened against him.

"I thank *you*, Mr. Hamlin," said the colonel in a lower voice—yet with a slight touch of his habitual stateliness in it, "for being here to bear witness, in the presence of this child, to my unqualified statement that a more foul, vile, and iniquitous falsehood never was uttered than that which has been poured into her innocent ears!" He paused, walked to the door, still holding her hand, and, as Mr. Hamlin stepped aside, opened it, told her to await him in the public parlor, closed the door again, and once more faced the two men. "And," he continued more deliberately, "for the infamous jests that you, Judge Beeswinger, and you, Mr. Wynyard, have dared to pass in her presence and mine, I shall expect from each of you the fullest satisfaction—personal satisfaction. My seconds will wait on you in the morning."

The two men stood up sobered—yet belligerent.

"As you like, sir," said Beeswinger, flashing.

"The sooner the better for me," added Wynyard curtly.

They passed the unruffled Jack Hamlin with a smile and a vaguely significant air, as if calling him as a witness to the colonel's madness, and strode out of the room.

As the door closed behind them, Mr. Hamlin lightly settled his white waistcoat, and, with his hands on his hips, lounged towards the colonel. "And *then*?" he said quietly.

"Eh?" said the colonel.

"After you've shot one or both of these men, or one of 'em has knocked *you* out, what's to become of that child?"

"If—I am—er—spared, sir," said the colonel huskily, "I shall continue to defend her—against calumny and sneers"—

"In this style, eh? After her life has been made a hell by her association with a man of your reputation, you propose to whitewash it by a quarrel with a couple of drunken scallawags like Beeswinger and Wynyard, in the presence of three painted trollops and a d——d scamp like myself! Do you suppose this won't be blown all over California before she can be sent back to school? Do you suppose those cackling hussies in the next room won't give the whole story away to the next man who stands treat?" (A fine contempt for the sex in general was one of Mr. Hamlin's most subtle attractions for them.)

"Nevertheless, sir," stammered the colonel, "the prompt punishment of the man who has dared"—

"Punishment!" interrupted Hamlin, "who's to punish the man who has dared most? The one man who is responsible for the whole thing? Who's to punish *you*?"

"Mr. Hamlin—sir!" gasped the colonel, falling back, as his hand involuntarily rose to the level of his waistcoat pocket and his derringer.

But Mr. Hamlin only put down the wine glass he had lifted from the table and was delicately twirling between his fingers, and looked fixedly at the colonel.

"Look here," he said slowly. "When the boys said that you accepted the guardianship of that child *not* on account of Dick Stannard, but only as a bluff against the joke they'd set up at you, I didn't believe them! When these men and women to-night tumbled to that story of the child being *yours*, I didn't believe that! When it was said by others that you were serious about making her your ward, and giving her your property, because you doted on her like a father, I didn't believe that."

"And—why not *that*?" said the colonel quickly, yet with an odd tremor in his voice.

"Because," said Hamlin, becoming suddenly as grave as the colonel, "I could not believe that any one who cared a picayune for the child could undertake a trust that might bring her into contact with a life and company as rotten as ours. I could not believe that even the most God-forsaken, conceited fool would, for the sake of a little sentimental parade and splurge among people outside his regular walk, allow the prospects of that child to be blasted. I couldn't believe it, even if he thought he was acting like a father. I didn't believe it—but I'm beginning to believe it now!"

There was little to choose between the attitudes and expressions of the two set stern faces now regarding each other, silently, a foot apart. But the colonel was the first to speak:—

"Mr. Hamlin—sir! You said a moment ago that *I* was —er—ahem—responsible for this evening's affair—but you expressed a doubt as to who could—er—punish me for it. I accept the responsibility you have indicated, sir, and offer you that chance. But as this matter between us must have precedence over—my engagements with that *canaille,* I shall expect you with your seconds at sunrise on Burnt Ridge. Good-evening, sir."

With head erect the colonel left the room. Mr. Hamlin slightly shrugged his shoulders, turned to the door of the room whither he had just banished the ladies, and in a few minutes his voice was heard melodiously among the gayest.

For all that he managed to get them away early. When he had bundled them into a large carryall, and watched them drive away through the storm, he returned for a minute to the waiting room for his overcoat. He was surprised to hear the sound of the child's voice in the supper room, and the door being ajar, he could see quite distinctly that she was seated at the table, with a plate full of sweets before her,

while Colonel Starbottle, with his back to the door, was
sitting opposite to her, his shoulders slightly bowed as he
eagerly watched her. It seemed to Mr. Hamlin that it was the
close of an emotional interview, for Pansy's voice was broken,
partly by sobs, and partly, I grieve to say, by the hurried
swallowing of the delicacies before her. Yet, above the beating of the storm outside, he could hear her saying,—

"Yes! I promise to be good—(sob)—and to go with Mrs.
Pyecroft—(sob)—and to try—to like another guardian—
(sob)—and not to cry any more—(sob)—and—oh, please,
don't you do it either!"

But here Mr. Hamlin slipped out of the room and out of
the house, with a rather grave face. An hour later, when the
colonel drove up to the Pyecrofts' door with Pansy, he found
that Mr. Pyecroft was slightly embarrassed, and a figure,
which, in the darkness, seemed to resemble Mr. Hamlin's,
had just emerged from the door as he entered.

Yet the sun was not up on Burnt Ridge earlier than Mr.
Hamlin. The storm of the night before had blown itself
out; a few shreds of mist hung in the valleys from the
Ridge, that lay above coldly reddening. Then a breeze swept
over it, and out of the dissipating mist fringe Mr. Hamlin
saw two black figures, closely buttoned up like himself,
emerge, which he recognized as Beeswinger and Wynyard,
followed by their seconds. But the colonel came not. Hamlin
joined the others in an animated confidential conversation,
attended by a watchful outlook for the missing adversary.
Five, ten minutes elapsed, and yet the usually prompt colonel
was not there. Mr. Hamlin looked grave; Wynyard and
Beeswinger exchanged interrogatory glances. Then a buggy
was seen driving furiously up the grade, and from it leaped
Colonel Starbottle, accompanied by Dick MacKinstry, his
second, carrying his pistol case. And then—strangely enough

for men who were waiting the coming of an antagonist who was a dead shot—they drew a breath of relief!

MacKinstry slightly preceded his principal, and the others could see that Starbottle, though erect, was walking slowly. They were surprised also to observe that he was haggard and hollow-eyed, and seemed, in the few hours that had elapsed since they last saw him, to have aged ten years. MacKinstry, a tall Kentuckian, saluted, and was the first one to speak.

"Colonel Starbottle," he said formally, "desires to express his regrets at this delay, which was unavoidable, as he was obliged to attend his ward, who was leaving by the down coach for Sacramento with Mrs. Pyecroft, this morning." Hamlin, Wynyard, and Beeswinger exchanged glances. "Colonel Starbottle," continued MacKinstry, turning to his principal, "desires to say a word to Mr. Hamlin."

As Mr. Hamlin would have advanced from the group, Colonel Starbottle lifted his hand deprecatingly. "What I have to say must be said before these gentlemen," he began slowly. "Mr. Hamlin—sir! when I solicited the honor of this meeting I was under a grievous misapprehension of the intent and purpose of your comments on my action last evening. I think," he added, slightly inflating his buttoned-up figure, "that the reputation I have always borne in—er—meetings of this kind will prevent any—er—misunderstanding of my present action—which is to—er—ask permission to withdraw my challenge—and to humbly beg your pardon."

The astonishment produced by this unexpected apology, and Mr. Hamlin's prompt grasp of the colonel's hand, had scarcely passed before the colonel drew himself up again, and turning to his second said, "And now I am at the service of Judge Beeswinger and Mr. Wynyard—whichever may elect to honor me first."

But the two men thus addressed looked for a moment strangely foolish and embarrassed. Yet the awkwardness was at last broken by Judge Beeswinger frankly advancing towards the colonel with an outstretched hand. "We came here only to apologize, Colonel Starbottle. Without possessing your reputation and experience in these matters, we still think we can claim, as you have, an equal exemption from any misunderstanding when we say that we deeply regret our foolish and discourteous conduct last evening."

A quick flush mounted to the colonel's haggard cheek as he drew back with a suspicious glance at Hamlin.

"Mr. Hamlin!—gentlemen!—if this is—er—!"

But before he could finish his sentence Hamlin had clapped his hand on the colonel's shoulder. "You'll take my word, colonel, that these gentlemen honestly intended to apologize, and came here for that purpose;—and—*so did I*—only you anticipated me!"

In the laughter that followed Mr. Hamlin's frankness the colonel's features relaxed grimly, and he shook the hands of his late possible antagonists.

"And now," said Mr. Hamlin gayly, "you'll all adjourn to breakfast with me—and try to make up for the supper we left unfinished last night."

It was the only allusion to that interruption and its consequences, for during the breakfast the colonel said nothing in regard to his ward, and the other guests were discreetly reticent. But Mr. Hamlin was not satisfied. He managed to get the colonel's servant, Jim, aside, and extracted from the Negro that Colonel Starbottle had taken the child that night to Pyecroft's; that he had had a long interview with Pyecroft; had written letters and "walked de flo'" all night; that he (Jim) was glad the child was gone!

"Why?" asked Hamlin, with affected carelessness.

"She was just makin' de kernel like any o' de low-down No'th'n folks—keerful, and stingy, and mighty 'fraid o' de opinions o' de biggety people. And fo' what? Jess to strut round wid dat child like he was her 'spectable go-to-meeting fader!"

"And was the child sorry to leave him?" asked Hamlin.

"Wull—no, sah. De mighty curos thing, Marse Jack, about the gals—big and little—is dey just *use* de kernel!— dat's all! Dey just use de ole man like a pole to bring down deir persimmons—see?"

But Mr. Hamlin did not smile.

Later it was known that Colonel Starbottle had resigned his guardianship with the consent of the court. Whether he ever again saw his late ward was not known, nor if he remained loyal to his memories of her.

Readers of these chronicles may, however, remember that years after, when the colonel married the widow of a certain Mr. Tretherick, both in his courtship and his short married life he was singularly indifferent to the childish graces of Carrie Tretherick, her beloved little daughter, and that his obtuseness in that respect provoked the widow's ire.

THE CONVALESCENCE
OF JACK HAMLIN

The habitually quiet, ascetic face of Seth Rivers was somewhat disturbed and his brows were knitted as he climbed the long ascent of Windy Hill to its summit and his own rancho. Perhaps it was the effect of the characteristic wind, which that afternoon seemed to assault him from all points at once and did not cease its battery even at his front door, but hustled him into the passage, blew him into the sitting room, and then celebrated its own exit from the long, rambling house by the banging of doors throughout the halls and the slamming of windows in the remote distance.

Mrs. Rivers looked up from her work at this abrupt onset of her husband, but without changing her own expression of slightly fatigued self-righteousness. Accustomed to these elemental eruptions, she laid her hands from force of habit upon the lifting tablecloth, and then rose submissively to brush together the scattered embers and ashes from the large hearthstone, as she had often done before.

"You're in early, Seth," she said.

"Yes. I stopped at the Cross Roads Post Office. Lucky I did, or you'd hev had kempany on your hands afore you knowed it—this very night! I found this letter from Dr. Duchesne," and he produced a letter from his pocket.

Mrs. Rivers looked up with an expression of worldly interest. Dr. Duchesne had brought her two children into the world with some difficulty, and had skillfully attended her through a long illness consequent upon the inefficient maternity of soulful but fragile American women of her type. The doctor had more than a mere local reputation as a surgeon, and Mrs. Rivers looked up to him as her sole connecting link with a world of thought beyond Windy Hill.

"He's comin' up yer to-night, bringin' a friend of his—a patient that he wants us to board and keep for three weeks until he's well agin," continued Mr. Rivers. "Ye know how the doctor used to rave about the pure air on our hill."

Mrs. Rivers shivered slightly, and drew her shawl over her shoulders, but nodded a patient assent.

"Well, he says it's just what that patient oughter have to cure him. He's had lung fever and other things, and this yer air and gin'ral quiet is bound to set him up. We're to board and keep him without any fuss or feathers, and the doctor sez he'll pay liberal for it. This yer's what he sez," concluded Mr. Rivers, reading from the letter: " 'He is now fully convalescent, though weak, and really requires no other medicine than the—ozone'—yes, that's what the doctor calls it—'of Windy Hill, and in fact as little attendance as possible. I will not let him keep even his Negro servant with him. He'll give you no trouble, if he can be prevailed upon to stay the whole time of his cure.' "

"There's our spare room—it hasn't been used since Parson Greenwood was here," said Mrs. Rivers reflectively. "Melinda could put it to rights in an hour. At what time will he come?"

"He'd come about nine. They drive over from Hightown depot. But," he added grimly, "here ye are orderin' rooms to be done up and ye don't know who for."

"You said a friend of Dr. Duchesne," returned Mrs. Rivers simply.

"Dr. Duchesne has many friends that you and me mightn't cotton to," said her husband. "This man is Jack Hamlin."

As his wife's remote and introspective black eyes returned only vacancy, he added quickly. "The noted gambler!"

"Gambler?" echoed his wife, still vaguely.

"Yes—reg'lar; it's his business."

"Goodness, Seth! He can't expect to do it here."

"No," said Seth quickly, with that sense of fairness to his fellow man which most women find it so difficult to understand. "No—and he probably won't mention the word 'card' while he's here."

"Well?" said Mrs. Rivers interrogatively.

"And," continued Seth, seeing that the objection was not pressed, "he's one of them desprit men! A reg'lar fighter! Killed two or three men in dools!"

Mrs. Rivers stared. "What could Dr. Duchesne have been thinking of? Why, we wouldn't be safe in the house with him!"

Again Seth's sense of equity triumphed. "I never heard of his fightin' anybody but his own kind, and when he was bullyragged. And ez to women he's quite t' other way in fact, and that's why I think ye oughter know it afore you let him come. He don't go round with decent women. In fact"— But here Mr. Rivers, in the sanctity of conjugal confidences and the fullness of Bible reading, used a few strong scriptural substantives happily unnecessary to repeat here.

"Seth!" said Mrs. Rivers suddenly, "you seem to know this man."

The unexpectedness and irrelevancy of this for a moment startled Seth. But that chaste and God-fearing man had no secrets. "Only by hearsay, Jane," he returned quietly; "but if ye say the word I'll stop his comin' now."

"It's too late," said Mrs. Rivers decidedly.

"I reckon not," returned her husband, "and that's why

I came straight here. I've only got to meet them at the depot and say this thing can't be done—and that's the end of it. They'll go off quiet to the hotel."

"I don't like to disappoint the doctor, Seth," said Mrs. Rivers. "We might," she added, with a troubled look of inquiry at her husband, "we might take that Mr. Hamlin on trial. Like as not he won't stay, anyway, when he sees what we're like, Seth. What do you think? It would be only our Christian duty, too."

"I was thinkin' o' that as a professin' Christian, Jane," said her husband. "But supposin' that other Christians don't look at it in that light. Thar's Deacon Stubbs and his wife and the parson. Ye remember what he said about 'no covenant with sin'?"

"The Stubbses have no right to dictate who I'll have in my house," said Mrs. Rivers quickly, with a faint flush in her rather sallow cheeks.

"It's your say and nobody else's," assented her husband with grim submissiveness. "You do what you like."

Mrs. Rivers mused. "There's only myself and Melinda here," she said with sublime naïveté; "and the children ain't old enough to be corrupted. I am satisfied if you are, Seth," and she again looked at him inquiringly.

"Go ahead, then, and get ready for 'em," said Seth, hurrying away with unaffected relief. "If you have everything fixed by nine o'clock, that'll do."

Mrs. Rivers had everything "fixed" by that hour including herself presumably, for she had put on a gray dress which she usually wore when shopping in the county town, adding a prim collar and cuffs. A pearl-encircled brooch, the wedding gift of Seth, and a solitaire ring next to her wedding ring, with a locket containing her children's hair, accented her position as a proper wife and mother. At a quarter to nine she had finished tidying the parlor, opening the harmonium so that the light might play upon its polished keyboard, and bringing from the forgotten seclusion of her closet two beautifully bound volumes of Tupper's "Poems" and Pollok's "Course of Time," to impart a literary grace to the centre table. She then drew a chair to the table and sat down before it with a religious magazine in her lap. The wind roared over the deep-throated chimney, the clock ticked monotonously, and then there came the sound of wheels and voices.

But Mrs. Rivers was not destined to see her guest that night. Dr. Duchesne, under the safe lee of the door, explained that Mr. Hamlin had been exhausted by the journey, and, assisted by a mild opiate, was asleep in the carriage; that if Mrs. Rivers did not object, they would carry him at once to his room. In the flaring and guttering of candles, the flashing of lanterns, the flapping of coats and shawls, and the bewildering rush of wind, Mrs. Rivers was only vaguely conscious of a slight figure muffled tightly in a cloak carried past her in the arms of a grizzled Negro up the staircase, followed by Dr. Duchesne. With the closing of the front door on the tumultuous world without, a silence fell again on the little parlor.

When the doctor made his reappearance it was to say that his patient was being undressed and put to bed by his Negro servant, who, however, would return with the doctor to-night, but that the patient would be left with everything that was necessary, and that he would require no attention from the family until the next day. Indeed, it was better that he should remain undisturbed. As the doctor confined his confidences and instructions entirely to the physical condition of their guest, Mrs. Rivers found it awkward to press other inquiries.

"Of course," she said at last hesitatingly, but with a certain primness of expression, "Mr. Hamlin must expect to find everything here very different from what he is accustomed to—at least from what my husband says are his habits."

"Nobody knows that better than he, Mrs. Rivers," returned the doctor with an equally marked precision of manner, "and you could not have a guest who would be less likely to make you remind him of it."

A little annoyed, yet not exactly knowing why, Mrs. Rivers abandoned the subject, and as the doctor shortly afterwards busied himself in the care of his patient, with whom he remained until the hour of his departure, she had no chance of renewing it. But as he finally shook hands with his host and hostess, it seemed to her that he slightly recurred to it. "I have the greatest hope of the curative effect of this wonderful locality on my patient, but even still more of the beneficial effect of the complete change of his habits, his surroundings, and their influences." Then the door closed on the man of science and the grizzled Negro servant, the noise of the carriage wheels was shut out with the song of the wind in the pine tops, and the rancho of Windy Hill possessed Mr. Jack Hamlin in peace. Indeed, the wind was now falling, as was its custom at that hour, and the moon presently arose over a hushed and sleeping landscape.

For the rest of the evening the silent presence in the room above affected the household; the half-curious servants and ranch hands spoke in whispers in the passages, and at evening prayers, in the dining room, Seth Rivers, kneeling before and bowed over a rush-bottomed chair whose legs were clutched by his strong hands, included "the stranger within our gates" in his regular supplications. When the hour for retiring came, Seth, with a candle in his hand, preceded his wife up the staircase, but stopped before the door of their guest's room. "I reckon," he said interrogatively to Mrs. Rivers, "I oughter see ef he's wantin' anythin'?"

"You heard what the doctor said," returned Mrs. Rivers cautiously. At the same time she did not speak decidedly, and the frontiersman's instinct of hospitality prevailed. He knocked lightly; there was no response. He turned the door handle softly. The door opened. A faint clean perfume —an odor of some general personality rather than any particular thing—stole out upon them. The light of Seth's candle struck a few glints from some cut-glass and silver, the contents of the guest's dressing case, which had been carefully laid out upon a small table by his Negro servant. There was also a refined neatness in the disposition of his clothes and effects which struck the feminine eye of even the tidy Mrs. Rivers as something new to her experience. Seth drew nearer the bed with his shaded candle, and then, turning, beckoned his wife to approach. Mrs. Rivers hesitated—but for the necessity of silence she would have openly protested— but that protest was shut up in her compressed lips as she came forward.

For an instant that awe with which absolute helplessness invests the sleeping and dead was felt by both husband and wife. Only the upper part of the sleeper's face was visible above the bedclothes, held in position by a thin white nervous hand that was encircled at the wrist by a ruffle. Seth stared. Short brown curls were tumbled over a forehead damp with the dews of sleep and exhaustion. But what appeared more singular, the closed eyes of this vessel of wrath and recklessness were fringed with lashes as long and silky as a woman's. Then Mrs. Rivers gently pulled her husband's sleeve, and they both crept back with a greater sense of intrusion and even more cautiously than they had entered. Nor did they speak until the door was closed softly and

they were alone on the landing. Seth looked grimly at his
wife.

"Don't look much ez ef he could hurt anybody."

"He looks like a sick man," returned Mrs. Rivers calmly.

The unconscious object of this criticism and attention
slept until late; slept through the stir of awakened life within
and without, through the challenge of early cocks in the
lean-to shed, through the creaking of departing ox teams
and the lazy, long-drawn commands of teamsters, through
the regular strokes of the morning pump and the splash
of water on stones, through the far-off barking of dogs and
the half-intelligible shouts of ranchmen; slept through the
sunlight on his ceiling, through its slow descent of his wall,
and awoke with it in his eyes! He woke, too, with a delicious
sense of freedom from pain, and of even drawing a long
breath without difficulty—two facts so marvelous and dream-
like that he naturally closed his eyes again lest he should
waken to a world of suffering and dyspnœa. Satisfied at last
that this relief was real, he again opened his eyes, but upon
surroundings so strange, so wildly absurd and improbable,
that he again doubted their reality. He was lying in a
moderately large room, primly and severely furnished,
but his attention was for the moment riveted to a gilt frame
upon the wall beside him bearing the text, "God Bless Our
Home," and then on another frame on the opposite wall
which admonished him to "Watch and Pray." Beside them
hung an engraving of the "Raising of Lazarus," and a
Hogarthian lithograph of "The Drunkard's Progress." Mr.
Hamlin closed his eyes; he was dreaming certainly—not one
of those wild, fantastic visions that had so miserably filled
the past long nights of pain and suffering, but still a dream!
At last, opening one eye stealthily, he caught the flash of the

sunlight upon the crystal and silver articles of his dressing case, and that flash at once illuminated his memory. He remembered his long weeks of illness and the devotion of Dr. Duchesne. He remembered how, when the crisis was past, the doctor had urged a complete change and absolute rest, and had told him of a secluded rancho in some remote locality kept by an honest Western pioneer whose family he had attended. He remembered his own reluctant assent, impelled by gratitude to the doctor and the helplessness of a sick man. He now recalled the weary journey thither, his exhaustion and the semi-consciousness of his arrival in a bewildering wind on a shadowy hilltop. And this was the place!

He shivered slightly, and ducked his head under the cover again. But the brightness of the sun and some exhilarating quality in the air tempted him to have another outlook, avoiding as far as possible the grimly decorated walls. If they had only left him his faithful servant he could have relieved himself of that mischievous badinage which always alternately horrified and delighted that devoted Negro. But he was alone—absolutely alone—in this conventicle!

Presently he saw the door open slowly. It gave admission to the small round face and yellow ringlets of a little girl, and finally to her whole figure, clasping a doll nearly as large as herself. For a moment she stood there, arrested by the display of Mr. Hamlin's dressing case on the table. Then her glances moved around the room and rested upon the bed. Her blue eyes and Mr. Hamlin's brown ones met and mingled. Without a moment's hesitation she moved to the bedside. Taking her doll's hands in her own, she displayed it before him.

"Isn't it pitty?"

Mr. Hamlin was instantly his old self again. Thrusting

his hand comfortably under the pillow, he lay on his side and gazed at it long and affectionately. "I never," he said in a faint voice, but with immovable features, "saw anything so perfectly beautiful. Is it alive?"

"It's a dolly," she returned gravely, smoothing down its frock and straightening its helpless feet. Then seized with a spontaneous idea, like a young animal she suddenly presented it to him with both hands and said,—

"Kiss it."

Mr. Hamlin implanted a chaste salute on its vermilion cheek. "Would you mind letting me hold it for a little?" he said with extreme diffidence.

The child was delighted, as he expected. Mr. Hamlin placed it in a sitting posture on the edge of his bed, and put an ostentatious paternal arm around it.

"But you're alive, ain't you?" he said to the child.

This subtle witticism convulsed her. "I'm a little girl," she gurgled.

"I see; her mother?"

"Ess."

"And who's your mother?"

"Mammy."

"Mrs. Rivers?"

The child nodded until her ringlets were shaken on her cheek. After a moment she began to laugh bashfully and with repression, yet as Mr. Hamlin thought a little mischievously. Then as he looked at her interrogatively she suddenly caught hold of the ruffle of his sleeve.

"Oo's got on mammy's nighty."

Mr. Hamlin started. He saw the child's obvious mistake and actually felt himself blushing. It was unprecedented—it was the sheerest weakness—it must have something to do with the confounded air.

"I grieve to say you are deeply mistaken—it is my very own," he returned with great gravity. Nevertheless, he drew the coverlet close over his shoulder. But here he was again attracted by another face at the half-opened door—a freckled one, belonging to a boy apparently a year or two older than the girl. He was violently telegraphing to her to come away, although it was evident that he was at the same time deeply interested in the guest's toilet articles. Yet as his bright gray eyes and Mr. Hamlin's brown ones met, he succumbed, as the girl had, and walked directly to the bedside. But he did it bashfully—as the girl had not. He even attempted a defensive explanation.

"She hadn't oughter come in here, and mar wouldn't let her, and she knows it," he said with superior virtue.

"But I asked her to come as I'm asking you," said Mr. Hamlin promptly, "and don't you go back on your sister or you'll never be President of the United States." With this he laid his hand on the boy's tow head, and then, lifting himself on his pillow to a half-sitting posture, put an arm around each of the children, drawing them together, with the doll occupying the central post of honor. "Now," continued Mr. Hamlin, albeit in a voice a little faint from the exertion, "now that we're comfortable together I'll tell you the story of the good little boy who became a pirate in order to save his grandmother and little sister from being eaten by a wolf at the door."

But, alas! that interesting record of self-sacrifice never was told. For it chanced that Melinda Bird, Mrs. Rivers's help, following the trail of the missing children, came upon the open door and glanced in. There, to her astonishment, she saw the domestic group already described, and to her eyes dominated by the "most beautiful and perfectly elegant" young man she had ever seen. But let not the incautious reader suppose that she succumbed as weakly as her artless charges to these fascinations. The character and antecedents of that young man had been already delivered to her in the kitchen by the other help. With that single glance she halted; her eyes sought the ceiling in chaste exaltation. Falling back a step, she called in ladylike hauteur and precision, "Mary Emmeline and John Wesley."

Mr. Hamlin glanced at the children. "It's Melindy looking for us," said John Wesley. But they did not move. At which Mr. Hamlin called out faintly but cheerfully, "They're here, all right."

Again the voice arose with still more marked and lofty distinctness, "John Wesley and Mary Em-me-line." It seemed to Mr. Hamlin that human accents could not convey a more significant and elevated ignoring of some implied impropriety in his invitation. He was for a moment crushed.

But he only said to his little friends with a smile, "You'd better go now and we'll have that story later."

"Affer beckus?" suggested Mary Emmeline.

"In the woods," added John Wesley.

Mr. Hamlin nodded blandly. The children trotted to the door. It closed upon them and Miss Bird's parting admonition, loud enough for Mr. Hamlin to hear, "No more freedoms, no more intrudings, you hear?"

The older culprit, Hamlin, retreated luxuriously under his blankets, but presently another new sensation came over him—absolutely, hunger. Perhaps it was the child's allusion to "beckus," but he found himself wondering when it would be ready. This anxiety was soon relieved by the appearance of his host himself bearing a tray, possibly in deference to Miss Bird's sense of propriety. It appeared also that Dr. Duchesne had previously given suitable directions for his diet, and Mr. Hamlin found his repast simple but enjoyable. Always playfully or ironically polite to strangers, he thanked his host and said he had slept splendidly.

"It's this yer 'ozone' in the air that Dr. Duchesne talks about," said Seth complacently.

"I am inclined to think it is also those texts," said Mr. Hamlin gravely, as he indicated them on the wall. "You see they reminded me of church and my boyhood's slumbers there. I have never slept so peacefully since." Seth's face brightened so interestedly at what he believed to be a suggestion of his guest's conversion that Mr. Hamlin was fain to change the subject. When his host had withdrawn he proceeded to dress himself, but here became conscious of his weakness and was obliged to sit down. In one of those enforced rests he chanced to be near the window, and for the first time looked on the environs of his place of exile. For a moment he was staggered. Everything seemed to pitch downward from the rocky outcrop on which the rambling house and farm sheds stood. Even the great pines around it swept downward like a green wave, to rise again in enormous billows as far as the eye could reach. He could count a dozen of their tumbled crests following each other on their way to the distant plain. In some vague point of that shimmering horizon of heat and dust was the spot he came from the preceding night. Yet the recollection of it and his feverish past seemed to confuse him, and he turned his eyes gladly away.

Pale, a little tremulous, but immaculate and jaunty in his white flannels and straw hat, he at last made his way downstairs. To his great relief he found the sitting room empty, as he would have willingly deferred his formal acknowledgments to his hostess later. A single glance at the interior determined him not to linger, and he slipped quietly into the open air and sunshine. The day was warm and still, as the wind only came up with the going down of the sun, and the atmosphere was still redolent with the morning spicing of pine and hay and a stronger balm that seemed to fill his breast with sunshine. He walked toward the nearest shade—a cluster of young buckeyes—and having with a certain civic fastidiousness flicked the dust from a stump with his handkerchief he sat down. It was very quiet and calm. The life and animation of early morning had already vanished from the hill, or seemed to be suspended with the sun in the sky. He could see the ranchmen and oxen toiling on the green terraced slopes below, but no sound reached his ears. Even the house he had just quitted seemed empty of life throughout its rambling length. His seclusion was complete. Could he stand it for three weeks? Perhaps it need not be for so long; he was already stronger! He foresaw that the ascetic Seth might become wearisome. He had an intuition that Mrs. Rivers would be equally so; he should certainly quarrel with Melinda, and this would probably debar him from the company of the children—his only hope.

But his seclusion was by no means so complete as he expected. He presently was aware of a camp-meeting hymn hummed somewhat ostentatiously by a deep contralto voice, which he at once recognized as Melinda's, and saw that severe virgin proceeding from the kitchen along the ridge until within a few paces of the buckeyes, when she stopped and, with her hand shading her eyes, apparently began to examine the distant fields. She was a tall, robust girl, not without certain rustic attractions, of which she seemed fully conscious. This latter weakness gave Mr. Hamlin a new idea. He put up the penknife with which he had been paring his nails while wondering why his hands had become so thin, and awaited events. She presently turned, approached the buckeyes, plucked a spike of the blossoms with great girlish lightness, and then apparently discovering Mr. Hamlin, started in deep concern and said with somewhat stentorian politeness: "I *beg* your pardon—didn't know I was intruding!"

"Don't mention it," returned Jack promptly, but without moving. "I saw you coming and was prepared; but generally—as I have something the matter with my heart—a sudden joy like this is dangerous."

Somewhat mystified, but struggling between an expression of rigorous decorum and gratified vanity, Miss Melinda stammered, "I was only"—

"I knew it—I saw what you were doing," interrupted Jack gravely, "only I wouldn't do it if I were you. You were looking at one of those young men down the hill. You forgot that if you could see him he could see you looking too, and that would only make him conceited. And a girl with *your* attractions don't require that."

"Ez if," said Melinda, with lofty but somewhat reddening scorn, "there was a man on this hull rancho that I'd take a second look at."

"It's the first look that does the business," returned Jack simply. "But maybe I was wrong. Would you mind—as you're going straight back to the house" (Miss Melinda had certainly expressed no such intention)—"turning those two little kids loose out here? I've a sort of engagement with them."

"I will speak to their mar," said Melinda primly, yet with a certain sign of relenting, as she turned away.

"You can say to her that I regretted not finding her in the sitting room when I came down," continued Jack tactfully.

Apparently the tact was successful, for he was delighted

a few moments later by the joyous onset of John Wesley and Mary Emmeline upon the buckeyes, which he at once converted into a game of hide and seek, permitting himself at last to be shamelessly caught in the open. But here he wisely resolved upon guarding against further grown-up interruption, and consulting with his companions found that on one of the lower terraces there was a large reservoir fed by a mountain rivulet, but they were not allowed to play there. Thither, however, the reckless Jack hied with his playmates and was presently ensconced under a willow tree, where he dexterously fashioned tiny willow canoes with his penknife and sent them sailing over a submerged expanse of nearly an acre. But half an hour of this ingenious amusement was brought to an abrupt termination. While cutting bark, with his back momentarily turned on his companions, he heard a scream, and turned quickly to see John Wesley struggling in the water, grasping a tree root, and Mary Emmeline— nowhere! In another minute he saw the strings of her pinafore appear on the surface a few yards beyond, and in yet another minute, with a swift rueful glance at his white flannels, he had plunged after her. A disagreeable shock of finding himself out of his depths was, however, followed by contact with the child's clothing, and clutching her firmly, a stroke or two brought him panting to the bank. Here a gasp, a gurgle, and then a roar from Mary Emmeline, followed by a sympathetic howl from John Wesley, satisfied him that the danger was over. Rescuing the boy from the tree root, he laid them both on the grass and contemplated them exercising their lungs with miserable satisfaction. But here he found his own breathing impeded in addition to a slight faintness, and was suddenly obliged to sit down beside them, at which, by some sympathetic intuition, they both stopped crying.

Encouraged by this, Mr. Hamlin got them to laughing again, and then proposed a race home in their wet clothes, which they accepted, Mr. Hamlin, for respiratory reasons, lagging in their rear until he had the satisfaction of seeing them captured by the horrified Melinda in front of the kitchen, while he slipped past her and regained his own room. Here he changed his saturated clothes, tried to rub away a certain chilliness that was creeping over him, and lay down in his dressing gown to miserable reflections. He had nearly drowned the children and overexcited himself, in spite of his promise to the doctor! He would never again be intrusted with the care of the former nor be believed by the latter!

But events are not always logical in sequence. Mr. Hamlin went comfortably to sleep and into a profuse perspiration. He was awakened by a rapping at his door, and opening it, was surprised to find Mrs. Rivers with anxious inquiries as to his condition. "Indeed," she said, with an emotion which even her prim reserve could not conceal, "I did not know until now how serious the accident was, and how but for you and Divine Providence my little girl might have been drowned. It seems Melinda saw it all."

Inwardly objurgating the spying Melinda, but relieved that his playmates hadn't broken their promise of secrecy, Mr. Hamlin laughed.

"I'm afraid that your little girl wouldn't have got into the water at all but for me—and you must give all the credit of getting her out to the other fellow." He stopped at the severe change in Mrs. Rivers's expression, and added quite boyishly and with a sudden drop from his usual levity, "But please don't keep the children away from me for all that, Mrs. Rivers."

Mrs. Rivers did not, and the next day Jack and his companions sought fresh playing fields and some new story-telling pastures. Indeed, it was a fine sight to see this pale, handsome, elegantly dressed young fellow lounging along between a blue-checkered pinafored girl on one side and a barefooted boy on the other. The ranchmen turned and looked after him curiously. One, a rustic prodigal, reduced by dissipation to the swine-husks of ranching, saw fit to accost him familiarly.

"The last time I saw you dealing poker in Sacramento, Mr. Hamlin, I did not reckon to find you up here playing with a couple of kids."

"No!" responded Mr. Hamlin suavely, "and yet I remember I was playing with some country idiots down there, and you were one of them. Well! understand that up here I prefer the kids. Don't let me have to remind you of it."

Nevertheless, Mr. Hamlin could not help noticing that for the next two or three days there were many callers at the ranch and that he was obliged in his walks to avoid the highroad on account of the impertinent curiosity of wayfarers. Some of them were of that sex which he would not have contented himself with simply calling "curious."

"To think," said Melinda confidently to her mistress, "that that thar Mrs. Stubbs, who wouldn't go to the Hightown Hotel because there was a play actress thar, has been snoopin' round here twice since that young feller came."

Of this fact, however, Mr. Hamlin was blissfully unconscious.

Nevertheless, his temper was growing uncertain; the angle of his smart straw hat was becoming aggressive to strangers; his politeness sardonic. And now Sunday morning had come with an atmosphere of starched piety and well-soaped respectability at the rancho, and the children were to be taken with the rest of the family to the day-long service at Hightown. As these Sabbath pilgrimages filled the main road, he was fain to take himself and his loneliness to the trails and byways, and even to invade the haunts of some other elegant outcasts like himself—to wit, a crested hawk, a graceful wild cat beautifully marked, and an eloquently reticent rattlesnake. Mr. Hamlin eyed them without fear, and certainly without reproach. They were not out of their element.

Suddenly he heard his name called in a stentorian contralto. An impatient ejaculation rose to his lips, but died upon them as he turned. It was certainly Melinda, but in his present sensitive loneliness it struck him for the first time that he had never actually seen her before as she really was. Like most men in his profession he was a quick reader of thoughts and faces when he was interested, and although this was the same robust, long-limbed, sunburnt girl he had met, he now seemed to see through her triple incrustation of human vanity, conventional piety, and outrageous Sabbath finery an honest, sympathetic simplicity that commanded his respect.

"You are back early from church," he said.

"Yes. One service is good enough for me when thar ain't no special preacher," she returned, "so I jest sez to Silas, 'as I ain't here to listen to the sisters cackle ye kin put to the buckboard and drive me home ez soon ez you please.' "

"And so his name is Silas," suggested Mr. Hamlin cheerfully.

"Go 'long with you, Mr. Hamlin, and don't pester," she returned, with heifer-like playfulness. "Well, Silas put to, and when we rose the hill here I saw your straw hat passin' in the gulch, and sez to Silas, sez I, 'Ye kin pull up here, for over yar is our new boarder, Jack Hamlin, and I'm goin' to talk with him.' 'All right,' sez he, 'I'd sooner trust ye with that gay young gambolier every day of the week than with them saints down thar on Sunday. He deals ez straight ez he shoots, and is about as nigh onto a gentleman as they make 'em.' "

For one moment or two Miss Bird only saw Jack's long lashes. When his eyes once more lifted they were shining. "And what did you say?" he said, with a short laugh.

"I told him he needn't be Christopher Columbus to have discovered that." She turned with a laugh toward Jack, to be met by the word "shake," and an outstretched thin white hand which grasped her large red one with a frank, fraternal pressure.

"I didn't come to tell ye that," remarked Miss Bird as she sat down on a boulder, took off her yellow hat, and re-stacked her tawny mane under it, "but this: I reckoned I went to Sunday meetin' as I ought ter. I kalkilated to hear considerable about 'Faith' and 'Works,' and sich, but I didn't reckon to hear all about you from the Lord's Prayer to the Doxology. You were in the special prayers ez a warnin', in the sermon ez a text; they picked out hymns to fit ye! And always a drefful example and a visitation. And the rest o' the time it was all gabble, gabble by the brothers and sisters about you. I reckon, Mr. Hamlin, that they know everything you ever did since you were knee-high to a grasshopper, and a good deal more than you ever thought of doin'. The women is all dead set on convertin' ye and savin' ye by their own precious selves, and the men is ekally dead set on gettin' rid o' ye on that account."

"And what did Seth and Mrs. Rivers say?" asked Hamlin composedly, but with kindling eyes.

"They stuck up for ye ez far ez they could. But ye see the parson hez got a holt upon Seth, havin' caught him kissin' a convert at camp meeting; and Deacon Turner knows suthin about Mrs. Rivers's sister, who kicked over the pail and jumped the fence years ago, and she's afeard o' him. But what I wanted to tell ye was that they're all comin' up here to take a look at ye—some on 'em to-night. You ain't afeard, are ye?" she added, with a loud laugh.

"Well, it looks rather desperate, doesn't it?" returned Jack, with dancing eyes.

"I'll trust ye for all that," said Melinda. "And now I reckon I'll trot along to the rancho. Ye needn't offer ter see me home," she added, as Jack made a movement to accompany her. "Everybody up here ain't as fair-minded ez Silas and you, and Melinda Bird hez a character to lose! So long!" With this she cantered away, a little heavily, perhaps, adjusting her yellow hat with both hands as she clattered down the steep hill.

That afternoon Mr. Hamlin drew largely on his convalescence to mount a half-broken mustang, and in spite of the rising afternoon wind to gallop along the highroad in quite as mischievous and breezy a fashion. He was wont to allow his mustang's nose to hang over the hind rails of wagons and buggies containing young couples, and to dash ahead of sober carryalls that held elderly "members in good standing."

An accomplished rider, he picked up and brought back the flying parasol of Mrs. Deacon Stubbs without dismounting. He finally came home a little blown, but dangerously composed.

There was the usual Sunday evening gathering at Windy Hill Rancho—neighbors and their wives, deacons and the pastor—but their curiosity was not satisfied by the sight of Mr. Hamlin, who kept his own room and his own counsel. There was some desultory conversation, chiefly on church topics, for it was vaguely felt that a discussion of the advisability of getting rid of the guest of their host was somewhat difficult under this host's roof, with the guest impending at any moment. Then a diversion was created by some of the church choir practicing the harmonium with the singing of certain more or less lugubrious anthems. Mrs. Rivers presently joined in, and in a somewhat faded soprano, which, however, still retained considerable musical taste and expression, sang, "Come, ye Disconsolate." The wind moaned over the deep-throated chimney in a weird harmony with the melancholy of that human appeal as Mrs. Rivers sang the first verse:—

> *"Come, ye disconsolate, where'er ye languish,*
> *Come to the Mercy Seat, fervently kneel;*
> *Here bring your wounded hearts—here tell your anguish,*
> *Earth has no sorrow that Heaven cannot heal!"*

A pause followed. and the long-drawn, half-human sigh of the mountain wind over the chimney seemed to mingle with the wail of the harmonium. And then, to their thrilled astonishment, a tenor voice, high, clear, but tenderly passionate, broke like a skylark over their heads in the lines of the second verse:—

> *"Joy of the desolate, Light of the straying,*
> *Hope of the penitent—fadeless and pure;*
> *Here speaks the Comforter, tenderly saying,*
> *Earth has no sorrow that Heaven cannot cure!"*

The hymn was old and familiar enough, Heaven knows. It had been quite popular at funerals, and some who sat there had had its strange melancholy borne upon them in time of loss and tribulations, but never had they felt its full power before. Accustomed as they were to emotional appeal and to respond to it, as the singer's voice died away above them, their very tears flowed and fell with that voice. A few sobbed aloud, and then a voice asked tremulously,—

"Who is it?"

"It's Mr. Hamlin," said Seth quietly. "I've heard him often hummin' things before."

There was another silence, and the voice of Deacon Stubbs broke in harshly,—

"It's rank blasphemy."

"If it's rank blasphemy to sing the praise o' God, not only better than some folks in the choir, but like an angel o' light, I wish you'd do a little o' that blaspheming on Sundays, Mr. Stubbs."

The speaker was Mrs. Stubbs, and as Deacon Stubbs was a notoriously bad singer the shot told.

"If he's sincere, why does he stand aloof? Why does he not join us?" asked the parson.

"He hasn't been asked," said Seth quietly. "If I ain't mistaken this yer gathering this evening was specially to see how to get rid of him."

There was a quick murmur of protest at this. The parson exchanged glances with the deacon and saw that they were hopelessly in the minority.

"I will ask him myself," said Mrs. Rivers suddenly.

"So do, Sister Rivers; so do," was the unmistakable response.

Mrs. Rivers left the room and returned in a few moments with a handsome young man, pale, elegant, composed, even to a grave indifference. What his eyes might have said was another thing; the long lashes were scarcely raised.

"I don't mind playing a little," he said quietly to Mrs. Rivers, as if continuing a conversation, "but you'll have to let me trust my memory."

"Then you—er—play the harmonium?" said the parson, with an attempt at formal courtesy.

"I was for a year or two the organist in the choir of Dr. Todd's church at Sacramento," returned Mr. Hamlin quietly.

The blank amazement on the faces of Deacons Stubbs and Turner and the parson was followed by wreathed smiles from the other auditors and especially from the ladies. Mr. Hamlin sat down to the instrument, and in another moment took possession of it as it had never been held before. He played from memory as he had implied, but it was the memory of a musician. He began with one or two familiar anthems, in which they all joined. A fragment of a mass and a Latin chant followed. An "Ave Maria" from an opera was his first secular departure, but his delighted audience did not detect it. Then he hurried them along in unfamiliar language to "O mio Fernando" and "Spiritu gentil," which they fondly imagined were hymns, until, with crowning audacity, after a few preliminary chords of the "Miserere," he landed them broken-hearted in the Trovatore's donjon tower with "Non te scordar de mi."

Amidst the applause he heard the preacher suavely explain that those Popish masses were always in the Latin language, and rose from the instrument satisfied with his experiment. Excusing himself as an invalid from joining them in a light collation in the dining room, and begging his hostess's permission to retire, he nevertheless lingered a few moments by the door as the ladies filed out of the room, followed by the gentlemen, until Deacon Turner, who was bringing up the rear, was abreast of him. Here Mr. Hamlin became suddenly deeply interested in a framed pencil drawing which hung on the wall. It was evidently a schoolgirl's amateur portrait, done by Mrs. Rivers. Deacon Turner halted quickly by his side as the others passed out—which was exactly what Mr. Hamlin expected.

"Do you know the face?" said the deacon eagerly.

Thanks to the faithful Melinda, Mr. Hamlin did know it perfectly. It was a pencil sketch of Mrs. Rivers's youthfully erring sister. But he only said he thought he recognized a likeness to some one he had seen in Sacramento.

The deacon's eye brightened. "Perhaps the same one—perhaps," he added in a submissive and significant tone "a—er—painful story."

"Rather—to him," observed Hamlin quietly.

"How?—I—er—don't understand," said Deacon Turner.

"Well, the portrait looks like a lady I knew in Sacramento who had been in some trouble when she was a silly girl, but had got over it quietly. She was, however, troubled a good deal by some mean hound who was every now and then raking up the story wherever she went. Well, one of her friends—I might have been among them, I don't exactly remember just now—challenged him, but although he had no conscientious convictions about slandering a woman, he had some about being shot for it, and declined. The consequence was he was cowhided once in the street, and the second time tarred and feathered and ridden on a rail out of town. That, I suppose, was what you meant by your 'painful story.' But is this the woman?"

"No, no," said the deacon hurriedly, with a white face, "you have quite misunderstood."

"But whose is this portrait?" persisted Jack.

"I believe that—I don't know exactly—but I think it is a sister of Mrs. Rivers's," stammered the deacon.

"Then, of course, it isn't the same woman," said Jack in simulated indignation.

"Certainly—of course not," returned the deacon.

"Phew!" said Jack. "That was a mighty close call. Lucky we were alone, wasn't it?"

"Yes," said the deacon, with a feeble smile.

"Seth," continued Jack, with a thoughtful air, "looks like a quiet man, but I shouldn't like to have made that mistake about his sister-in-law before him. These quiet men are apt to shoot straight. Better keep this to ourselves."

Deacon Turner not only kept the revelation to himself but apparently his own sacred person also, as he did not call again at Windy Hill Rancho during Mr. Hamlin's stay. But he was exceedingly polite in his references to Jack, and alluded patronizingly to a "little chat" they had had together. And when the usual reaction took place in Mr. Hamlin's favor and Jack was actually induced to perform on the organ at Hightown Church next Sunday, the deacon's voice was loudest in his praise. Even Parson Greenwood allowed himself to be non-committal as to the truth of the rumor, largely circulated, that one of the most desperate gamblers in the State had been converted through his exhortations.

So, with breezy walks and games with the children, occasional confidences with Melinda and Silas, and the Sabbath "singing of anthems," Mr. Hamlin's three weeks of convalescence drew to a close. He had lately relaxed his habit of seclusion so far as to mingle with the company gathered for more social purposes at the rancho, and once or twice unbent so far as to satisfy their curiosity in regard to certain details of his profession.

"I have no personal knowledge of games of cards," said Parson Greenwood patronizingly, "and think I am right in saying that our brothers and sisters are equally inexperienced. I am—ahem—far from believing, however, that entire ignorance of evil is the best preparation for combating it, and I should be glad if you'd explain to the company the intricacies of various games. There is one that you mentioned, with a—er—scriptural name."

"Faro," said Hamlin, with an unmoved face.

"Pharaoh," repeated the parson gravely; "and one which you call 'poker,' which seems to require great self-control."

"I couldn't make you understand poker without your playing it," said Jack decidedly.

"As long as we don't gamble—that is, play for money—I see no objection," returned the parson.

"And," said Jack musingly, "you could use beans."

It was agreed finally that there would be no falling from grace in their playing among themselves, in an inquiring Christian spirit, under Jack's guidance, he having decided to abstain from card playing during his convalescence, and Jack permitted himself to be persuaded to show them the following evening.

It so chanced, however, that Dr. Duchesne, finding the end of Jack's "cure" approaching, and not hearing from that interesting invalid, resolved to visit him at about this time. Having no chance to apprise Jack of his intention, on coming to Hightown at night he procured a conveyance at the depot to carry him to Windy Hill Rancho. The wind blew with its usual nocturnal rollicking persistency, and at the end of his turbulent drive it seemed almost impossible to make himself heard amongst the roaring of the pines and some astounding preoccupation of the inmates. After vainly knocking, the doctor pushed open the front door and entered. He rapped at the closed sitting room door, but receiving no reply, pushed it open upon the most unexpected and astounding scene he had ever witnessed. Around the centre table several respectable members of the Hightown Church, including the parson, were gathered with intense and eager faces playing poker, and behind the parson, with his hands in his pockets, carelessly lounged the doctor's patient, the picture of health and vigor. A disused pack of cards was scattered on the floor, and before the gentle and precise Mrs. Rivers was heaped a pile of beans that would have filled a quart measure.

When Dr. Duchesne had tactfully retreated before the hurried and stammering apologies of his host and hostess, and was alone with Jack in his rooms, he turned to him with a gravity that was more than half affected and said, "How long, sir, did it take you to effect this corruption?"

"Upon my honor," said Jack simply, "they played last night for the first time. And they forced me to show them. But," added Jack after a significant pause, "I thought it would make the game livelier and be more of a moral lesson if I gave them nearly all good pat hands. So I ran in a cold deck on them—the first time I ever did such a thing in my life. I fixed up a pack of cards so that one had three tens, another three jacks, and another three queens, and so on up to three aces. In a minute they had all tumbled to the game, and you never saw such betting. Every man and woman there believed he or she had struck a sure thing, and staked accordingly. A new panful of beans was brought on, and Seth, your friend, banked for them. And at last the parson raked in the whole pile."

"I suppose you gave him the three aces," said Dr. Duchesne gloomily.

"The parson," said Jack slowly, "*hadn't a single pair in his hand*. It was the stoniest, deadest, neatest *bluff* I ever saw. And when he'd frightened off the last man who held out and laid that measly hand of his face down on that pile of kings, queens, and aces, and looked around the table as he raked in the pile, there was a smile of humble self-righteousness on his face that was worth double the money."

A GENTLEMAN
OF LA PORTE

HE was also a Pioneer. A party who broke through the snows of the winter of '51, and came upon the triangular little valley afterwards known as La Porte, found him the sole inhabitant. He had subsisted for three months on two biscuits a day and a few inches of bacon, in a hut made of bark and brushwood. Yet, when the explorers found him, he was quite alert, hopeful, and gentlemanly. But I cheerfully make way here for the terser narrative of Captain Henry Symes, commanding the prospecting party:—

"We kem upon him, gentlemen, suddent-like, jest abreast of a rock like this"—demonstrating the distance—"ez near ez you be. He sees us, and he dives into his cabin and comes out ag'in with a *tall hat,*—a stovepipe, gentlemen,—and, blank me! gloves! He was a tall, thin feller, holler in the cheek,—ez might be,—and off color in his face, ez was nat'ral, takin' in account his starvation grub. But he lifts his hat to us, so, and sez he, 'Happy to make your acquaintance, gentlemen! I'm afraid you ex-perienced some difficulty in getting here. Take a cigyar.' And he pulls out a fancy cigar-case with two real Havanas in it. 'I wish there was more,' sez he.

" 'Ye don't smoke yourself?' sez I.

" 'Seldom,' sez he; which was a lie, for that very arter-noon I seed him hangin' ontu a short pipe like a suckin' baby ontu a bottle. 'I kept these cigyars for any gentleman that might drop in.'

" 'I reckon ye see a great deal o' the best society yer,' sez Bill Parker, starin' at the hat and gloves and winkin' at the boys.

" 'A few Ind-i-ans occasionally,' sez he.

" 'Injins!' sez we.

" 'Yes. Very quiet good fellows in their way. They have once or twice brought me game, which I refused, as the poor fellows have had a pretty hard time of it themselves.'

"Now, gentlemen, we was, ez you know, rather quiet men —rather peaceable men; but—hevin' been shot at three times by these yar 'good' Injins, and Parker hisself havin' a matter o' three inches of his own skelp lying loose in their hands and he walkin' round wearin' green leaves on his head like a Roman statoo—it *did* kinder seem ez if this yer stranger was playin' it rather low down on the boys. Bill Parker gets up and takes a survey o' him, and sez he, peaceful-like—

" 'Ye say these yer Injins—these yer *quiet* Injins—offered yer game?'

" 'They did!' sez he.

" 'And you refoosed?'

" 'I did,' sez he.

" 'Must hev made 'em feel kinder bad—sorter tortered their sensitiv' naters?' sez Bill.

" 'They really seemed quite disappointed.'

" 'In course,' sez Bill. 'And now mout I ask who you be?'

" 'Excuse me,' says the stranger; and, darn my skin! If he doesn't hist out a keerd-case, and, handin' it over to Bill, sez, 'Here's my kyard.'

"Bill took it and read out aloud, 'J. Trott, Kentucky.'

" 'It's a pooty keerd,' sez Bill.

" 'I'm glad you like it,' says the stranger.

" 'I reckon the other fifty-one of the deck ez as pooty— all of 'em Jacks and left bowers,' sez Bill.

"The stranger sez nothin', but kinder draws back from Bill; but Bill ups and sez—

"'Wot is your little game, Mister J. Trott, of Kentucky?'

"'I don't think I quite understand you,' sez the stranger, a holler fire comin' intu his cheeks like ez if they was the bowl of a pipe.

"'Wot's this yer kid-glove business?—this yer tall hat paradin'?—this yer circus foolin'? Wot's it all about? *Who* are ye, anyway?'

"The stranger stands up, and sez he, 'Ez I don't quarrel with guests on my own land,' sez he, 'I think you'll allow I'm—a gentleman!' sez he.

"With that he takes off his tall hat and makes a low bow, so, and turns away—like this; but Bill lites out of a suddent with his right foot and drives his No. 10 boot clean through the crown of that tall hat like one o' them circus hoops.

"That's about ez fur ez I remember. Gentlemen! thar wa'n't but *one* man o' that hull crowd ez could actooally swear what happened next, and that man never told. For a kind o' whirlwind jest then took place in that valley. I disremember anythin' but dust and bustlin'. Thar wasn't no yellin', thar wasn't no shootin'. It was one o' them suddent things that left even a six-shooter out in the cold. When I kem to in the *chapparel*—bein' oncomfortable like from hevin' only half a shirt on—I found nigh on three pounds o' gravel and stones in my pockets and a stiffness in my ha'r. I looks up and sees Bill hangin' in the forks of a hickory saplin' twenty feet above me.

"'Cap,' sez he, in an inquirin' way, 'hez the tornado passed?'

"'Which?' sez I.

"'This yer elemental disturbance—is it over?'"

" 'I reckon,' sez I.

" 'Because,' sez he, 'afore this yer electrical phenomenon took place I hed a slight misunderstanding with a stranger, and I'd like to apologize!'

"And with that he climbs down, peaceful-like, and goes into the shanty, and comes out, hand in hand with that stranger, smilin' like an infant. And that's the first time, I reckon, we know'd anythin' about the gentleman of La Porte."

It is by no means improbable that the above incidents are slightly exaggerated in narration, and the cautious reader will do well to accept with some reservation the particular phenomenon alluded to by the Captain. But the fact remains that the Gentleman of La Porte was allowed an eccentricity and enjoyed an immunity from contemporaneous criticism only to be attributed to his personal prowess. Indeed, this was once publicly expressed. "It 'pears to me," said a meek newcomer,—who, on the strength of his having received news of the death of a distant relative in the "States," had mounted an exceedingly large crape mourning-band on his white felt hat, and was consequently obliged to "treat" the crowd in the barroom of Parker's Hotel,—"it 'pears to me, gentlemen, that this yer taxin' the nat'ral expression of grief, and allowin' such festive exhibitions as yaller kid gloves, on the gentleman on my right, is sorter inconsistent. I don't mind treatin' the crowd, gentlemen, but this yer platform and resolutions don't seem to keep step."

This appeal to the *Demos* of every American crowd, of course, precluded any reply from the Gentleman of La Porte, but left it to the palpable chairman—the barkeeper, Mr. William Parker.

"Young man," he replied severely, "*when* ye can wear

yaller kids like *that* man and make 'em hover in the air like summer lightnin', and strike in four places to onct!—*then* ye kin talk! *Then* ye kin wear your shirt half-masted if ye like!" A sentiment to which the crowd assenting, the meek man paid for the drinks, and would have, in addition, taken off his mourning-band, but was courteously stopped by the Gentleman of La Porte.

And yet, I protest, there was little suggestive of this baleful prowess in his face and figure. He was loose-jointed and long-limbed, yet with a certain mechanical, slow rigidity of movement that seemed incompatible with alacrity and dexterity. His arms were unusually long, and his hands hung with their palms forward. In walking his feet "toed in," suggesting an aboriginal ancestry. His face, as I remember it, was equally inoffensive. Thin and melancholy, the rare smile that lit it up was only a courteous reception of some attribute of humor in another which he was unable himself to appreciate. His straight black hair and high cheek-bones would have heightened his Indian resemblance; but these were offset by two most extraordinary eyes that were utterly at variance with this, or, indeed, any other, suggestion of his features. They were yellowish-blue, globular, and placidly staring. They expressed nothing that the Gentleman of La Porte thought—nothing that he did—nothing that he might reasonably be expected to do. They were at variance with his speech, his carriage, even his remarkable attire. More than one irreverent critic had suggested that he had probably lost his own eyes in some frontier difficulty, and had hurriedly replaced them with those of his antagonist.

Had this ingenious hypothesis reached the ears of the Gentleman, he would probably have contented himself with a simple denial of the fact, overlooking any humorous incongruity of statement. For, as has been already intimated, among his other privileges he enjoyed an absolute immunity from any embarrassing sense of the ludicrous. His deficient sense of humor and habitual gravity, in a community whose severest dramatic episodes were mitigated by some humorous detail, and whose customary relaxation was the playing of practical jokes, was marked with a certain frankness that was discomposing. "I think," he remarked to a well-known citizen of La Porte, "that, in alluding to the argumentative character of Mr. William Peghammer, you said you had found him lying awake at night contradicting the 'Katydids.' This he himself assures me is not true, and I may add that I passed the night with him in the woods without any such thing occurring. You seem to have *lied*." The severity of this reception checked further humorous exhibitions in his presence. Indeed, I am not certain but it invested him with a certain aristocratic isolation.

Thus identified with the earliest history of the Camp, Mr. Trott participated in its fortunes and shared its prosperity. As one of the original locators of the "Eagle Mine" he enjoyed a certain income which enabled him to live without labor and to freely indulge his few and inexpensive tastes. After his own personal adornment—which consisted chiefly in the daily wearing of spotless linen—he was fond of giving presents. These possessed, perhaps, a sentimental rather than intrinsic value. To an intimate friend he had once given a cane, the stick whereof was cut from a wild grape-vine which grew above the spot where the famous "Eagle *lead*" was first discovered in La Porte; the head originally belonged to a cane presented to Mr. Trott's father, and the ferrule was made of the last silver half-dollar which he had brought to California. "And yet, do you know," said the indignant recipient of this touching gift, "I offered to put it down for a five-dollar ante last night over at Robinson's, and the boys wouldn't see it, and allowed I'd better leave the board. Thar's no appreciation of sacred things in this yer Camp."

It was in this lush growth and springtime of La Porte that the Gentleman was chosen Justice of the Peace by the unanimous voice of his fellow-citizens. That he should have exercised his functions with dignity was natural; that he should have shown a singular lenity in the levyings of fines and the infliction of penalties was, however, an unexpected and discomposing discovery to the settlement.

"The law requires me, sir," he would say to some un-mistakable culprit, "to give you the option of ten days' imprisonment or the fine of ten dollars. If you have not the money with you, the clerk will doubtless advance it for you." It is needless to add that the clerk invariably advanced the money, or that when the Court adjourned the Judge instantly reimbursed him. In one instance only did the sturdy culprit—either from "pure cussedness" or a weaker desire to spare the Judge the expense of his conviction—*refuse* to borrow the amount of the fine from the clerk. He was accordingly remanded to the County Jail. It is related—on tolerably good authority—that when the Court had adjourned the Court was seen, in spotless linen and yellow gloves, making in the direction of the County Jail—a small *adobe* building, which also served as a Hall of Records; that, after ostentatiously consulting certain records, the Court entered the Jail as if in casual official inspection; that, later in the evening, the Deputy Sheriff having charge of the prisoner was dispatched for a bottle of whiskey and a pack of cards. But as the story here alleges that the Deputy, that evening, lost the amount of his month's stipend and the Court its entire yearly salary to the prisoner, in a friendly game of "cut-throat euchre," to relieve the tedium of the prisoner's confinement, the whole story has been denied, as incompatible with Judge Trott's dignity, though not inconsistent with his kindliness of nature.

It is certain, however, that his lenity would have brought him into disfavor but for a redeeming exhibition of his unofficial strength. A young and talented lawyer from Sacramento had been detained in some civil case before Judge Trott, but, confident of his success on appeal from this primitive tribunal, he had scarcely concealed his contempt for it in his closing argument. Judge Trott, when he had finished, sat unmoved save for a slight coloring of his high cheekbones. But here I must again borrow the graphic language of a spectator: "When the Judge had hung out them air red danger signals he sez, quite peaceful-like, to that yer Sacramento Shrimp, sez he, 'Young gentleman,' sez he, 'do you know that I could fine ye fifty dollars for contempt o' Court?' 'And if ye could,' sez the shrimp, peart and sassy as a hossfly, 'I reckon I could pay it.' 'But I ought to add,' sez the Gentleman, sad-like, 'that I don't purpose to do it. I believe in freedom of speech and—action!' He then rises up, onlimbers hisself, so to speak, stretches out that yer Hand o' Providence o' his, lites into that yer shrimp, lifts him up and scoots him through the window twenty feet into the ditch. 'Call the next case,' sez he, sittin' down again, with them big white eyes o' his looking peaceful-like ez if nothin' partikler had happened."

Happy would it have been for the Gentleman had these gentle eccentricities produced no greater result. But a fatal and hitherto unexpected weakness manifested itself in the very court in which he had triumphed, and for a time imperiled his popularity. A lady of dangerous antecedents and great freedom of manner, who was the presiding goddess of the "Wheel of Fortune" in the principal gambling-saloon of La Porte, brought an action against several of its able-bodied citizens for entering the saloon with "force and arms" and destroying the peculiar machinery of her game. She was ably supported by counsel, and warmly sympathized with by a gentleman who was not her husband. Yet in spite of this valuable coöperation she was not successful. The offense was clearly proved; but the jury gave a verdict in favor of the *defendants,* without leaving their seats.

Judge Trott turned his mild, inoffensive eyes upon them. "Do I understand you to say that this is your final verdict?"

"You kin bet your boots, Your Honor," responded the foreman with cheerful but well-meaning irreverence, "that that's about the way the thing points."

"Mr. Clerk," said Judge Trott, "record the verdict, and then enter my resignation as Judge of this court."

He rose and left the bench. In vain did various influential citizens follow him with expostulations; in vain did they point out the worthlessness of the plaintiff and the worth-lessness of her cause—in which he had sacrificed himself. In vain did the jury intimate that his resignation was an insult to *them.* Judge Trott turned abruptly upon the fore-man, with the old ominous glow in his high cheek-bones.

"I didn't understand you," said he.

"I was saying," said the foreman hastily, "that it was useless to argue the case any longer." And withdrew slightly in advance of the rest of the jury, as became his official position. But Judge Trott never again ascended the bench.

It was quite a month after his resignation, and the Gentle-man was sitting in the twilight "under the shadow of his own vine and fig tree,"—a figure of speech locally interpreted as a "giant redwood" and a mossy creeper,—before the door of that cabin in which he was first introduced to the reader,—

when he was faintly conscious of the outlines of a female form and the tones of a female voice.

The Gentleman hesitated, and placed over his right eye a large gold eyeglass, which had been lately accepted by the Camp as his most recent fashionable folly. The form was unfamiliar, but the voice the Gentleman instantly recognized as belonging to the plaintiff in his late momentous judicial experience. It is proper to say here that it was the voice of Mademoiselle Clotilde Montmorency; it is only just to add that, speaking no French, and being of unmistakable Anglo-Saxon origin, her name was evidently derived from the game over which she had presided, which was, in the baleful estimation of the Camp, of foreign extraction.

"I wanted to know," said Miss Clotilde, sitting down on a bench beside the Gentleman—"that is, me and Jake Woods thought we'd like to know—*how much* you consider yourself out of pocket by this yer resignation of yours?"

Scarcely hearing the speech, and more concerned with the apparition itself, Judge Trott stammered vaguely, "I have the pleasure of addressing Miss—"

"If you mean by that that you think you don't know me, never saw me before, and don't want to see me ag'in, why, I reckon that's the polite way o' putting it," said Miss Montmorency, with enforced calmness, scraping some dead leaves together with the tip of her parasol as if she were covering up her emotions. "But I'm Miss Montmorency. I was saying that Jake and me thought that—seein' as you stood by us when them hounds on the jury give in their hellish lying verdict—Jake and me thought it wasn't the square thing for you to lose your situation just for me. 'Find out from the Judge,' sez he, 'jist what he reckons he's lost by this yer resignation—putting it at his own figgers.' That's what Jake said. Jake's a square man—I kin say *that* of him, anyhow."

"I don't think I understand you," said Judge Trott simply.

"That's it! That's just it!" continued Miss Clotilde, with only half-suppressed bitterness. "That's what I told Jake. I sez, 'The Judge won't understand you nor me. He's that proud he won't have anything to say to us. Didn't he meet me square on the street last Tuesday and never let on that he saw me—never even nodded when I nodded to him?'"

"My dear madam," said Judge Trott hurriedly, "I assure you you are mistaken. I did *not* see you. Pray believe me. The fact is—I am afraid to confess it even to myself—but I find that, day by day, my eyesight is growing weaker and weaker." He stopped and sighed.

Miss Montmorency, glancing upward at his face, saw it was pale and agitated. With a woman's swift intuition, she believed this weakness explained the otherwise gratuitous effrontery of his incongruous eyes, and it was to her a sufficient apology. It is only the inexplicable in a man's ugliness that a woman never pardons.

"Then ye really don't recognize me?" said Miss Clotilde, a little softened, and yet a little uneasy.

"I—am—afraid—not," said Trott, with an apologetic smile.

Miss Clotilde paused. "Do you mean to say you couldn't see me when I was in court during the trial?"

Judge Trott blushed. "I am afraid I saw only—an—outline."

"I had on," continued Miss Clotilde rapidly, "a straw hat, with magenta silk lining, turned up so—magenta ribbons tied here"—indicating her round throat—"a reg'lar 'Frisco hat—don't you remember?"

"I—that is—I am afraid—"

"And one of them figgered silk 'Dollar Vardens,'" continued Miss Clotilde anxiously.

Judge Trott smiled politely, but vaguely. Miss Clotilde saw that he evidently had not recognized this rare and becoming costume. She scattered the leaves again and dug her parasol into the ground.

"Then you never saw me at all?"

"Never distinctly."

"Ef it's a fair question betwixt you and me," she said suddenly, "what made you resign?"

"I could not remain Judge of a court that was obliged to record a verdict so unjust as that given by the jury in your case," replied Judge Trott warmly.

"Say that ag'in, old man," said Miss Clotilde, with an admiration which half apologized for the irreverence of epithet.

Judge Trott urbanely repeated the substance of his remark in another form.

Miss Montmorency was silent a moment. "Then it wasn't *me*?" she said finally.

"I don't think I catch your meaning," replied the Judge, a little awkwardly.

"Why—ME. It wasn't on account of *me* you did it?"

"No," said the Judge pleasantly.

There was another pause. Miss Montmorency balanced her parasol on the tip of her toe. "Well," she said finally, "this isn't getting much information for Jake."

"For whom?"

"Jake."

"Oh—your husband?"

Miss Montmorency clicked the snap of her bracelet smartly on her wrist and said sharply, "Who said he was 'my husband?'"

"Oh, I beg your pardon."

"I said Jake Woods. He's a square man—I can say *that*

for him. He sez to me, 'You kin tell the Judge that whatever he chooses to take from us—it ain't no bribery nor corruption, nor nothin' o' that kind. It's all on the square. The trial's over; he isn't Judge any longer; he can't do anything for us —he ain't expected to do anything for us but one thing. And that is to give us the satisfaction of knowing that he hasn't lost anything by us—that he hasn't lost anything by being a square man and acting on the square.' There! that's what he said. I've said it! Of course I know what *you'll* say. I know you'll get wrathy. I know you're mad now! I know you're too proud to touch a dollar from the like of us—if you were starving. I know you'll tell Jake to go to hell, and me with him! And who the hell cares?"

She had worked herself up to this passion so suddenly, so outrageously and inconsistently, that it was not strange that it ended in an hysterical burst of equally illogical tears. She sank down again on the bench she had gradually risen from, and applied the backs of her yellow-gloved hands to her eyes, still holding the parasol at a rigid angle with her face. To her infinite astonishment Judge Trott laid one hand gently upon her shoulder and with the other possessed himself of the awkward parasol, which he tactfully laid on the bench beside her.

"You are mistaken, my dear young lady," he said, with a respectful gravity,—"deeply mistaken, if you think I feel anything but kindness and gratitude for your offer—an offer so kind and unusual that even you yourself feel that I could not accept it. No! Let me believe that in doing what I thought was only my duty as a *Judge,* I gained your good-will, and let me feel that in doing my duty now as a *man,* I shall still keep it."

Miss Clotilde had lifted her face towards his, as if deeply and wonderingly following his earnest words. But she only said, "Can you see me in this light?—at this distance? Put up your glass and try."

Her face was not far from his. I have forgotten whether I have said that she was a pretty woman. She had been once prettier. But she retained enough of her good looks to invest the "Wheel of Fortune," over which she had presided, with a certain seductive and bewildering uncertainty, which increased the risk of the players. It was, in fact, this unhallowed combination of Beauty and Chance that excited the ire of La Porte—who deemed it unprofessional and not "on the square."

She had fine eyes. Possibly Judge Trott had never before been so near eyes that were so fine and so—expressive. He lifted his head with some embarrassment and a blush on his high cheek-bones. Then, partly from instinctive courtesy, partly from a desire to bring in a third party to relieve his embarrassment, he said—

"I hope you will make your friend, Mr. ——, understand that I appreciate his kindness, even if I can't accept it."

"Oh, you mean Jake," said the lady. "Oh, *he's* gone home to the States. I'll make it all right with *him!*"

There was another embarrassing pause—possibly over the absence of Jake. At last it was broken by Miss Montmorency. "You must take care of your eyes, for I want you to know me the next time you see me."

So they parted. The Judge *did* recognize her on several other occasions. And then La Porte was stirred to its depths in hillside and tunnel with a strange rumor. Judge Trott had married Miss Jane Thomson, *alias* Miss Clotilde Montmorency—in San Francisco! For a few hours a storm of indignation and rage swept over the town; it was believed to have been a deep-laid plan and conspiracy. It was perfectly well understood that Judge Trott's resignation was